PRAISE FOR KATHERINE REAY

"In this story of war, deception, and absolution, we find also a tale of sisters, love, loss, and all of the unspoken things in between. A history of heroism and tragedy unfolds bit by bit through letters that illuminate the past and change everything one woman thought about her family—and her own journey forward. Carefully researched, emotionally hewn, and written with a sure hand, *The London House* is a tantalizing tale of deeply held secrets, heartbreak, redemption, and the enduring way that family can both hurt and heal us. I enjoyed it thoroughly."

—Kristin Harmel, *New York Times* bestselling author of *The Forest of Vanishing Stars* and *The Book of Lost Names*

"*The London House* is a thrilling excavation of long-held family secrets that proves sometimes the darkest corners of our pasts are balanced with slivers of light. An expertly researched and marvelously paced treatise on the many variants of courage and loyalty, Reay seamlessly weaves present and precarious past as one young woman finds strength where others found betrayal. This is a brand-new side of fan-favorite Reay: wonderfully balancing her hallmarks of smart heroines and inimitable voices blended with an urgent jolt of suspense. Arresting historical fiction destined to thrill fans of Erica Roebuck and Pam Jenoff."

—Rachel McMillan, author of *The London Restoration*

"The town of Winsome reminds me of Jan Karon's Mitford, with its endearing characters, complex lives, and surprises where you don't expect them. Reay has penned another poignant tale set in Winsome, Illinois, weaving truth, forgiveness, and beauty into a touching, multilayered, yet totally cozy story. You'll root for these characters and will be sad to leave this charming town."

—Lauren K. Denton, bestselling author of *The Hideaway*, for *Of Literature and Lattes*

"In her ode to small towns and second chances, Katherine Reay writes with affection and insight about the finer things in life—from the perfect cup of coffee and the right book at the right time to enduring friendships, the power of community, and the importance of not giving up on your loved ones or yourself. Reay's fictional town of Winsome, Illinois, lives up to its name and will leave more than a few readers wistfully dreaming of moving there themselves."

—Karen Dukess, author of *The Last Book Party*, for *Of Literature and Lattes*

"Reay understands the heartbeat of a bookstore."

—Baker Book House, for *The Printed Letter Bookshop*

"*The Printed Letter Bookshop* is both a powerful story and a dazzling experience. I want to give this book to every woman I know—I adored falling into Reay's world, words, and bookstore. Powerful, enchanting, and spirited, this novel will delight!"

—Patti Callahan, bestselling author of *Becoming Mrs. Lewis*

"Dripping with period detail but fundamentally a modern story, *The Austen Escape* is a clever, warmhearted homage to Austen and her fans."

—*Shelf Awareness*

"Reay handles . . . scenes with tenderness and a light touch, allowing the drama to come as much from internal conflict as external, rom-com–type misunderstandings . . . Thoughtful escapism."

—*Kirkus* for *The Austen Escape*

"Reay's sensually evocative descriptions of Italian food and scenery make this a delight for fans of Frances Mayes's *Under the Tuscan Sun*."

—*Library Journal*, starred review, for *A Portrait of Emily Price*

"Katherine Reay is a remarkable author who has created her own sub-genre, wrapping classic fiction around contemporary stories. Her writing is flawless and smooth, her storytelling meaningful and poignant. You're going to love *The Brontë Plot*."

—Debbie Macomber, #1 *New York Times* bestselling author

"Book lovers will savor the literary references as well as the story's lessons on choices, friendship, and redemption."

—*Booklist* for *The Brontë Plot*

"Reay treats readers to a banquet of flavors, aromas, and textures that foodies will appreciate, and clever references to literature add nuances sure to delight bibliophiles. The relatable, very real characters, however, are what will keep readers clamoring for more from this talented author."

—*Publishers Weekly*, starred review, for *Lizzy & Jane*

"Katherine Reay's *Dear Mr. Knightley* kept me up until 2:00 a.m.; I simply couldn't put it down."

—Eloisa James, *New York Times* bestselling author of *Once Upon a Tower*

"Book nerds, rejoice! *Dear Mr. Knightley* is a stunning debut—a first-water gem with humor and heart. I can hardly wait to get my hands on the next novel by this gifted new author!"

—Serena Chase, *USA TODAY*'s *Happy Ever After* blog

The

LONDON
HOUSE

ALSO BY KATHERINE REAY

Dear Mr. Knightley

Lizzy & Jane

The Brontë Plot

A Portrait of Emily Price

The Austen Escape

The Printed Letter Bookshop

Of Literature and Lattes

NONFICTION

Awful Beautiful Life, with Becky Powell

The

LONDON
HOUSE

*A
Novel*

KATHERINE REAY

HARPER **MUSE**

The London House

Copyright © 2021 Katherine Reay

Published by Harper Muse, an imprint of HarperCollins Focus LLC.

Interior design by Mallory Collins

Library of Congress Cataloging-in-Publication Data

Names: Reay, Katherine, 1970- author.
Title: The London house : a novel / Katherine Reay.
Description: [Nashville] : Harper Muse, [2021] | Summary: "An uncovered family secret sets one woman on the journey of a lifetime through the history of Britain's WWII spy network and glamorous 1930s Paris in an effort to understand her past, save her family, and claim her future"-- Provided by publisher.
Identifiers: LCCN 2021024177 (print) | LCCN 2021024178 (ebook) | ISBN 9780785290209 (paperback) | ISBN 9780785290216 (epub) | ISBN 9780785290223
Subjects: BISAC: FICTION / Epistolary | FICTION / Romance / Contemporary | GSAFD: Love stories.
Classification: LCC PS3618.E23 L66 2021 (print) | LCC PS3618.E23 (ebook) | DDC 813/.6--dc23
LC record available at https://lccn.loc.gov/2021024177
LC ebook record available at https://lccn.loc.gov/2021024178

Printed in the United States of America

21 22 23 24 25 LSC 5 4 3 2 1

MBR and MMR—
Thank you for the most extraordinary research trip.

We can only see a short distance ahead, but we can see plenty there that needs to be done.

—ALAN TURING, FROM "COMPUTING MACHINERY AND INTELLIGENCE"

PROLOGUE

Caro hugged Martine, whispering close to her ear. "I won't be back. It's too dangerous. Christophe is a threat to you now. You must see that. He'll take his chance when he needs the money or the protection. He will turn you in."

"Schiap keeps me safe."

Martine had grown thin in the months since Caro left France. Her light auburn hair, usually pulled back into a neat chignon, hung loose. Her eyes, usually assessing and sharp, looked worn and narrowed with suspicion and fear.

Caro sensed Martine didn't believe the lie she offered. She also knew how hard it was to lay down those lies. She had once believed them as well—that because Elsa Schiaparelli controlled every design, button, stitch, and memo; dotted every *i* within her domain; and directed her growing empire with swift efficiency, she wielded the same control outside it—and that her power was good, fair, and honest.

"Schiap's gone. Anything she offered you is gone. This place?" Caro gestured to the four walls of the small workroom and beyond them to encompass every inch of the ninety-eight-room mansion that held the House of Schiaparelli. "It's open because the Germans allow it to be so. They are the ones offering protection because their wives shop here. And it won't last. Don't be naive."

She shoved the pouch, a thick canvas sack filled with seventy-five thousand francs, into Martine's shaking hands. "Take this money, pay your contacts, then use the rest to get out. I've given you names and now you have money. Hurry and get it done."

Tears filled Martine's gray eyes. She pushed out a whisper. "This is my home."

Caro gripped her shoulders hard. She could feel every bone. They'd grown more pronounced and Martine's thick wool dress no longer hid their sharp angles. "Not now. Maybe someday again, but you have to live to see it."

Martine cringed and tried to pull away.

Caro tightened her hold on her friend's fragile frame. "Get to Spain. Use my name as your sponsor for the British. Promise me?"

A light shifted outside Martine's workroom window. She clutched at Caro's arm. "You need to go. Christophe is on security tonight. He'll be back soon. That cut?" She looked to Caro's covered forearm. "He'll do worse now. Without thought."

Martine dropped her voice and moved closer to Caro as if needing to whisper, despite their being the only two in the small room. "He's open now. He flaunts their gifts, his new power. He—" Martine pressed her lips together, unable to finish her sentence.

"Collaborates." Caro supplied the final word.

"It's a dirty word, a dirty thing."

"You've made my point." Caro stepped even closer. "You're running out of time. He will turn you in to the Germans. The stories of what they are doing to Jew—"

"*Arrêtez.*" Martine stiffened and wrapped her arms around herself. Her dress looked to swallow her small frame. "Do you think I do not know?"

"I've stayed overlong." Caro studied her watch. "I've got to leave. I have somewhere I—" She stopped. "Use the money for your contacts, but save enough for you. Do you understand?"

"This is my home," Martine repeated, shaking her head as if willing the changes in Paris and in life to disappear. Tears spilled down her cheeks. "I will try. I will—"

Caro hugged her friend tight. "Promise me, because I can't come back. I need you to promise me."

Martine nodded into her shoulder.

It was enough. It had to be.

Caro stepped out of Martine's sewing room and into the salon's back hall. The walls were covered with years of first draft sketches and photographs of gowns, workers, and opening shows. It was her favorite spot in the entire mansion.

For all the glitz and glamour encased within the House of Schiaparelli, this narrow hall, with original drawings pinned into the plaster and photographs of the seamstresses, designers, and mannequins who worked there, told the true story. It embodied the life of the House—Schiaparelli's brilliance as well as the dedication and dogged determination of the team that supported her.

Caro stopped at her favorite drawing. Not the infamous Lobster Dress nor the design of Schiap's famous perfume bottle. The Butterfly Dress. A soft, delicate creation from 1937 that embodied hope, life, and love in a whisper of pale-pink silk.

She slid the sketch from its pin. She had purchased one for Margo from the first batch stitched. Perhaps, she thought, Margo would like the drawing as well, Perhaps she'd wear the dress. Perhaps she'd believe in herself again and let in hope, life, and love once more. Perhaps . . .

Missing her twin . . . remembering . . . distractions dulled one's senses. Caro blinked to focus her mind and bring herself back to the present.

A second late.

An unseen force hauled her to the ground.

Splayed on the cobblestones, palms cut by gravel, she looked up to

Christophe's cold, chiseled face. His eyes glinted like ice in the watery lamplight.

"I thought I got rid of you last time," he growled.

"You're rid of me now. I came to say goodbye to Martine. We were friends. Only friends." In her fear, Caro realized she was offering unnecessary information. She silently chastised herself as she scrabbled backward, out from beneath him. "You'll never see me again." She rose and stepped back.

He lunged for her. His hand completely encircled her bicep and sent tingles down the length of her arm, numbing her fingers.

"*Non.*" He pushed her toward the courtyard's entrance. "The Carlingue will get you this time. There's good money in traitors."

Caro pulled back. Her leather soles slipped on the cobblestones and she lost her footing. Christophe counterbalanced her move, hauling her upright and forward.

The French Gestapo, the Carlingue, was as brutish as the German iteration—perhaps more so in an effort to impress their occupiers. But what was worse, they would know her. Christophe would tell them exactly who she was and what she was. A prize.

This was why Dr. Hugh Dalton had not wanted her involved. This was why Sir Frank Nelson asked her to stop.

If she hurt the war effort . . . if her loss or death was used to promote anti-British propaganda . . . or worse, if she was tortured and the Germans publicized it for ransom, power, position, or trade concessions . . . To hurt the British effort and morale was more than she could bear.

Caro twisted in Christophe's grip again. He squeezed tighter, to the point she thought her arm might break.

What had she done?

ONE

A call came in. May I forward it to you?"

"Of course." I'd quit asking the receptionist who was calling months ago. Mednex had a main line, but as we each had company cell phones, the CEO hadn't put landline phones on our desks. She simply forwarded calls.

"Caroline Payne," I announced at the click.

"Caroline? It's Mat Hammond. I don't know if you remember me from college, but—"

"Mat? Of course." I felt myself straighten. "I remember you."

Three simple words accompanied a complex picture. *Mat Hammond*. The Greek boy with the electric smile and the soft, dark eyes. Funny. Determined. Brilliant. Challenging . . . A close friend. Somehow I'd forgotten that last part, and it struck me with an odd note of longing.

"I wondered . . . I mean, I thought you might not." He paused.

I waited, unsure how to step into the silence that followed his comment.

When it tipped toward uncomfortable, he rushed to fill it. "I'm working on a project for the *Atlantic*, and I need to ask you a few questions."

"Oh. I'm sorry." Oddly disappointed, I reached for a pen. Fielding questions about our company's new immunotherapy drug was above my pay grade. "You need Anika Patel, but she's unavailable today. Let me take your number and I'll have her call you."

"It's not about your company; it's about you. Well, about Caroline Waite."

"Who?" Surprise arced my voice. I recognized the name, but it could have no meaning to Mat or anyone outside my family.

"Your great-aunt? Twin sister to your grandmother, Margaret Waite Payne?"

"I know who my grandmother was, but why are you calling about her sister?"

"It might be easier if we met in person . . . I'm in the lobby."

"What?" I stood and looked over the cubical partitions as if, eight floors up, I'd somehow see Mat's lanky frame leaning against a doorjamb.

"I didn't even know we were both in Boston until earlier this week," he continued. "Please . . . this is no good over the phone and email is no better. It won't take long."

I dropped to my seat. "I'll be down in a minute."

Caroline Waite. That was a name I hadn't heard in years—twenty years, to be exact. I'd been named after my great-aunt. But once I'd learned that she died in childhood from polio, I'd lost interest in her. Even at a young age, I thought it felt wrong to be named after someone best known for dying young.

Mat Hammond was another name I hadn't heard in years—six, to be exact. He was the first boy I met on campus my freshman year. We bumped into each other entering the dorm. He, buried beneath a box of books. Me, swamped by a down comforter. We became friends, good friends—at least from his perspective. I'd always hoped . . .

I stepped off the elevator and scanned the lobby. Mat was momentarily forgotten as my chest filled with the same expansive feeling I got every time I stepped within it. I loved our building's lobby. My father always said it didn't matter where you lived or in what type of building you worked, but I disagreed. Buildings bore personalities. They held our secrets and carried the weight of our lives, our families, our work, and our dreams. The grandeur and significance of Mednex's lobby had become symbolic of how I viewed Mednex's work and my place within it—something small participating in something grand.

Ours was the newest company fighting one of humanity's worst foes—cancer—with a groundbreaking protocol that supercharged the body's cells as our latest weapon. There was something so fundamental and old school, yet cutting edge, about the idea that we could equip our bodies to withstand and conquer this most invasive assault.

Our building's lobby embodied that synergy. Its 1920s art deco designs and lines, the pink marble-patterned floor and the dark wood and gold filigreed interior storefronts of the shops circling it gave it a dignity and gravitas missing from steel, glass, and concrete. It exuded history, stability, and solidity, while offering the latest amenities, including a security system that worked on a biometric scan . . . and the best coffee shop around.

It was next to this door I found Mat. He studied me rather than greeted me. I had anticipated a warm smile but banished the thought before my face reflected it. This was business. Friendship, it seemed, had died long ago.

Physically he looked the same, other than the slight curl to his hair around his ears. He certainly still had the same straight nose and jawline most women would die for—or pay thousands to obtain—and I knew full well his scruffy three day shadow hid an equally chiseled chin.

That was one thing I hadn't inherited from my grandmother—twin sister to the Caroline in question—her square jaw. With her dark hair, bright blue eyes, and that gorgeous Grace Kelly jaw, I saw her as the most beautiful woman in the world.

The saddest too.

As I crossed the lobby, Mat—looking every bit the academic I always suspected he'd be—pushed off the wall and met me midway.

We stalled, side-shifted, then awkwardly stepped into a semi-hug and back-pat while our hands got stuck between us mid-handshake.

"You haven't—"

"Wow. It's been a lo—"

We stopped and started and sputtered to another stop. I opened my mouth to try again, but he stepped back and gestured first to my hand then to the coffee shop. "Your hand is freezing . . . Can I buy you a coffee?"

I nodded and rubbed my hands together, feeling both embarrassed and exposed. Within a few steps and no words, we stood in line. Two black drips later, we sat across from each other tucked next to a window.

"Okay . . . Where to begin." He circled his cup with both hands.

It wasn't a question, so I didn't try to answer. It wasn't congenial, so I didn't start a round of "What have you been up to lately?" I simply sat and waited.

"I'm an adjunct instructor at BC, but I have a side job that, in the craziest of small world ways, leads me to you."

He scrunched his nose. "That didn't help . . . The humanities don't pay much without tenure, so on the side I do research for families. I trace lineage, make albums, digital programs, anything they want to give Grandma for Christmas. It usually starts with 23andMe or something, and the wife discovers she's German or English, and wouldn't royalty be fun? Then a friend tells them about me because all these people seem to know each other, and I've been doing this for years. So I get hired to do a deep dive on the family and present their history with a big bright bow."

Mat sucked in a gulp of air, as he hadn't drawn a breath since *"I'm an adjunct . . . ,"* and I choked on my coffee. "Someone in my family hired you? How? Who?"

There was no way that could be true.

"No." Mat watched as I swiped at the table between us with my napkin. "Your family name came up in my current project and . . . it's an interesting story that, if I do it right, the *Atlantic* wants for a feature article. Not one about the Arnim family, who hired me, but about yours."

His smile flattened into a vulnerable sheepish thing that made me wary.

"You've lost me. Can we start over?"

Mat took a sip of coffee. "A couple years ago, the *Atlantic* picked up some pieces I wrote on history and how we remember it. World War Two stories about all the monuments under construction at the time, both in England and here. My guess is that the look back was as commemorative as it was therapeutic . . . When people feel anxious about the future, and globally we've been through the wringer, they look to the past and tangible reminders that things ended well before and, therefore, can again. I   "

He pressed his lips shut as if realizing he'd gone off topic. "My current idea isn't about the stories we want to remember. It's a counterpoint perspective, featuring a story most—your family specifically—would rather forget. My belief is that those stories, your story, also provide a sense of hope. They assure us that when bad things happen, life continues, and that we humans are resilient and endure. Hope emerges from tragedy."

He stalled and stared at me. Barely understanding, I stared back.

"In World War Two, no one can deny there was a real mix and mess of loyalties. It must have felt like the world was ending and life would never be the same. What's more, the enemy was sometimes within your own home." He dipped his hand toward me as if I could relate to that point. "In France, you've got Free France, Occupied France, brothers and sisters turning on each other. In England, you've got the Mitford sisters fawning over Hitler, Edward and Wallis Simpson, and even Edward's agreement to the whole German plan to get him back on the throne before he got shipped off to the Bahamas . . . There are lots of stories that show family life was real and messy and carried consequences."

"Okay?" I drew the question long.

"Your great-aunt is one of those stories. A woman, daughter of an earl, no less, who worked as a secretary for the Special Operations Executive, then crossed the great divide and ran away with her Nazi lover? You have to admit, it's compelling."

He took another sip, assessing me over the rim of his cup. When I said nothing, he set it down. "I didn't do that well . . . I practiced how to reach out to you a million times this past week because, while I could hand it in as is, I know you. I didn't want this to surprise you or hurt you if you read my name on it. I also hoped you might comment."

"Comment how?" I sat back. "You've found the wrong Caroline Waite, Mat. My aunt died from polio in childhood. I'm named after her. I should know."

Mat mirrored my defensive cross-armed slouch. His eyes drew tight as he watched me. "Is that what you've been told?" He reached into his messenger bag, pulled out a standard manila file, and opened it. The top page was a photocopy of a short letter in Courier type, with the salutation handwritten in a large swirling script.

He slid it across the table.

20 October 1941

My dear John and Ethel,

It is with real sorrow that I write this letter, for it brings you, I am afraid, very bad news about your daughter, Caroline Amelia Waite.

Without permission, she boarded a transport boat to Normandy on 15 October and was identified

outside Paris two days later. She joined German
Gruppenführer Paul Arnim, with whom we have confirmed she had a previous romantic connection.

I am beyond sorry, John and Ethel. I can only
imagine how hard this news will sit with you.
She did good work at the Inter Services Research
Bureau and we did not anticipate this action. I
want to reassure you she was not involved in anything delicate that should incite your concern
for our efforts.

That said, I do not write these words without
heartbreak for your loss.

I send this letter with consideration and
sympathy.

Hugh

I slid it toward him. "Impossible. This is dated 1941."

"Do you know who Hugh Dalton was?" Mat tapped on the name.
"He was the Minister of Economic Warfare, tasked to form the SOE,
the Special Operations Executive. They called it the Inter Services
Research Bureau, the ISRB, but that was a front."

His chair screeched as it scraped forward across the stone floor,
closer to the table, closer to me. We hovered inches apart. I resisted the
urge to shift back in retreat.

"It was a whole new idea, Caroline, set on espionage, sabotage,
reconnaissance, and establishing guerrilla resistance groups. Rough
and tough stuff, modeled on IRA training and tactics from the Irish
War of Independence. It's incredible really . . . No gentleman, and
back when it started in 1940, certainly no lady, was part of it. Women
weren't actively recruited until 1942 as spies, so your aunt probably
worked—"

He drew another slow breath. "The beginning," he said more to himself than to me. He used to do that in college. He'd get carried away with a theory or an idea then need to remind himself to go back to the beginning and bring the rest of us along. Sometimes I sent us down conversational rabbit trails just for the fun of setting him off.

The memory brought a fleeting smile. Fleeting because Mat didn't recognize it, reciprocate it, or make any gesture at all that we'd once been more than a cold call about a story.

With a frown, he continued. "The Arnim family hired me for a project. He's the Gruppenführer mentioned in the note. His granddaughter owns all these famous dresses he bought for his wife from a salon in Paris, so after checking his German files, that's where I headed to start building texture for their project. Two names popped up—your aunt's and a Christophe Pelletier.

"Pelletier was the salon's security guard and general bully, arrested and sent to Auschwitz in November 1941. He died in 1943. Your aunt, however, proved more interesting. She worked at the salon, knew Arnim there, then headed home when the Germans invaded France—almost a year after the declaration of war. Following her trail to England, I found her involved with the SOE and the Gruppenführer mentioned in the file. My guess is that she was his lover turned informant."

Mat straightened the paper between us. "It's beyond anything I could have imagined. Think about it—I get hired by a family in New York to trace their German lineage, and here we are with an incredible story, having coffee in Boston."

"But it's still wrong . . . It can't be my aunt."

Mat's brown eyes lit a notch brighter. His excitement fueled the gold flecks along their edges before he caught something in mine. The light dimmed with a crinkle of concern. It was so swift, gentle, and kind, my breath caught. He was suddenly the boy I once knew.

"Do you really not know?" His gaze flickered. "It's true, Caroline. This is your aunt." He spread his hand across the paper. "And it's not dangerous, if that's what concerns you. This story can't hurt your family. It was eighty years ago. But it does have a great angle and contemporary significance. How we deal with pain and adversity remains relevant no matter how long ago it happened."

I opened my mouth to protest, but he cut me off with a raised hand. "I'll be gentle with her, but I'm not wrong . . . I did some digging. Dr. Dalton and your great-grandfather knew each other well. I expect Dalton wrote this personally because they were friends."

Mat opened the folder again. "I have this." He handed me another page. "And this." Another. "Your aunt met with Dalton and the SOE head, Sir Frank Nelson, a couple times. She worked there for over a year before this final note was sent to her family."

He sat back and stared at me for a few moments before running his hands through his hair and leaning forward, as if ready to go into battle again. "Don't you see? When she joined the Nazis, a lie had to be created. Even if she just typed memos, the truth would've hurt the narrative. If it had been made public that a peer's daughter had worked for the SOE and defected that early in the war, it could have ended it right there. British morale was low and the country was vulnerable. That's part of my point. Your family didn't get to grieve her loss properly, because this hung over her . . . There's a lot to say here."

"There's nothing to say, Mat." I pushed at his paper pile. "That's not my aunt."

We sat at a stalemate for five seconds or five minutes. My head spun too fast to process time properly. All spinning stopped with his next sentence.

"Your father says I'm right."

"What?" I tipped back so fast the legs of my chair snagged on the uneven stone floor.

Mat lunged for me, grabbing my arm. He let go the instant I was upright.

"You talked to my father?"

"Briefly. I thought that was the more direct connection, and you and I haven't spoken in years. He threatened legal action."

I felt my eyes widen. Threatening legal action did not sound like my dad at all. "That proves you're right?"

"His tone did. A person doesn't get that scared or stern over a lie, but over an unfortunate truth . . ." Mat started to replace each of his memos within his folder. "Look, Caroline, I don't know why your dad got so upset or what you've been told, but your aunt knew Paul Arnim and she ran away with him."

I gripped my coffee cup tight. The warmth felt good against my now freezing fingers. "How does the Arnim family feel about this? They're paying you. They can't want you to publicize that he was a Nazi."

"No . . . He isn't part of the article. They knew he was a German officer and I need to tell them about this, of course, but I'm not writing about him for publication." Mat slid his chair back. "You know what? I'm sorry, Caroline. This was a mistake. I—I shouldn't have called."

He returned his folder to his bag and pushed up and out of his seat. This time I reached for his arm to stay the motion. His eyes locked, first on my hand clutching his arm, then on my face. He dropped back into his chair.

"Are you sure you've got this right?" I asked.

In college, we'd been friends—good friends—at least for our first two years. I had trusted him, relied on him . . . had a crush on him. And while there was a distance, a coolness between us now, I knew Mat was still trustworthy. He wouldn't lie.

"I'm sure."

I let go of his arm and spread my fingers across the wood table. I

needed something firm, something real to hold. "You can't put anything in your article about us meeting here, and that I knew nothing
about this." I bit my lip. "Please."

"Why not?"

"Because I can't learn this . . . here . . . from you. I get that it fits.
I mean, you want to know how three generations dealt with pain, and
turning a blind eye is certainly one way, but you can't understand what
we've been through."

My mind raced with memories, questions, implications, and
consequences. Each felt as empty and dark as the thought before it,
bringing an instant swirling headache and a sense of weightlessness—
perhaps a little like Alice felt careening down that hole.

"No one has told me any of this. Ever."

Mat's lips parted in silent disbelief.

"Can you wait? A couple days?" A plan formed as I spoke, my
brain barely able to keep up with its delivery. "I'll talk to my dad, find
out what is true and what is not, and in exchange for the time, I'll
comment."

He raised a brow. "You'd do that? For a couple days' time?"

"Today's Friday. We can meet Monday?" I felt my voice rise into
the territory of pleading and dropped it with a short cough. "When's
it due?"

"Next Friday. One week. But, Caroline, I don't want to give you
the weekend just so you can think up ways to change my mind or stop
me. Marketable work like this is the difference between a tenure track
hire or creating puff documentaries for rich families while babysitting
undergrads. I can't risk losing this."

"I just want time. I promise. We'll sit down Monday and talk it
through. And I want to read the article."

Mat ran his hand over his hair again. His dark bangs stuck up
with the motion. "I'm not doing a hatchet job and you know it. You

know me. The whole point of this is to do something good, to examine how history is real and messy, but that it isn't objective or defining."

"I need to read it, Mat, because that's where you are wrong. If what you say is true, then it has been defining. And I can't let it hurt my father more, not now." This time my voice did betray me.

"What's wrong?" Mat stilled. "Is he okay?"

I shook my head.

"I'm sorry."

"Not your fault." I shrugged, feeling embarrassed and exposed all over again. I pointed to Mat's bag. "Can I have that letter? The Dalton one?"

"It's a copy. Keep it." He pulled it from his folder.

I tore off a corner of the page and reached for his pen. "Here's my email and cell. Send me the article and your number. I promise to call you Monday morning, if not before."

"I'm not agreeing to change anything, Caroline, and in the end, I don't need your permission or a quote."

"Fair enough." I pushed my chair back. "You won't submit until you hear from me?"

"Agreed. If you call before Friday." Mat glanced up as he tapped my information into his phone. "You haven't changed a bit, you know."

My heart skipped, then stopped.

His head shake told me that wasn't a good thing.

TWO

Coming up from the Charles/MGH stop, I stalled. Right would take me home—an airy, light, and bright two-bedroom apartment off Charles Street. Left, a couple blocks east, and a few streets up Beacon Hill, and I'd be at my dad's house. Not my childhood home. My dad's house.

I was so tempted to turn right. I was tired and, regardless of whatever the truth proved to be, seeing Mat again was messing with my head, and the conversation with my dad was going to be rough. Nothing was ever easy between us.

I crossed the street and headed up Beacon Hill.

As a kid, I always loved Acorn Street. True to my belief that buildings have personalities, those houses exuded love. Dad once commented the houses were "diminutive" because it was where the trade workers who serviced the larger houses on Chestnut Street, one block over, lived. I didn't care who had once built or lived in them—I just knew they were special. I dreamt I lived on that tiny stone street, too narrow for cars, with its small houses tucked tight. Families within them must always bump into each other. Even a family of three, like my own the year I turned eight, would have to squeeze through narrow hallways, twist to pass each other in a tiny kitchen, and get tangled up on a single couch to share popcorn on movie night.

I grew up on Chestnut Street, with all the roominess, comfort, and coldness that implied. We had two stairwells. A sitting room that

Dad never entered. A study Mom never stepped foot in. And a third floor all for me. I was the envy of my friends.

It was desperately lonely.

I turned left onto Acorn Street and paused as I always did. To Dad, moving houses last year was a way of sorting his life, perhaps closing a door. To me, he moved into my dream home—only years after the dream had died and we'd all left home.

I walked up the sloped hill and rang the doorbell at number 9. A chill made me shift within my thin cardigan. The sun, nowhere near setting on this June evening, was cut early from this narrow street.

"Caroline?" Dad stood on the step above me. He looked taller in the shadows, thinner. His salt-and-pepper hair was ready for a cut. "I didn't expect to see you this weekend."

He stepped back, inviting me inside. I bumped into him squeezing past. I couldn't help but wonder—had we lived here before, would bumping into each other have forced us to relate and heal? Or would we have broken even faster?

As I continued down his short hallway toward the kitchen, I noted the subtle smell that followed me. Mint and the Acqua di Parma cologne I'd given him two Christmases past. It made me smile . . . and hope.

I called behind me, "I almost dropped by your office at lunch today, then remembered you're working from home Mondays and Fridays. How do you like it?"

"I'm still getting used to it." He sighed. "Ferdinand put out to pasture."

I laughed as I stepped into his bright white-marble kitchen. Dad didn't have a robust sense of humor, but he did have a deep well of literary allusions, and a surprising number came from my favorite children's stories.

"Ah . . . That's where Ferdinand wanted to be."

"True." Dad flipped the switch and the kitchen glowed from a series of pencil-sized lights. "It was a bad analogy." He looked down at his hands as if calculating his life's wear and tear within each knuckle. "I am not where I want to be."

Rather than console or chide, as neither was wanted, I shifted my attention from his kitchen to the office space next to it. The previous family had probably used it as a breakfast area, but Dad had separated the space with a set of glass French doors to create an office overlooking his walled garden. "Why reserve the best view for a meal I never eat?" had been his reasoning.

"Dad, you've still got unopened boxes."

He looked past my outstretched hand to his office. "I'm getting there."

"It's been a year. This is not 'getting there.'" I toggled my fingers in air quotes.

"Did you come to harp at me?" If his voice held any emotion, it was curiosity. Mild curiosity. In fact, if the last year proved anything, it was that mild was Dad's dominant characteristic.

"No." I wilted. I had come to ask tough questions and didn't know how to begin and that made me nervous. Dad and I only had one constant conversation topic—my inconstancy or, better termed, my failures. He never pushed at me—that wasn't his style. He simply asked enough questions, in just the right tones, to let me know I wasn't measuring up.

Dad lifted his chin. "How's work? Are you still liking it? You've been there . . . almost a year now?"

And so we began.

I perched on one of his high stools and spread my hands across the marble island. I recognized the gesture from earlier that morning at the coffee shop and saw it for what it was—a reach for understanding, connection. At the very least, I found the marble refreshingly cool and slightly bracing.

"Eleven months." I added a shade of perky to my tone. "All that patent work I've been doing? Well, the FDA approved Xyantrix and we're going to market in December."

"In six months? That's fast."

"It's a good protocol, Dad." I stretched my arms farther across the counter. There was no hiding the significance of the action, my reaching out for relationship. I pulled them back. "It will really help people. It's a huge advance in immunotherapy. It gives support so the body can fight cancer rather than relying on a drug to kill it and, unfortunately, all the good cells with it."

The word *cancer* hovered between us, a specter always in our periphery now. Dad fidgeted with several loose papers resting on his counter.

"I handled all the FDA filings." My voice rose in a shameless beg for approval.

"You did?" He looked at me, hands still. "Shouldn't the company's lawyer have handled that? It's complicated stuff."

"She signed off on everything, but I did the legwork. I had the courses my second year. I've learned a ton, both about the law and about cancer. Did you know—"

He raised a hand. "You still have a chance to finish. If you'd get through your last year of law school, you could direct and manage that work yourself. It's foolish to—"

"Stop." I raised a hand in reply. "Leaving law school was the right decision and I don't regret it . . . I came back. I came back to be here . . ." I pressed my lips together, unable to walk that road any farther. The *with you* hovered between us.

He wasn't looking at me regardless.

"It's good work. I'm helping people. At least, I hope I am."

He smiled. It was small and fleeting, but it was there. "You have a good heart, Caroline. You always have." Then, as quickly as the connection formed, it evaporated.

Dad straightened. Time to get to business. "Now, to what do I owe this pleasure? I'm sure you didn't come to sign me up for Xyantrix or ask advice about your life."

I looked around. I wasn't ready for a serious conversation. We'd already skirted several in the five minutes I'd been there. I certainly wasn't ready to ask if he'd lied to me my whole life. I wasn't ready to ask what was true and what was fiction.

I pointed to the boxes in his office. "I've got nothing going on tonight. Why don't we order a pizza and I'll help unpack the rest of those."

Dad dismissed the suggestion with a wave of his long fingers. "If I haven't needed what's in them by now, perhaps I'll simply give them away."

"Don't say that. There could be important things you don't want to lose."

Dad blinked, but his bland expression didn't change. "You're right." He reached into a drawer and handed me a pair of scissors. "You begin and I'll call Florina for a large sausage and olive."

I sliced open a box and was pulling out the last flat object wrapped in cream moving paper when Dad joined me. I unwrapped a picture of our family taken when I was about two and placed it on Dad's desk next to the six I had already unpacked. I'd been right—and not surprised—to find the box filled with a collection of family pictures he hadn't missed.

Dad glanced at the seven pictures propped on his desk before sliding the scissors off a copy of the *Harvard Law Review* and slicing into another box. "So . . . ?"

It was easier to work than look at him. I hauled another box from the corner. "I saw Mat Hammond today. He said he spoke with you."

Dad worked his way into the box for a few beats before answering. "He did. He said you were friends in college. That, of course, didn't change the conversation. If he prints his story, I said I'd pursue legal action. I should have guessed he'd contact you. What did you say?"

"What was there to say? He claimed Aunt Caroline was a Nazi and I told him she died when she was seven. But he had a letter from 1941. I brought it with me." I stepped over the mess of packing paper to grab my bag from the kitchen.

Dad followed me.

I handed him the sheet.

"I don't understand." He glanced between the sheet and me.

I pointed to the page. "Me neither, but those are your grand-parents' names and there—"

"No, I don't understand why you told him that. The childhood polio story isn't going to put him off, Caroline." I pulled back as Dad shoved the paper into my hands. It crumpled between us. "He's right and you, of all people, know that. I hoped a bluff would stop him, because if he goes to print, there's nothing I can do." Dad's hands dropped to his sides. "You can't sue over the truth, but lying only makes it worse."

"I didn't know I was lying."

Dad stared at me and I'd never felt less like his daughter. His stare was blank—I was a conundrum or a mystery he'd never encountered.

"Are you serious?" he finally asked. "How can you not remember that day? We only found out because of you."

"Me?" I perched on the stool again. Something dark and shapeless crept into the corners of my mind. A rainy day. A stiff conversation. Shock and hurt.

Dad lowered himself onto the stool next to me. His eyes never left mine and I struggled not to look away or even blink.

"We were at the London House. You were eight. I remember because it was our first trip after . . ." He ran out of words. We always did when confronted with my sister. "Jason couldn't come, and you went digging about in that infernal attic. You found a trunk full of diaries and letters, papers and books. It spilled out from there."

"What spilled out from there?" I felt like I was leading a witness in a law school evidence class.

Dad straightened his neck. Every time he made that gesture, a sharp retreat of his chin, he reminded me of a turtle. There was so much we avoided. So much we never said. I was more familiar with that gesture than I was with anything else about my father.

He pushed off the stool and stepped back into his study. I followed.

He unwrapped the object he'd left lying on top of the box. A stapler. "I've been missing this."

"What spilled out from there?" I repeated the question, slowly with perfect diction. That got his attention.

"I don't want to talk about it. It's in the past and it will remain there, at least for us." He busied himself digging through packing paper. He straightened, another cream paper–wrapped mystery in his hands. "We don't need to comment on his article or even read it. I won't tread that ground again. I can't. I—"

Dad stopped, and it felt as if he'd started to fall into memories before he recalled I was standing there to witness it. He looked straight at me. "I've tried and tried to believe that what one does in this life matters, that what came before doesn't have to taint it, but I was wrong. This betrayal has followed me my whole life, and now its publication will bookend my entire existence." He blew out a long, measured breath. "Please, Caroline. Don't make it worse. Don't speak to that man again."

"I have to." I felt my face warm. "In exchange for time to talk to you and to read his article in advance, I agreed to comment." I rushed on. "It's important to know what he's going to say before it comes out."

"No, it's not. Beyond the event itself, there's a narrative that plays here. What did Shakespeare say? 'The evil that men do lives after them; the good is oft interred with their bones.' I'm sure there was some good to my aunt. Even my mother couldn't disguise how much she loved her, but . . . What she did? I somehow doubt eighty years has made us more forgiving or less interested in the misfortunes of others. There is no point in engaging with any of this. Ever."

Dad swept a hand over his face, pulling at his eyes, his cheeks, and his neck with the downward motion. He looked a lifetime older than his seventy-two years. I wondered if the cancer was changing him faster than he was letting on. But again, that was something he'd never tell me.

He sighed. "How do you think it felt growing up in that . . . in that choking blackness and never understanding why? Until that day, I never understood what was different about us, why there was no light or peace in our home."

My lips parted. In describing his childhood, he had described mine.

He pulled the paper from the object he held in his hands. He gripped it tight and I noticed his nails whiten with the pressure.

He placed the picture on his desk with all the others. It was one of our family, the last photo in which we were whole, taken in the summer of 2002 right before Jason left for college. Amelia had her arm wrapped around me tight in a protective posture. Only one year older, but she always looked after me. Our matching grins formed the picture's focal point.

"When is enough enough?" Dad sighed.

I nodded, but not in agreement.

THREE

We only found out because of you."

I rolled over and watched the first strands of day creep through the crack in my curtains. The light was just enough that I could discern the scattering of purple tulips across the cream fabric. I had been so excited to hang those last year.

I left law school to be near my dad, to help him bear and navigate a cancer diagnosis that arrived only weeks before. He didn't need me, perhaps didn't want me, but I felt a compulsion to be near, to help, to . . . I didn't even know anymore what I'd hoped to accomplish. The irony of it was that I had loved law school. Despite my dad's constant chirping about my inability to finish anything, until Jason's call last June, finishing was never in question.

Days after my arrival, Dad secured a sale on the Chestnut house and paid the movers to deliver everything I wanted to my new apartment. It felt like a new beginning with boxes full of my books and treasures, and a few I'd asked to be saved from Amelia's room. It was her small chair that now sat in the corner of my bedroom. Her old dresser that held my clothes.

I huffed in the approaching dawn. A therapist would have a field day with these thoughts and this room—with my whole life actually.

I opted not to stay last night to help Dad unpack, and left before the pizza arrived. He had set his jaw against talking about the only subject that mattered to me. He'd done it so many times—about school, my jobs, his diagnosis, his treatments, that I recognized it more swiftly this time—and I lied. I claimed forgotten dinner plans with friends and fled.

Rather than make plans with friends and redeem the lie, I came home, ordered my own Florina pizza, and ruminated over endless questions with no answers. I also checked my email every five minutes. Mat hadn't sent his article.

Then it happened . . .

Around three in the morning, I was either too curious to throw up barriers or too tired to keep them standing strong, and answers emerged. They played out slowly in that netherworld between cognizant thought and subconscious dreams.

I'd been wearing a new pair of jeans. They'd been a November birthday gift I'd saved for our early Christmas trip to London. After all, my jeans were the latest cut and "London is so cool," my friends said. They had all either visited themselves or pretended well. Oddly, I had never traveled there, despite my dad being British and his family descending from the "peerage," as Mom called them.

And bangs. I had just cut a full set of bangs. Stress haircutting, one would call it today. It was the same then—we just didn't have a name for it. What a mistake! My new bangs shot to the sides of my forehead, never laid flat, and never looked right. Two tufted horns pointed downward at my temples, the left side curling up and out.

It also rained our entire trip. We hardly left the London House, as I gather the great monstrosity had been called for generations, and no one came in. Grandmother was quiet and seemed heavy with sadness. I remembered how that surprised me. She wasn't the same grandmother who had come to Boston only six months earlier for a summer visit, or even three months before for my sister's funeral. She had talked to me then, played games, and even helped me bake cookies.

In London, she moved slowly, as if through water. She seemed shadowed, as if only a memory of her walked those halls and sat in the front sitting room. Oddly, she reminded me of my dad. Sometimes, even back then, I wondered how to react to him. He never gave me anything to push against—to challenge, to confront, to love.

I hardly recalled my grandfather at all. He was there, I know. In the shadows. Stern. Unyielding. Disappointed. He said a terse good morning at breakfast then ventured out to his club each day. I believed his "club" to be a place where men read, talked, sat, and smoked pipes. The same things my father did every day in Grandfather's wood-paneled study at the house—minus the pipe.

Mom sat with Grandmother. She stayed by her side, asked and answered questions, met her every request, and when the silence pressed down like a weighted blanket, she read. In many ways, I recognized how alike they looked and acted—despite not being related. That had not occurred to me before that trip and wasn't remembered until this morning.

I explored.

The London House filled me with awe. Its personality was dark and foreboding as it rose up four floors before me that first morning. Mom rushed me out of the back seat while the limousine driver unloaded our bags. When I tried to follow him to the side of the house and a door at street level, he shook his head and gestured to the front door, bright blue and five steps up from the sidewalk. Mom and Dad had already climbed the stairs.

The plaster and painted white-brick house sat perched at the end of a long street filled with identical houses, each one adjoined to its neighbors in a pristine row. Upon entering, I knew it was full of history and that old glamour Mom always raved about in the black-and-white movies we watched.

The front entry reached two floors high with a curved staircase flowing up to the right. There were indents in the plastered walls set with sculptures. The windows reached floor to ceiling. And there were countless rooms. I spent a day racing through them all—closets, pantries, sitting rooms, antechambers—and days exploring them fully. I was thankful for the endless opportunities to get lost, and the infinite ways to avoid the oppressive silence of the front sitting room.

Stories and secrets lay hidden in each room and I was desperate to discover them. I remembered that—I was hungry to understand something, anything, about who I was and where I came from. Although my mom had been welcoming and open when I was young, my dad was always more remote, and somehow, perhaps because I was named after his side of the family and looked very much like his mother, I felt a yearning to be close to him. Amelia had looked like Mom.

I found snippets of life in each and every room. Leather-bound books with cracked spines. Old coloring pages. Silver brushes. Dolls. Pens, letters, clothing, games, tiny boxes . . . chests cleared out except for the occasional treasure tucked deep in the back. A fan, a lipstick, a comb, a glove. Tiny items that told me nothing but made me feel not so alone.

I was alone because Jason wasn't there. I was alone because Amelia was gone.

I wouldn't have been in the attic that day if either of them had been with us. Amelia and I never needed anything more than each other to occupy us. We made up games, puzzles, and challenges. There wasn't a riddle we couldn't solve together. But Amelia had been killed by a car running a red light three months earlier. I was a few feet ahead of her and, turning back at precisely that instant, saw the whole thing.

We had created a massive Rube Goldberg machine the day before. It spanned across our two bedrooms, and I wanted to see if the change I'd thought up during math class might make it work. So when the "Walk" light flashed, I ran. Over halfway across the street, I spun around to call, "Hurry up!"

That moment stopped me this morning, as it always did. It

brought its usual slowed-time and high-def visuals, along with a hot flash of panic. Everything in those split seconds was magnified into a lifetime and I saw it all again. I felt it all again.

It took—I have no idea how long it took . . . But eventually my mind settled and drifted back to the London House.

Jason was a college freshman that fall and had a couple weeks of classes before winter break. Had he been with us, he would have taken me to the shops, the sites, the parks, and the museums. Who goes to London and doesn't see the Tower, the London Eye, Buckingham Palace, the Princess Diana Playground, Piccadilly Circus, or take in a West End show and eat dim sum for lunch in Chinatown? At eighteen, Mom and Dad would have let him go and they would have trusted him to take me. It would have relieved them of the burden.

Alone, I explored—and on day four, I found the attic.

The narrow stairs opened into a large room. On day one, Mom called it the nursery and said kids, including my dad, played, learned, lived, and slept up there with a nanny until they were about five years old. Then, also according to Mom, they got sent away to school.

Behind this front room was a short hallway with doors on either side. Maids' quarters, she told me, and bedrooms for the family's children. She said my grandmother and her twin sister had slept there when they were girls, and their father and his siblings before them. I felt sad as I realized that without siblings, my dad would have stayed up there all by himself.

Mom hadn't taken me through the small door at the end of the hallway that first day, and that was where I headed that fourth afternoon.

It was a storage room, wood-paneled like Grandfather's study, but the similarity ended there. The wood lining his room was smooth and polished. The mahogany so dark and shiny you could see your reflection, and so smooth that when I ran my hand down the wall I was reminded of Mom's silk dresses. I did the same here and came away with a fine coating of splinters as if I'd rubbed the cactus that sat in Jason's window well. I brushed my hand against my jeans and most of them fell away. A few dug deeper.

There was a series of dormer windows along both sides of the room that let in the low afternoon sun on one side and the gray of evening on the other. I walked to one and stepped up on something to see outside. Looking down I surveyed the gravel courtyard behind the house and the side garden. Looking across I could see where the buildings ended at the entrance to Kensington Gardens. Mom promised we'd walk there, but we hadn't yet.

That's when I felt my breath hitch—both then and now. Back then I realized I'd never visited the gardens, at least not on that trip.

At three o'clock this morning, I realized I was headed toward a moment I had never allowed myself to revisit. A moment I had willfully forgotten.

I smoothed out my breath and exhaled long and slow. It was time . . .

The room overflowed with furniture, boxes, knickknacks, and who knows what else. Lifetimes were stored in that dark space, much of which was draped in white sheets. The object that served as my perch was covered as well. I stepped down and pulled away the sheet and watched the dust dance like fairies in the slanted sunlight as it sank again to the floor. A large trunk sat before me. It had gleaming brass corners and the leather was scratched and worn smooth.

The lock was loose. I jiggled it and it released. The lid tipped far enough to rest against the window ledge, allowing me to dig through books, sets of white gloves, dried flowers, pictures, letters tied with ribbon, two dolls—one with creepy glass eyes that opened when I held her upright—and jewelry. There was a leather sleeve with a large gold locket inside. I opened it and found two girls. Beautiful girls. I knew I was looking at my grandmother and her twin sister, Caroline. The one who'd died young. The one for whom I was named.

Something was wrong with the picture and I dropped cross-legged onto the floor to study it. They didn't look like girls. They looked Jason's age or older. And even though the pictures were black-and-white, I could tell one of the girls wore dark eyeliner and her lips were a deeper tone than her sister's. *Makeup,* I thought. She was glamorous and, again, I was reminded of those old movies with Greta Garbo, Grace Kelly, and Myrna Loy that Amelia, Mom, and I had watched together.

I rested the locket beside the trunk and reached for a packet of letters. They were tied with a black ribbon, frayed thin and soft by time and use. I pulled one letter from the center and shifted to the light to read. The writing swirled in loops and dips. Whoever had written it had much to say and I couldn't read a word of it. The letters crashed into each other and danced across the page in tight lines. But three things were clear—then and early this morning.

The date . . .

October 7, 1941

My grandmother's name . . .

Dear Margaret,

And my great-aunt's signature . . .

Love,

Caro

Having recalled that, the rest washed over me. I couldn't have stopped the onslaught of remembrance if I wanted to. It wasn't distant. It was yesterday. It was now. And Dad was right—it changed everything.

I had raced down and down and down again before sliding across the marble hall and into the front room. Dad and Grandfather were there and I remember being surprised, then worried I was late for dinner.

"Look, Grandmother. I found a letter to you." I held out the page. "It's from your sister, Caroline."

Mom laughed. It was light and clear and indulgent. "Sweetheart, I hardly think a little girl wrote a letter that long. Why don't you . . ."

Her words drifted away as I handed her the open locket. Confused, she looked to my grandmother, but Grandmother was focused on me.

She reached for me and her hand trembled as she wrapped it around mine. It was cold. Icy like my hands get today when I'm anxious or nervous. Although hers were bone thin and gnarled at the knuckles, she gripped me tight and I couldn't pull away.

"Margaret?" Mom shifted toward her. "What is this? You're both much older in this picture and the letter is dated 1941."

"I wouldn't go to Paris with her. Maybe if I had . . . or lived with her here . . ."

"What do you mean? In 1941? Paris?" Dad towered over us. Grandmother stared at him, almost through me, as if Mom and I had vanished.

"She betrayed us . . . I had to lie. I loved her"—she glanced to my grandfather then back to her son—"more than anyone, and we shared everything. But in the end, it seems, we both had our secrets."

Grandmother's voice softened with a faraway quality. "I was bold and fearless, until I wasn't. Then she was. We were always opposites, from the very beginning. As we grew she became the brightest spot in any room. Me the wallflower, no one noticed. Then she left."

"Left? But, Grandmother—"

Mom wrapped an arm around me to signal silence.

Grandmother sat looking at my dad. "I told you she died as a child, but she grew, and she joined the Nazis in France. She had a lover we never knew about and we never saw her again."

"Impossible. You used to tell me stories of your childhood. You had adventures before she died. I named our daughters after her because . . . because you loved her."

"I did . . . I still do."

Dad shifted his attention to his father, who sat in an armchair near the window. Not part of the cluster near the fireplace.

"Your mother never should have told you those stories." Grandfather's voice fell heavy. "They served no purpose but to fill you with fantasies. There was nothing to do but forget and move on."

"I could never do that." Grandmother shuddered as if an unpleasant film was playing in front of her and she wanted it shut off. "But we weren't to talk about her. Not once after that night. Father was very clear. Then after the war, the nation came together, but there was still fear. Among our friends. Everywhere. For years we said she died in the war, and everyone forgot."

"Then why the polio story? You said she died as a child."

She regarded my father again. "You were young. You saw her picture and started making a hero of her. She was magnetic and lovely and you wanted to know so much. I couldn't have you hate her. Or what if you researched the war, found the truth, and tried to find her? So I lied. I said the pictures you found were of someone else and I packed every piece of her away again. I left her young and innocent so you could keep her and love her."

Grandmother pressed her lips together as if fighting memories or tears, I wasn't sure which. "I couldn't survive otherwise."

"Survive?" Grandfather cut in. "Margaret, is that what you

call this? If you had simply let her go, we could have done better than this."

"I'm not the only one who held tight," she barked at him. "Nine years. You waited nine years before you—"

"Before I what?"

"Married me." She deflated into the armchair.

Grandfather's glare was sharp and hard. It cut like steel. "I let her go and yet you still punished me." He rose and dusted the knees of his trousers. It was a rote action and, once accomplished, he was at the door before he said anything more. "Please don't wait on me for dinner this evening. I'll dine at the club."

Thinking back now, I didn't see my grandfather again that trip. In fact, I never saw him again. The next time we traveled to London was eight years later, in 2010, for his funeral. We crossed the Atlantic on a Tuesday and flew back two days later.

My dad did not follow him out the door that evening—he wasn't invited. He stared at his mother so long that Mom called his name three times before he registered her presence.

"Jack. Perhaps you should sit down."

Without answering or sitting, he returned his attention to his mother. "So it was my fault? All my questions?"

"You found a picture of her from a visit home from Paris. She'd become so sophisticated. I told you the lie I wanted to believe, that none of it ever happened. I had only told you childhood stories, the golden ones before my illness, before her love story, before her treachery, so it was easy to end your questions there by saying the picture was of someone else."

"What really happened?" Dad dropped to the settee.

"It doesn't matter now. It doesn't affect you."

"How can you say that? We're here, right now, because it does . . . this house . . . my whole childhood. Grandmother never left her room; you never smiled; Father hates everybody. You sent me away to the States."

"I did what was best." My grandmother's conviction crumpled with her next breath.

"I was fifteen."

"I was heartbroken." She tried to reach for my dad's hand, but he pulled it away. "I wanted you to be free. Your father, me, this house . . . It's been so very heavy."

Recalling how old and frail she looked in that moment surprised me anew this morning that she lived fourteen years after that evening.

Mom tugged at my arm then and slid her hand down until she reached my hand. Squeezing it tight, she led me from the room. "We should let them talk."

We turned at the door as my dad called to me. "Not a word, Caroline. Do you understand me? We will not speak of this or share it with anyone."

I could only nod. It wasn't Dad's request that kept my silence all these years—it was the lost look in his eyes. The hollowness of utter defeat.

I turned to my mom after the door closed behind us. "We can put the letter back. Wasn't it long enough ago we could just put the letter back and no one would know?"

"That's what we'll do. Come on." She started climbing the stairs. "We'll put it away and everyone will feel better in the morning."

Mom's tone was soothing, but her eyes were wide with surprise and concern. "They just need to talk. Your dad and grandmother will sort it out. Don't you worry."

We did put the letter back. I retied the black ribbon myself. But Mom was wrong. Nothing got sorted. No one felt better.

And it didn't stay secret.

FOUR

I sat up and reached for my phone: 5:25 a.m. It was much too early to call anyone or do anything. I had wanted to call my brother the night before, but old admonitions held firm. Although I hadn't recalled the exact words until the morning's early hours, the weight of secrecy, of some undefined and unspoken promise, had pressed upon me since speaking to Mat.

Does Jason know?

I pulled on a Tracksmith top and shorts and laced up my shoes. I hadn't taken a long run since my last marathon, but ready or not, this was the morning I needed one.

I headed out my apartment door and turned left on Charles Street in the direction of the Appleton Bridge and the bike path. To the Boston University Bridge and back would give me six miles—enough to settle my mind without injuring my cold legs. I hadn't thought about when I'd begin running again. Usually after a marathon I rested for several weeks then started back slow, running a couple miles every other day for the first few weeks, and gradually built from there. Not this time. I'd gotten caught up in trying to make life work—trying to do my best at Mednex, help Dad in any way he'd let me, and reconnect with friends—catching short runs whenever I could. Two weeks turned into seven months.

I huffed a long breath as I reached the path in an effort to clear my head. The sun caught my attention and I paused to watch it rise in a wonderful orange tipping to yellow. As it gained degrees in the sky, shadows dissipated and the Charles River burst to life. I continued my run, heading southwest as boats hit the water and fellow runners poured from the nearby buildings onto the path.

I stopped again at mile three to check my email—clearly the run wasn't long enough yet to distance my thoughts.

Mat Hammond.

I dropped to the nearest bench and breezed past his brief email to the attached article.

To: Jessica Burgess, Editor, The Atlantic
Fr: Mat Hammond
Re: Divided Loyalties: The Importance of a Multifaceted Approach to Our Past

In a time that necessitates reaching for the past to understand our present and navigate our futures with greater intention, there is a call to memorialize our shining moments, our sacrifices, and our heroes. As we grapple with the aftermath of a world pandemic, tumultuous elections, social upheaval, the rise of sectarian interests, intolerance, and financial uncertainty across the globe, we find ourselves examining the past to find the firm footing our present fails to provide. Some contend that by studying humanity's victories, we set our course toward the future on a more durable foundation.

Contrary to popular ethos, I have found greater growth and understanding come from our failures. It is the fallen who reveal to us our humanity, our perseverance, our yearning for right, our resilience, and our determination to stand after stumbling. While such stories of human frailty, weakness, and betrayal are ones we'd rather forget, as they leave us vaguely uncomfortable, I contend their fragmented light is more reflective of truth and provides a more substantive ground upon which to build a better future. They remind us of our shared experiences, mercy, and grace.

The past several years have seen burgeoning interest in WWII, from memorials to books, films, television shows, and even fashion. We've read about British and American citizens enamored with the Nazis; we've seen reenactments of the lives and loves of the Duke and Duchess of Windsor; and we've read several bestsellers introducing us to the Mitford sisters in England and the scandals surrounding Americans Florence Gould and Charles Lindbergh, whose loyalties lay with Germany as well. Yet their betrayals and sympathies danced in the periphery, away from battle and the front lines. We can accept or dismiss them as fits our will.

However, some crossed those lines. They carried their sympathies to battle and betrayed their countries, to the devastation of their families and, had it been known at the time, to the scandal and heartbreak of their nations. Such stories were not made known then. They were hidden, buried in files, and locked away. If known, they could cause a break in morale, a fracture in the united front, and harm a nation's will to endure and to ultimately succeed.

Caroline Amelia Waite is one such name and hers is one such story. To understand who she was and what she did, one must examine her roots.

Born in 1918, an identical twin to Margaret Georgiana Waite, Caroline was the daughter of John Thomas Waite, the sixth earl of Eriska, and his wife Ethel. Lord Eriska served as an admiral in the British Fleet from 1915 to 1917 and was awarded the Knight Grand Cross of the Order of the Bath for his service in WWI. Beyond that, he was close friends with David and Bertie growing up—men we remember as the short-reigned Edward VIII, turned Duke of Windsor, and King George VI.

Upon returning home in late 1917, Eriska married the young Lady Ethel Blaremont in February 1918. Later that year, daughters Caroline and Margaret were born. They were the girls in the twin bows, the patent shoes, the lace dresses, and the winning smiles. They were the girls playing on the lawn while their nannies looked on and their mother and father entertained their king and queen on numerous occasions and conversed on the most familiar terms with Winston Churchill, a close family friend. They were the girls with the idyllic life one now imagines while watching *Downton Abbey* or early episodes of *The Crown*. In fact, the two families were so close, some historians surmise that Princess Margaret, while named for family, was also named for Margaret Waite—only twelve years her senior.

At sixteen years of age, in 1934, the inseparable twins parted ways. Margaret stayed at the family estate, Parkley, in Derbyshire, while her twin sister attended Brilliantmont in Switzerland, an international school still educating Europe's elite. At eighteen, rather than return home to Derbyshire or to the family's London residence, Caroline set off to Paris to work with modernist dressmaker Elsa Schiaparelli, one of the twentieth century's most famous designers, known for her avant-garde styles, artistic collaborators—Salvador Dalí and Jean Cocteau, to name two—and her Communist leanings. In the late 1930s, Schiaparelli was setting the fashion world aflame with innovative designs, such as the wrap dress as well as her knits, and provocative stylings like the

Lobster Dress (1937) worn by *the* Wallis Simpson, Duchess of Windsor, on her honeymoon, and the even more shocking Tears Dress unveiled a year later.

It was at the House of Schiaparelli's place Vendôme salon, commonly referred to as the Schiap Shop, that Caroline met a German industrialist turned Gestapo officer and began an affair. Although relations between France and Germany were contentious from the 1939 declaration of war, the two sides existed in a tense stalemate during the Phoney War, with ideas and business mixing between private citizens from each side on a daily basis. All that ended when the Germans flooded France on May 10, 1940.

At that time, Caroline returned to London to work for the Auxiliary Transport Service and found her way to the offices of Churchill's newly formed Special Operations Executive, under the cover of the Inter Services Research Bureau. This new division of "ungentlemanly warfare" was tasked by Churchill to "set Europe ablaze" and was modeled after IRA tactics learned in the Irish War of Independence. Led by Dr. Hugh Dalton, the minister of economic warfare, the SOE was charged with everything from gathering intel to fomenting discord and revolutions in occupied countries.

While Caroline most likely worked in the typing pool at the SOE, her intimate knowledge of Parisian customs, culture, and events at the highest levels of society would have proved invaluable for a spy organization desperate to gain a foothold in France.

In October 1941, her work at the SOE ended in betrayal and the following letter was sent to her parents:

[INSERT PHOTOCOPY OF ORIGINAL LETTER HERE – TO COME]

The implications of the letter are staggering. Dr. Dalton and Eriska had worked several committees together under Prime Minister Chamberlain and his successor, Sir Winston Churchill. The men knew each other well and one can only assume this missive, what was said and what was left unsaid, was presented in the most personal and discreet terms both to uphold Eriska's honor and privacy and to protect SOE secrets.

Nothing is known regarding the whereabouts of Caroline Waite after that October date in 1941. Did she run away with her lover? Return to Germany with him after the war? Flee to South America as so many officers did in the late 1940s and 1950s?

While it is easy to pose myriad questions, it is reductive to condemn her choice. The 1940s were a tremendous time of upheaval in world events, in ideology, and in the governing tides of the Zeitgeist. In many ways, it was not unlike our own time. The future felt cloudy and uncertain at best. And, as is often the case, in such uncertainty, the young break free from the confines of their predecessors and seek new ways to find assurance, stability, and a way forward. One has only to look at women's fashion, as perhaps Caroline did when working for Elsa Schiaparelli, to see this. Post WWI, hems rose, necklines sank, and the iconic flapper emerged. Post WWII, luxurious fabrics and a focus on the hourglass New Look, as made famous by Dior, commanded society's favor. Trace fashion through the later half of the twentieth century and you'll continue to find changes indicative of our political and cultural ethos. We instinctively seek ways to redefine ourselves and emerge new across all spectrums of society and of life.

A lesson for today can be drawn as we look back. We need to be cognizant of the nuances, the emotions, the humanity, even the fragility of our own determination. We need to take in the collective experience and concede that we often hold our own lens with rigid determination. To condemn our predecessors for wrong choices is to condemn ourselves and the missteps, mistakes, and misunderstandings we now promulgate.

Yet the past often binds us. Words and stories have power. And what we are told, we often believe . . .

Upon receiving Dalton's notification in 1941, Caroline's father, Lord Eriska, rejoined the Navy. He had been serving in a consulting capacity during the early days of WWII, but within forty-eight hours of learning of his daughter's duplicity, he submitted his name for a command. Six months later, German U-boats sank his ship in the North Sea.

Upon news of her husband's death, Caroline's mother sold their Derbyshire estate, held within her husband's family for three hundred years and employed as an Army hospital at the time, and moved with her remaining daughter Margaret to the family's London home.

The family closed ranks.

Yet three generations later, Margaret's family thrives in the United States. Son John Randolph Payne, "Jack," who came to the States in 1965 for boarding school and founded the Boston law firm Swartz, Payne, and Lennox, still lives and works in the Boston area.

During a discussion, Payne commented:

[INSERT COMMENTS FROM JACK.]

[REACH OUT TO CAROLINE??]

FIVE

REACH OUT TO CAROLINE??

tapped my phone off. Unable to move or think, I closed my eyes and let the sun warm my face.

I hadn't known about my great-grandparents, their connections to Churchill or to the king and queen, my great-grandfather's service, or his awards. The Derbyshire estate. The idyllic childhood. Heck, the most I knew about London and England in the twentieth century came from *Masterpiece Theater* on PBS.

It was time to break that promise made long ago—a promise that was only remembered earlier this morning. I needed Jason.

Cutting through Charlesgate Park, I finally hit his townhouse on Saint Botolph Street at 7:00 a.m. A perfectly respectable time for a family with a five-month-old baby to be awake. And, if I knew my young niece, Carolina pulled her mom, if not both her parents, from bed at least two hours before.

I rang the bell in my signature style. Two short, one long. Gabriela answered immediately and pulled me into a hug. "Thank God."

"Watch it." I leaned back. "You'll get all sweaty."

"That won't be the worst thing that gets on me today. She's all yours to clean up. I tried peas this morning and it was a disaster." She stepped into the house and I followed her.

"Peas? Can't say I blame her."

Gabriela smirked and led me down the hallway to the kitchen.

I called after her, "I've got news that'll make you regret naming your daughter after me."

"Again?" I could hear her eye roll.

I rounded the corner from the hall to the kitchen and into their small back family room. I dropped to the floor next to Carolina's bouncy seat. "It's not the polio thing."

"Or the 'can't find the right job' thing? The 'dropped law school' thing? Or the 'I'm not worthy' thing?"

"I never said that last one."

"Didn't have to," Gabriela chirped from their pantry.

I refused to take the bait. My sister-in-law had a horrible habit of implying she knew different—and better.

Instead I looked around and absorbed what, to me, felt like the happiest home on earth. Jason and Gabriela's townhouse danced with light and color even on the cloudiest days.

The daughter of Mexican and Colombian parents, and with more style in her pinkie than I contained in my whole being, Gabriela had transformed their white-walled home into a utopia of color, texture, and design. I used to wonder how my decoratively pallid brother could stand it. Then I realized Jason and I shared something in common—we needed people in our lives with vibrancy and color, perhaps because we had somehow and somewhere lost our own.

Maybe that was true for me, but I might have been projecting onto Jason. The moment Gabriela set eyes on him, it was like he was the keeper of all the world's color and excitement. She glowed. Before I headed to law school, Jason had come to support me at a work fundraiser and, naturally, had to meet my boss. He was surprised to find Congressman Morris's chief of staff only a few years older than me, and even more surprised when she agreed to go out with him.

"Baby!" I cooed as I tickled Carolina's bare feet. "I'm a little sticky, but you don't care, do you? You're green and you love your aunt." I unstrapped her and held her high above my head to blow kisses on her pea-glopped onesie.

I looked beneath the upheld baby to find Gabriela frowning at me. "Stop calling her Baby. Use her name."

I scrunched my nose at my sister-in-law.

It had been a running debate when Carolina was born. It was Gabriela's idea. She wanted to honor her heritage, as did Jason, but she also wanted to honor me as representative of Jason's family. I was against it—honoring me. Honoring her heritage was a great idea.

But having never liked my name, nor believing I was worthy of any child's emulation, I used to bring them lists of suggestions until Jason told me to shut up.

"You're my sister and the closest thing to a sister Gabriela's got. So suck it up and be grateful."

I never said another word, but I still found it hard to embrace.

"Where's Jason?"

"Asleep. He had a twenty-four-hour shift so I'm trying to keep her quiet."

"You're not loud, are you?" I whispered to Carolina. She had changed in the few weeks since I'd seen her. Her eyes were still coal black, her hair equally dark, but it had grown in a little more and no longer carried the curls her mother sported. It looked stock straight.

"She's looking more like my brother." I winked.

"Don't say that. My mom is coming next month. She's a little territorial and thinks your family got the name. We've got to give her the looks."

"Harrumph. See? It wasn't a good concession at all." I sat at their breakfast table and bounced Carolina on my lap. "I need to talk to Jason. And to you."

"This sounds serious."

"It is."

She gestured toward the front of the house. "To the window with you. Change her on your way and I'll get us coffee and wake your brother."

Gabriela and Jason's home sat on the corner of Saint Botolph and Albemarle and featured the most amazing semicircular window well in the living room's corner. Right when they moved in, she had a cushioned seat specially fabricated and filled it with pillows. She then designed and built a high semicircular table to fit into the niche to hold food, drinks, books . . . whatever was needed to make the corner one's sanctuary. It was where we always talked, especially when life felt tough.

I grabbed a cloth from the kitchen, a fresh onesie from the small bin Gabriela kept in their pantry, and curled into a corner of the window well to wiggle Carolina into fresh clothing.

Within minutes Gabriela set three coffees on the table. Right as she turned toward the stairs, a soft chuckle reached us both.

"This looks cozy. Shall I leave you two?"

I flapped my hand. "I came mostly for you. Did we wake you?"

"Nah. I set an alarm. I find if I sleep more than nine hours after a shift I get groggy. Best to keep my circadian rhythm in sync."

"Of course." I chuckled. "Wouldn't want your rhythm getting off."

He scowled as only an older brother can and crossed the room to drop beside me. Rather than hug me, he tucked me tight under his arm and ruffled my hair, pulling it in every direction from my ponytail.

"Stop, you bully," I whined.

"Bully? You ghosted me again." Jason released me. "I have texted you for dinner almost every week since you got back. I don't know which is worse—that my sister refuses to have a single dinner with me or that I keep asking."

"You have a family. I don't want to take your time."

Jason gave me the evil eye, then relented as he always did. He looped an arm around my shoulders and squeezed. "Well . . . it's good to see you." He then shifted his gaze to his daughter. It was so full of love and longing, I held Carolina out to him. No doctor gets enough time with their family.

"Did you know Aunt Caroline was a Nazi?"

"What?" Jason's yelp startled his daughter and left no doubt in me. He knew nothing.

I briefly tried to remember what that Christmas had been like. Had he come home from college days after our return and no one said anything? Did we really act as if nothing had happened?

I answered the questions as quickly as they surfaced. Yes and yes. No one said anything about London because no one was saying anything at all. We'd all retreated to our metaphorical corners to heal after Amelia died. Except we never healed. And Jason, if I recalled correctly, decided to return to campus a week early that break.

I emerged from this trip down memory lane to find both Jason and Gabriela staring at me. "Sorry . . ."

With that, I dove in. I laid out Mat Hammond, his article, and everything as I knew it, beginning with our grandmother and great-aunt's birth in 1918 and hitting upon that afternoon in 2002. I then handed my phone, with Mat's article still displayed, to Jason, who leaned toward his wife to share the screen. After Carolina grabbed for it several times, I lifted her from his arms.

Jason laid the phone on the table. "What'd Dad say?"

"He refused to talk about it. He said he threatened to sue Mat, but it was just a bluff. He simply hoped he'd drop the story."

"Dad? Wow. This must have really shaken him."

"Your poor father." Gabriela sighed. "To have all this churned up.

He must feel so hurt, even threatened. And right as you're trying—"
Carolina distracted her with a fist to the eye. Grabbing her daughter's
hand, she finished with, "I'm just so sad for him."

"You're trying what?" I asked my brother.

Jason leaned back into the window. "I want him to get another
opinion from Sloane Kettering in New York. There is so much he can
do, but he's taken the most minimal path at Mass General. Someone
needs to knock some sense into him. It's like the man wants to die."

My chest tightened. "He won't go?"

"Like you say, he refuses to talk about it."

"But you two"—Gabriela cut between us—"don't you understand
better now? This is family. This has formed him." She pressed her
hand against her heart. "This betrayal pressed upon him his whole life.
I understand you say you learned this twenty years ago, but we feel
things even when we cannot name their cause. This has always been
with him, hovering, wounding."

"He said something like that last night." I rubbed at my eyes.

Jason clamped a hand on my knee. "You didn't cause this, kid."

I looked up at him.

"I know what you're thinking."

With ten years between us, Jason and I agreed we grew up in different families. His memories were filled with baseball games, model
trains, family dinners, and one-on-one excursions with Dad. I remembered little before Amelia's death, making my childhood all the more
somber, solitary, and shadowed—with me at fault for the change.

I liked hearing his stories, and loved imagining them to be mine.
More than that, our personalities were as different as our stories. He,
always direct and determined. Me, seemingly more scattered, unsure
where to stand. I often wondered if looking at the same thing, we'd
understand the other's description. Our perspectives were night and day.

Yet despite all those differences, Jason always saw me. He tried to understand. And he was right about the invitations—every week for the past year, he'd invited me to dinner. Just the two of us. To talk. To connect. And I had shied away each and every time, certain I'd disappoint and let him down, certain if I accepted, he'd see through me and never call again.

I drew my legs beneath me. "First Amelia, then a few months later this . . . I can't help but think that since 2002 I've been a constant reminder of the worst things that ever happened to Dad."

Jason folded me into a hug. "I'm sorry I wasn't around much. That was a rough year."

Despite my best efforts, the tears started to fall. When I finally sat back, Jason did what Jason has always done for me. He handed me a Kleenex and began to problem solve. "Now that you know, what's next? You need to help Dad."

Part of me wanted to retort, "What do you think I've been trying to do every day this past year?" while the saner part didn't want to share that nugget of my psyche.

"While I was running here, I wondered if I should go to London." I looked between them. "There's still that trunk of letters. Maybe I'll find something that can soften the narrative, something to make all this not so horrible for him. To make me not so horrible."

"That's a lot to hope for."

My jaw dropped. So did Jason's.

Gabriela covered her mouth in surprise. "I didn't mean it like that. I meant you may not find anything to redeem or soften this, and you have to be able to accept that. You also have to believe what this man wrote." She handed me my phone. "That good can come from tragedy. It's in every line here. You must see how illogical it is for you to be held captive by this, much less feel responsible."

"It doesn't feel illogical."

"Go." Jason cut across us both. "If you need me, call." He stood, lifting Carolina high above his head just as I had done earlier. "And tell Mom I say hi."

Gabriela smiled then bit her lip. "Just don't tell your dad until you're back."

SIX

The plane touched down at five in the morning on Sunday, London time. The sun was just breaking across the sky, piercing the gray with sharp strands of pink golds. It'd been six years since I'd been there and that was only for twenty-four hours.

I was a senior in college at the time. I flew over with Dad; Mom was already there. They'd been divorced three years by then and, I gather, she'd crossed the Atlantic six months earlier to care for Grandmother, her ex–mother-in-law, in her final months—as odd as that sounds. Odder yet, Dad hadn't visited his mother at all.

I remembered walking up the stairs to the London House's front door that morning and not knowing what to do.

"I'm sorry," I said when Mom answered the door. Nothing more. At the time, I wasn't sure if I was sorry my grandmother had died, sorry my dad had never come over, sorry for the weight my mom carried, or sorry that I—as Dad had purchased the tickets—was flying out with him the next day and leaving her to handle everything alone. Again.

Now, as I thought back, I wondered if my sorry had been based on my own doubts that, facing the same situation, I might not have given six months to my mother.

"Me too," she replied cryptically and pulled me into a hug. "I understand better after these months."

Her voice was sad and resigned, and hinted at a greater story. Rather than continue, she ushered me into the hallway. And, in the chaos of those twenty-four hours and then because she never moved back to the States following that trip, I forgot to ask.

I grabbed a cab outside Heathrow and headed to Eaton Square in Belgravia and to the London House. Before I could collect my thoughts or work out an approach, I once more found myself standing at the base of the five steps wondering what to say and do. Turning, I watched the sun dapple the trees of Eaton Square Gardens, opening through the wrought iron gate across the street, and wished I could head that direction.

Twisting back, I stared up at my family's "London House" as it had stood for two hundred years, shouldered on one side against the massive row of matching homes and wrapping around the corner on the other, the masthead to a long white ship. The broad blue front door was now painted a high-gloss black.

I could not step forward.

Four deep breaths and I forced myself to step up and ring the bell. Time moved faster than my ability to lay a plan, and the door swung open.

"Hi, Mom."

"Caroline?" She stepped onto the landing and pulled me into a hug. She held me tight and I felt myself melt into her. I breathed her in. A mixture of jasmine, lily, and something fresh and green enveloped me.

"I came to visit you."

"I see that." Her voice tripped across notes in a half laugh, half question. She glanced behind me. "No luggage?"

"Just this." I lifted my shoulder bag. "I'm only here for a couple days."

She stepped back. "This is getting curiouser and curiouser. Come inside, my little fly."

Mom always did that when we were very young. When everything else felt grim and gray, or Dad launched into a litany of book quotes—dark ones from Tolstoy, Shakespeare, or Dante—to make his point, she'd take a different tack. She'd wield the same tools, but with a lighter touch. She never made Dad wrong, but she lifted us up. I had not noticed until her counterbalance was gone—and that was long before she actually left.

As she closed the door, my jaw tipped open. The London House was unrecognizable. Gone was the foreboding and dark home of my memory. I gaped inside a front hall that was light, bright, almost joyful, and hinted at more airy beauty beyond. It knocked me off balance. It changed everything.

She smiled with excitement. "I take it you like?"

"I like." My eyes scanned the front hall, ceiling to checkerboard marble floor and back up again. "You did this?" I blinked, unsure how so much light could come from . . . "How?"

"I spent three years and twice the amount I should have, but this house deserved it. And it was a good project for me. And a wonderful use of Margaret's money."

"Has Dad seen it?"

"Of course not." Mom scoffed. "He'd never willingly come here. When your grandmother left it to me? I can't imagine that sits well, but it's his legacy, Caroline, and yours." She pulled at my arm. "Come see. I have so much to show you. Then we'll get to why you're here . . . I can't believe you are. I've imagined this . . . First let's stop in the kitchen and I'll put on some coffee."

Mom was red, flustered, and flapped her hands. She seemed eager to see me. Delighted even. She spun on her heel and waved for me to follow.

We walked through the front hall to a set of back stairs that had been widened in her renovations. What had been small, cramped stairs with uneven rises, leading to a dark kitchen and a warren of rooms surrounding it, was now a showpiece. Well-lit, broad wood stairs, stained dark brown, curved downward and led to an equally dark floor, stained in a chessboard fashion mirroring the marble floor above. But this iteration of the game board was dark upon dark. Deep brown–stained wood checkered against a deeper black. The effect was striking against the kitchen's fresh white and blue. White marble counters. White lacquered cabinetry. Glass doors revealing beautiful white-and-blue china, blue glassware and serving dishes. It was also flooded with morning light as the kitchen's entire rear wall was comprised of three sets of glass French doors leading to the walled garden.

"It's spectacular. Where'd you get this table?"

Standing in front of the doors was a rough wood table with seating for at least sixteen. It was smooth and irregular as if hundreds of years of cooking and cleaning had worn their stories into it.

"It was in a storage closet aside the garage. I expect a couple hundred years ago, it was the kitchen's main counter and cooking space and, rather than throw it away—because nothing in this house ever got thrown away—someone shoved it into a closet that was once part of the stable. You know, that back west corner?"

I shook my head.

"Anyway, I had it hauled out and I rubbed it down myself every night with oil for a month. It was a cathartic experience. Better than therapy."

Something incongruent caught my eye. Something massive and royal blue.

"What is that?"

"My oven. Come see. It's an AGA and it's my favorite thing in the whole house. It's always on and always warm. It heats this room all by itself. I had to take a class to learn how to use it. You can't adjust any of those compartments."

She stepped away from the stove and went through the motions of preparing coffee. As soon as it was steeping in her French press, she turned back to me. "While this rests, we'll tour the other floors then come back down here."

The first floor—an American's second floor—was equally transformed. The bedrooms no longer sported peeling wallpaper, water-stained ceilings, and soiled carpets.

The floors here were an interwoven parquet. Mom had used very few rugs. That struck me as I recalled always feeling damp and cold during my short visits. She grinned when I commented.

"The floors are heated. I did it throughout the whole house. It not only keeps everything drier—eleven percent drier—but it feels wonderful. I just couldn't bear to cover them."

Mom led me through the four bedrooms flanking the sides of the house, saving the front center room for last. I turned back at the doorway.

"Why'd you pick that corner one for your room? You should have this one."

She smiled, small and mysterious, as she led me around the doorway into the room.

It was mine. So clearly mine.

It was not exactly like the room I'd grown up in, but of the same value and texture if you'd combined mine with my sister's. She had used our colors—greens for Amelia, purples for me—but in a far more sophisticated manner. The walls were covered in a cream paper, with hand-printed, raised white stripes running down every few inches. The curtains hung straight, with no tiebacks or frills, and puddled onto the wood floor. They looked as if someone had taken a bridal bouquet of deep, rich flowers and thrown them onto the fabric. The flowers had scattered and, rather than assault you with chaotic color, they teased you closer. The bed was draped in white with the same floral fabric covering three Euro shams across its headboard. A chartreuse reading chair and ottoman sitting in the corner brought out the greens. The room also had a small desk.

"I hoped you'd come someday."

I turned to her. Unable to speak, I nodded. Then to fill what felt to be an uncomfortable silence growing, I did what I always did. I pushed Jason between us. "What did Jason say?"

Mom smoothed over the comparison I hadn't explicitly made. "Ten years is a big age gap. I was so different for you both. We were all different after Amelia, and I made so many mistakes . . . We'll talk." She squeezed my hand. "Come see the rest of the house."

I swallowed. I blinked. I followed my mom down the hallway.

As we made our way to the top floor, I envisioned the abandoned nursery, the playroom, the series of servants' quarters, and the dark wood–paneled attic that had occupied my last thirty hours of thought.

The west half was now one long open room. Its walls were painted a warm cream, and it held reading chairs set in the dormer window bays. Bookshelves lined the walls, and a massive, high wood table stood in the center of the room.

"I designed this myself. I come up here to work on things, wrap gifts and such. It's nice to be able to stand."

She opened double doors to the east side, revealing a fully appointed one-bedroom apartment. I raised a brow.

"I planned this floor for Jason's family or yours someday to have privacy when you come to visit." She smiled. "Or for someone to live in when I get old."

"Mom."

"Don't 'Mom' me. I may be ten years younger than your dad, but it'll happen." She pushed open a panel of wall where I hadn't noted the outline of a door. "The attic is still back here. I had it thoroughly cleaned and sealed and added lighting and better shelving, but for the most part, I left it untouched."

"It's really nice, Mom."

I stepped back into the large room with the high table. It was a stunning house, and only up here, looking at a worktable—the most basic thing in the home—did I realize how enormous it was and how lonely she might be.

She must have trailed my thoughts. She shrugged. "I also come up here to sit or when life feels big. Sometimes we need smaller spaces to confine us, comfort us. I refinished it first and even lived up here for a couple years while working on the rest of the house."

"Mom." I sighed. Something hard softened within me.

She smiled. It was less buoyant this time. "None of that. It's so good to see you. I . . . I have so much I want to say."

"I came to talk about Grandmother and that letter we found all those years ago." My reply felt curt. It sounded curt.

"I see." She tilted her head. "Let's head back downstairs then."

Nothing more was said until we sat at the broad table, coffees in hand, with a slice of homemade zucchini bread sitting in front of me. I wasn't hungry—and hadn't been for the last couple days.

"I can't believe you're here." Mom's eyes widened as if she was absorbing every detail of my face. "Tell me about life. How's your job?"

"Good." I nodded. "It's busy, but good."

"But?"

I wrapped both hands around my coffee, unsure how to start, how to explain. My relationship with Mom had been fraught for years, but in some ways it was more honest and forthright than my dealings with my dad. She'd been more open and approachable once upon a time, and that memory lingered—as clearly did my longing for that time because she could still sneak in between the chinks in my armor. It was both soothing and disconcerting.

I drew a deep breath to keep focused on the here and now. "I like it, but it's not what I want to be doing. I loved the law. It fit how I think, and it felt personal. What I do now might help humanity, but I never see or know the individual."

I picked at a corner of the zucchini bread, surprised I'd shared so much and made myself vulnerable to her opinion, or to her dismissal.

"You're twenty-eight." She reached for my hand and squeezed her assurance. "There's still time to find what you want and where you want to be."

"Not so much." I chuckled, hoping it didn't sound as disillusioned as it felt. "Jason sent me a terrifying article that these years aren't the throwaways everyone says. They're 'formative.'" I made air quotes to make light of an article that had kept me awake for two nights after I read it.

"Oh, your brother." Mom laughed. "To have three parents is not easy, dear."

"But he's not wrong. A couple of my friends have babies. Two more are finishing law school. My college roommate is the youngest partner ever at Bain and Company, and the medical research Callie is doing is groundbreaking."

"Okay, not *that* much time." She lightened her comment with a smile. "What brings you here? Why do you want to talk about the letter?"

"I came to set our family ablaze."

"What?" She set down her cup.

"I read it on the plane. It's what Churchill told some guy when he started Britain's first real spy division in World War II. He was 'to set Europe ablaze.'"

"This sounds dangerous."

"It feels dangerous."

To come here, to pursue this search, meant breaking another cord with my dad. So few tied us together, I feared that breaking this one might sever us completely.

"You'd better start at the beginning."

And so I did . . .

When I finished, she pushed away from the table and set a kettle on the stove. "No more coffee for me or I'll get jumpy." She pulled a tea tin from the shelf. "I hoped that afternoon would set your father free. I'd never understood why he was so closed, aloof. I thought it was a British thing and he'd warm up, and when we first met, he wasn't so much that way with me." She glanced at me. "Or when Jason was young. He was warmer, more giving. There was an endearing eagerness about him. But even then it felt like work and not his natural disposition. Then Amelia died and perhaps we both stopped trying." She looked straight at me. "Not perhaps. We did stop. I'm so sorry, dear."

"I'm not here for that." I pulled my head back, just as I'd seen my father do countless times, unable to tread where she was leading. "I want to talk about that afternoon."

Mom nodded. "I think every fear he had got named that day."

My name.

I pressed my lips tight to keep from saying it. It would sound churlish, childish, and self-centered. But it was how I felt and—calling to mind the look he threw me as I left the drawing room that long-ago afternoon—I realized I'd felt that way for twenty years.

Mom sighed as she crossed the kitchen to me, tea in hand. "It wasn't her name so much, but the reality of her. It was the lie they told and the fear behind it. That lie took on a life of its own and formed their family—our family, in a way. Caroline changed from a bright spark, one he chased to bring his mother joy when nothing else could, to a shadow from which no one was ever going to escape."

Her words drew me back to my Friday meeting at the coffee shop. Mat had said something about the fact that how we absorbed and translated history mattered and that it was never objective. The emotions we brought to it changed it. At the time, I associated his comments with world events; now they struck close to home. Aunt Caroline's betrayal changed us all. My failure changed us all.

Mom continued, "When one approaches death, I suspect life looks different. Your grandmother's perspective certainly changed. She was racked with guilt those final months—for not being bold, for not being more forthright with her sister, for not forgiving her husband, for feeling trapped and weak and unable to break free, and for lying to your dad and sending him away. For so much. It was heartbreaking and she was all alone."

"You were here."

"I was alone right beside her," Mom whispered. She then flashed a smile as if hoping the emotion would follow the action. "But you're here now."

"I need to see the letters, Mom. Do you have them?"

"I do . . . all of them."

SEVEN

Mom refused to give them to me right away. She looked over her teacup and stared at me while delivering her edict.

"What do you mean, not yet?"

"This might not be as easy as you think. Rest for a couple hours. We'll go for a long walk and grab tea at the Orangery. Then we'll get them from the attic."

"Is this a joke? I just told you my flight home is Tuesday." I pushed back, a little annoyed that she was playing a protective and concerned mother now.

"Then you'd better head upstairs for your nap quickly."

I opened my mouth to protest again. But she had the letters and I had only forty-eight hours.

As I walked back up the flights of stairs, I recognized something small unfurling within me. There was something novel, enticing, and comforting about being taken care of. I supposed we never grow out of that longing—and, I had to admit, the prospect of a nap, food, and finally getting to walk through a London park was compelling.

I washed my face, brushed my teeth, and collapsed onto the bed while Mom's comment about how this was the lie that formed our family played on a soft repeat. It sounded dramatic, yet I suspected she was right.

A rap on my door sat me up straight.

"Are you awake?"

"I don't think I slept."

She stepped into the room. Her shoes made soft squeaks on the floor. "It's noon. You slept."

"Four hours? I've wasted time." I tossed back the covers and threw my legs over the edge of the bed.

"Not at all. Grab some comfortable shoes and let's get going. It's about a two-mile walk."

We headed up Belgrave Place into Knightsbridge and entered Hyde Park at the Mandarin Hotel. It was bustling and sunny and glorious. Black cabs zipping down the streets, smartly dressed pedestrians in Belgravia, fast-paced tourists in Knightsbridge, and a more relaxed early summer Sunday scene once we hit the park—kids ran along the paths, riders on horseback trotted the outer dirt-and-gravel path, and blankets dotted the grass as far as I could see.

"You'll love the Orangery. They refurbished it and Kensington's rear gardens a few years ago. The architect, the same one who designed Britain's World War Two Normandy memorial, did a beautiful job retaining its history while bringing it into the present."

I scanned the room as the hostess seated us at a corner table next to a tall arched window. Mom was right. While I didn't know what it had been, what it was was spectacular. I felt like I had stepped into a Regency novel with delicate food to match the pristine high walls with their ornate top moldings, arched doorways, and floor-to-ceiling windows you could step through if you needed to beat a hasty retreat or get to an assignation in the gardens beyond.

I dropped my napkin into my lap, wondering at the small world nature of it all. The past. Respect. Translation. Adaptation. The things we reform; the things we let go.

I hoped I could do as well.

After lunch we walked home. Few words were spoken. I wondered if Mom felt as I did—that we were about to pass a point of no return. Our mood reminded me of walking into class on the day of a law final.

No one ever spoke. What was ahead absorbed our focus, charged the air around us, and held our futures in its grasp. It was either that, or Mom and I simply had little to say to each other after so many years.

We entered the house through the side door I remembered from years before. Although we had walked out the front, it was clear this was the entrance Mom used most. The small mudroom had a soapstone floor, already worn with water spots and life. Three pairs of Hunter boots stood sentinel in a tray—one the most startling orange color. Several coats hung on thick wood pegs and shelves held a variety of baskets to drop objects within. She plopped her house key into one and her handbag within another.

She then led me up the back stairs to the top floor. We came out at the workroom with its high center table. But rather than stand empty, the table now held three large cloth bins.

"While you slept I emptied the trunk. There was no way we were going to be able to lift it so I filled these. These are all letters." She pulled at one bin. "At least what I thought were letters—all the packets tied in ribbons. This one holds books. I assume they are Margaret's diaries." She walked around the table and laid her hands on the third bin. "And this last holds papers, odds and ends, and a few photographs."

She pointed back toward the attic. "You can also go through the trunk. There are still dolls, clothes, and lots of stuff in there, but I think this is what's pertinent to your search."

"Thank you."

"You're welcome." She paused, a question flickering across her face before she verbalized it. "Can . . . Can I stay? Can I help?"

I pulled out one of the four high stools. "You've never been through this? Not while you were here with Grandmother all that time? Not after?"

"Back then I felt it would have been a huge invasion into her privacy. Besides, Caro—that's what she called her sister—was all she wanted to talk about those last months. After almost eighty years of silence, she couldn't stop. I got to know both Margaret and Caro that way."

Mom dug through the bin of odds and ends and pulled out a photograph. "Then I didn't want to search. I wanted Caro to be for me just as Margaret remembered her. Despite everything that happened, your grandmother adored her twin."

She handed me the photograph. Two young women captured from the waist up. Lovely women. Mirror images. Yet different. One had her long dark hair pulled back. The other wore her hair short, curled close to the jawline, much like I'd seen in *Downtown Abbey* and *Foyle's War*. The one with long hair seemed wide-eyed and anxious or sad, I wasn't sure which, and the short-haired girl's head tipped back as if the camera caught her mid-laughter. Her bold joy was infectious. It made me smile and wonder why her mirror image, standing so close I couldn't find the line between their shoulders, wasn't joining in the fun.

"You look like them." Mom tucked a strand of my dark hair behind my ear.

I wanted to disagree, but I couldn't. For the first time, I saw rather than simply accepted what I'd been told. Before me were two iterations of me. The same wide, light blue eyes, dark hair, and square jaw—although my jaw was not so pronounced. Both my parents had brown eyes and Mom, a heart-shaped face.

"You and Dad said that, but I never saw myself in Grandmother."

"She was very changed by the time you knew her."

I turned the picture over. The year 1936 was written on the back. "They would have been eighteen? I assume Caro has the short hair?"

"Yes. She moved to Paris that year. Perhaps this was taken on a visit home." Mom nodded at the table. "Where do you want to begin?"

"I'm going to start with the letters." My thinking was that Caro's letters would provide the best insight into her story.

"I'll sort through Margaret's diaries." Mom stacked six identical books—all brown leather, hardbound with cream pages tipped gold at the edges—on the table. "The last book ends in October 1941."

"October 20, 1941, was the day of the notice Mat gave me, when they told her parents Caro ran off with her German."

"Margaret must have stopped writing . . ." Mom shifted as if trying to get comfortable. "She told me about that night, and what followed."

I waited for her to continue, but she didn't. Lost either in thought or in memory, Mom opened one of the diaries and began to read. I dropped my head and focused on my own task. The letters. I was tired of talking, guessing, and wondering anyway. I wanted to find answers—from the source.

I lifted out the packets of letters and placed them before me. The envelopes varied in size, and they did not seem to be organized by date but rather by importance. Some were crisp. Read once and put away. The ones in the first packet I pulled out felt soft with handling and wear. They held spots of ruined ink as if tears had fallen on them. My heart hurt for a woman who must have loved her sister very much—and, according to my mom, mourned her all her life.

Fanning through the stacks, I found most letters featured a swirling script that looked as if the writer's brain moved faster than the pen, which raced to catch up but never succeeded. There was something hurried about the penmanship, frenetic and excited, with the letters sloping close and up to the right in an endless chase.

One bundle came from a different writer. The pen had moved straight up and down, creating rigid letters. Instinctively, I knew those were not written by my aunt. No one thought to have impulsively run away with her Nazi lover could have such stiff, precise penmanship.

I reached for the topmost letter, one from the packet bound by the worn ribbon, created by the racing hand, and unfolded the soft linen pages.

EIGHT

HASTINGS, ENGLAND
17 MAY 1940

Dearest Margo,

I can't imagine your dinner conversation after I telephoned this evening. I thought Mother was going to convulse and expire right there. Father sounded near tears as well—and that says something. But you, dearest sister, your trembling "Thank God" was all I needed.

I was with you, hugging you tight. Our short conversation wasn't enough. There is so much filling me right now and no one to tell. I asked a WAAF senior section leader billeted here for pen and paper. I am warm, bathed, and dressed in clothes also borrowed from her. She is shorter than we are, so I look like I waded from France this morning. If I had, I would keep walking home to you. But that's impossible.

First I must be fed and, if I can be helpful, I must answer a million questions. They gave me a meal upon landing and that was the first I'd eaten in two days. I packed a bag when I left Paris, but that ran out quickly. Everything on the road ran out quickly.

Tonight I will live vicariously through you right now. Mrs. Dulles will have finally lightened Parkley's menu with spring and, as soon as she heard I was safe, most likely whipped up a treat. I'm hoping for champagne and my favorite custard and, if my salvation doesn't warrant that, please don't tell me. Let me dream I am worthy of a full month's rations of butter and cream and a little black market bubbly if Father has drained the cellar.

Tell him I'm sorry, Margaret. I tried to say it on the telephone tonight, but the line wasn't clear and emotions ran too high. My apology is for a quieter time. I can't imagine what favors Father pulled to secure passage for me, but I suspect the cost was high. Even after missing my ship, his telegram and Ambassador Campbell's letter got me out. Thousands waited in Brest for passage that I fear won't come without a longer wait and a higher cost.

We never saw it. We believed the *Ligne Maginot* would hold. We believed all those newly arrayed French soldiers sauntering through the Place de la Concorde represented a fraction of the thousands upon thousands ready to fight. We believed because the alternative was unthinkable. We believed what we were told. Propaganda.

I should have known better. After all, we were told the British were responsible for all our deprivations as well, and not the Germans. I knew that to be a lie.

In the end, the Maginot Line did hold. Each bunker stands untouched. The Germans bypassed it completely, swarming through the Belgian Ardennes with enough planes and tanks to scatter our defenses like paper soldiers easily blown in the wind.

As soon as we got word at the Schiap Shop, panic ensued and I became an instant outsider. That hit me hard, Margo. I felt I belonged here—there—but, as I said, the propaganda has been very anti-British over the past several months. Nevertheless, no one ever pointed a finger at me—until May 10 when I became an enemy, an outsider, and even my closest friends jeered.

"This isn't your country. See to yourself."

Dear Martine secured a ride west for me with her boyfriend, Pierre. Schiap would have helped, but she had left before. She left May 1 to visit Lyon in the South. It makes me wonder now . . . Maybe some of us did know.

I tried to make the ship, Margo. Tell Father that. Upon receiving his telegram, I hopped in Pierre's truck and headed west. I didn't wait a second. Neither did anyone else. All Paris, all northern France, emptied in a day, clogging the roads. People walked as their cars ran out of petrol, then died as German planes dropped bombs and fired upon the largest routes south and west.

Pierre drove me one hundred kilometers out of the city that first day before his truck died as well. I talked my way onto the back of a lorry to Orléans and caught a night train from there to Rochelle. I traveled for five days. I missed the first ship and broke down right there on the docks. A captain took pity on me and, seeing the letters, granted me a spot on his vessel.

I—

You'll never guess!!! There is more to add, dear one, and since you'll get this letter before you see me, I have to share here. We don't keep secrets, right? We never have and I'll not be the one to put a barrier between us now.

For one, I plan to head straight to the London House. I will spend this morning giving the officers here anything and everything I know about Paris and what's going on there, then I will head to London. There is work to do and George has inspired me to get to it.

Yes, George is here. Well, he was . . . I must start at the beginning. It's so exquisite it's bursting out of me, and telling you will let me relive it.

George knocked on my door as I was writing to you last night and, upon answering it, I burst into tears. I have never been so happy to see anyone in my life. He caught me as I dropped to the floor and held me tight. He came for me, Margo. Not last night, but in Saint-Nazaire. He expected me to make Father's reservation and had taken leave to meet me and escort me home. He said he was devastated when I didn't show, but he had to come back. He was needed on duty and no one had any word about me.

But when I arrived yesterday a friend called him and he came. I clung to him so tight I thought I'd never let him go, but he laughed and said he needed to feed me. So off to a wonderful little restaurant for fish and chips we went. Despite not having a real meal in weeks, and very little in the past several days, I could barely eat. I simply couldn't focus on anything but him. He looks gorgeous, Margo. We've been writing to each other, but I hadn't seen him since last year and never in his uniform.

I felt so loved that happy tears flowed all through our meal. He kept reaching across the table to squeeze my hand, to assure me I was safe and admonish me to keep eating. He couldn't believe my stories about how Paris was a study in deprivation. And I couldn't believe all I saw here. Sandbags, blackout curtains, ration cards, and a tension and wariness, an alertness that matched my own. You tried to tell me in your letters; I simply wouldn't listen. I held tight to my own imaginings for you—picnics with ginger beer, cold sandwiches in the sunshine, and cake. I've dreamt about a lot of cake in the past year. Is Derbyshire the same? Is Parkley as dark and barren? I've been so selfish, Margo. I never asked.

George assured me you are well. I didn't know about your work, though, or Father's. He reminded me that no one could tell who was reading our letters. At first, I thought he meant Schiap. She opened every piece of mail regardless if it was addressed to her or not. Her control was so tight. But then I recalled she started sending her letters through government friends and diplomatic pouches long ago, long before I ever did. It really is true, isn't it? Enemies are everywhere now.

But not last night . . .

George walked me back to my room and hesitated at the door. I looked up in wonderment at his expression. It was so tentative, innocent, and yearning. He's twenty-six, Margo, and I was not his first. If I didn't know it then, I certainly know it now. He's quite skilled. But, to his credit, he made me feel like I was his first, and his only.

I've gotten ahead of myself. Back to the door . . . At his hesitation, I turned the key in the lock and pulled him inside without a word. You would have been so impressed with my cool demeanor despite my heart beating into my throat. Every cell in me was alive and focused solely on him. In an instant, we were devouring each other. I couldn't get close enough, fast enough. Nor could he. I breathed him in and was lost. He hesitated only once more as he

---

I sat up straight and looked out the window to ground myself as to when and where I was. And, if I was being really honest, to make sure my mom was focused on her own work and not watching me. I felt a little hot and flushed, not only by what I'd read but by imagining what came next. The page had been torn and nothing more remained.

Turning it over, I found the letter's closing at the top.

He's gone back to his base now. He has a mission tonight. He wouldn't tell me what or where because it's confidential and he doesn't want me to worry. How can I not? Life has just begun, Margo, and who knew it could taste and feel so sweet.

I'm heading to the London House this afternoon and will register for an assignment there. I hope to see Father and deliver both my apologies and my thanks. Does he still attend military meetings at Whitehall? I'll telephone Parkley if I don't find him.

Come to London, Margo. There is so much more to tell you. We'll curl into your bed like we used to and I'll share every detail. To share with you is not kissing and telling—and I'll get to relive it once more.

I love you, dearest.

Caro

I unfolded the next letter, hoping for more of the story, more of that night, but the pile was not chronological. The next letter was dated several months later and, like the first, it was soft and worn from continuous reading.

The order of the bundle didn't feel random. While part of me wanted to search for George and Caro's next chapter, another part wanted to understand my grandmother and how she approached these letters. Why were these four tied separately? Why wasn't this ribbon pristine like the others, but soft and frayed instead?

Something about these four letters mattered to Grandmother—which meant they mattered to me.

NINE

LONDON HOUSE
26 AUGUST 1940

Dearest Margo,

I'm sorry I yelled last night. London is more unnerving than I anticipated and that bomb dropping three nights ago made it feel real and dangerous. Reports say it was one of the first direct hits to the city and more will come. Part of me wants you here with me. The better part of me wants you to stay far away and safe at Parkley.

But I can't leave, Margo. Please don't ask again. I know you feel working here rather than at home is reckless, but I need to be here. I've put in for a transfer to the Inter Services Research Bureau and hope it will come through soon. This other work is important, Margo. I feel it in every fiber of my being. And it can't be done in Derbyshire.

I need to apologize on another count as well. I wasn't very kind about Mrs. Bevington's death. With all your other duties, placing her children cannot be easy. But I miss them—the children—and you still see them at home. You hear them. Blame that insensitive outburst on ugly jealousy.

You wrote to me last year that they'd all left London, but I couldn't envision what that meant—the quietude, the loss of hope. The clubs are hopping at night with plenty of laughter, but it's that frenetic kind, with the high notes trying to outrun reality. I've heard them before. I've pushed them out before. We drank too much, laughed too loud, and yelled about how fine we were in Paris, especially in Montmartre, talking art and revolution until the wee hours of the morning. We felt invincible. How little we knew.

It's no different here. London carries those same frenzied tones trying to fashion a new reality from thin air as the world crashes around us. Only now we know we are vulnerable—and there is no young hope, no skipping girls and naughty boys pulling their bows, to counterbalance our fear and chase the demons away.

I got a letter from Martine yesterday. She relayed that the Schiap Shop remains open under some sort of police protection. She didn't go into specifics and I bet she doesn't know them. Schiap trusts Martine with everything that requires a needle, but she knew Martine didn't share her political leanings, and I'm sure everything is more tense now. Martine remarked that Schiap is more mercenary than Communist these days. I can believe it, but I fear Martine should not write it.

Because if the House of Schiaparelli stays open, it provides Martine and others work, salaries, and a modicum of protection. I wrote back advising her not to think deeply about its cost and to certainly not write about it. If she does, and gets fired for it, she'll be on the streets. No Jewish woman could survive that, not with the Germans in charge.

There's a cold efficiency about the Nazis, Margo, a soulless cruelty that still makes me shudder. We laughed at them after war was declared and nothing happened. Like England, we called it the Phoney War and remarked on their absence from Paris. After all, it had been a great game when I first arrived to make fun of their stiff stomping as they ran drills in their embassy's courtyard. They were like guard dogs held back on chains, dressed in a horrid brown. We wanted to rattle them, shake their chains, fully believing those strong links kept us safe. Then, even before the declaration of war, they were suddenly all gone. Gone to fight other enemies.

It was an illusion. They were always our enemy. While they were fighting in the east, swelling their ranks, they were lying in wait until the time came to devour us. Their strength, their speed, their inhumanity is terrifying. I tasted it those few days I remained after the invasion, racing west, and I can feel the fear in Martine's missive. The Nazis are ravaging all of France and Pétain's Vichy government is letting them.

Martine says they hold Dunkirk up to them as a show of British cowardice and report that our blockades continue to keep their food and fuel scarce, rather than German gluttony. I hate that she thinks that about us, about me. I hate that all France might. I must remember that I can't believe what I read or hear; I must believe what I know to be true.

I know you, Margo. That is why I fell apart and yelled so badly on the telephone. You keep me safe, and sane.

Thank you for sending me that care package and for telephoning, despite Father's grumbling over the expense. Please know I heard you last night. In many ways, I can't deny I want to come home. But . . . I can't. Father and Mother need you. We both know I have hurt them again and again, and I can't imagine that will change. I never meant to. It's just that things got tangled between us and I'm not sure the threads will ever run straight.

Father wrote to me last year that I was "amounting to nothing." I hope he doesn't truly feel that way, but words have power and those now sit between us. You don't believe that. I can feel it. Remember that. Remember that no matter what happens tomorrow, next week, or next year, you and I are one—and you, of course, are our better half.

Yours, as always,

Caro

My eyes scanned the words again. *Amounting to nothing.* They weren't simply words on a page. Crossing eighty years, they were daggers. While I hadn't heard that exact configuration, I'd felt the black abyss of similar statements. *Quitting law school after two years is a waste . . . You need to grow up . . . Finish anything . . . Stop acting like a child and commit.*

That particular dynamic between my father and me solidified when I was eight. Perhaps he retreated in his grief or disappointment. Perhaps he really thought so little of me. I didn't know his side of our story. I only knew mine. I pulled away in fear, in sorrow, and in guilt for being the child still alive and, perhaps, chased anything and everything I thought might assuage that agony.

Amounting to nothing. Yes, I could understand that pain.

Rather than dwell on it, I turned to the next letter and noted that we were going back in time . . .

PARIS
16 JUNE 1937

Dearest Margo,

Did you see the Lobster Dress in *Vogue*? Gene Tierney, that American girl at school, used to say, "A picture is worth a thousand words." I suspect she'll end up in the movies someday saying plenty more than that—but I digress.

Boy was she right! A thousand words! A thousand hours! A thousand sexual innuendos!

Please tell me you saw it! And don't try to convince yourself you're above it, because I know you—better than I know myself most days. If Mrs. Dulles still lets the maids keep that magazine stash in the silver closet, run *tout suite* and grab this month's American *Vogue*. They gave Wallis Simpson an eight-page spread.

We Brits didn't give her so much respect—then again, she stole our king, so we shouldn't have.

In fact, now they're my problem, not yours. The happy couple plans to live here. Wallis simply *adores* the French—actually she loves the Nazis, but we won't go there. There's talk all over Paris of a Nazi lover who sends her seventeen red flowers each and every day. Enough about that . . .

Back to the dress!

The Lobster Dress. That's what we called it during design and now it's what everyone around the world is calling it. Hardly a surprise with a large lobster straight down the front. I say "down" because Dalí wanted it up. He wanted his large crustacean to snap up at Wallis's private parts. Seriously, how disgusting can the man get? Schiap won that argument—along with a few others.

I worked on the bodice. Well, Martine did, but after hours we sat in her studio and worked together. Her workroom is my second home. It's off the back of the salon and has incredible light. It's large enough that Martine put a small bed in there to collapse upon when Schiap is at her most demanding and wants it NOW! The woman really has no patience. So more nights than is reasonable, Martine stays and sews late. I piled the bed with pillows she let me make from fabric scraps and shared with her all the city's gossip. They really are gorgeous pillows, Margo.

Martine is fascinating to watch work. Nothing at all like when I used to mend our dresses. She's a genius. She's our age with three generations of dressmakers in her family, so I guess it's in her blood. For the Lobster Dress, she fashioned the bodice from only two layers of tulle and thin supports the width of fish bones. That's what undergirds the silk—created by the famous Sache, of course. The whole dress weighs less than a pound. And no wonder—look carefully—the waist is practically transparent!

Wallis Simpson came to the House last spring. We shut the whole place down for her, brought in champagne, and Dalí was his most charming. He found her especially alluring and practically drooled all over her. Everything has sexual connotations for the man. Telephones. Lobsters. Anything. Meeting Wallis brought it all to the forefront. There is something about her, even I'll admit that, an instinct that's both predatory and sexual.

She fell in love with the design, along with half the House. She outfitted her whole trousseau with the Lobster Dress as its crowning glory—besides Edward, of course. He's the real crown, *non?* Dalí was apoplectic with delight, rubbing his hands together like a greedy child and pulling out the side of his mustache in nervous energy. I hate how he twists it around his fingers when aroused. It's disgusting.

At first Schiap demanded his lobster follow Wallis's hip line—I'm having trouble calling her Duchess—like she wears her leaf motif to emphasize her shoulders and hips. But Dalí won the day and, as I said, stuck the crustacean right between her legs. He won that round, but Schiap won the next and fanned the tail over her private parts rather than the snapping claws. It's equally provocative, though not quite so aggressive.

Then there was the mayonnaise. You should have heard the uproar over that. It escalated into a yelling match of such violence, I locked the salon's front door so no one could walk in. Schiap screamed she'd never work with Dalí again if he slathered the final dress with the huge jar of mayonnaise he brought to the salon. For once, he believed her.

Don't share these details with Mother, please. I wrote her a very different letter this evening. One that won't generate another lecture about the immorality of my work. Because it's not immoral, Margo—it's new and modern, and it's the way we are meant to dress.

Fabrics should skim the body like a living skin. We should be able to move, breathe, and live. Fashion isn't merely about clothes—it's about design, ideas, innovation; it's theological, political, fundamental. It reveals the soul through draping the body. It's about a woman making a statement on how she sees her place in the world and in eternity. I'm getting dramatic, and you hate that, but it's all true. Besides, Mother is a hypocrite. She bought two trunkfuls of Schiap's knitwear from the London salon. Should I remind her how free and comfortable she found all those soft knits?

The Lobster Dress started something new here, Margo. Schiap has always been daring, avant-garde, and fearless, but a new energy fills the air now. She and Dalí were thick as thieves last week, and this morning they called the whole salon together. I can't even describe their new collaboration. It's all white, red, pink, and brown. She called it the Tears Dress. I thought she meant tears, like drops of water from one's eyes, and I envisioned a gorgeous ephemeral creation of blues and greens—water touched by light. Something perhaps less structured than the Lobster Dress, with more transparency. But she meant tears—like tearing meat. Grinding, chewing, masticating. I'm not kidding. The white silk dress has structured rips to expose red, pink, and brown layers, which will be sewn beneath as if you're ripping through pearly skin into the animal, into the woman underneath.

A few of us squirmed in our seats as Dalí got overly graphic in his description. It's daring, but Schiap won't let it get out of control. She's brilliant, but she's also pragmatic. She knows what sells and what doesn't. She knows which way the wind blows.

Dalí? He's crazy. You'd hate him—most of us do. He has to be the center of every moment. You've never met anyone so in love with his own needs and so ready to pitch a temper tantrum like a five-year-old if they're not met. You'd love his wife, though. Gala is capable, firm, ten years his senior, and, for the most part, manages him well—and tolerates his dalliances with a generous eye. But she isn't always around and she wasn't here when he described the Tears Dress. I really wish she had been because there are some images I'll never forget and her presence might have tempered the show.

Or . . . you could have been here to watch it with me. We would have then gone out for dinner and wine, curled up in my apartment, and laughed all night together.

Come to Paris, Margo. We've been apart long enough. And while you'll counter my request and say "you come home," please know that is impossible. Someday, perhaps, you'll understand. Someday, perhaps, the veil will be lifted between us and we can see each other clearly again. Everything changed when you were sick. I can't think about that summer and the despair I felt that I might lose you, without catching my breath and growing hot with panic. But you are well now and we are nineteen. We are our "own women" as Mother used to say—though I doubt she says that now. It was fine when we were young and she felt she had time to mold us. Now she keeps calling me a "girl," as if saying it can turn back the clock.

Nevertheless, we are grown and we could have such fun here together. We could breathe deep, work, and be free. Father is worried about nothing. He and Sir Churchill have been sounding the doomsday gong for years and, yes, there is turmoil in Germany, but when isn't there? Our new prime minister says all is well. If Father can't trust an old friend like Chamberlain, who can he trust?

You need this, Margo. You need to spread your wings, and Paris is the perfect place to fly. It's alive, moving, and racing—and I am here to catch you.

No more . . . Just come.

Love,

Caro

PARIS
5 SEPTEMBER 1939

Dearest Margo,

Try to understand. I'm not being hardheaded or stubborn, petulant or selfish. I endured hearing all that from Father. I wouldn't have telephoned if I had known what was coming. Schiap was furious with me for using the salon's telephone, and then to have everyone in the room hear Father yell . . . It was beyond embarrassing.

But your cold silence was worse and your parting shot— "Tresse"—was completely beyond the pale.

How dare you say that to me. How dare you call me that. I'm doing what's right, Margo. How is me staying here, working where I love, in a country I adore, a betrayal of all Father believes in? He's the one who taught us to think, listen, and stand up for what is right. France is equally at war! And on England's side!! I can do my bit for the war effort here. People here will suffer just as much, if not more than in England, and this is my home now.

Fine . . . I was wrong about the Munich Agreement. I'm sorry I ever quoted that "everlasting peace" bit. But Father didn't need to throw it in my face. I wasn't the one who said it. Remind him it was the prime minister.

And what makes him so sure Herr Hitler will turn his eyes west from Poland? Hitler has what he wants and now France and England have made their stand. It's probably all over and, in days, we'll see Hitler back down. Even if he doesn't, I refuse to accept I'd be safer in one country at war than in another equally at war, simply because Father says so.

I expected vitriol and disdain from him, Margo, but not from you. Never from you. Has the gulf between us grown so wide you couldn't stand beside me? Even if I am wrong, you are my sister, my twin. How can you not support me? I never asked to leave, by the way. I was sent away. Do you feel I betrayed you on that front as well? Because if you do, you are wrong. I was the one betrayed.

I'll have you know I sat outside your bedroom for days until Father hoisted me into that car to London. Do you have any idea how horrible that was? To leave you? Fearing your death every moment? I lived banished from everyone I loved and just when I thought I could come home, I was cast off to Switzerland. Brilliantmont was wonderful. I'm not saying it wasn't, but I didn't choose it, Margo. None of it was my choice. Now when I finally find a home I created and I love, you condemn me? I expected it from Father. I have endured it for five years from Father. But you? Who is the real Tresse here?

I will always love you, but this struck deep.

Caro

P.S. I can't believe I'm doing this . . . I've enclosed a jacket I designed. I'm so angry with you right now, I can barely write, but I still want you to have it. I made it for you, and England is now required to carry identification papers just like we must. Martine and I have been working on this for weeks. Schiap likes it and may offer an iteration of it in her next collection, but you get the first model. My model.

It has twelve pockets sewn into it. Clearly you can see the six across the front. Don't you love the buttons? Now search for the other six . . . I think it will take you some time. Sliding precious items into those will protect them. I defy anyone to find something thin and sleek in a few of those pockets. And, speaking of thin and sleek, I'm getting diabolical . . .

For some reason this idea of concealment has captured my

imagination. I started with one of the basic brassieres Martine developed for the Lobster Dress a couple years ago and, rather than reinforce it with the bone, I rolled sheets of paper tight and slid them in. I then left a one-centimeter thread hanging loose, right beneath the arm. That tiny thread allows the wearer to release the rolled papers at a second's notice. Rolled, however, I don't think anyone else could ever find them, even in an official search or interrogation. Martine couldn't find them and she's brilliant. I have no idea what use it is, but it was a challenge and right now, Martine and I stay in more often than we go out. I need ways to focus my mind and thoughts.

I won't deny the declaration of war has brought changes. Paris has ramped up in a frenetic passion that Martine and I find unsettling. I used to love the pace and flavor of the nightclubs and parties, but they've soured. I'm sure it's the same in London. Perhaps only dear Parkley remains untouched in its northern woods.

But, despite all this, dear sister, there's no place I'd rather be. Try to understand.

C

Tears had smudged the ink and wrinkled the paper with pock marks, and somehow I knew they hadn't come from the first reading. At that reading, perhaps Margaret had been too angry to hear Caro's hurt beneath her defiance. But as time wore on, I felt sure my grandmother felt all her sister's love.

The postscript revealed the depth of their connection. And by the soft folds and worn edges, it was clear my grandmother had returned to this letter, to this moment, and to this pain again and again.

I sat back and considered the four letters, tied together in their own black ribbon, apart from the rest. Each represented different aspects of my aunt, different aspects of her relationship with her twin, and different moments my grandmother felt compelled to revisit.

They meant something then and I couldn't help but feel they were equally important now.

TEN

How late do you think you'll be up?"

I tapped my phone to reveal the time. Eleven o'clock. I'd been reading for over nine hours with only a short dinner break.

I looked up, pulled off my glasses, and rubbed my eyes. I scrubbed them to the point of pain trying to wake them up, wake me up, and clear my head.

"You'll get bags and wrinkles that way." Mom laughed at me.

"That's the least of my worries." Stars skittered across my vision with the release of pressure. "I'll crash soon. I should've slept on the plane."

"Quit now and get back to it tomorrow."

I pushed up from the stool and arched my back. "I don't have much time, Mom. It's going to require some sacrifices."

"How noble," she said dryly as she poked a finger through the scattered papers. "What have you found?"

"Tons . . . Well, not much that refutes Mat's article, but a lot about Grandmother and her sister." I plopped down again. "It's touching, scorching, uplifting, and sad. For the most part, it's really sad. They were so close. Maybe twins are closer than mere sisters."

Mom stilled. We both drifted to Amelia. Only in such close contact, with her or with Dad, did I feel Amelia's absence so strongly. I always thought we would have weathered her loss better together, but when together, her memory pushed us apart. Perhaps we were all frightened of happiness, or of seeing and feeling it in each other.

I traced a line of the letter sitting in front of me. "Losing Caro would feel to Margaret like she lost herself."

"She never recovered," Mom added.

I looked up. Neither of us were talking about Caro and Margaret. Yet neither of us could make the leap.

I tapped the table—the first to back away. "To catch you up, I've been reading Caro's letters in the order they were bound rather than chronological because these first four were tied separately and were the most worn. They seemed special to Grandmother, which made me wonder if the others were in order of importance as well. But I'm beginning to think no. I don't sense she returned to most of these, so now I'm sorting them in chronological order."

I reached to my left and gently picked up the first four letters I'd read. They were old, delicate, and so worn I feared they could disintegrate at my touch. Yet I couldn't help but touch them. They felt vital to me. In just four letters, I knew my grandmother and my aunt—and I loved them both.

I passed them across the table to my mom. "In these, you get Caro arriving back in England in 1940, a later letter about her work, and a fabulously fun letter from Paris with a description of Elsa Schiaparelli's famous Lobster Dress you've got to read." I pointed to my computer. "Tap that on and you'll see a picture of the duchess of Windsor in it." I waved my hand back to the letters now lying in front of her. "And I have to read a section to you."

I walked around the table and picked up the first letter, donned my glasses, and prepared to take Mom back in time . . .

I started at *George walked me back to my room* and read to the torn end of the description.

"That's it. The page is ripped off there." I flapped the page. "Either Grandmother was a prude and it offended her, or she was afraid their father might read it. Either way—"

I looked up, expecting flushed cheeks, wide eyes, and a compressed smile. Instead I found Mom in tears wearing the most tender, heartbroken look I'd ever seen on her—and I had held her hand when she buried her daughter.

"What?"

"She was neither. Margaret wasn't a prude and she wasn't protecting Caro from their father . . . To think that was her most important letter." Mom swiped at her eyes with her pinkie fingers. Unlike me, she delicately moved her fingers across the lower lids from corner to corner.

She blew a shaky breath and continued. "She couldn't bear it, tore it, then returned to it to remind herself, to make sure she never forgot and believed for a single second that he could actually love her. She probably read it over and over for self-preservation."

"Mom?"

"My heart breaks for her. Because he did, Caroline. When I was up here earlier, I read a few from that last stack. His handwriting is the up-and-down stiff one you remarked on. His letters were affectionate and sweet and open. He did love her, always as a close friend. They could've been happy . . . but she couldn't let herself believe it was real or that it could grow. She poked herself with this thorn again and again."

"You're going to need to slow down." I reached for the block-lettered stack. I hadn't read any of them yet. "These letters are from George? To Margaret?"

"Only Caro ever called him George. It was his middle name."

I felt my lips part with the realization.

Randolph George Payne. My grandfather.

"I . . . Did you know? Did she tell you?"

"Not about that letter, no. But in those last months, she told me all about Caro and her George, and how Randolph hated his middle name and only ever let Caro call him that."

Mom perched beside me. "It's one of the many things we talked about. Regret. Only at the end could she see what she'd done her whole marriage. She pushed him away. She felt second-best her entire life. She always believed he only married her to protect her and Ethel out of duty. He waited nine years for word from Caro."

"So he didn't believe she ran off with a Nazi?"

"I don't know what he believed. It was never spoken of until Margaret's last months. She chose to believe it. Perhaps there was no alternative that felt better. I just know he stayed by Margaret's side all those years, but didn't marry her until 1950. Then your father was born ten months later." She rubbed at her eyes again. "To feel so alone and to imagine every touch, look, or loving word was meant for her twin. That's what Margaret did to herself."

"That's why he married her, but why'd she marry him?"

Mom sat straight. "I expect you'll find that in the diaries. She adored him her whole life. I doubt she had any idea of the twists and turns her heart would take."

Mom reached into the box and pulled out a black-and-white photo. Two men close together. One perhaps sixteen or seventeen, the other broader, more assured, even smarmy, and in his early to mid-twenties.

"The younger is Randolph, your grandfather, and the older is his brother Frederick. They grew up with the "Waite Girls," as they were called. Their parents were best friends. The stories she told about their childhoods. It felt magical."

I studied the picture, imagining magical. Nothing about my grandfather conjured such images for me, but looking at this young man, I could see it. He was alive. Handsome and tall with light hair and a smile that lit his whole face. Mischief danced in his eyes.

Mom gestured to the letter still resting in my hands. "I suspect that was why she ripped it and why she returned to it. First in despair, then as a barbed reminder of her real situation."

"But it wasn't her real situation."

Mom shrugged. "How we feel can become our reality, Caroline. Nothing is objective."

Mat. Again.

I hadn't thought of him in years, yet memories of him surrounded me. The two of us leaning across library cubicles in college debating history, perspective, and weekend plans. The two of us organizing our schedules so we could take at least two classes together each quarter. His constant chirping about how we created our reality by what we chose to keep, what we chose to remember, and what we called truth.

"So he gave up." I sighed.

"'There are very few of us who have heart enough to be really in love without encouragement.'"

"That sounds like Dad." I raised a brow.

"His quotes were sometimes spot on. Credit that one to *Pride and Prejudice*'s Charlotte Lucas."

We sat in silence for a few minutes. She scanned the piles of papers. My mind felt numb.

"Speaking of your dad," she ventured. "I didn't want to ask earlier, but what did he say when you told him you were coming here?"

"I didn't tell him."

"Oh, honey. Didn't you say he threatened to sue the reporter?"

I twisted to face Mom straight on. "He was just upset."

"Exactly . . . This is upsetting for him." Mom studied me with equal directness. "You're doing this to help him?" Her eyes softened. "He may not see it that way."

"Does he ever?"

She laughed. It was small, sad, even a touch self-deprecating. There were layers within it I could barely trace before it ended. "Be careful, sweetheart. What you're learning here . . ." She waved her hands over the letters and the bin of diaries I hadn't touched yet. "None of this ended in 1941. That's where it began, and these bands stretched over the years and bound us all, especially your dad."

She pushed off her stool and walked toward the stairs.

I called after her, "You aren't going to tell him, are you?"

She turned back. "It's not my story to tell. I'm bringing you coffee before I head to bed. You'll need it."

She disappeared from view and I returned to the letters, far more intrigued now by a love story than my family's history, but wondering, perhaps, if they were one and the same.

ELEVEN

A t midnight, I called Mat.

"Hello?" He sounded distracted. I grimaced as I did the math in my head. Seven o'clock on a Sunday night.

"It's Caroline. I'm sorry. I didn't realize the time. You're probably eating dinner."

"This is fine." I heard background chatter. "Hang on. Let me grab my computer." Voices called out. "I've got a few friends over for burgers. Are you ready to comment?"

"No," I exclaimed. I felt like once he turned on his computer everything would be set. There'd be no turning back. No room for what I wanted to propose. "I didn't call for that. In fact, I called to say you've got it wrong."

"How's that?" Mat's voice fell in fatigue-tinged sarcasm.

"I have all Caroline Waite's letters to her sister and all my grandmother's diary entries covering the same time. Caroline was British—loyal British—and she had a lover, but not a German. He was an Englishman named George. And she mentioned your Paul Arnim—openly, as a good man in love with his wife." I pulled that letter toward me. The one that inspired the call.

"Listen to this, from a letter dated March 3, 1940:

"'There's a German industrialist in Paris—Paul Arnim. I've mentioned him before. He's about forty, and his wife the same, with two small children you want to eat up. Schiap is horrified when the kids come to the salon, but they are angels. Last night at the party,

Mrs. Arnim was anxious, almost skittish. I didn't understand why until I was delivering a gown to her in one of the dressing rooms. I gather they leave for America soon and she was frightened. While all soldiers were, of course, recalled to Germany last year, Mr. Arnim, like many private citizens, stayed for his work. Something has now changed. Her voice pitched high as I raised my hand to knock on the door and I heard Mr. Arnim say, "We will be fine, my love. Trust me. I will always be with you.'"

"That's not a man involved in an illicit affair, Mat."

When he didn't reply, I rushed on. "She goes on to write about how he'd been in the salon several times before and how they'd become friends—how anything Caro set aside for his wife, he purchased. Caro wouldn't do that or write that way if she was going to betray the woman. Not only that, it doesn't fit anything I've read about her."

I drew a breath. My spiel had felt like the mock trials in law school, but with less breathing. Now I awaited the verdict. The silence drew out between us.

"Mat? Are you there?"

"I'm here. And . . . I didn't have any of that. Nothing in my files says Paul Arnim left France before his conscription and subsequent transfer east. You've simply got a husband placating a wife."

"Or a trail to follow."

"It's irrelevant, Caroline. He's not mentioned in the article."

"He's the basis of your unvalidated assumptions about my aunt," I ground out.

"Unvalidated—" he shot back then stopped. "Are we done here? I've got guests."

Something in his tone flashed a memory of another night, another fight, another hurt long ago. Our senior year. The last time we spoke. I took a deep breath to stay in the present.

"Look, this is going wrong . . . I didn't call to fight. I called because it's different. The story feels different from anything I expected, and I think if you were to read all this, you'd change your mind."

"Perhaps I would." He sighed. "But the affair is irrelevant. Yes, it adds color to her defection, and love affairs add marketability, but I'm talking about history and how we remember it, change as we examine it, and grow from it."

"But we haven't grown from it." The words slipped out.

Mat had no quick retort. Instead silence again filled the line. He had stepped away from wherever he was before and I could no longer hear the din of chatter in the background.

"I'm sorry, Caroline. When I reached out to your dad and to you, I had no idea this was news for you. I . . . I don't know what to say."

"Say you'll help me?"

"Fine." He sighed. "How?"

"I figure if you're wrong about the affair, you could be wrong about a lot else. Just read the letters."

"Fine," he repeated. "I'll meet you tomorrow."

"Sorry . . . no . . . I forgot that part. I'm in London." I wrinkled my nose. "But I'm flying back Tuesday and I'll bring them with me. You've got to see some of this. I've read about World War Two politics and rations, some Nazi named Dubbell who made passes at Caro when she first arrived in Paris, and incredible nights in restaurants and clubs. And you were wrong about her being a secretary. When she got back to England, she worked in fabrics. She wrote Margaret that ISRB sent her to Arisaig and Morar in Scotland for a couple months to develop new zippers and canvas. And she didn't agree with Schiaparelli's politics at all. In fact—"

"What did you just say?"

"Caro wrote that Schiaparelli was mercenary and implied that, despite being a Communist, she was spying for the Germans."

"Everyone suspected that. The FBI had her under surveillance the whole time she lived here during the war. I mean about Arisaig and Morar? She wrote about those towns? She mentioned them?"

"Of course. Unless you're Tolkien, you can't make up those names." I expected Mat to laugh. He didn't. "Mat?"

"I—" He stalled out. "I don't think she was a secretary."

"That's what I'm telling you. She worked fabrics. Designed uniforms."

"There was no manufacturing anywhere near those towns, Caroline. There were no fabrics in the Scottish Highlands . . . But there was demolition and paramilitary training. Could your aunt have been a spy? Impossible. She'd be the first . . . the first woman? That would make her defection huge . . ." Mat's voice drifted away.

"Wait. What?"

"You need to stay." His voice snapped from contemplative to directive. "You need to get over to the National Archives. I can send you what file numbers to request, but they're a mess so you'll need to canvas everything from the time Caro left France to that October 1941 letter. No, you'll need to go beyond. Get files for the next year at least. Then—"

"Slow down. I don't know what you're talking about."

"This is a bigger story, Caroline. If she got training, if she was a spy, this is something new."

"I'm trying to tell you—"

"And I'm telling you —"

We started talking over each other.

"Stop," I cried out. "We aren't getting anywhere. Just come and read everything for yourself. We'll go to the Archives together."

Mat huffed a long, loud breath. "Caroline, as much as I want this story—and maybe even to help you—I don't have that kind of money. I already used most of the Arnim family's deposit for my last trip to Paris and London. It's not good business to use everything you're paid just to do the job."

"I'll pay half your ticket."

"What?" Mat scoffed. I heard typing in the background. "You want to pay over a thousand dollars? One way."

"I need you." I blurted the words before thinking them through. They hung between us, heavy with the past, the present, and some undefined future. Three words never felt more weighted and, in many ways, terrifying, but I couldn't let him turn me down.

I felt his intake of breath and rushed to cut him off. "I'm hiring you. I don't want a presentation about my family, but I need answers. I'm hiring you to research my family, with me. You just said this is a bigger story, so it's a win-win for you."

"I can't write what I want if you hire me. Is that what you're doing? Tying my hands? Because—"

"No." The word came out strong and clear. I knew what it felt like to be backed into decisions by guilt or by trying to please another. *Pick this school . . . Take this job . . . Go home to help*. "What you write is up to you and I'll sign anything you want that says that."

I imagined him rubbing his brows together with his thumb and forefinger as if trying to ease tension in his brain. He'd done it during our chat at the coffee shop. He'd done it during long-ago late-night study sessions.

"I can only imagine what's in those letters," he muttered before raising his tone back to full volume. "Look, Caroline, if I want a full-time job and, better yet, best yet, a tenure track position, I need to become a voice in the public forum, an expert outside academia, because that's what it takes now. The old 'publish or perish' is now 'panel, publish, promote, or perish.' I can't let one article go because another may or may not be better."

"I get it." I slowed my breathing. "I'm not trying to trick you . . . Unless you choose otherwise, Friday remains your deadline with your current story. Just consider other possible angles."

As I stated the words, something shifted within me. I wasn't talking to Mat, the guy who was writing an article about my family; I was talking to Mat, my friend, my secret crush, the smartest guy in the room, and the kindest. Yes, I wanted answers for me, but I also wanted something for him. I'd hurt him our senior year—in ways I was only now recognizing. Not only that, but he'd filled my thoughts over the past forty hours as surely as my aunt and grandmother had. The cacophony of emotions jangling within me was hard to sort and harder to silence—I just knew he was a vital part of whatever this was.

"Trust me, Mat. There's something here. Something good, for both of us. I can feel it."

"Why did I ever call you?" he whispered over the line.

It made me smile. I recognized that tone. Mat was coming to London. "What's that flight you were looking at?"

"This one leaves Boston at ten o'clock, connects in New York, and flies to Heathrow at 11:30 p.m. Tonight."

"Book it." I sounded confident, but I was shaking inside. A well of hope had opened within me over the letters, over my aunt, and now over Mat. I was desperate to hang on to it. "Please. You said you aren't teaching this summer; you're doing research on your own time. We only have until Friday."

With a little more back-and-forth—and complaints that he had to kick out his dinner guests—he booked the flight.

"Thank you, Mat. This means a lot to me. It's not history. It's . . ." Here we came to the heart of it. The heart Jason saw right away. "It's my family. My father needs this. So do I."

"What if you don't like what we find?"

We.

"It'll be the truth." My statement settled within me. I felt comfortable with it. "We've lived in lies long enough."

TWELVE

I sat stunned by what I'd done. It was both harder and easier than I imagined. I stared at my phone. It had been the medium of a revolution over the past several minutes, and I was unsure how to approach the fallout. I quickly left a message on my boss's voicemail asking for more days. Then, still nervous, I texted Jason. Someone needed to know what had just happened.

> Finding a treasure trove of information in London. I called Mat, the Atlantic writer, and invited him over. I think I can change the article.

Instantly the three dots appeared . . .

> I hope you know what you're doing.

I waited. No more dots. I hoped I did too.

I laid my phone on the table and rustled through the piles of letters before me. "I blame you," I whispered.

After all, she was responsible for this. Caroline Amelia Waite—not only for the events eighty years ago but for those of the last ten minutes.

But how could she not change me? All day, I'd read about a woman who chased life and made bold choices. She was only twenty-three when she defected or disappeared or died in 1941, yet she had lived far more than I had, despite my already being five years older. Her words had left me feeling as though I'd experienced nothing, stood for nothing, hoped for nothing.

And those recriminations weren't wrong. In my heart, I acknowledged I was biding my time, wasting it really, in hopes of finding someplace I belonged. But I wasn't chasing it. I was waiting for it to come to me. I was waiting—like Sleeping Beauty for her prince—for my life to come.

No more.

It felt as if my destiny was tied to my aunt's. If I could find her story, I could start my own. Because that's what it would take—finding her story by discovering the truth. Her letters revealed that, in many ways, she ran from the same demons I did—the same feelings of loss and displacement, abandonment and regret. I was so tired of running, and running in a gray, hazy world compared to the vivid color she evoked.

She wrote of the frenetic Paris scene, hashing out political arguments deep into the night in Montmartre, just as the Lost Generation had done the decade before her. She wrote of weighing Schiap and Dalí's Communism against Fascism and how those ideas differed from her childhood dinner discussions at Parkley with the likes of Churchill and even King George VI at the table. She conveyed dynamic scenes through her descriptions of the House of Schiaparelli, with its lobster- and circus-themed parties, and Germans and Parisians in a silent, taut standoff. She marked the movements of people from two nations sitting side by side in cafés and then, with the declaration of war, the tense anticipation that held France captive awaiting her enemy's return. And when the Germans did storm across the border, she wrote of the devastation of France. She wrote of love and life, with a passion when she referred to George, and with concern and wonder over who was going to make the first move in another true World War—and who the last.

There was so much to learn. Mat knew how to conduct the research and I possessed the letters. Perhaps one could inform the other and together we could find the answers.

We.

The word pulled me in. Caro referred to Margaret as such—the better half of her "we." It was alluring and inviting to think in those terms, to not be alone.

It was late. I was tired. Mat, I reminded myself, was not my friend now. He had been, once long ago, but years had passed between us. I needed to be careful not to presume too much and not to trust him too far.

But he had answered my call and listened. He was coming to London. I couldn't help letting hope creep close.

I picked up one of Margaret's diaries to pair with Caro's letters. I needed a timeline, context, and a better understanding of what exactly I'd invited Mat into.

I'd barely begun when Mom came up the stairs with coffee and a slice of cake on a tray.

"What's this?"

"I couldn't decide if you needed a sweet dessert to end your day or a savory one to start it." She set down the tray and placed the plate and coffee before me. "I landed in the middle and made you a lemon olive oil cake."

I smiled. A lemon olive oil cake whipped up in the middle of the night. It was an image and an offering I never expected from my mom. After Amelia died, I'd made my own breakfasts, lunches, and even dinners.

"Are you finding answers?"

I picked at a corner of the still-warm cake. "More questions than anything. I think putting the letters in chronological order to read in tandem with the diaries will give me the most complete picture."

"Why don't you get some sleep?" She gestured to the letters. "Tuesday is still a day away."

I rubbed at my eyes again. I was wired, not tired, but they still stung. "We need to talk about that. I'm not going home Tuesday."

"What about your job?" She straightened and the air charged between us.

Mom let the last word drift up and float between us. Dad's domain was criticizing my "life choices." But she was clearly attempting to pick up his baton. I almost laughed at the internal war she waged: say something, stay quiet, launch, act cool.

I waited. It was a visual standoff and she blinked first.

She tucked in her lips and, with a tiny hitch, dove into the waters. "Don't you think that's risky? You've had such trouble sticking to things and enjoying them, and I thought you liked this job. You said it was important to you, and with whatever it's called going to market—"

"You're right," I conceded. "But this is more important, Mom, and I won't come this way again. None of us will, especially not Dad."

"I don't want you to give up your present chasing a past that can't be fixed. It's not your job."

"What if it is? And I'm not convinced they aren't one and the same. We're a mess, if you haven't noticed." She flinched at that, but I kept going. "Once that article is written, our pasts are closed; I feel it. It's how Dad's thinking. Whatever happened here—Amelia, our family, however little is left of us—won't matter even if Dad lives to see it and I'll—" I scrunched my nose, forbidding my eyes to fill with tears. "I'll, again, be the one at fault. This is my lifeline. Don't you get that?"

"Honey." Mom reached across the table and seized my hand. "None of this was ever your fault. It started long before you were born, and what happened to us, with Amelia, was never your fault either. You can't honestly believe that."

"Rationally, no, but . . . ." I looked at her. Part of me wanted to back away from everything between us; another part was so tired and worn I wanted to burst through. "No one ever told me it wasn't."

My words felt sharp and piercing. I readied myself for Mom to decamp with the accusation, but rather than recoil, she surprised me again. She softened further.

"I'm so sorry . . . So much time has passed." She looked around the room. "I started to understand in those final months with your grandmother, then refinishing this house helped." She slid her palm across a few bare inches of wood peeking through the scattered papers. "The physical work helped."

Mom returned her attention to me. "I disappeared on you. I gave up on . . . on everything for a long time. I'm sorry about that. I'm so sorry, darling."

I felt my lips drop open and pressed them shut. Cake lodged in my throat.

"It was never your job to save us," she whispered.

"You stood there—" I rubbed the back of my hand against my nose. "Then you left. You both just left and . . . I can't do this. I need to get back to work."

She reached for me, but let her hand drop just before contact. Something she read in my eyes made hers flicker. "I hope you'll forgive me." She paused a beat before adding, "Someday."

I wasn't sure what she'd seen. Anger? Maybe. Hurt? Definitely. Maybe she saw I was empty. My mind was suddenly fuzzy and tired. I couldn't process more than the task at hand.

We sat for a few minutes before she spoke again. "What will you tell work?"

"I left a voicemail that I was here on family business and asked for the week. I went for Dad's 'assumptive close.' Now I pray they don't fire me . . . And there's more." I told her about Mat and his impending arrival. "Can he stay here?"

"Oh, Caroline McKeenan Payne."

I straightened. When either of my parents used my full name, it was never good.

"He can. But if you're looking for truth, you're going to have to start offering it as well. You need to call your dad." She gestured to my cake and coffee. "Finish that. You'll need the energy. Then call him."

I ate a real bite this time. The sharp and sweet, savory and tart, tasted in perfect balance. "There's something to be said for the old adage that what he doesn't know can't hurt him."

"His whole life was framed by what he didn't know." Mom shook her head with a cynical, hopeless semi-chuckle. Her eyes glistened. "I thought you came to end that."

THIRTEEN

I spent over an hour organizing the letters. All were dated, but they were terribly mixed up. A few had second and third pages nestled into different letters. I linked words, thoughts, handwriting styles, and ink colors. As I worked, I began to get a sense of when my aunt was upset and when she felt relaxed. She pressed her pen hard and the slope of her writing increased when under stress.

Once I got them in order, I pulled out the first diary and began, skimming some entries and savoring others. Margaret first started writing in 1928, years before the first 1934 letter, and, I suspected, those early days would be my best introduction to these twins.

14 November 1928

Today we are ten!

Mother gave me a beautiful copy of *Cinderella*, my favorite fairy tale. I told her I was getting old, but she says one never outgrows beautiful books and can never start a proper library too soon. She has given both Caro and me hand-painted books every birthday for our whole lives. I suppose we are already starting our libraries. She gave Caro *Briar Rose* with drawings that look like oil paintings. My book's pictures are made from watercolours.

Briar Rose has always been Caro's favorite fairy tale. I think she likes the idea of the princess sleeping until true love comes. She and I tease that I want to go to the ball—in my own carriage— and she wants the ball and the prince to come to her.

Father gave us each journals. That's what he called you. A journal. Mother said you are a diary and that you don't look like anything we would use. You are brown leather and your pages have gold-tipped edges, and you are heavy. Caro's journal is navy. Father frowned at Mother and said serious thoughts go into journals and frippery into diaries. He expects serious thoughts from us, but I think you are a diary.

I didn't say that, but I did say I would write in you. It's odd writing to no one, so I will call you Beatrice, after Beatrice Potter. Mother reads her books to us at bedtime. I love Mrs. Tiggy-Winkle and Jemima Puddle-Duck, but I like Squirrel Nutkin best. Caro says that's odd because Squirrel Nutkin is a teasing bully who got what he deserved. Maybe that's why I like his story. There is a kind of proper justice there. And he learned his lesson.

But when things feel really bad, like after I've gotten into trouble, Mother always reads Peter Rabbit. He misbehaved and, rather than losing his tail, he was put to bed with chamomile tea with his mother nearby. That's nice, isn't it? Sometimes I also need someone to be nearby. That's you now.

It's our birthday today. We are ten. I told you that. We. Sallie and Rebecca get mad when Caro and I speak about "we" and "us." Sallie says her mother calls that the "royal we" and not for us to use. But we are "we." There are two of us with nothing between us. Mother made us wear matching dresses today and Father gave us matching diaries. That proves Sallie is wrong. Rebecca joined her, but as she only repeats what Sallie says, I didn't bother talking to her about it.

The girls are spending the night tonight. Friends never stay without their parents, but Mother says we are very grown up. Everyone is dressing for supper. Poor Betsy is in Sallie's room fixing her hair. That will take forever. But Betsy had better hurry because supper is served at eight, with no exceptions, and Mother says we can have the dining room all to ourselves. I suggested we play hide-and-seek throughout the house afterward. I also want to stay up until sunrise tomorrow. Caro said no to both. She says we'll get in trouble. Caro hates to get in trouble.

But this is a birthday that only comes once a decade. A "great round number," Father said smiling this morning. They are very important numbers and maybe that means we won't get into trouble after all.

25 December 1928

Dear Beatrice,

It's Christmas! There is snow! Tiny flakes of white make the whole wood look new. Father says we can stay up late tonight to play games. I will write more later . . . I must go. Caro is calling.

2 January 1929

Dear Beatrice,

You aren't a Beatrice at all. You are a Beatrix, but how was I to know that? I found Mother's box of all Beatrix Potter's tiny books up in the nursery today. We never read them ourselves and I had never seen her name before. Beatrix . . . Isn't that a funny name? But you can't be a Beatrix now . . . I'm sorry. You're stuck with Beatrice.

11 August 1930

Dear Beatrice,

I'm horrid. I said I would write in you, then Betsy put you in my bookshelf and I forgot about you. From the spine you look very much like a book I'm supposed to read but don't want to. The Paynes are coming for the weekend. Lord Latimore—Father calls him "Payne"—is his oldest friend, and his family comes every year for a long weekend before their sons go back to school. Frederick and Randolph aren't any fun at all. Father used to joke that he had two girls so that each Payne boy could have a good wife, but Mother says Frederick is wild so he stopped joking about that. We never liked it anyway. Frederick is twenty and returns to Oxford in a few weeks.

Randolph will turn sixteen while he's here, so Mrs. Dulles is preparing a special cake. And I must be fair, he was nice last summer. I had made a fort at the beginning of summer and filled it with books and pillows. Then after our trip to Scotland, I forgot all about it. When we were fishing down by the South Field, I saw it and ran to see if my books were ruined. I crawled in the door, a tunnel made through the branches, and my right hand landed on a nest of squirrels. It was terrifying and I remember scrabbling, screaming, and claws and grey fur everywhere. All the sticks came tumbling down and the next thing I knew I was getting hauled out by my ankles. Randolph didn't say a word as he hoisted me into his arms and ran back to the house. I could hear Caro sobbing behind us and Frederick laughing on the riverbank.

I didn't get bitten, but my arm and my cheek got scratched very badly. Father sent for Dr. Barlow, who looked over each mark with a magnifying glass. He declared no bites and Mother cried.

Mrs. Dulles cleaned me up and put a thick, stinky ointment on my arms then wrapped them in gauze. My legs were scraped up too, but that was because of the branches. She said her grandmother's ointment would keep everything from scarring and she was right. One year later and there is not a single mark on my cheek, and those were really deep.

I wonder if Randolph will notice or remember that day.

17 August 1931

Dear Beatrice,

I grabbed his book and ran. Caro rushed back to the house, and first he ran after her, then mid-lawn he turned my way and stopped. It was exciting, like a lightning bolt had struck between us. I can't explain it any other way.

He started chasing me.

I ran behind the garage and headed to the South Field. That's my patch and I know every inch of that land. There's a steep slope beyond Mother's gardens that leads to the river.

But I forgot Randolph likes to fish and he's been here often enough to know what I'd be thinking. He headed straight for where I was planning to go.

To trick him, I climbed the fence to the orchards instead.

That was my mistake.

Squish. I stepped on the biggest, freshest, smelliest cow patty ever. Then I slipped and fell backside-flat into it.

Randolph was upon me in seconds. First he stared. I will always love him for that. He didn't laugh. He reached down and pulled me up despite the muck. "Are you hurt?"

I lifted his book. It was covered like the rest of me. "I'm sorry. I ruined your book."

That's when he burst out laughing. "Oh, Margo Moo, you're never boring."

He swung an arm around me and walked me back. He was covered by the time we reached the kitchen door, but he didn't seem to mind. I didn't at all. He's seventeen. That's not overly far from thirteen, is it? I'll be thirteen in two months. Ages merge as you get older. Father is seven years older than Mother.

Anyway, Randolph left me at the side door with Mrs. Dulles screaming for Betsy to bring me a robe.

Caro came and sat beside me as I bathed. I told her everything, except how it felt. I didn't know how to explain it. Would she understand lightning? Or the tiny bubbles that filled my heart? Or that I didn't smell anything at all because everything was beyond beautiful?

I could see by her face she would think I was crazy, along with smelling gross.

"Why are you smiling?" Caro asked me, looking confused that I wasn't more upset.

I pushed it all down, and I lied. "You'd smile if you were finally clean."

Was that wrong, Beatrice? I wish you could talk. You see, we share everything. Caro and I made that pact long ago because it's just the two of us.

But I meant what I wrote—it feels like bubbles and I never want them to end. I think I love him, Beatrice, and I want to keep this delicious secret all to myself.

And maybe someday, I'll get to keep Randolph as well.

2 December 1931

Dear Beatrice,

I'm in trouble again . . . and Caro keeps passing notes under my door. She won't risk opening it. She never takes chances. Father calls her "quietly compliant." She is everything I am not. She walks; I run. She sits; I squirm. She discusses; I protest. She's certainly never had her mouth washed out with lye soap.

"I don't want to grow up," Caro whispered last night.

"What?" I pushed back against the pillows to sit fully upright. "I can't wait."

We got a lecture during last evening's supper about "comporting ourselves with greater decorum."

"Don't you want to be on your own? Like we said? When we

turn eighteen, we'll live in the London House. Father will let us go if we're together." I nudged her.

She and I have talked about it for years, but last night she shrugged.

"You can't change your mind. You promised, and Father will never let me go alone . . . Come on." I bumped my shoulder into hers again, harder this time. "We'll get to see things, do things, say things. In the magazines, girls have shorter hair now, shorter hems, and they're out doing stuff. Amelia Earhart flew across the Atlantic Ocean, and when I go to Egypt to become a famous archaeologist, you can come with me."

I reached for her in my desperation because if there is one thing that is true, it is that my freedom is tied to her. "We'll have fun, Caro, I promise. While I study, you can work in a shop for a couple years. Do whatever you want. You can be a dressmaker. You're amazing with your drawings and sewing. You can work for whoever makes all those beautiful dresses in *Vogue*."

She guffawed.

"No. It's true. Father will see the world is changing."

"In a few years, you'll be married." Caro mimicked Mother's voice so perfectly my jaw fell open. She then continued in her own voice. "If they have their way it'll be to one of those awful Payne boys."

"Why is Randolph awful?" I felt everything within me still.

Caro smiled and imitated Mother again. "Not ideal. After all, he is the second son with no title and no money, but he is a sweet young man."

"True." I laughed. None of that bothers me at all. "You can marry that bully Frederick, get all his money, leave him wherever you like, and come stay with me at the London House when I'm in town, or travel with me to Africa . . . I'm never marrying."

She laughed because she knew I was lying. We do that some-times. We say things to see if they fit. This one didn't. I'll marry Randolph if I can. He'll come with me on expeditions. Because, if I'm honest, I know Caro won't. She isn't like that. She's "quietly compliant." But I do need to get her to the London House. If she doesn't at least go there, I'll never step beyond.

Yet even that is in question now. Caro left me last night with a hug and a parting comment that kept me awake and made my insides feel twisty today, which was probably why I decided to see if I could slide the servants' stair rail all the way from the fourth-floor quarters to the kitchen. I wanted to do something daring and it was raining too hard to go outside. I fell off at the final turn and cracked the wood railing. Father heard it and punished me.

Last night she said, "Don't be disappointed if it doesn't come true, Margo. I like your dream, but Father will never let it happen."

It wasn't what she said, but how she said it. She wasn't unhappy about it. It didn't make her angry. She accepted it. She sounded pleased that he has us hemmed so tight, as if she found comfort in that.

She would feel that way. He loves her best. He sees her. He asks her opinion on things at the table far more than he asks mine. But you can't talk to someone or care about them, much less love them, if you can't see them.

But you can be angry when they trespass into your world and make a mess or cause a ruckus. Like today.

Like yesterday, if I'm being honest—again. That was another banner day for me.

Father made me walk up and down the front stairs forty-seven times after hearing me run yesterday morning.

Trent found me and asked, "Why forty-seven, miss?"

"Because Father says 'this is the forty-seventh time we've

addressed this issue.'" Caro might imitate Mother perfectly, but no one mimics Father like me.

Trent laughed, then blanched and hastened away. I looked straight down and found Father had emerged from the library right beneath me. "Add another forty-seven for good measure, Margaret."

"Yes, Father. My pleasure." I stomped—just a little.

No wonder Caro wants to stay and I can't wait to go.

FOURTEEN

I sat in awe of my grandmother. From later letters, I had gotten the impression that Caro held all the spark and fire while Margo was the more demure, even submissive twin. Caro constantly admonished her sister for being quiet, compliant, fearful, and timid. Margaret's early diary entries defied that assumption. This was a girl I wanted to call my friend. A girl who climbed everything she could find, made games and puzzles out of anything around her, and wanted something so personal and uniquely hers that she named her diary Beatrice. She wanted to explore the world, dig up the past, and understand history. She wanted to try new things and live in Egypt. She wanted to find a place to stand. She wanted to see and be seen.

Time slipped away as I kept reading about her capers, hopes, and dreams, along with her sister and her Randolph. I soon found myself in the fall of 1932 with my fourteen-year-old grandmother.

14 November 1932

Dear Beatrice,

Father gave us new journals today. He said that you should be full by now. I didn't tell him only half your pages are filled. Caro confessed she had never written in her diary at all. Not to him, of course. To him, we both nodded, thanked him, and lied.

She confessed that moments ago. She just left my room.

We celebrate every birthday this way, and have forever. After the party or whatever Mother and Father plan, we climb into my bed and go over the day and the year. It was a good year for Caro. But not for me. It was a good day for me. But not for Caro.

Would it surprise you that despite being always together and seeing the same things, hearing the same words, and eating the same foods, we see, hear, taste, and feel things completely differently?

I've been at odds with Father all year. I'm wild, immature, scattered, everything I shouldn't be. I also grew two inches—and that makes me, for fourteen years of age, overly tall. We're identical, but Caro hasn't gotten her inches yet. I wonder when she does if she'll have done something wrong too, or will it be the exact right and proper time for her two inches of growth?

But the tables got turned today. Father asked my opinion then said something nice when I gave it. It upset Caro.

"He was being a dear," I told her.

Caro pushed back against my headboard. "Stop trying to sound like Mother."

"Stop criticizing Father," I snapped back. "He's easier on you anyway, so why are you complaining? I get one nice comment in a year and you're sniffly?"

That caught her because she knows it's true. Caro never gets in trouble and I never get a compliment. She is quiet, obedient, and a *modèle jeune femme*. I learned that in our French text and Mother actually nodded to Caro as the example. Yes, she is the model young woman that I am not.

It could make me really angry, but it doesn't. She is all those things to the world, but she's honest with me. When we are alone, Caro is open and fun and even daring. There is a part of her she only shares with me. Sometimes I worry how much she pressures herself to appear perfect. I fear it's only going to get worse as we become "young ladies" and French ones at that . . .

For another birthday surprise, Mother hired Mrs. Langston's daughter to tutor us in all things French. Language, culture, style . . . I rolled my eyes and got a stern look from Father.

Claire, Mrs. Langston's daughter, came for tea. She is *très chic* and has spent the last two years teaching in Paris. She said we can no longer speak English in her French class of two. She also said that, with her guidance, we will read and speak fluently within the year. She let us pick French names to make it more fun. She said playing a role helps one step into a culture. Father gave his great nod of approval, citing *The Merchant of Venice* as proof that role-playing focuses one's energies and distills their character—whatever that truly means.

I am Bebe Dupont. Isn't that glamorous? Caro made up Nanette Bellefeuille. She has always loved the name Nanette. Her first doll, a beautiful porcelain French doll that still sits in her room, is named Nanette.

After tea with Claire, we scrambled out of our dresses and got to do my favorite thing in the whole world. Betsy even anticipated the adventure and was waiting to help us into our gear. We went fishing!

The last hatch of the season always occurs around our birthday and it happens as the sun drops to about thirty-five degrees. The sun was getting right to that point as we ran in our waders to the river. Creighton had already laid a fire.

"The caddis flies are good. We will eat well this evening." He shooed us off the bank.

After only a few casts, we had enough for a grand dinner. I caught three fat trout and Caro caught two. We ate one and Creighton carried the others home as we didn't dare spoil our appetites for supper. Mother and Mrs. Dulles would never forgive us. Birthday dinners are always extravagant.

Creighton was talkative today. I consider that another birthday present. He told us about the Great War while we ate our fish. Mother would scold him if she knew, but we promised not to tell. She doesn't like any talk of war, any disagreement at all.

He didn't talk about the battles so much as he did about the smell, the smoke, and the burned flesh—not like the fish at all, he said, but "acrid," he called it, like when I singed my hair on the candle last Christmas. He said despite the cold and the rain and the mud that got into every crack and crevice of his body, it was that burning smell that has never left him.

"Sounds linger," he said. He can still hear massive booms in his head, even while working the silent gardens here at poky Parkley. I wonder if that's why he is so quiet at times and doesn't seem to hear us when we talk to him, even when we stand only a few feet away.

His stories put me in my place, Beatrice. I've always considered myself brave, but I didn't feel brave listening to him. War sounds terrifying. I think I should be more respectful when Father talks about it. He served in the Navy during the Great War and was awarded a medal. If he saw even a fraction of what Creighton saw, I understand why he watches Europe so closely. How could the world ever endure such horrors again?

19 December 1933

Dear Beatrice,

It's been so long since I've written in you. I can't seem to get into the rhythm of "daily recordings" as Father recommends, and life has been terribly busy. But I am glad you are here, and when I come to you, I feel so much better.

The world is topsy-turvy. Even here in Derbyshire, we feel it. Father gave a full lecture tonight on the "state of affairs." He does this more often lately. He has always wanted us to be informed and aware, but there's now an urgency to his manner that concerns me.

It upsets Mother. She says we should be spared such talk. But even though it's unnerving, I'd rather know. Besides, Father has always been this way. Whenever guests come, Caro and I stay at the table. We never speak, but we listen. We've listened to King George VI, Sir Churchill, Prime Minister Baldwin, Dr. Dalton, and so many others I can't begin to name.

Tonight Father walked us through what's going on in Germany. They elected a new chancellor in January of this year, but then by bullying and intimidation he became dictator in March. Now Herr Hitler refuses to pay the reparations outlined in the Treaty of Versailles. I gather if he doesn't repay England the money Germany owes her, she can't repay America. It starts a whole chain of events. But worse than going back on a signed treaty, Hitler is rearming Germany. He walked out of the Geneva Disarmament Conference in October, and Father is concerned because every other country, including ours, wants disarmament. The current prime minister, MacDonald—he's never come for dinner—wants peace and has based his government on that and a balanced budget. Rearming England would run a deficit, especially with no reparation payments coming in.

Father says Sir Churchill is apoplectic. He hasn't been here to stay for a long while—so I haven't heard him myself—because he's sequestered or something. When I asked what that meant, Father said Churchill is out of favor at present and is concentrating on his writing. I understood that—I constantly say things that get me "out of favor."

How much of this is real, Beatrice? That's what I want to know. Father's opinions counter Prime Minister MacDonald's.

Despite Germany's actions, most believe peace will remain. In fact, a man just won a seat in the House of Commons from East Fulham on a platform of peace and passivism. He supports disbanding our entire armed forces, and he won in a landslide.

Who is right? Who is wrong? Do they even see the same thing?

To drive his point home last night, Father told us that Herr Hitler endorsed a one-day boycott of all Jewish shops and businesses last April 1. He also forced book burnings all summer and into the fall.

Books. I can't imagine burning books. What is next?

When I asked that question, Father stared at me hard. I could tell he agreed, but he wanted me to take my thinking to its logical, abhorrent conclusion. I shuddered because I suppose I know—the Jewish people.

After all, he banned them for a day, didn't he?

FIFTEEN

After calling it quits at four in the morning, I woke early Monday. I credited adrenaline. Mat was to arrive at noon and there was a lot to do before then. I had only read the diaries as far as 1938 and, in my exhaustion, felt I'd missed much.

Before I let Mat dig into the private lives of Margo and Caro, I had to better understand what he would read, what he might find, and where it would lead him. I had to protect them as best I could—I had to protect myself. I loved them.

I heard Mom moving about outside my room as I dressed. When I was growing up, she always had a ritual at home, and alone here now she seemed to maintain it. As she moved from her bedroom to the kitchen, she would stop by every room touching base. "Freshening," she called it. If a glass needed replacing or I'd left a bowl in the upstairs sitting room, she'd carry it downstairs. When I was in high school and would take full meals up to my attic rooms, she started carrying a laundry basket through the house each morning.

I hadn't thought about it before, but after reading Caro's letters and Margaret's diaries and learning how much they cared—yet how often they misunderstood and missed each other completely—I realized Mom's "freshening" was a form of care. She was reaching out to me, perhaps, in the only way she could back then—yet I never saw it.

Once dressed, I headed straight to the attic and perched on the same stool I'd vacated only a few hours before. I pulled the 1934 pile to me to start again. My 2002 was their 1934—the year that changed everything.

That summer, at sixteen years old, Caro and Margo split for the first time. The *we* became *me* and *you*.

29 August 1934

Dear Beatrice,

You thought I forgot about you, didn't you? I've been sick. This is the first time in over a month I can sit up in bed. The first time in a month Mother and Mrs. Dulles have left me alone. I can't blame them.

They thought I would die. Everyone did, I gather. I have to confess, at times I wished it myself. There were long stretches of between-time in which my throat felt seared shut and my brain swelled much larger than my skull could hold. The heat and pain consumed me and I wanted it to stop. Father sometimes quotes Dante's *The Divine Comedy* to us and a favorite line is, "The path to paradise begins in hell." Paradise to me was simply relief from that hell—by any means possible—and I'll confess this to only you—I prayed for death.

What I didn't know until this morning, however, was how close I actually came and how it affected everyone else. Mother put her hand on my head this morning, declared my fever gone, and promptly burst into sobs. She frightened me. Only after she left did Betsy explain that two nights ago, she had to change my sheets three times. I kept sweating through them and Dr. Barlow declared me past hope.

Father just left me. I think Mother sent him up to make sure her newfound hope had foundation.

"Dr. Barlow said if you survived Sunday night you'd heal fast. You're cool to the touch and your eyes aren't glassy." It felt like Father was making an official pronouncement over me.

I expected him to nod and leave, but he didn't. He dropped onto the edge of my bed. "It's awfully good to see you, my dear."

That's when I comprehended how bad things had been and why Mother looks pale, thin, and haggard, and Mrs. Dulles only slightly less so.

"It's awfully good to be seen."

Father ran his index finger down my cheek and tapped the tip of my nose like he did when we were little. "I'll go find you something to eat. We need to get a little colour back into you."

Mother met him at the door.

He pulled her into a hug. "Time for you to get some rest, Ethel. You must breathe again, perhaps even sleep. We didn't lose her."

3 September 1934

Dear Beatrice,

"We didn't lose her."

Those words have played in my head for days now. Mother has hovered incessantly so I've had no time to write, no time to think. Not that my brain allows for much of that right now. Even the sunlight through the window hurts.

I'm so weak, Beatrice. And pale. Betsy brought me a hand mirror yesterday after my bath and I didn't recognize myself. I should have known from the bath. I used to like my curves. Even my breasts were a good size. They're gone. I'm flaccid, flat, and, I'm not exaggerating, my ribs stick out farther than my breasts.

And my hair used to shine. It now lays as drab and lifeless as I feel. Can bones feel limp? Mine do. I'm also a strange colour—a sort of pasty yellowish white that gives way under my eyes to the grey-blue circling them. They are still blue, but a faded and dull blue with no spark. They don't look like me. I don't look like me.

Mrs. Dulles often clucks her tongue and says the eyes are the windows to the soul. It never used to be good when she said that. It meant she knew I'd done something wrong and that I should confess and get it over with—and she was always right. But when she said it yesterday, I bit back.

"Thank you for pointing that out. Don't you think I see it?"

"Your body and soul are only bruised, Little One. Let them heal."

Little One. She called me, and only me, that when we were young. It used to make me feel warm and safe. She then hugged me tighter than anyone has yet. I almost cried. Mother seems afraid of touching me. Perhaps I'll break.

Mother also won't let Caro visit.

This morning, I got forceful. "I'm well. Send her up after lunch."

When she didn't, I walked next door to Caro's room to find her. It felt sterile, like she hasn't been there for some time. I suspect they've moved her to a far guest room, but no one will tell me. They keep changing the subject.

I don't remember the last time I saw my sister. I counted back to what I could recall and got to mid-July . . . We were planning the Paynes' visit for the first week in August. Frederick had commitments in town before classes began and Randolph was heading to Oxford early for rowing. Mother also told us that Frederick might not come at all because he was visiting Miss Adele Bennington's family and would most likely propose to her.

I teased Caro that her future husband was straying. She laughed and said good riddance to the man, but good for Adele.

"How's that?" I asked.

"She is one of five sisters and he inherits it all. Everything in the Payne family."

"Who wants any of it if Frederick's included? He's dreadful," I teased and moved on to a new topic.

But it bothered me all night and I didn't sleep well. I tossed and turned, wondering how that would feel. To inherit nothing, not even the bed you slept in or the chest that held your clothes, simply because you were born second. I didn't have to wonder actually. I heard it often in the way Randolph's father spoke to him, like he didn't matter, at least not as much as Frederick mattered.

I remember finally falling asleep that night feeling grateful that nothing like that would ever come between Caro and me.

With no sons, and us being twins, Father always said his decisions were easy. "Right down the middle." He would raise his hand and slice an imaginary line between us. It always made us giggle—until we grasped how seriously he meant it. Right down the middle also meant he expected us to take our duty, our educations, and our futures, including his estate, very seriously.

For our part, we decided long ago that I would take the London House and Caro would keep Parkley. She's always seen herself growing old here with tons of children and I've always wanted to leave—and I'm not entirely sure about children either. There's a whole world beyond Derbyshire and for sixteen years I couldn't wait to see it.

I'm not sure about any of that anymore . . . Maybe I'll feel like me again when I gain a stone or two. Maybe I won't. From my window, Mother's garden is spectacular with roses, hollyhocks, hydrangea, and peonies. It's lush and colourful and alive, and I've never seen anything more beautiful.

There isn't anywhere in the world I'd rather be right now.

Here, I am safe.

7 September 1934

Dear Beatrice,

I can barely write. The Paynes never visited and Caro isn't here. She hasn't been here for weeks.

The Paynes came a couple weeks after I got sick, picked up Caro, and drove her straight to London with them. Caro stayed with them for a week until Mother had the London House opened and Claire Langton hired to chaperone her—all summer long.

"When is she coming home?" I asked.

"Tomorrow, dear, but it's been a hard summer and your sister . . . she's been acting out. Your father and I feel it's best for you and your recovery if she goes to school for a few months."

"You promised never to send us to Harrogate." That sat me straight. Caro wouldn't survive boarding school, and certainly not without me.

"Not Harrogate, dear. Claire believes Brilliantmont in Switzerland will be best. Caro is so proficient in French. She's fluent."

"Am I going with her?"

"No." Mother sank to the side of my bed. "You are not well enough to go anywhere right now. We must protect your health."

Mother refused to answer any more questions and soon fled the room to avoid them.

As much as I want to know about Caro, I also want to know about Randolph. I didn't dare ask, of course, but he was there, Beatrice. Caro stayed with his family for a week. Then after that, their home is only blocks from the London House on Eaton Square.

I—I can't think right now. I wish you were real, Beatrice. I wish you were real and could tell me this is all going to be, as Sallie says, tickety-boo.

This does not feel tickety-boo.

10 September 1934

Dear Beatrice,

Caro did come home and left just as fast. She is different. Harder. Older. I can't describe it, but I feel it. She cut her hair. It's short now, right below her chin. It's very chic. I've seen it in the magazines Mrs. Dulles lets the maids keep in the silver closet. She knows we read them—the only one who doesn't know is Father.

Caro also wears red lipstick. It was a beautiful colour, but I didn't say that. I didn't say anything. I was shocked and I was hurt.

She breezed in, kissed me, hugged me tight, and for a second I thought she was mine again—my twin, my other half. But as she turned away, a sharpness flashed through her eyes as she faced Mother and goaded her.

"It's a wonderful shade, isn't it, Mother? All the rage now."

Mother told her to wipe it off immediately. They stared at each other a full minute before Caro, with calm purpose, walked to the water closet. Her message was clear—she was obeying on her terms and soon she wouldn't. Mother's eyes widened before she schooled her expression and left the room to "check with the kitchen." Mother never "checks with the kitchen."

"I can't stand it here." Caro returned and balanced on the edge of my small sofa. She looked tense and rigid, ready to flee.

I pushed back against the headboard to shift upright. "I'm here."

She jumped up and flopped onto my bed, throwing her arms over me. "I don't mean that. I'm sorry I'm being a beast, but you don't know what it's been like."

"You're right. I've been here fighting for my life. How was your summer?"

"Don't be that way. It wasn't my idea to go to London. Father sent me. I called every day. They told you, right?"

"For a week."

"Trent told you that, did he? He always did like you best. But why call if no one was going to tell me anything? And I don't know what Father is going on about. I never stepped out without Claire or George."

"Who's George?"

Caro beamed and my heart leapt for her. She was in love. She was so clearly in love. I had never seen it before, not in real life. In the films it's all amorous prose, fake swoons, and eyelash batting. But Jane Austen got it right—it brings a "bloom" and Caro had it. Her cheeks glowed rosy and a sheen lit her eyes. She was transformed. She was radiant. I almost told her about Randolph right then and there, knowing she could understand. The emotion, the highs, the lows, the bubbles—we could share it together.

She continued faster than I could draw breath to begin.

"Remember how he used to hate it when we called him that?" She laughed.

My head filled with a heavy weight and I tried to remember a George we knew.

"Come now . . . George." She poked me in the arm.

Her poke shot the answer straight to my head, then to my heart. "Randolph George? Are you talking about Randolph?"

"Who else?" She squealed and wrapped me tighter in her arms. "It started the week I stayed with them. I was so angry. I was picking on him, being terrifically nasty, but he didn't stop me. He knew I was hurting. Then one night, after I'd gone to the London House with Claire, he came to pick me up for dinner and I forgot. I called him 'Randolph' and he spun on me as we walked through Hyde Park. He clasped my hand, Margo, and said, 'I like being George to you.' Then walking on, he didn't drop my hand. I've called him George ever since."

I could barely breathe. My heart beat so fast I was sure she could feel it. I've lost so much weight, I could see it. My linen nightgown quivered, and I pushed her away. She hardly noticed and shifted her weight to sit beside me, still lost in her story.

"He's working at a legal firm this summer between terms,

though I expect he's back at Oxford now. He was leaving either at the end of last week or by the end of this week . . ." She sighed and draped herself across the foot of my bed, facing the ceiling. "He was wonderful, Margo. He came by, invited me out for walks, to tea, to dinners. He went on and on about you. Seriously, it was the first thing he asked every day—what I'd heard and how you were. You two always did have a 'thing' between you."

She sang the word *thing* as if it was bright and playful and belonged to a child.

I clung to it anyway. "Every day?"

"Every day." She smiled at me. "Then I think he realized how hard it was on me because I had no answers. No one here would tell me anything. They all swooped around you and forgot I might care. Mother started lying. Only when I could catch Betsy on the telephone did I believe I was getting even a partial truth." She propped herself up and stared at me. "But you're okay now, right? You are truly well?"

I assured her I was and we chatted until she was called to supper. I still take a tray in my room. She offered to stay with me, but I didn't want her. I couldn't breathe, I couldn't speak, and I wanted to cry. Alone.

I hate her, Beatrice.

I want to hate her. I want to yell, scream, cry out, and call her "Tresse." Then she would know. She would know how much she has hurt me. We made up the name years ago as a code for the worst kind of betrayal—for Mother when she betrayed us to Father simply because she refused to deal with us, for Trent when he told Father that one of the maids got pregnant, for Sallie when she stole Rebecca's boyfriend last Christmas. *Traîtresse.* Traitor. Tresse.

I did none of those things. I bit my tongue so long and so

hard, I tasted blood. It's not her fault. I've sat here for hours trying to make it her fault. But it's mine. All mine.

I never told her, Beatrice. I am the one who broke the pact. We always said we would tell each other everything and I kept Randolph secret. Now it's too late. I can't let her know. I won't be humiliated like that. What could I do? Ask her to give him to me? To not love him anymore?

She came back after supper. "Are you tired? I have a few more stories to share and it's so nice to be with you again."

She described every detail, every heartbeat, and every wonderful moment of the summer because that's what we do. We tell each other everything.

Every loving sigh pierced like a dagger.

I couldn't help myself, Beatrice. The moment she left, I climbed from bed and crossed my room to the mirror over my dresser and stared at this ghost I have become. We were once the same. Now I am night. She is day. I am death. She is life.

And Randolph kissed her.

She told me that before she left. She climbed to the head of the bed and curled into my pillows next to me. "Everything every-thing?" she questioned.

"Of course." I closed my eyes.

"I love him, Margo." She twisted to me and grabbed my hands. "I have missed you. You are the only one I can tell and I know you two are close, but you're my sister so you can't tell him. This is between us . . . Father would never let anything happen until I'm eighteen, and I don't want George feeling complacent that I'll just sit waiting for two years. After all, there are plenty of handsome boys in Europe."

I pulled my hands away and pressed them into my eyes so hard stars burst beneath the lids.

"Are you okay?"

"They burn." I looked to the window. "It was sunny outside today. At night, when I'm tired, they hurt."

"I'm so selfish. I must let you rest."

I sank into my covers and she skipped from the room. When excited, Caro has this half skip to her step. I always thought it was a very adorable trait and was glad to see she hadn't outgrown it, as I feel she's outgrown me.

Then another thought crept across me . . . I bet "George" finds it adorable too.

SIXTEEN

I sat holding the 1934 diary in my hands. It was after this point that the letters started. Caro left for Brilliantmont in Switzerland and nothing was ever the same between them.

My heart hurt for Margo. This was the beginning of a heartache that lasted a lifetime, despite marrying the man she loved. Part of me wondered why she and Randolph could not bridge the distance between them. Why had she or they held on to Caro and the past so tightly?

The entries revealed Randolph clearly enjoyed Margo's company, laughed with her, had fun with her, and was incredibly concerned when she got scarlet fever. They were true friends. The entries also revealed Margo's illness fundamentally changed her. It was deep within every line, within every comparison to her twin, within every new fear she penned within Beatrice. She emerged from her illness timid, a shadow of her former self, and retreated both within her home and within her soul. *But why?* I thought to myself. *She didn't die. She lived.*

The irony of my indictment struck me—I was the one who survived that day, yet how well did I embrace life?

My heart hurt for Caro as well. In many ways, I related to her journey better. I wasn't sent away—at least not physically when Amelia died—but banishment can take many forms, and it changes you. It can harden you. Mom didn't get up to see me off to school. She no longer greeted me after school in the kitchen to chat through the day. Dad rarely made it home from work for dinner. Then, within months, Mom stopped cooking altogether and each of us became responsible for our own meals and our own lives. I remember how that hurt. Dinner was where we came together. All five us at the table. But within one fall, Jason left for college and Amelia left for good. I was alone.

Like Caro, I found ways to cope. I went home with friends, studied at their houses, ate dinners with their families. I avoided our cold, silent house as much as I could, to the point that even if Mom and Dad had reached out, I might not have noticed. I stopped seeing them, just as they had stopped seeing me.

And, as I allowed myself to draw closer to true honesty, I still held tight to that hurt, that ache. I fed it, figuratively keeping one arm outstretched against my mom and against the world. Maybe I understood Margo better than I wanted to admit.

I set the diary aside and picked up the first stack of letters. Fall 1934. Caro had just arrived at school . . .

BRILLIANTMONT, LAUSANNE, SWITZERLAND
14 NOVEMBER 1934

Dear Margo,

Happy birthday, dearest!

There's a surprise party for me this afternoon. No one can keep a secret around here. I'm excited and I'm having fun, but I miss you today—more than I thought I could.

I'm sorry I'm not coming home for Christmas. It would have been fun to celebrate together, and I should not have let Mother relay that message to you. You deserved to hear it from me.

I tried to telephone this morning to wish you a happy birthday and to explain, but the line was full of static and Father forbade me from making any more transnational telephone calls. A letter will have to do.

Renée invited me to Paris for the Christmas holidays and I

can't refuse such an opportunity. Yes, seeing Paris after all our studies will be a treat, but her father has also promised to make introductions for me. He is a silk manufacturer and works with Elsa Schiaparelli, Coco Chanel, and others. Wouldn't it be extraordinary to work in fashion, Margo? And not just any fashion—French haute couture. Renée's father can make it happen.

Isn't that incredible? You're the one who told me it could come true and I could be a dressmaker. I never believed it. I never saw my life reaching beyond Parkley, but I do now. I have been forced to, and perhaps that is as it should be.

And speaking of a future . . . Payne stopped by Geneva last week and George came with him. Payne sounded just like Father with his grave concerns of "rising nationalism." It made me miss home and our long suppers terribly.

But then he left the table during dessert to meet a colleague in the lobby and my mind moved to other matters. George reached for my hand. He looked me straight in the eyes and said, "Most of the time unexpected things don't bode well, but you give me hope. You are unexpected."

I'll confess to you, dear sister, I had begun to wonder if we were a summer fling. Me, sixteen. Him, twenty. But we weren't.

He slowly leaned toward me and I found myself drinking in every aspect of his approach. His eyes are a delectable brown. They remind me of a light treacle, and his skin is translucent. You can see the blood rise in his face. It's adorable because you really can see what he's feeling, as well as those tiny shadows where his razor didn't scrape close. And his lips . . . My gaze dropped from his eyes to his lips and I couldn't look away. His lips hovered only an inch from my own. We were so close I felt his soft exhalation.

Time stops, Margo. It stopped then and I wondered what to do. Mother's voice came to me, tight and precise, admonishing me to play demure and turn away despite every fiber of my being pushing me forward to close that inch. Turning a hair's breadth either direction would have done it. One degree of tilt would have broken the taut thread between us. But I couldn't move. I didn't want to. We stayed so close yet so far for several heartbeats before George leaned back with a longing sigh. There was a tantalizing promise in that sigh, Margo. I could taste it.

As soon as the bill was paid, he tucked my arm within his and escorted me outside the hotel at a pace I could hardly match. Around the corner there was a small wooded park, and George marched me through it without speaking until we were deep in the foliage. There he stopped and looked around. Just as I shifted my focus from his face to the park, he captured my lips in his and had pressed me so close there was no space, no air, nothing at all between us.

It was perfect, Margo. Time stretched and we stood enfolded within each other forever, and he tasted like chocolate. When he finally pulled back, I couldn't breathe.

Oh, he liked that. You should have seen his eyes—so sure of himself and of me. Part of me hated being so easily read, but another part felt powerful. I put that look in his eyes. I was the girl he wanted that badly. The game is over now . . . He knows he won. I am his. Yet I won too. He is mine.

After another lengthy kiss that really was a conversation in another, truer form, he wrapped an arm around me and walked us back to the hotel lobby and the car his father arranged to return me to school.

"Until next summer?" He handed me into the car.

I nodded and blushed a red streak I'm sure was terrifically unattractive, but I couldn't do or say anything more. There were and are no words.

All week I have wanted to write to you and this is my first

chance. Even now, I have only a few moments before class. How I wish you were here and we could room together and talk like we used to. Nothing is the same, Margo, and I'm afraid it will never be again. ~~I wish I could be home.~~ Never mind that I wrote that. I don't wish it, Margo. I love it here, and I sense life would squeeze tight there.

Why don't you come? You aren't sick now. You are as strong as ever, if you would just believe it, and if you could convince Mother of it.

You'd love it here. The school sits at the base of a mountain. Not the hills we see in the Lake District, but real snowcapped mountains where you can't find the tops some days because the clouds don't reach that high.

You'd like the girls. Well, not all the girls. There are three from the United States who would make you laugh. They talk like something is sitting on the back of their tongues, flattening them out. But they are bold—you'd love that. Bolder than you ever were! And they brought books . . . I've never read such writing, Margo. You would love them. I gather there was a group of American writers who lived in Paris several years ago and one of them dubbed their group the Lost Generation. Their ideas are incredible and their new ways of writing fresh and innovative. Find some if you can. Order a few from Hatchards on Piccadilly. Ask for Hemingway, Fitzgerald, Stein, Cummings, and Eliot. Well, T. S. Eliot is British now, but he was born American.

Oh, and keep them from Father. He is not going to appreciate the artistry of these novels and may well be offended by their politics.

I miss you, my darling sister. Give Mother a kiss for me and tell Father I send my love.

Always yours,

Caro

P.S. Did Mother give you a heart necklace? I assume she did—we always receive matching gifts, and that makes me smile. When next I'm home, let's trade. I'll wear the *M* and you wear the *C*. That way we will always be together. Love you!!

BRILLIANTMONT, LAUSANNE, SWITZERLAND
12 JUNE 1936

Dearest Margo,

It feels wrong to graduate without you. Daily life is one thing, but the milestones? We should celebrate those together. Since you can't be here next week, promise we will celebrate turning eighteen together—but I don't want that ball Mother keeps going on about, do you? Discourage her if you can, then come to Paris to celebrate with me.

Because I am not coming home.

I need your help, Margo. I have received a job offer to work at the famous House of Schiaparelli in Paris. I'll be an assistant, secretary, whatever you want to call it. I won't touch design work, not at first, but that may come later. Elsa Schiaparelli! The Schiap Shop in Paris! Can you believe it? It's beyond anything I ever imagined.

I'm traveling with Renée on the 5:34 p.m. train following the ceremony next Friday. Her father has secured us an apartment merely blocks from Schiaparelli's salon. We'll settle in over the weekend and I'll begin work the following Monday.

I will write Mother and Father after I'm settled. They never planned to come see me graduate, so they shouldn't be surprised when I make my own plans.

And soon you can be my first guest! What fun we shall have!

All my love,

C

PARIS
23 JULY 1936

Chère Margaret,

Paris est vivant! Absolutely pulsating with life!

I work all day, my feet never touching the ground; it's so fascinating. Then at night, we head to the Montmartre neighborhood and I soar higher. It's not the drinking or anything like that. It's the ideas, the creativity, and the passion. The Lost Generation—I learned Gertrude Stein started the term, but Ernest Hemingway made it famous in that book I told you to read, *The Sun Also Rises*—is long gone, but the heat and the spark of new thinking remain. We carry the baton now.

Please console Mother if she needs consoling. Father's letter said she was desolate, but I suspect it's his new tack. His threats to cut my funding didn't go far as I'm making my own money now. If he decides to try silence next, that is nothing new for me.

But you? Please don't be silent. I couldn't bear it. Write to me again soon and tell me of life at Parkley. It's not that I don't love home, Margo, I do. I just don't fit there anymore, not like you do.

I suspect you'll refuse again, but I won't stop inviting you . . . Come visit! I have a charming flat on the rue Chabanais with Renée. You'll love her. She's more like you than me—she's smart, forthright, and practical. She keeps me on budget and food in our pantry.

I saw Greta Garbo last week. Truly, I did. She stopped at the salon on her way back to America. Schiap dresses her, along with Katharine Hepburn and Mae West. You should see Mae West! Schiap designs long lines except when it comes to her. The bust on that woman! It's her defining feature and Schiap accentuates it in the most cunning ways. And you won't believe this, but Schiap is using Miss West's form, her bust-line fashioned in glass, as the bottle for her new perfume. It will be Shocking! By name and by nature.

Everything here is shocking, Margo—in all the best ways. There are so many things to taste, experience, think, discuss, and debate. At home, we were fed one way of doing things and one way to think. The door cracked open at Brilliantmont, but here it's been blown off its hinges. There are so many ideas, and not little ones—big ones about people and the ways we should live and how we should be valued for our work—and my views matter. I don't sit silent at the table listening and absorbing. I share my thoughts and truly contribute to the formation of new thinking, as well as new designs now.

I want you to taste it all, Margo. Please come visit.

Your loving if slightly impatient sister,

Caro

SEVENTEEN

I heard Mom's shoes squeak on the stairs. "Good morning . . . I brought you coffee. More coffee, I should say. This can't be healthy." She set the carafe on the other side of the table and stared at me. "Please tell me you haven't been at this all night."

She pointed to the green notebook in which I'd started jotting down the details I thought might be worth remembering.

"I got sleep. I promise. In fact"—I tapped my phone to bring up the clock—"I've only been awake an hour." I laid my hand on the letter I'd just finished. "I'm pairing the 1936 diary entries with the letters."

I stretched my back as Mom handed me a mug. "They had fun, Mom. They were the best sisters. Then scarlet fever came along and, with it, George." I heard my voice. It was critical. Clearly, deep within, I was on Margo's side, maybe even Caro's, but I blamed "George" as an interloper into my family's happiness.

I was being unfair, far from objective, and crazy illogical. There would be no family, no *me,* without Randolph George Payne. He was integral to their story and vital to my own.

Was objectivity possible here? Emotions ran high and there were two sides to this relationship—even a third side once I weighed in. Is objectivity ever possible? Could Margaret understand her sister? Could I, across eighty years, understand either of them? My head started spinning and I wondered what Mat would think about all this, what he might say, and what he would write. I took a sip of coffee to banish him from my mind. It was strong, hot, black, and just how I liked it.

Mom sat across from me. "Margaret told me she contracted scarlet fever at sixteen and folded in on herself. That's how she phrased it. While penicillin had been discovered by then, it wasn't in regular use until the '40s. Scarlet fever was deadly and it almost got her."

"Did she tell you their parents banished Caro to London? Probably to keep her safe, but neither saw it that way."

"No . . ." Mom whispered the word long as she reached for a letter. "She viewed that summer as the beginning of her end. And when she got really honest about it, she said it was an end of her own making. She didn't talk much about what Caro did or didn't do."

"How of her own making?"

Mom leaned on her elbows. She seemed more comfortable this morning, more willing, even eager to stay. "She mentioned Caro changed and that she couldn't keep up, but she said it was because she got scared . . . grief, fear, guilt, pain . . . They can transform you in ways so fundamental you can't recognize yourself."

I sat straight. Something within me sparked at Mom's words and I felt myself leaning forward.

She watched me for a moment. Her gaze seemed to reach for me and I realized how much I missed her. It was a hollow feeling in my chest that made my breath shudder as I inhaled.

"When something bad happens," she continued, "it's easy to blame someone else, and in some cases maybe it is their fault, but that doesn't matter. Not in the end. What does matter is how long we hold on to that hurt or that anger. We can magnify the pain, making it worse and worse until it devours us, or we can forgive it and get on with life. Margaret felt she clutched at her pain and after"—Mom's focus darted around the room—"my work and my time here, I would say I've done the same."

In some cases maybe it is their fault. I swallowed. This was the closest we had come to the truth. Two options lay before me. Confront. Retreat. I chose the road most traveled. I sidestepped.

"Funny . . . I feel I relate better to Caro."

"Do you?" Her question revealed surprise.

"She was sent away and never invited back in. What happened to her was a betrayal and she felt second, left out, and cut out. She couldn't trust that they loved her." I bit my lip and shrugged off a familiar tight ache. "Only Margaret. She still believed Margaret loved her. But she was out of reach."

"And the fear Margo carried?" Mom reached toward me and, without thinking, I leaned back. It was so small and quick, I registered the action after I'd made it. These twins left me jangly and jumbled. Young. Insecure.

Mom wasn't wrong. I understood my grandmother all too well.

She pulled her hand to her side. Without another word, she pushed off her stool and headed toward the stairs. "I'll make us a little breakfast. Come down in about a half hour?"

I nodded and as she started down, I called after her, "When did you start to cook . . . again?" There was a yearning to my voice that embarrassed me. To counterbalance it, I had twisted my tone on "again" and it came out sharp. It felt like I'd asked, *When did you decide to become a mom again?* without the protection of sarcasm. I wondered what I'd do if she didn't have the answer I wanted, or needed.

Her head tilted as she considered my question. "As I said, your grandmother and I were a lot alike . . . We started cooking together when I first arrived, before she grew weak. I think we had both missed that connection. There is a relational beauty to food, to cooking. Gifts I had forgotten, and I'm sorry for that."

She smiled. The longing in her voice matched her soft smile, but she said nothing more.

I sat there staring at the top of the stairs as she descended, wishing our conversation had gone further, wishing I'd said more, asked more questions, been able to accept her touch . . . something. Anything.

But I hadn't and, once again, I was sitting alone in an attic space.

Noon found me standing at the WHSmith bookstore outside Heathrow customs. I watched each bleary-eyed passenger exit the double doors. Mat's plane had landed only twenty minutes before so I figured these were passengers from an earlier flight, yet I still scanned the faces.

There he was, red eyes staring right back at me, sporting an unexpected grin. "It's crazy. They've got this whole customs thing down here. I barely paused."

"Same when I arrived. I hadn't thought about how fast it was." I pointed to Nero Coffee a few shops to my right. "Do you want a coffee?"

"Yes. Otherwise I might finally sleep now that I want to be awake."

I led the way with no more words. There was something different about him. Granted I'd only seen him once in six years for approximately forty-five minutes on Friday, but in that time, I thought I'd pegged him pretty well. Still tenacious. Intelligent. And hurt . . . Somehow that emotion struck me during our meeting. It had hung between us. It was gone now.

Last night, when I called Dad about Mat coming to London, he had ended our short talk with, "No matter what we've been through or how you feel I've failed, I asked you to stop and leave this be. I can't do this, Caroline. Goodbye."

His goodbye sent my heart to my throat again. It had struck me throughout the night and morning with unexpected force. There was a finality to that quietly spoken word that stunned me. There was no anger. Only bottomless disappointment—which was far worse.

I'd pushed it away during my reading, but with Mat standing next to me, Dad's was the only voice I heard.

"You're quiet." Mat turned to me in line.

"My dad . . . He's not happy you're here."

Mat raised his brows in question. They got momentarily lost in dark bangs that had been swept back at our meeting. He put his hand on my shoulder for the briefest touch before pulling it back in confusion or embarrassment. I couldn't tell if he had surprised himself or thought he might offend me.

"I can only say this. No matter what we find, I won't blindside you. There are real ripple effects for your family here."

That brought a sputtery laugh. "Tsunamis."

"Possibly."

We ordered him a large dark roast and headed out to Mom's black Peugeot.

I stepped back as he, with ease and familiarity, walked from the trunk to the left side of the car and dropped into the front seat before he recognized what he'd done.

He gripped the steering wheel. "This isn't going to work." He climbed out and circled the car. "You could've said something."

"And missed that?" My first true smile in days broke free.

With that simple exchange, I somehow felt okay with him again. While I had brought him here to prove his article wrong, in that moment, it didn't feel as if I needed to prove him wrong. Those were two very different things.

As I drove out of Heathrow, following my phone's GPS and announcing each turn out loud so I didn't mess up, I gave him an overview of what I'd found.

"Roundabout to the third exit. Stay to the left . . . Caro and Margo split in 1934 . . . turn left . . . Caro went to boarding school . . . left lane. Turn."

"Should I be worried?" Mat waved a hand toward the road.

"Yes. Do you know they let people drive a full year here on their foreign licenses? On the wrong side of the road? I looked it up to make sure I could do this."

"You've never driven here before?"

"I've barely visited." I glanced over at him and almost missed a right-hand turn. I veered to the right as he screamed out, "Swing wide. Swing wide!"

"Right." I wrenched the steering wheel left to miss an oncoming line of cars. "No more talking. Either direct me or start praying. Your choice."

As we approached Belgravia, I felt more comfortable. The roads were less crowded, giving me time to think before reacting.

"You're safe now." I peeked over at him. He sat grinning and turned to the window in a pathetic effort to keep me from seeing.

"It wasn't that bad."

"No, it wasn't." He laughed. "But you muttered to yourself the entire time . . . just like when—" He stopped with a head shake. "Never mind."

"What?" A tingly bubbly feeling caught me by surprise.

"I was thinking about our run from campus security sophomore year when our dorm party got shut down. You got lost."

"It was dark." I threw him an indignant glare. But he was right. I got lost running across a campus I knew like the back of my hand. I never could navigate my way down a straight road.

I shook my head, to myself rather than him, and refocused my attention on the road.

After a few turns, Mat spoke again. "What more have you found?"

Something had changed in the timbre of his voice. It felt as if a subtle line had been drawn between yesterday and today—and we were to stay in the present.

"You're going to love these two. Caro and Margo, they called each other. I haven't learned about Caro's war work yet—I've been reading their early years—but I've learned so much history." I glanced at him again. "I started to make a list of things that struck me last night. Caro was bold and daring, but loyal. She was also in love, and not with Paul Arnim, like I said on the phone."

"A steamy romance doesn't preclude another affair."

"If you're going to be difficult, I'm taking you back to Heathrow."

"How is that difficult?"

"I tell you a fact and you're argumentative, drawing your own conclusion. You always do that. You haven't even read anything yet and—"

"Always?" Mat scowled. "I don't recall talking to you in seven years. You know nothing about my 'always.'"

"Seven? We graduated six years ago." I scowled right back.

"You ghosted me senior year. It doesn't count."

"Ghosted you?" The car followed my head jerk and I quickly brought both back in line.

Mat huffed a short, concise breath. "I told myself we wouldn't get into all this and it took—what—an hour? Let's stick to history." Mat added quietly, "Their history, I mean."

"Sure . . . but . . . I feel like I need to apologize for something."

I kept my eyes on the road, but I could feel him staring at me. I got the impression he was trying to work out what to say.

He settled on, "I promise you don't."

I pulled the car through Eaton Mews North toward the garage at the back of the house. I was about to say more when Mat leaned forward, mouth dropped wide, to see all four stories rising above us. "You've got to be kidding me."

"I know, right?" I pulled Mom's car into the garage. "Welcome to the London House."

EIGHTEEN

S ticking to task, I started sharing more of the letters and the early
 years of sisterly hijinks while we climbed the short flight of stairs
to the kitchen.

Mom called out as I hit the top riser, "Caroline, your father is
here to see you."

I stopped so suddenly Mat bumped into my back.

"Whoa . . . sorry." He gripped my shoulders to keep us both from
toppling downward.

I flapped my hand to shush him as Dad's voice carried across the
kitchen. "I didn't want to believe it was true."

Rounding the corner, I found myself face-to-face with him. A
glance at the table, laden with coffee, toast, jam, and a bowl of berries,
revealed he'd been there for some time. Mom had added a champagne
ice bucket full of red, purple, pink, and white delphiniums as well. It
was a cozy, colorful scene.

"How?" I gestured to the spread.

"After we spoke, your brother called. He filled in some blanks you
omitted and suggested, rather demanded, I get over here."

"Jason told you to come? Here?"

I looked between my parents and felt Mat step behind me. Mom
moved in front of me, creating a barrier between me and Dad. It was
such an incongruent sight—my mom protecting my dad, or me—I
blinked.

"Let's take a moment." She crossed between us and stretched out her hand. "Mat Hammond? It's nice to meet you. You'll be on the fourth floor. I converted it into an apartment and I think you'll be comfortable there. The room outside it is also where Caroline has been working."

"No." Dad's voice draped over us.

Mat looked between us. "That's okay, Mrs. Payne." My mom's name lifted like a question, and he glanced at me as if unsure that's what he was to call her. He rushed on. "There's a cheap hotel by the British Library. I got a room there last time I was here. I can crash there again."

"You're welcome to stay here . . . The letters are here."

"No," Dad repeated. This time it came out in a strangled whisper. Like he wasn't so much against the idea as he was pained by it.

Mom turned to him. "He's here, Jack. That ship has sailed." She tapped me on the arm. "Caroline, your conversation with your father can wait while you show Mat upstairs. He can shower and rest while I prepare him some food."

I nodded and we left, Mat carrying his messenger bag and small suitcase, and neither of us saying a word.

At the top, I showed him the apartment to the left of the large room and let him wander through it alone. After he placed his bag on the stand, he rejoined me and stepped toward the high table. Sunlight flooded this room as it had the kitchen and I didn't want to leave. It felt warm and safe three floors from my dad.

"Are you going to be okay?" Mat asked.

"Most likely not."

He looked down at the piles on the table. "You go talk to your dad. I'll shower, get settled like your mom said, then come back down for food. I won't touch a letter until you're ready."

"Thank you." I headed back down the stairs, pausing in the hallway outside my room to send a text to Jason.

You traitor! This is my project and I chose to tell him exactly
what I wanted him to know. Now he's here. If he puts an end to
this, we'll never know the truth. Happy now?

The three dots for an impending reply popped up immediately. I
checked the time. Eight o'clock in the morning in Boston. Jason had
probably been at the hospital for hours already.

Very happy. I'm sorry you're upset, but I'm trying to put fight in
Dad. I want him to live, C. Not saying you don't, but if I have to
pit him against you—so be it. You first. Cancer next. Text me
how it goes. I've got Sloan Kettering set for next Friday.

I sighed. How was I to reply to that?

I couldn't, so I didn't. I slid my phone into my back pocket and
descended two more flights to the kitchen.

Dad sat alone, small and slumped, at the enormous table. He
pointed behind him toward Mom's mudroom and office nook. "She
went to write down the address for our lunch reservations. I gather
food will soften our conversation."

"It's her fix for everything it seems." I pulled out the chair across
from him. "How are you here so fast? Were you on Mat's flight?"

"I caught the 10:00 p.m. United flight. I assume he was on the
11:30 p.m. American I also looked at. Your mom said I just missed you."

I wondered what would have happened if he'd been early enough
to catch me. Would I have stayed and sent Mat a text sending him
straight back home? Would Dad have confiscated the letters and diaries? Could he still?

"There." Mom's overbright voice silenced us. "I had a reservation at
a wonderful restaurant for Caroline and myself, but then Mat came . . .
Well, it won't go to waste. If you leave now, you'll just make it."

"But?" I pointed to the ceiling.

"I'll take care of him." Her decisive tone was new. Granted, I hadn't been around my mom for years, but she had always been more of an "if you think so . . ." or an "if that's what you want . . ." kind of person. An absent person who hadn't cared enough—after telling me exactly where I fit in her world—to put up a defense or an offense ever again.

She started to clear the dishes from the table. "You need a proper meal, and talking in public might be the only way not to escalate this. There's no point going any further if you two can't get on the same page. Head out the front door, grab a cab, and here's the address." She handed me, not Dad, a slip of paper.

As we walked to the street corner, better to find a passing cab, I studied my dad. I'd always considered him a mild man. Salt-and-pepper hair—the most basic of spices, and used sparingly—with a disposition to match. His profession bolstered the image. Transactional law didn't require a lot of emotion. It required knowledge and acumen, attention to detail.

But I was wrong. He wasn't mild mannered. He was resigned. Fearful. Lost. It became clear in that tortured "no" moments earlier. Such a short word to carry so much power.

Margo's Mrs. Dulles was right. The eyes are the windows to the soul and, now looking, really looking, I saw so much in my dad. I saw what I'd only heard and failed to understand years before—my mom yelling across our living room days before she walked out. "If you'd only talk to me. Give me something, Jack. Help me. I'm hurting like you, but we can't live like this anymore." I finally saw what Jason confronted every time he asked a colleague to consult on Dad's diagnosis only to have our father back out. I saw why, after years of pushing and prodding to connect, I could never reach him. He simply wasn't there.

How long had Mom, or anyone, tried to push this boulder uphill only to have him tuck tight and roll down again?

Now it was up to me? I was to be the juggernaut that got him fired up to feel, to fight, to live?

Jason certainly had high expectations.

NINETEEN

All this churned within me as the cab drove north through Knightsbridge, around Green Park toward Regent's Park. It dropped us off at a modern glass office and amphitheater complex along the canal.

"Down the ramp to the left." The cabby pointed. "You can't miss the Prince Regent."

We wandered down the semicircular drive and, at the end, stopped. The London Shell Company's Prince Regent restaurant sat before us. On the water.

"It's a boat." I stated the obvious.

We stood there staring and speechless. The *Prince Regent* was a long canal boat. I could see that the restaurant inside was light wood, large windows, and white tablecloths. If the idea of a boat leaving land and trapping me with Dad hadn't felt so intimidating, I'd say the *Prince Regent* looked charming.

Dad scoffed. "I'm not in the mood for tourist food and a canal tour through the zoo to Camden. There is nothing enticing about this prospect."

Dad digging in his heels made me dig in my own.

"We need to talk." I pointed to the boat. "There's our table for two."

Dad's eyes widened in surprise. I surprised myself. But I was mad—and beyond tired. I had come here to help, maybe not to start the fight Jason wanted, but to offer another option—hope—for all of us. And foolishly, I'd let it grow. Somewhere along the way, my desire to simply understand and offer a palatable comment morphed into vindicating my aunt, rewriting my family's story, and saving my dad. The absurdity of it would have been laughable, if not so tragic. Especially as I was now cast as the villain in our story, the "Tresse" as Margo and Caro would have called me.

As we stepped down the boat's four steep stairs into the dining area, I noted a map on the wall outlining our path and timeline through the canal. I chuckled as we waited by the stern's galley kitchen to be seated.

"What's amusing?"

"You. Me. Mom. This is what we've come to . . . a two-hour tour in hopes we'll talk and, in public, in hopes we'll behave."

Dad chuckled too.

I watched the hostess seat the couple who entered before us at a four-top with another couple they clearly didn't know. My eyes widened at the thought of trying to talk to my dad with another couple leaning and listening in.

"Are you the Paynes?" A woman about my age with flaming red hair gestured to Dad with a teasing smile. "You're our last guests to arrive. We were going to raffle off your table in a minute."

"That would have been a shame," he murmured.

As we walked toward the boat's bow, I noted the tables. Each was draped in white linen with a bouquet of fresh flowers in the center and antique cutlery flanking china plates. No setting matched. Each was unique and lovely. The glasses were old as well. Vintage with gold inlay. The 1930s type. This was no slipshod affair.

As we sat, a waiter came over with two delicate glasses, each a quarter full of brown liquid. "Here's an apple cider brandy made in Somerset to start off your lunch."

I enjoyed a sip while he laid the menus next to our plates.

"And here," he continued, "is a map of our route and a menu. You don't have a choice about either, but some find it nice to know where they are going and what they'll eat along the way. If you have any questions, let us know."

He stepped away and the boat pushed off the side of the canal.

"This is ridiculous," Dad muttered. "What was your mother thinking?"

I couldn't join in his disdain. I didn't feel sour anymore. The atmosphere, the cider, everything about this situation was incongruent and surprising. I felt that darn ray of hope seep back within me. "A tasty time-out?"

Dad arched a brow, but before he decided what more to say, our first course arrived. A modern twist on fish and chips.

Glancing to the menu, I read aloud, "'Torched Mackerel, Blood Orange, Monk's Beard, Smoked Garlic and Anchovy Sauce with Straw Potatoes.' I'm not sure how it will taste, but it sounds great."

Dad took a bite and his features relaxed. "It's surprisingly light."

We ate the dish in silence and only after it was cleared did Dad speak. "I want you to stop this."

I set down my glass. Mom had also ordered the wine pairings—this course featured a light Sauvignon Blanc—and I was very happy to have both the softening effects of a sip of good wine and the seconds of stall time it offered while I set down the glass.

"It's not what you think, Dad, and Mat's story isn't what he thought either. We can find . . . well, I'm not sure what we'll find, but it's amazing so far. They were amazing. And it's your family. Your history."

"That's my point. It is my history and you should respect my wishes. And what is this 'we'?" He let the word linger. "You and this young man are not a *we*, Caroline. He has encroached into our lives, wants to expose us, and you align yourself with him?"

"You act like he's an enemy, or that it's you or him. What if you're both wrong?" I shifted forward in my seat, glancing around to make sure no one was paying attention to us. "I said it was your history, but I'm your daughter. It's just as much mine. I remember that day, Dad. I didn't before, but I do now. Can you recall what you said to Grandmother? She said it happened before you were born and it didn't affect you. You shot back that you felt the burden, the black void it created every day of your life. You said those words. Don't you think I feel that way?"

I swirled the light liquid around my glass. "I came home to be with you. I live a few blocks away and you don't see me. You see my failures, but do you see me? And if you—" I couldn't say the word. "I don't want what we've had to be all there will ever be."

I felt a stillness around us. Despite my best efforts, in such a small space, with no soft surfaces to dampen the noise, my whisper had garnered attention.

"This will ruin even that, Caroline."

"So be it. There isn't much to ruin." Tears pricked my eyes, but I refused to blink.

The two of us had leaned so far toward each other in our effort to talk quietly, we jumped back as the waiter, slightly flustered, lowered the next course between us.

"Here we have Fowey mussels and saffron potatoes in a curried cauliflower velouté." He reached for a wine bottle sitting on the ledge running the length of the boat. "And Chef is pairing it today with a Viognier."

"Thank you." I pressed the linen napkin to my lips to gain my composure.

When the waiter stepped to the next table, I turned my attention back to Dad. "How can you not want answers?"

"'Better the devil you know than the devil you don't,'" he quoted with no humor.

"You can't be serious."

He was. His eyes rounded and there was a yearning within them, fleeting as it was, that rendered him young for a heartbeat. Young and so alone I felt myself sink into the chair.

"I'm sorry," I said.

We sat in silence for several minutes. Then Dad picked up his spoon and ate a few bites. I followed.

As we finished the course and the boat entered a long tunnel running underneath the highway, he spoke again. It was a strange experience, hearing his words disembodied by the complete dark surrounding us.

"I lived my entire life believing a set of facts that made sense to me. My parents never loved each other, most likely didn't love me much, yet perhaps just enough to push me out to find a new life when neither had more to offer. How it all started? I never knew. Perhaps the war. I remember growing up in its aftermath . . . Even born in 1950, I was ten before the city looked and felt whole again. So, you see, it didn't matter what caused our pain. It simply was."

We emerged from the tunnel. He sipped his wine. Then, eyes fixed on me, he resumed talking. "Then twenty years ago, you stumbled upon a letter and everything changed. There was a cause. A person. A secret. Shame got added to that brew. I simply want it all to go away."

I stared at my plate. I had nothing to counteract that.

"I'm tired, Caroline. I'm seventy-one years old. I've lost enough. I'm too worn out for more."

I tapped the stem of my wineglass. It was so delicate. My eyes traveled to the tablecloth, the flowers, the cutlery, and the tiny bits of saffron sauce still marking our white plates in yellow. *One should enjoy this experience*, I thought. I glanced to the tables around us. Couples smiling, tasting, laughing, and making friends with the others seated with them. I wondered how much my dad had missed, how much I had missed, by focusing on what was absent rather than what was in front of us.

"Jason hoped your coming here would be a good thing."

Dad smiled something small, almost indulgent. "Jason hopes for a lot of things."

"As do I, Dad, and respectfully, I can't give up." I raised my hand. "Please, before you say anything, let me tell you some things I've learned. First of all, your parents did love—they both loved Caro . . . Caro was Grandfather's first love and Grandmother knew it. He held on to her memory, the hope of her return, for years."

"Caro?" Dad shifted his gaze out the window.

"That's what they called her. And she called your mom Margo," I offered, then waited, unsure what he was thinking.

He nodded to himself, as if reliving a memory. "I hated him that day. It was right before I left for the States and they were arguing. I came to the stairs because I thought it was about me. I first heard Mother clearly. She said something about Father loving someone better than her. He spit back, 'I did and she's gone. When are you going to let her go . . . I can't breathe here.' He went on to say he'd once loved her. My mother. He used that word, 'once.'"

Dad faced me again. "That's when I figured out there was someone else. I thought she was still alive; that it was ongoing. I've always thought . . . It doesn't matter what I thought."

We sat still for a long time. Me digesting. Dad reliving.

The boat turned around and eventually we entered the tunnel again. Dad continued, "I thought he wanted to leave her. I almost wanted him to because then . . . then she might be happy. Someone could be happy."

I bit my lip, wondering what to reveal and what to keep secret. There had already been too many secrets.

The boat pushed into the light as I spoke. "Your father first loved Caro. From Caro's letters to Margaret, it's clear he wanted to marry her. He waited a long time after she disappeared, maybe hoping she'd come back. I sense he married Grandmother to protect them—only she and her mom were left—but it soured because . . . because . . . your mom had always loved him. She had loved him best, and he had loved Caro best."

"They lived with a ghost between them." Dad sighed. "That's worse than an affair. Ghosts never age and they never die."

Memories overtook us again. They had to, as I expect we were both parsing through the ghosts and the losses between us.

"True." I shrugged. "Their worlds revolved around Caro and, from what I'm reading, I suspect that never changed." I dragged the tines of my fork through the bits of sauce from a light pasta course still dotting my plate. "There were some pretty passionate scenes Caro wrote about to Grandmother. She'd have had a hard time ever forgetting them."

The heartache of the torn page settled over me. Years of diary entries and letters now sat between me and that first letter and I knew, with a deep certainty, Margo tore the page from despair, perhaps even envy, yet she returned to it again and again so as to never feel comfortable and let herself fully fall in love again. An odd and painful form of self-protection to which I could fully relate.

Yes, Dad was right: a ghost lived between them.

Dad kept his eyes trained out the window. I couldn't tell if he was annoyed, disillusioned, or even listening anymore. The boat had already passed back through the London Zoo and was chugging through the outer circle of Regent's Park. We ate our next course in silence, Cornish hake with Jerusalem artichokes, as we traveled the straightaway toward the landing.

Dad poked at his last bite of fish. "This was my father's favorite fish. He liked it prepared just like this. He used to take me fishing when I was young. He loved to fish. He said Mother had once loved to go fishing, but she never joined us. I certainly can't imagine my mother ever fishing. She was so dour and serious . . . I haven't thought about that in years. I haven't thought much good about either of them in years."

"You should get to know her, Dad. She was feisty and bold. She fished, climbed trees, fought squirrels . . . You should read her stories."

Dad's eyes rounded in surprise. He looked again like a small boy before he banked his wonder. I could almost see the walls grow within his mind. He was stepping away once more. "I've buried her, Caroline. Both of them, and I can't keep going back there. Please. No more."

I tucked in my lips so as not to retort, plead, or even speak, as one waiter removed our plates and another set dessert before us.

Staring down at a Yorkshire rhubarb fool, and feeling like one myself, I risked a next step. "You spoke of ghosts, Dad. There are so many in our lives." His eyes flickered with alarm. I continued, "We have to go back. We have to go back or we'll never move forward. Maybe this is where it all began."

"What began?"

"This holding on so tight that no one can breathe, no one can live."

Dad laid his fork onto his plate and sat back. "You're being dramatic."

"Do you know why I went to law school?" A slight widening of his eyes told me he didn't. Even though I'd told him again and again, he'd never heard me. "When Mom left, you once commented how we'd all gone. I came back after college, bounced around jobs, but we never connected. I thought if we had law school in common, maybe we'd find a way to talk, to be together . . . And maybe it would have worked because I loved it. I didn't drop out because I'm 'flighty,' Dad." I gave the word the emphasis he always did during our life talks.

"I quit because I wanted to be with you. I wanted to help you . . . because we're family. Despite everything. And unless you do something, unless you meet with the doctors Jason keeps finding, or you take your cancer more seriously, we're running out of time. I don't want us to end like we are now"—I scanned the restaurant—"sitting at a table on a boat because that's the only way we'd willingly sit and talk to each other. Maybe even listen."

I looked out the window, letting the quiet stretch between us. I expected him to step into it, to say something, anything.

He didn't.

I finally turned back to find him staring at his plate. "And what if I'm right? I've already found extensive holes in Mat's assumptions. If Caro loved Grandfather, then she probably didn't have an affair with a German. And if she didn't have an affair with a German—if that's not true, the very premise behind her supposed defection—then what else isn't true? Possibly all of it. That means you lived under a lie. Your mom, your grandmother, your father . . . all believed a lie. And that blackness you talked about can be lifted, and maybe mine as well. Maybe I'll do something good, and we won't be paralyzed by the bad."

"This is nonsense. None of it matters anymore."

"That's not true." I thumped the table so hard silverware rattled against china. Heads turned.

I lowered my voice. "It may be the only thing that does matter."

Dad watched me, and for a second I thought he was going to relent. Scenes, scenarios, emotions, and memories played through his eyes. As he brought himself out, and back to me, a hard glint met my gaze.

He dabbed the corners of his mouth with the crisp white napkin, his eyes never leaving mine. "I came because you are my daughter. I came because . . ." He narrowed his eyes, not at me, but at something behind me, that past he claimed no longer mattered. "Because no one came for me and I wanted to offer you that—and your brother goads well. But perhaps this was inevitable with both of you. One generation never truly understands the perspective and needs of another."

The boat bounced against the side of the canal as they moored it.

Dad folded his napkin and laid it perfectly aligned with the edge of the table to the left of his plate. "Goodbye, Caroline."

I shot up to stand as he did, twisting my napkin in my hands. "You don't mean that. Come back to the house with me. Read some of the letters. You'll see. You'll love her—both of them."

Dad surveyed the table before returning his attention to me. "You say you like your job, Caroline. I hope you don't lose it over this fruitless and destructive chase. That would be a shame. Please thank your mother for the lunch and tell her I'm heading straight for Heathrow." He glanced at his watch. "If I hurry, I can still catch the five o'clock to New York."

He walked to the back of the boat and climbed the four steps to the landing.

I dropped back into the wooden chair and didn't realize I was crying until the woman at the table next to me handed me a tissue.

What was I going to text Jason now?

TWENTY

The house was quiet when I returned. I climbed the stairs and found Mat sitting on my stool, absorbed in a letter.

I couldn't wrestle the energy to be annoyed. I felt as wrecked as my dad had looked. Perhaps I was a fool after all—and about to be betrayed. "You said you would wait for me."

Mat dropped the letter as if it burned him. "I tried. Your mom brought me up here and pointed to your piles. She said I had to get to work. She was pretty forceful."

I slumped onto the stool across from him. "That sounds like her lately. Where is she?"

"She went to the grocery store. She wants to make us chicken pot pie tonight."

I smiled. "She's turned into Thomas Keller . . . It was my favorite as a kid. I'm surprised she remembered."

"Lunch didn't go well?"

"That's an understatement." I rested my elbows on the table.

"Maybe this isn't the best approach."

"As Mom says, that ship has sailed. I've crossed a line and there's no going back, so can we please find something good?"

Mat scrunched his brows together and offered me a small, flat smile. "Let's get to work."

He returned to the letter he was reading and I reached for the diary nearest me. I sat for who knows how long seeing nothing. The letters blurred on the page as lunch replayed through my memory on a perpetual reel—all those moments I could have handled differently, all those missed chances for . . . what, connection? Understanding? Nothing had changed in twenty years. I was still that same kid chasing my dad, wanting him to see me. Taking us off land hadn't altered that reality.

"I envy you all this."

I looked up to find Mat sitting straight, stretching his back, surveying the attic space. I followed his gaze. The room was large, clean, beautifully restored—a source of envy in most circumstances. Not unlike my attic bedrooms on Chestnut Street.

"It's a house. It's big. It's grand, but it's still a house." I returned to staring at the page in front of me.

"But what a house." Mat whistled.

"I used to feel that way about your family . . . Remembering your stories, I still do." I scanned the room again. "This has been in my family for at least a couple hundred years, maybe more, and my grandmother, my dad's mom, left it to my mom after she divorced my dad. Somehow that feels messed up to me."

I looked back at him. "It's what you do in a house that matters. You used to call home every Sunday night to be a part of your family's dinner. We'd be doing homework and I'd pretend to read while you talked, but every word . . . Those are some of my favorite memories from freshman year."

I shrugged away Mat's stunned expression. This confession had a point, and it felt imperative to get it out, to state it, and maybe be done with it. I didn't want to bring up the past. He'd made it clear in multiple unspoken ways that wasn't wanted. But this trip down memory lane was all about the present.

I continued, "Whereas I just went to an amazing restaurant and I want to throw up because, instead of having good conversation with all that good food, my dad basically served me an ultimatum. I am to stop this or not have a relationship with him, not that I really have one." I shook my head. Talking wasn't helping after all. "I guess . . . just be careful what you envy."

"You're coming around to my way of thinking." Mat offered me a knowing smile. "History reflects humanity. It isn't one-dimensional, or even two-dimensional; it's multifaceted and far more complex and nuanced than we allow."

I rolled my eyes. At the coffee shop, he said I hadn't changed. Neither had he. "A simple acknowledgment or some understanding would be fine here."

"Yes, well . . ." He chuckled with humor, and a note of something tender and sad. "Nothing was ever simple with you. I'm sorry about lunch, about all of it." A flush of red crawled up his neck. He cleared his throat and pointed to the diary still in my hands. "You've been staring at that page for at least a half hour."

I blinked and nodded to the letter at his elbow. "Read those in conjunction with this." I handed him the diary. "Those letters will make more sense in tandem with the diary. And here . . ."

I reached to the pile in which I'd placed Margaret's four worn and beloved letters. The ones she had tied with their own black ribbon and read so often they'd softened almost to the point of disintegration. "Here's a letter from 1939. But be really careful. These four were tied separately. They were important to my grandmother."

"Got it." Mat seemed startled by my change in subject, but didn't comment. He ducked his head and got to work.

I pulled another diary closer to begin annotating it. Yet, once again, I found myself staring at nothing, listening to soft words I wanted to savor on repeat.

"Yes, well . . . Nothing was ever simple with you . . ."

12 March 1938

Dear Beatrice,

Hitler invaded Austria today. Overran and absorbed it into Germany, more like. Father has been worried he would do this. He and Sir Churchill are among the few, he says, and that concerns him even more.

But I'm not home, so I have no idea what he'd say tonight—I wouldn't want to hear it. It would be more than I could handle right now.

I'm at the London House and I hate it. Caro came from Paris for the weekend and invited me to visit. Things have felt so fractured between us lately that I conceded and travelled by the train yesterday morning. It's been nothing but eating, drinking, and talking nonsense about buttons and dresses. Haute couture and bad politics.

Ugh . . . I have to go. It's my last night here and we're meeting a few of her friends for dinner and drinks. This isn't a set we knew growing up. I have no idea how she knows them, but she does—and we can't survive an evening without them.

13 March 1938

Beatrice,

It's three o'clock in the morning and I'm tired of waiting up and I'm mad. Couldn't it have just been the two of us tonight? Was that an unreasonable request?

Caro is still out, but I came home hours ago. I said I had a headache, but really I was fed up. She and her friends drank, laughed, and looked at me like I was an archaeological find pinned to one of those display boards at the Natural History Museum.

I was so cute, they said. What they meant was my provincial ideas were so antiquated and passé, they've become cute. Furthermore, I am an idiot. They didn't say it, but everyone's tone dripped with condescension. I couldn't possibly understand that Hitler's Anschluss was inconsequential. Only imperial England would think that way. The world is a much broader place with a wider scope of belief, loyalty, and truth. And, after all, Austria was Germany's to begin with—how can we begrudge them annexing an integral part of their national heritage? And, in the grand scheme of life and the movements of history, wasn't it to be expected? My opinions were merely defined by my father's perspective, which is sadly outdated and just plain wrong.

Bollocks!

Of course, I didn't say that. That particular word got my mouth washed out with soap at least three times as a child. But, while it would have expressed my anger perfectly, they would have laughed at it, with a "How quaint . . . Is that the strongest word you can say?"

Instead I sat there mute and they left off me to canvas Schiap's latest political statement, designed within the lines and fabrics of her newest collection.

They think I'm frivolous?

If Father heard Caro tonight, he would be devastated. Forget Modigliani or F. Scott Fitzgerald and all those writers she fights with him about—he'd worry about his own daughter!

Worst of all, I felt stupid. I felt as provincial as they thought me, with my hair still long and with my pink lipstick I bought when I was fourteen and found in the London House's powder room this evening. My clothes were worse. I know nothing of fashion. I care nothing for fashion. Caro did suggest I borrow something of hers, but the way she offered wasn't kind.

"Are you sure you don't want to borrow this? Or this? Or . . ."

Is there a better way to tell your sister she's an embarrassment? There is . . . You laugh at her.

Someone commented about my dress and I replied, "With
war coming, I have no use for anything fancy. I spend most of my
days helping the tenants and managing the estate."

I wanted to show I worked, like they do. Instead I sounded like
I had a silver spoon shoved down my throat. Caro didn't like that
at all. She glared at me, and I got the sense none of these friends
know anything true about her. It disintegrated from there . . .

"War isn't coming. Hitler's satisfied. He'll stop now. You'll see."

"You're wrong," I declared. "Hitler is a real threat and that
Anschluss, as he calls it, was not the peaceful annexation they want
us to believe. It was the subjugation of a nation and Hitler's ideas are
radical and dangerous, and people are suffering, and many dying."

The whole table quieted. Caro, who had been gentle with me
when I first arrived and only glared at me when I misstepped, had
grown weary of protecting me from her friends. Rather than ease
the harsh silence between us, she diverted their attention with a
joke at my expense. Everyone laughed and the awkward moment
was over—for them.

I never spoke again. My headache wasn't really a lie. I had one
from that instant on.

But, Beatrice, sitting there passively listening was worse.
I might parrot Father, like Caro says, but she parrots Elsa
Schiaparelli, Dalí, and all those other designers and artists. They're
Communists. Supposedly that's the opposite of Fascism, but I'm
not sure how if both give the government control of everything and
human life matters little.

At least it's over. We leave for Parkley today. Father insisted
that if she came to England, she needed to come all the way home.
The next few days should be very interesting.

PARIS
1 APRIL 1938

Dear Margo,

I'm sorry I haven't written you back. I'm still trying to forgive you. I don't think you meant harm, but repeating my conversations to Father was wrong. You betrayed me, Tresse.

There, I said it. You deserve it.

He has written for me to come home and I have penned my refusal. There is no danger here and, if I want to go out with my friends and ponder new ideas, that is my business—just as staying home safely tucked under Father's wing is yours.

If your apology was sincere, I'll ask you to put in a good word for me. If you were lying and have any inclination to betray me again, I ask that you keep out of this.

I can't come home, Margo. How can you not understand? There is no room for me there. I'll suffocate.

This is where I belong. This is where I can breathe, create, and live. I am beyond fluent now. I think and dream in French. No one can tell I'm not a native speaker.

And there is no war. I'd like to remind both you and Father of that salient fact. This unrest will settle down. The salon is busier than ever and that wouldn't happen if France, if the world, was marching toward war. People would retrench.

Schiap has her finger on the pulse of things. I've never known anyone to read the times, clothing, or politics so well. Did you see her latest collection? The Circus collection is whimsical. Fun. Daring. Decadent. Do you really believe that is the aesthetic Paris would snap up on the eve of war?

At the collection's opening, the place Vendôme mansion—all ninety-eight rooms—was packed with light, colour, and chaos.

Acrobats tumbled through the upper-story windows from high ladders propped against the outside walls. Mannequins strolled the rooms, with performers leaping up and around them like popcorn. The girls wore hats fashioned like ice cream cones—all thirty of us. Martine and six others came from design and sewing to work the boutique while I managed the runners for our exclusive clientele working the dressing rooms. I think I now know of every dalliance in Paris. I certainly saw a few trysts I'll never forget.

It's life, Margo. You can't hide from it. You seem to think it's all disingenuous or, worse, frightening. But it's real and creative, and it's touching. There was one tender moment amidst the festivities I'll never forget . . . There's a German industrialist, Paul Arnim, who has been frequenting the salon. The Germans made his family move to Paris last year to run some company and he said, for his wife's sake, he plans to make the best of it—I gather that means buying expensive clothing. You should see all he has purchased for her!

Anyway, that night I was helping Mrs. Arnim into a selection of gowns in a dressing room. She commented to her husband how disheartening it was that no man was with his own wife. Right in front of me, he stepped forward, kissed her passionately, and whispered, "You are all I see."

It was the most romantic thing I've ever seen or heard. You see nations; I see people. No one wants a war, Margo. No one. If you were here, you'd understand better. France was devastated in the Great War. We are still rebuilding and no one is bent on tearing it all down again.

As I write this, I miss you. I'm angry, but I miss you more. I miss talking to you, working things out together, and finding where we stand. I choose to believe you are still on my side. And because I believe that to be true, I would never lie to you . . .

Despite all this decadence, or maybe the decadence is a reaction to reality, there is fear here. I can taste it. I'll also concede there are soldiers here—German ones on leave, I think, alongside our French. Actually, that should prove something. If war between France and Germany was a heartbeat away, as Father says, they wouldn't dare visit. Their conflict is to the east, clearly, but Paris holds nothing but good food, wine, and culture for them.

Father isn't alone in his concerns, I'll be fair and admit that. A couple weeks ago, Schiap was snappish and cut off Martine for expressing her political anxieties. She doesn't allow such talk in her salon and she punished Martine by reassigning her for a week to work shipping out of the basement—it was better than being fired. Penance paid, Martine is back in her studio, needle in hand.

So, yes, tensions exist. It may all come down to the passing of an age. Don't you expect every age experiences the sour fear of letting go of the past before it can burst forth in a fully new present? Growing pains . . .

In the end, I suspect we are both right, dear sister. We are at the edge of a precipice. The difference is you believe we will fall, while I choose to believe we will soar.

Time will tell who is right.

I love you,

Caro

P.S. I know we talked about me visiting again this summer, but I don't think I will. I'm not trying to punish anyone, but life is busy and coming home to fight with Father, or with you, is not enticing. Your world and mine feel too far away to bridge right now. If it were only the two of us, I believe you and I could make it, but Father and Mother will never allow me to carry an original thought through Parkley's front door.

Please come here, Margo. I will welcome you with open arms, show you all around town, dress you beautifully—and we will have fun like we used to.

XXO

TWENTY-ONE

3 July 1938

Dear Beatrice,

It's my last day in Paris. Mother insisted I come for soaps and knits, but she sent me for Caro. It was so obvious it was insulting she didn't just come out and say it.

She did say to tell Caro she worries.

"A sneeze makes Mother worry," Caro retorted. "Your sneeze, that is."

I glanced away, feeling weak and embarrassed that I couldn't deny it. Mother grows apoplectic whenever I catch cold.

But after two days, after two minutes, I sensed the futility of this mission. Caro is never going to come home with me. I will take home a trunk of outrageously priced soaps, clothes, and linens—I don't think Mother fathomed how scarce and dear such items are becoming—and I will leave my sister behind.

I will leave her behind because she doesn't see the problem.

"You see demons everywhere. Herr Hitler and his Wehrmacht are not coming here. Austria was Germany's before and now it is again. End of story."

"There are German soldiers all over Paris," I shouted back. I never shout.

"This isn't England, Margo. It's the cultural capital of the world and an easy train ride for all of Europe. They aren't here to fight. There's no war. Of course there are visitors in Paris."

Visitors.

She continued, "Besides, if it ever came to it, the Germans do not touch the numbers of French soldiers. We've been building up the army for the past couple years. That, along with the Maginot Line, will keep Hitler from ever glancing to France."

"We?" I retorted. "In a recent letter you said France was worn out and couldn't handle another war. You're switching stories, dear sister, and if Father were here, he'd say, 'The lady doth protest too much.'"

She set her head at a sideways angle like she did when we were children and I had done something senseless that landed me in trouble. "Don't let them do this to you, Margo."

"Do what?" I felt cool, as if all the blood had dropped to my feet. There was never any pretending between us. I knew where she was headed—again.

She stated it anyway. "Make you afraid. Of everything."

I'm so tired of being perceived as weak and afraid by everyone, including Caro—who more than anyone should know my strength. I saved her more times growing up than she can count, yet she looks at me now as if I'm a cowering simpleton swooning on a couch.

I've changed. I can't deny that, but when I look around, the world has changed equally if not more so. As Caro told me months ago, should we not change with it? Perhaps my change isn't one toward cowering fear, but toward a better understanding of the real dragons out there. Fear can be a rational and appropriate response.

I stiffened my spine and spat out words that tasted bitter and hard, but surprisingly good. "At least I'm seeing clearly. Look around, Caro, because the tension is palpable here. You can taste it. You can smell it. It covers every surface, oozes into every pore.

The Germans are not here for vacation. They may say that, but their arrogance, their swagger—they know something you all don't. They know they have won before they've begun to fight. They sneer as they toss their cigarette butts into the streets as if this is dirty ground and they will own it, and when they do, they will destroy it."

I straightened my spine more, if that was even possible. "Your soldiers? They won't outnumber the Germans. Their rearmament has been gaining speed for years, back when Hitler ceased paying reparations, and your President Lebrun and Prime Minister Daladier are hiding like the rest of them, not standing against him at all. And you and your friends? You do nothing. You talk about clothes, act urbane with your new politics, as if it's all theoretical and carries no real consequences, then you race to drink, race to laugh, and race to find meaning when it's all crumbling around you—and despite me coming to get you and bring you back where you are loved, you'll stay in this cesspool and do it again tomorrow. Until your tomorrows run out."

Caro and I stared at each other. The sound of my breathing and cars passing on the road outside filled the space between us. I counted breaths waiting for her to speak.

One . . . two . . . three . . .

"Our conceptions of love and home are very different, Margo. I wish, for once, you could understand that."

She cloaked those final sentences in velveted steel and not in the anger I expected. She looked sad, forlorn. I've sensed that before and I've pushed her to share with me, but she won't. I can't reach whatever has hurt my sister. Perhaps that's the problem. She can't reach me either.

Instead of staying and hashing it out, she swiped at her eyes, grabbed her handbag, muttered something about the work, and left.

She hasn't returned.

4 July 1938

Dear Beatrice,

Caro came in late last night. She crawled onto the bed I'm sharing with her and said one word: "Stay."

I rolled over and hugged her. She knows I cannot and, for some reason, she will not come home with me. But one thing is certain: my dear sister sees far more than she lets on. She senses fully what is ahead, yet she won't give in. There is something broken in her that has become defiant, that wasn't there when we were kids. It scares me and I suspect I am to blame.

"You can work for Schiap," she whispered. "Not in design. You're not creative at all, and you can't sew." She laughed and I laughed with her.

When we were young and I got us into scrapes, Mrs. Dulles taught us to mend our own dresses. Caro loved it. She was the one who loved everything quiet, everything home, everything cozy. She was going to stay there, happy forever. I was the one who couldn't wait to leave and set the world on fire, explore new continents, dig up treasures, and make history.

How differently we grew.

She continued in a gentle, pleading whisper, "You'll love it here and you're stronger than you think. You always were. You led. I followed." She tugged one of my curls. "You've just forgotten."

We lay silent and comfortable, dreaming of a world that we once imagined could be ours, before she spoke again. "Does Father talk about me?"

"He wants you home," I replied.

"That's not the same thing and you know it." She rolled over. Her back to me. She felt I'd betrayed her, again, and perhaps I had. After all, we promised to always be honest and I hadn't answered her question.

But other than to demand her return, Father doesn't talk about Caro—ever.

PARIS
19 JULY 1938

Dear Margo,

I miss you already. Martine agrees you should have stayed. In contrast, I believe I should have sent her with you. It's only been two weeks since you left, but much has changed. Or maybe you put thoughts into my head and I see demons where there are only misunderstandings.

Yet misunderstandings didn't paint words across buildings all over Paris. They are real and evil. Gangs have defiled the city by painting "Death to the Jews" on buildings and bridges over the past several nights.

Martine was trembling when I entered her studio this morning. She is Jewish and she is scared. Her parents died a few years ago and she looks to Schiap for guidance. But Schiap is a Communist, hates the Nazi Party, and declares they will never take over France. She may be right, but her blustering feels overly brash and bold for what I see around me. What's worse is that I know she'll go to any lengths to preserve all she has built. The salon's clientele is increasingly German and she has no problem with that.

Yesterday Schiap dismissed Martine's fears and ordered her, along with a whole group of us, outside to wash walls. My heart broke for Martine having to scrub away such hatred. I fear Schiap's insensitivity, bravado, maybe even greed, will harm Martine in the end.

Paul Arnim came in today. I shared with him Father's concerns and your observations. He is German and he is kind. I expected reassurance from him. He didn't offer any and he didn't dismiss your fears as I did. He did say, however, he doesn't expect the Germans to show any interest in France.

It was the first ray of hope I've had in days.

There's so much I want to tell you, Margo. So much I didn't say while you were here. I will be home soon and we can talk. Not to stay, please don't misunderstand, but for a visit. Life is too short, Margo, to cut out the ones we love. I refuse to be the one who stops trying to bridge the gap between us. If you won't come to see me more often, I must come to you.

All my love,

Caro

PARIS
30 SEPTEMBER 1938

Dearest Margo,

Are you all feeling better now?

I must confess, you got into my head during your last visit and I've been glancing over my shoulder into dark shadows all summer. But now I feel the weight lifted. There is truly nothing to worry about. The wireless reported today that the Munich Agreement is signed. England, France, Italy, and Germany all agreed that part of Czechoslovakia rightfully belongs to Germany and, now that it has been given over to them, there will be peace.

Prime Minister Chamberlain said it himself, "peace with honor," adding that it was "peace for our time." It makes my heart soar. I didn't realize how tense I'd become over all this until this morning. Father must breathe easier now. He must believe our own prime minister.

On another bright note . . . George was here yesterday! He is working with the Cunard-White Star Line and showed up at the salon before lunch. He gave me no word of warning and what a stir he created!

He walked in with such a confident swagger that every woman stared at him, looked him up and down, and rushed to assist him. Their reaction surprised him and he tried to act all shocked and modest, but he loved every minute.

"*Il est à moi, mesdames.*" A little singsong "He is mine" and everyone stepped away. George's eyes lit like fireworks. It was a tantalizing and powerful feeling.

Then he kissed me. Right then and there. He pulled me close and dipped me just like in the cinema. You should have heard the giggling. He never would have done such a thing in all England, but it's different here. It was right and wonderful and I wish it had lasted longer.

But all good things must come to an end. After a quick lunch and a few more kisses around quiet street corners, he left for meetings. Last night he had meetings as well, and I saw him only briefly before he left early this morning.

He promised he will come again. He promised he will schedule more meetings in Paris. I hope he does because while I had convinced myself I needed this period of my life, Margo, and I have enjoyed every moment, I miss George. Desperately. He's been so patient, and we'll be twenty soon . . . a very marriageable age, don't you agree?

He mentioned me coming home. Not to Parkley, not to the London House, but to him. He danced around it, though, and if he wants a reaction from me, he must get braver. He's seen a lot of pain, Margo—more than I think we can understand. His trust is hard to win, and he's wary of family, of love, and he's so tender. He breaks my heart while lifting it high.

Goodness! I'd marry him tomorrow if he asked. Don't you dare tell him that!

How I wish you were here so we could talk about this. I could share with you every moment of those few short hours and you could reassure me that all will be well, that he will ask, that we will marry, and that we will live happily ever after, like Briar Rose all those years ago—my prince will come.

He also mentioned Adele is expecting a baby. The idea of Frederick as a father gives me the shivers. That poor baby!

I must go, dear one, but write to me soon.

Love,

Caro

10 October 1938

Dear Beatrice,

Caro ended her last letter with "write to me soon" and I should. I get out the pen. I pull out the paper. I write "Dear Caro," and I go blank. For ten days I have gone blank each time I start to write anything. I couldn't even write to you. Writing makes it real and I—I'm having trouble bearing it.

But it is real. I can see it in my mind's eye. I can feel and taste it. We are the same height, Caro and I. We hit Randolph at the same place when he pulls us close, me as a friend, her as a lover. We each nestle perfectly within the hollow beneath his shoulder. I imagine he dips a girl well. He's always been strong. Then I feel that kiss, and taste those peppermints he loves, and an emptiness beyond anguish engulfs me.

He didn't visit Parkley, as he said he would this summer. He wrote me a short note about being busy with work and travel, yet he mentioned nothing about Paris. He has always told me before when he visited Caro, but not this time. He must feel it—lovers need their secrets.

Father has heard from Payne that Randolph is in love. Father smiles indulgently and says Caro is fickle and that her "infatuation" with Randolph cannot last—much to his dismay, for he'd love to have a "Payne Boy" for one of his daughters.

He's wrong. Father has misjudged Caro so completely I wonder if he ever saw her at all—if he sees either of us. Caro is loyal. She endures and has strength beyond imagining. When we were young, I was the fickle one, always changing my mind, acting out, and getting us into trouble. Never Caro.

If he looked closely, he would recognize it now. All that loyalty and capacity for love and sacrifice is still there. It is simply directed elsewhere. She is loyal to Elsa Schiaparelli, to France, to her George, and—still—to me.

Blind loyalty can also go too far. She quoted Prime Minister Chamberlain in her letter and his inane "peace in our time" comment following the Munich Agreement last month. Did she not hear Sir Churchill's retort? Could his voice not break through her notions of what the present looks like and what the future holds? How could she dismiss someone who knows so much, and who has taught us so much at our own table over the years?

Sir Churchill was almost frightening in his disdain and adamance. "You were given the choice between war and dishonor. You chose dishonor and you will have war." Sir Churchill didn't mince his words. He never does.

War is in the air. It is a specter that grows strong, dark, and heavy. I pray it doesn't pounce before Caro wakes.

I need to write her now. It's time.

Thank you, Beatrice, for helping me settle my thoughts—and my loyalties.

TWENTY-TWO

t's not enough." Mat laid down his last letter. "I'll give you she is no hard-core Fascist, but she is drinking the Kool-Aid." He raised his brows in reply to my glare. "Come on, she dismisses obvious German armament and encroachment; her worldview has changed dramatically, and she has no problems with Elsa Schiaparelli's politics and mercenary nature. She admires, even romanticizes, Paul Arnim. I suspect she's a little in love with him."

"And his wife?" I leaned forward.

"She helps the case. Watching their interactions, Caro sees a man who she thinks loves well. You said George had trust issues . . . It only takes a heartbeat for a woman to believe she can be the object of that kind of ardent devotion. It's almost cliché."

My eyes widened before I could bank my expression. This was an unexpected insight into Mat, inconsistent with the man I once knew.

"Bitter?" I quipped. He shot me a dark look. "Come on." I mimicked his earlier exasperation. "You pick. Nineteenth-century novelist? Misogynist? Or that little tirade was born from experience."

His face flushed and he focused on his hands. "Experience, but that doesn't mean it isn't true."

"It does mean you can't be objective. Your preconceived notions, your lived experience, affect everything." I echoed his tone and delivery, as well as his theory.

"Remind me to stop talking to you." Mat refused to look up.

"I wasn't being serious. Hey—" I stalled.

I had pushed him. In my nervousness to smooth over whatever had derailed us in the car, my distressing lunch with Dad, and the tiny bubbles I felt sitting here, I had hurt his feelings.

Mat had said nothing was easy with me all those years ago. It wasn't the words, those could be taken any number of ways—some not good at all—but it was the way he'd said it. Soft. Nostalgic. Warm. His voice had held an undertone of longing that pulled at me—as if "nothing easy" had been the highlight of his freshman year just as listening to him laugh and tease with his family had been mine. It led me to wonder what I had missed all those years ago. While I looked for ways to be close to him—study, research, grab a snack, meet at a party, start a debate—had he been looking for ways to draw close to me?

Back then, I'd felt alone in that odd push-pull feeling. I had wanted him near. I craved it. Yet sometimes he felt too close, like he could see through me. And his eyes . . . What had Caro written? Treacle. Mat's were a deep golden brown that, from the moment we met, invited my confidence and my trust. It was often that alluring pull that drove me to push back. It was both exhilarating and terrifying to feel so transparent and known to him. *"Nothing was ever simple with you."*

I watched the top of Mat's head, unsure what to do or what to say to make things right again. The air in the room took on a sharp and discordant charge. To apologize felt like it would only highlight his embarrassment and my insensitivity.

Instead I pushed the letter I'd just finished in front of him. "Have you read about George? For yourself?"

"He just visited her in Paris." Mat still didn't look up.

"You can't think there's anything romantic with Arnim."

Mat bit back, "Yes . . . they've got true love." He raised his head and stared at me. "We should quit."

Something needed to be said.

"I'm sorry about just now, but you have to admit"—I lifted my hand to stop his rebuttal—"what you say isn't uncommon, but it's not a given."

"You're right. It's not a given. But—" He climbed off his stool to stretch. "We need more. None of this is getting us anywhere. I had a good article, Caroline, and it's gone. There aren't answers here, merely holes. Tons of them. I can't submit what I wrote now. This is worse than if I never proposed that article in the first place."

He stepped back to the table. Letters, diaries, our notebooks and laptops covered every available inch. "The information I found in the Archives during my first research visit? These contradict most of it. According to the Arnim family and the German records I've searched, he sent his family to the States in early '40. He stayed in France with his companies. Did he go with them? Then return? Did he even love Caro? There's no affair hinted at in these letters. And, I'll concede, she seems to love George . . . I thought I was better than this."

"You are. In fact, this is what you posited all along. Nothing is simple." I used the same words he'd given me. He had meant them as a form of comfort and I hoped he'd take them the same way now. "Humans are messy. Their history is going to be messy."

"True, but inconvenient when you're ready to publish."

"Do you want to stop?"

He looked at me. His eyes flashed an angry retort, but he didn't articulate it, and he extinguished it quickly—rather, another thought replaced it. This one he didn't articulate either. He simply ran his fingers over the letters as if asking them to reveal their secrets and tell him the true story.

"I should. I have enough to please the Arnim family, and I have to turn down the *Atlantic* anyway. I suppose it's a good price for you . . . a thousand dollars on a plane ticket to scuttle your problem?"

I opened my mouth, but he held up his hand. "I didn't mean it like that, I promise. I'm mad at myself. Not at you. That came out wrong."

"Why don't you wait? It's only Monday. You could have something great by Friday." I walked around to the side of the table, only a corner away from him. "I still need answers. I still need your help."

"What answers, Caroline? Knowing about your aunt isn't going to fix your father. This isn't a cure for cancer and you don't know it won't cause more pain." He gripped his chin, thumb spread to one ear, fingers to the other, as if struggling with a thought, or with a decision. "I had no idea . . . You weren't kidding about tsunamis. And what happens if we do find something? You think it will be better, but are you ready to accept if it's worse? Much worse?"

A true smile—a little sad, but no less true for that—accompanied my shrug. He sounded like Caro's description of her sister. *"You believe we will fall, while I choose to believe we will soar."*

"I've already released the tsunami. Maybe with the truth, it'll have been worth it." I laid my hand across a pile of letters. "You talked about resilience within the human spirit. I have to believe the truth will bring that."

I reached across the table and handed him the several letters I'd just annotated. "Here are a few choice letters from 1939 into 1940. Tell me when you get to the April 1940 letter. I have the next one set aside."

Mat laid them down and held out his hand. "Hand it to me now. If we're going to do this, let's get it over with."

I stepped back. "I want to know when you get to it. It's a turning point, after which everything changes."

He nodded, not in agreement, but in acquiescence. He was willing to take that first next step.

I plopped onto my stool again, my mind swirling. Two minutes before, I'd been out. Mat defeated. Article abandoned. Yet, rather than agree, accept, and offer him a ride to the airport, what had I done? I opened the door wider—and pushed him through it.

1 September 1939

Dear Beatrice,

I'm exhausted. I can't feel my feet. I've been standing all day and can barely keep my head up, but I have to write to you because I have to write to someone. I have to get this out. Sobbing hasn't helped.

Caro isn't here—writing to her won't help, as she won't understand. I can't imagine things are better in Paris, but perhaps they haven't done what we've been forced to do. Can they truly see a world we do not?

The children started leaving the cities today. They are calling it Operation Pied Piper, as if a cute name makes it less devastating. Not that the name is all that cute—I've never liked that story.

But that's who I was today, the Pied Piper playing my happy song, as we led thousands of children onto trains, with wide red eyes, runny noses, and looks of stoic determination no child should be asked to fabricate.

There were two sisters who passed through Chesterfield and almost brought me to tears. They looked like Caro and me, and they were so scared. I smiled and laughed and straightened their bows—with shaking hands.

Everything is a bit of a game, isn't it? That's what we were told to project today—make it a game and be buoyant, assuring, and compassionate. And if we play it well, we will win. Our children will be safe. But when you see it through the eyes of a child, reality crashes through the illusion. It's not a game and we will never be the same again.

We checked the brown tags hanging from each of their necks as they disembarked the trains and ushered them into the unknown. To safety? I'm not sure. All I know is I loaded scared children into packed train cars, lorries, buses, and family cars, sending them to places they'd never heard of, to people they've never met.

What awaits them at the end of the line?

To make it all worse, Caro's latest letter to Father arrived tonight—and from a diplomatic pouch through Whitehall. I wonder that she does not sense the irony in that, while she claims to be safe, she sends her letters through Father's diplomatic connections to ensure their safety.

She refused to come home—again. She said if war happened, France and England would be united in it. Therefore, how could it matter where she was?

But it matters, Beatrice. We are family.

Randolph visited last month. The Cunard-White Star Line was making changes and he offered Caro passage from their last open port on France's west coast. He said it was urgent as the port would close soon—it may be closed already. That precipitated most of last month's quarreling across telephone lines and in letters. Randolph confirmed that people are having trouble fleeing many cities throughout Europe. Controls are tightening. Nazi controls. He sounded as grim as Father. But Caro never budged.

Why would she? If you read her letters, you'd think she doesn't have a care in the world. The salon this. The salon that. Schiap's Zodiac collection. New designs for the Modern Comedy collection. The latest opening. The glamorous parties. On and on . . .

Father and Randolph versus Caro.

Who is lying? Or is everyone seeing the same thing, but unable to face it in the same way? Or can no one see the truth at all? Is there truth here? Or only perspective?

Caro has never been blind, or stupid. It makes me question what she truly sees and what she's about. Years ago I would have said I'd be the one to defy Father and do what I want when I want. But the world flipped upside down. For me? Years ago. For everyone else in the world? It's still tumbling.

She sent me a dress. Amidst all this chaos, Caro sent me a dress. It lays across my sofa near the window and it is light and airy and perfect. I can't bring myself to hang it in the closet. I can't stop looking at it. I can't bear to own it either.

"George loves it," she wrote. "When he visited in August, I modeled it for him because if it looked good on me, it will look smashing on you."

But we don't get everything the same, do we, Beatrice? The same clothes? The same experiences? The same love?

If I could be anything, I would be this dress. It's easy to see why Randolph loved it. It's the palest shade of pink silk, with butterflies dancing across the entire dress. Caro said it's one of Schiaparelli's best designs and that it will be famous someday. It reminds me of our childhood, a sublime happiness I thought would never end—

All good things come to an end.

3 September 1939

Beatrice,

It is official. We are at war.

PARIS
4 APRIL 1940

Dearest Margo,

I need you. I don't know what to do and I can't reach you . . .

I tried to telephone you today, but you were out. Trent assured me you would get my message. Did you try to telephone me? It never rang and I'm beginning to wonder if the lines no longer work. Or it might have been that we didn't hear it as the salon was terribly busy today—probably our last busy day.

The boutique is bare. While most can't afford anything beyond the essentials, if they can get ahold of those, those who can are absorbing goods at a frenzied rate. Schiap is out of town—she's been out more than in lately—and without clear direction, we closed the boutique early. Raw goods are so hard to come by we have no stock to refill the shelves. The news says it's because the British are blockading goods to all Europe to thwart the Nazis, but looking around at the gluttonous wealthy Germans, I suspect they are the ones hoarding. Although we are at war, if you can call this stalemate a war, German private citizens still live here and still have money to spend.

Paul Arnim came in today. I thought he was coming for a gift for his wife, but he pulled me aside instead. He said his family was sailing for America, without passes, at midnight tomorrow and I was to do the same.

His words weren't casual, Margo. They were pointed. He then said something about not being subscripted in '35 but being sent to France to work and build capital, but now everything had changed. He had new orders. At first I didn't understand. He's not in the military, he's here, in Paris.

He gripped my arm and articulated each word slowly, as if speaking in code. A chill went through me and my mind blanked.

"I want you to tell your friend Martine," he added. "She is in greater peril than you. She doesn't understand what is coming. Exit papers will be impossible soon."

I am sending this through a diplomatic pouch. Before Schiap left, she said it was the only secure way to send information, and Ambassador Campbell has always been so kind to me. I've sent letters this way before, but now I feel it's the only way. These words are only for you, Margo. Even Schiap cannot know what I've written here.

For the first time, I'm scared. Not so much for me, but for Martine. She has no family to protect her and we hear stories. We hear stories of Jews being beaten. We hear stories of them vanishing in the night. We hear stories of them being rounded up all across Europe and forced into cordoned-off areas, into ghettos. We hear stories of whole families fleeing. We hear of work camps and detainment facilities in Germany.

I know the French would never allow such atrocities here, but they exist. The wolves are real and they are at the door. I know you would never chide me for my foolishness, but I am feeling the weight of it now.

What have I done?

Love to you, dear one.

Caro

"Studying it isn't the same as reading someone's letters, is it?" Mat broke our focus. "I remember that about Anne Frank's diary from high school, but I'd forgotten how much . . . This feels very real."

"It's why I called you. I liked Margo and Caro as soon as I read the first letters. I want to do my best by them."

"Can't blame you." Mat chuffed. "I like her. I like both of them. There is something so sincere and earnest about each of them. I didn't expect that . . . Honestly, I can't believe Caro could be a spy, for either side. She's so open. Maybe she really was working fabrics."

"Where are you now?"

"I just finished the April 1940 letter from Paris. You have the next one?"

I handed him the May 17, 1940 letter. The torn letter. "Here's where it all begins. Caro comes home and . . . It isn't fabrics. There's a different energy from here on out. It's like she's playing a game of sleight of hand. I can feel it."

I watched him read, unable to return to my own work.

Mat sat straight. His lips parted. He cleared his throat as he reached the end. And, just like me, he turned the page over, certain there had to be more. He looked up, smiled, and jokingly pulled at his sweater's collar. "Wow . . . Your aunt got a little steamy there."

"Just a little." I grinned.

Mat returned to business. "We need to follow up on George. Maybe through his records, we can prove the Arnim thing is a misdirect and figure out what really happened."

I realized he hadn't read any of the diaries yet. Although I handed him one, he had yet to open it. Mat didn't know who George was. "You're agreeing with me?"

"Caroline, my article's current iteration is blown. If I don't come up with something better, I'm sunk. Try to keep up."

Without waiting for me to "keep up," he started pacing across the room. "If the Arnim information was a ruse, who initiated it and why? Google George." Mat pointed to my computer. "Let's see what more we can find on him." He ruffled through the pages. "Do you have a last name? There isn't one in any letter I've read—"

"I already know what happened to George."

"You do?" He stopped.

"He married Margo."

"But . . ." Mat blinked. "That would make him . . . your grandfather? George married Margo?"

"Randolph George Payne married Margo in early 1950." I scrunched my nose. "It's about the saddest love story you can imagine. Margo loved Randolph and he loved her, but not like that letter, which she read, lots." I gestured to it. "In fact, I think she kept it close to keep the wound fresh and remind her to never love him deeply."

"Why didn't you say all this hours ago? I never would have considered leaving." Mat smirked. He was teasing me now. "This crap sells . . . Forget history. People love a good romance, and unrequited love is even better."

After the May 17 letter, Mat was hooked. It wasn't the unrequited love story but the tidbits of secrets and spy-craft Caro dropped like crumbs along her path. He caught hints and references that had alluded me and commandeered everything from 1938 to 1941, with a pen clenched between his teeth.

"So . . ." He pulled the pen from his mouth as the evening sun shot through the west-facing windows and French doors. "Arnim sailed to the United States? Maybe. If so, the Reich called home all officers and he'd been conscripted by that time. To not return would jeopardize his family. Then what happened?" He shuffled through his notebook, tapping his pen against the table with his other hand. "He was promoted to Gruppenführer on February 22, 1941. That's an official record placing him in Paris, and a transfer order was issued on October 17, 1941, to Tula . . . the Battle of Moscow."

Mat stilled and stared at me. "Then nothing more. I couldn't find a single notation in any file on him. He didn't report for duty in Russia. Nothing. That, along with that note to Caro's parents, seemed to imply they both left their countries and ran. But now, maybe not. Moscow was a disaster for the Germans, so losing track of him may not be surprising."

Without waiting for me to comment, Mat pulled another pile of letters to him and started again.

After the third long soliloquy, I stopped trying to answer. He wasn't talking to me but having a full-on research discussion with himself, his laptop, and his pen and paper.

He worked that way for hours, reading, notating, turning pages in his black Moleskine notebook, reconciling what he'd found months ago in the National Archives to what the letters and diaries revealed tonight.

Rather than answers, he found more questions.

"I give up." He threw the pen down after one in the morning and pulled over his computer. "We'll just have to go back."

"Go back?"

"To the National Archives at Kew." He started typing. "Grab your driver's license and your passport. We'll need them to get you a Reader Pass so you can get access to the files. Once we have your pass number, I'll start ordering them."

That's how we ended the night. Exhausted around three in the morning, files ordered, I headed to my room to crash for a few hours, while Mat stayed, still racing through the letters and still talking to himself.

TWENTY-THREE

We got off the train and Mat led us down Richmond's Ruskin Avenue.

"About today . . . There are going to be a ton of files. Thin sheets of paper, most of which will mean nothing to us, but any little clue—name, date, event, place—near Caro's name, we record and chase down. That's how I found your aunt. A notation in Arnim's file—Schiaparelli's employment files in Paris, the ATS, ISRB, and then I stumbled on Arnim all over again. We find a thread and we start pulling."

"How many files did you order?"

"Twelve, for now. There's more than you can imagine in there, and it's a mess. You'll find papers from SOE North Africa and an operational log from France in the same file. We're looking for a needle in a haystack and in only about ten percent of the haystack."

I felt my face scrunch in confusion. "Ten percent?"

"Most of the European SOE files burned in a records fire in 1999."

"You're kidding."

"No . . . We have to accept we may not find anything more than what we already know."

"What aren't you telling me?" I stopped and stared at him. He was awfully excited for someone who needed to "accept we may not find anything more."

He beamed at me. Lips pressed together. Eyes dancing. My heart simultaneously sank and rose.

"What? What did you find?"

"There was so much in those letters, Caroline. And once I paired them with the diaries . . . You might not have caught it all, but Baker Street, the Irregulars, references to books, Tube stations, people like Nelson and Selwyn Jepson. She was spilling the tea. She didn't share secrets, per se, but she gave enough clues that now, with files no longer classified, it paints a picture. A really complete picture."

"A picture of what?" I couldn't move and Mat couldn't stand still. He started walking down the street. I raced after him. "Hey! Slow down. A picture of what?"

"A spy. When I threw it out yesterday I wasn't being serious. But I am now. It all became clear around four this morning. But I need proof. Proof and time to write it up by Friday." He grinned down at me, racing on, one long stride after another.

At five nine, I can usually keep up with anyone, and Mat's only about six two. Yet I had to run to catch him again.

I grabbed his arm. "What does that mean?" It didn't sound good. From my perspective, it sounded a lot worse. This was no longer a private shame but an international one?

"It means a shift in history, Caroline." His smile was a broad thing fueled by endless coffee and the entire tin of shortbread cookies Mom had delivered at midnight. "My article before was positing that your aunt worked for the SOE as a secretary, maybe in records or something, as that was common. But it was about how we view history, how it affects us, changes us, and we grow, rebound, and move forward. But what if I can prove your aunt was the very first female SOE agent? Her dates signal she was on board in 1940, putting her at the very beginning with Giliana Gerson and Virginia Hall. Earlier even—and they weren't British. See? That's a game changer. The stuff of history books and careers. This is no longer a discussion about nuances and perspectives but a seismic shift in the actual events themselves."

"And if she defected?"

"Again, seismic shifts in how we look at that time. A defection like that, if known, would have changed everything for the SOE and the British war effort. A tsunami on a global scale." He bounced on the balls of his feet.

I pulled at his forearm to stop the bouncing. He dropped his attention to my hand, white with pressure and still clutching his arm.

He calmed. "Something this big requires hard proof, Caroline. We're far from that."

I looked to the National Archives building in all its colossal cement solidity, then back to him. "I . . ." I was suddenly afraid of what we might find. For all my talk about putting ghosts to rest, the idea that Caro's story could be bigger —and worse—had not felt like a probability. How much had the letters and diaries really taught me about my aunt?

Mat threw an arm around my shoulders. He squeezed and turned us both to face forward. He started us walking. "You can trust me, Caroline. I won't blindside you and this will all be okay. Remember, we're still at the beginning."

"It's the end I'm worried about."

Mat and I turned our separate ways in the front lobby. He rode the elevator straight to the third floor Reading Room. I climbed the stairs to Security on the first floor to pick up my pass. Although I was only a few minutes behind him, he was already deep within a file by the time I dropped into the chair next to him.

He lifted a stack from his desk and gently laid it in front of me. "I pulled six folders from my locker. You can only have three out at a time, so you take these three."

Three large, brown trifold folders sat in front of me. Each tied with a cloth ribbon. I opened the first and found that the thin copy pages inside were bound with strings like a three-ring notebook. The pages crinkled with every turn.

"Is there any order to this?" I whispered.

Mat leaned toward me. He smelled of citrus and something rich, like cedar. "Within each folder, it's a loose reverse chronological. Just start reading. Take pictures of anything interesting. No flash." He held out his hand. "Give me your card."

I reached into my pocket and handed it over. He sniggered at the picture. My hair looked flat, eyes dull, and skin oddly yellow.

"It's not that bad." I nudged him. "The lighting was terrible."

He raised a brow I read to mean *nice try* and continued with his thought. "Now that we're here, I'm going to request three more files on each of our cards. You start reading."

While he left the room for the computers outside, I began.

Page after page after page of . . . Egypt?

He returned as I was shutting my first file and reaching for the second. "Nothing interesting?"

"Lots, but in Egypt. 1943." I lifted another folder toward me. It was heavier than the last, and that one had been filed with at least one hundred sheets of the thin copy paper. "We'll never get through all this."

"One page at a time." Mat chuckled. "Welcome to my world. Research is worse than watching paint dry or a pot boil. You'll soon figure out what's important and what's irrelevant, and it'll go faster."

I opened the folder and hit a name I knew on page one. "Hey . . . Dalton . . . Church—" I clamped my mouth shut, annoyed that I hadn't schooled my excitement and examined everything first. Alone.

It wasn't that I would hide information or lie to Mat; it was that I wanted to know whatever it was, no matter how good or bad, before he did. To me, they were family. To him, they were an article—now a career-making one.

It was too late.

Mat was out of his seat, hovering over me in an instant. "These are the memorandums that formed the SOE."

He carefully turned one page after another before returning to the very first. I sat feeling like I did at age six when Amelia grabbed my I Can Read! book and read it to me.

18 July 1940

My Dear Prime Minister,

I will do my best to carry out the additional duties you wish me to undertake.

Yours very sincerely,

Hugh Dalton

"Look how they hand-wrote the salutations and the signatures." Mat moved back to his chair and scooted it closer to mine. "I saw these before, but it never gets old. This is history, Caroline."

I glanced at him. His eyes had taken on a softer sheen than the electric glow of our conversation outside. Outside, he had scared me—he reminded me of Veruca Salt from *Willie Wonka and the Chocolate Factory* with her "I want it *now.*"

I didn't feel that way looking at this Mat. This was the Mat who brought me coffees in the library as we rushed to finish papers. This was the Mat who ate a whole box of Red Vines with me at *The Avengers* opening night. This was the Mat who said history was multifaceted, nuanced, and complex, and had walked me through his ideas late into the night. This was the Mat who really did smell wonderful and was, at that moment, looking straight at me from not more than six inches away.

"What?" I blinked, having completely missed his comment.

"He wrote that. Churchill. With his own hand." Mat turned the pages, going back in time from when Dalton accepted Churchill's commission to Churchill's initial request.

I traced my finger over the letter's handwritten parts. "16 July 1940 . . . Dear Dalton . . . Yours sincerely, Winston Churchill."

Mat grabbed for my hand and held it. "You can't do that."

"It's his real signature. Isn't it amazing?"

"It's in pencil. It won't be amazing for long if everyone rubs their greasy fingers over it."

I suppressed a smile. "I washed my hands and I bet we're the only people to request these files in years."

"That's not the point." A ghost of a smile lingered on Mat's lips as he studied the signatures. I was sure he wanted to run his finger over them.

"Quick swipe?" I shoulder bumped him.

Without moving his chair away, he shifted his attention back to his own file. "Turn the page, Payne, and keep reading."

Minutes later, he pulled at my arm. "Interesting as that is, it's a little early for Caro. Shift over here." He tapped the folder in front of him. "This is the file in which I found the note and meeting references about your aunt. In light of the letters, read it together?"

I nodded and we began . . .

MOST SECRET PRIVATE MEETING NOTES

6 August 1940

Hugh Dalton

I met with Caroline Waite at 1900 hours today. Major Selwyn Jepson joined as Miss Waite, serving in the ATS, laid out her abilities and connections within Paris and offered her assistance on fact-finding missions. We outlined the impossibility of her proposal. I added that I was a longtime friend of her father and he would not appreciate her involvement or my endorsement of such activities. My answer displeased her and I suspect we have not heard the last from her.

Major Jepson, concerned with her social and political importance, believes she cannot play any role in our operations. She knows more than most due to family and personal connections, and that alone makes her a strategic risk.

I will reach out to Miss Waite's commanding officer at the ATS to garner increased assignments to fill her time and energies.

MOST SECRET PRIVATE MEETING NOTES

10 September 1940

Memorandum of a meeting between Miss Caroline Waite and Assistant Information Officer Sir Frank Nelson.

Miss Caroline Waite, who returned from Paris on 17 May and is currently serving in the ATS, had a preliminary conference with Dalton and Jepson on the evening of 6 August. She told them how pleased she was to have an opportunity to consult with them and proposed herself as an intermediary to increase communication between France and England, which is slender at present.

In today's meeting with Frank Nelson, Miss Waite noted that German propaganda in Paris throughout the past year has harmed the French impression of British care and involvement. Miss Waite again proposed using her person and contacts to acquire and disseminate information into Paris via her work in fashion and her position within Parisian social circles.

Nelson, after listening with extreme interest to Miss Waite's exposition, expressed his agreement in general with what she said. He added, however, that her position in society and potential loss (of life) could cause extreme backlash to reconnaissance and information gathering efforts as ministerial opinion was presently wary of this new warfare tactic.

Miss Waite conceded his point but remained unconvinced that the cost outweighed the benefit of her involvement.

She then stated that she had found her own way back to Paris and had remained there from 27 August to 6 September. She outlined the location of German offices, troop numbers, new laws and restrictions instituted, and the general tone of French morale.

Nelson ended the meeting by asking Miss Waite to take no further action until he contacted her. He will meet with Dalton to discuss next steps. Nelson suspects Miss Waite's interests will not wane and that her private travels could put both her and British interests in jeopardy.

"Remember her letter to Margaret? About two weeks after this?" I pulled up my phone and scanned through the countless letters I'd photographed until I found the one I needed.

Enlarging it with two fingers, I handed Mat the phone.

"A couple weeks ago I transferred to a new research team, the Inter Services Research Bureau (ISRB). My work revolves around what we do and how we can do it better. Last week, I sorted countless defective uniforms and proposed new zipper designs. It sounds silly, but it's a good use of my skills. You would be surprised at how many zippers are needed for military uniforms, and the cost of replacements and repairs, in time and in monies, when they break. So if Churchill's next radio address speaks of increased productivity and resulting victories, credit me and my zipper research.

"I laugh, but it actually is quite serious. All of it is. And if ever I forget, I glance over to Rose Tremaine who sits next to me. She was shy at first but has grown to trust me. She confided in me this morning that she returned to Paris at the end of last month. She wouldn't tell me how she did it, and I don't want to know. I chastised her for her foolishness, but then she burst into tears and I stopped. It breaks her heart what's happening to her beloved home, and she is so afraid for her family. Every day she arrives early, stays late, and never comes out with us at night. I wonder if she feels she has something to prove. She doesn't. We like her very much.

"War is a strange and terrible thing, Margo. Even fighting side by side, it can tear us apart."

Mat returned my phone and as I scrolled through the letter again, something caught my attention. I gestured to his file and slid him mine. "Trade with me?"

Mat had said Caro's name never came up in the file after this meeting. Not until that final letter to her parents, but . . . I clamped my hand on Mat's shoulder so hard he flinched.

"We're so stupid. It's here and she told us, by telling Margo." I shifted the file between us. "Who is named Rose Tremaine? In real life? No one. It's not a person—see here? It's capitalized on every page."

Mat furrowed his brow.

"Code names are capitalized." I tapped my phone, still open to the letter we'd read moments before. "She writes about Rose, but Rose wasn't a real person who sat beside her. Rose was fiction, a code name." I returned to the file and turned the page. I pointed to *ROSE* typed in three different places. "And again." I turned another page and tapped on *ROSE* once more.

Mat nodded, catching on. "Caro is never mentioned after this point, and Rose was never mentioned before." He scanned the page. "Without the letters, that connection is impossible . . . We have to be sure."

"Rose from *Briar Rose*, Caro's favorite fairy tale. Tremaine, the stepsisters' last name from *Cinderella*, Margo's favorite fairy tale. They got the books for their tenth birthdays." I leaned back, cycling through all I remembered. "And she writes about Rose in Paris at the end of last month—exactly when Nelson reported Caro was there. How likely is it two random women working in the same office were in Paris, without permission, at the same time?"

"Not very . . . So Caro is Rose?"

I nodded. "Rose is Caro."

"We've got to prove it."

We.

The word had opened a world of longing when I first encountered it in Margo's diaries. *We are ten . . . We are "we."* Even when arguing, the sisters were on the same side. They were united. I missed that with my sister. I had missed it with anyone in my life, if I was completely honest.

It was a powerful word—an elusive, beautiful word of belonging. When Mat first used it on the phone that night, it sparked something deep within me—for me. Then Dad threw it in my face at lunch.

We.

Here it was again. Mat and I had been bandying it about for the last few minutes as if it was common, a given, and understood between us. I checked my enthusiasm, or my vulnerability—they somehow felt one and the same—and reminded myself Mat hadn't meant anything significant by using the pronoun. To him, it was merely a word, a substitute for a noun, quicker than referring to each of us individually. But I couldn't deny, within it, within this "we," I didn't feel alone and our task didn't feel so daunting.

We sat studying files as fast as we could for the next four hours, taking pictures of every page on which ROSE appeared, and recording notes as to the file, record number, and any other information we hoped could be useful. I wrote straight through a pen and moved on to another.

My stomach then growled so loud neither of us could ignore it any longer.

Mat laughed and closed his folder. "Let's head to the café and feed you."

We sat at a small table to compare notes after purchasing coffees and two plates of lamb vindaloo from the cafeteria.

"Remember the memo about landing at Brest?" I tilted my phone to him.

CONFIDENTIAL
14 November 1940
To: Army Command
Fr: Nelson, Frank

Are you landing at Brest? If so, I have an agent I would like to send with you. Please let me know if you have space.

"That was Margaret and Caro's twenty-second birthday and I think the agent who needed a ride was Caro/Rose. Margaret wrote in her diary that Caro refused to come home and was unreachable by phone on their birthday and for several days after."

I searched my notebook for notes on the diary entry but was unable to find them. I kept talking as I leafed through each page. "Then she wrote that she got a call from Caro eight days later, on the twenty-second, claiming she'd been sick and had stayed in the London

House's basement, unable to go to work or to an approved shelter, blah, blah, blah. Margaret wrote it all in her diary that night."

"I remember that. She thought Caro was lying to her, something she felt Caro had never done before." Mat picked up his phone. "Google says Brest wasn't in German hands at that time. The Soviets won it in battle in 1939 and held it until '41. While they had a non-aggression pact with the Nazis in '39, Stalin played both sides. Maybe there was a secret place the British could put in?"

I scrolled to the next photo, the picture of a file page I'd taken moments before, and handed my phone to Mat. "There had to have been because she called her sister the night she came back. November twenty-second."

MOST SECRET CIPHER TELEGRAM
22 November 1940
To: Jepson
Fr: Nelson

ROSE returned from Paris today. Meeting tomorrow 0800.

TWENTY-FOUR

After our quick lunch, we each grabbed another stack of files from our lockers and Mat requested three more for each of us. It felt like a race. Not against each other but for the truth—and against time. The Archives closed at seven o'clock.

Finding little over the next several hours, I felt the energy between us diminish. We slumped in our chairs and turned pages more slowly. Until Mat laughed out loud. All heads in the quiet room turned our direction.

"You've got to hear this," Mat whispered.

"'Major Golding has antagonized the staff to such a degree that I have had to resume control, and he fails to carry out my instructions to an alarming degree. His continued presence on my staff is a waste of public funds. He criticizes the policy of the British Government and my conduct of the work of this section in the presence of private soldiers and foreigners. He is unreliable and slothful to a remarkable degree. In my opinion he is unfitted for employment in any post demanding discipline and dependability.'

"Signed 'Colonel, G. S.'"

"Slothful. I need to remember that."

"It reminds me of some of the students in my TA sections," Mat quipped.

"Do you like teaching? I didn't realize when we were seniors that you were going on for a doctorate." I faced Mat.

From his expression I couldn't decide if he was considering the question or me. We'd been so close once I should have known that, no matter what had happened our final year of school.

"I do. I didn't at first. I suspect eighteen- and nineteen-year-olds have little respect for twenty-two- and twenty-three-year-olds, but now I'm a decade older than they are and there's a little distance we recognize. The dynamic works. They act like I might know something." He winked at me. "I never let on when I don't."

"What would you tell them about all this?" I drummed my fingers on the file in front of me. "A student finds a thread, one that pulls in lots of directions, yet can't pull a definitive answer from any one of them—nothing that answers the main question. Was Caroline Waite a traitor or a hero?"

Mat drew closer, clearly understanding my deeper question. "I'd counsel caution, even more so than when I wrote my now defunct article. The letters opened up their humanity for me and changed the facts considerably. They were sisters who were funny, touching, kind, jealous, and in love—tragically with the same man. Everything written about them should carry that humanity. I'm not sure I got that before."

He sat back. "But to answer your question, I would still encourage them to pursue it, wrestle with it, chase down all those threads, draw conclusions, and write something up. I'd push them to get to the point where their ideas are firm enough to commit them to writing, discussion, grading, publication, anything. We have to take our thinking that far because we can't learn from history if we don't press to understand it. And if we don't understand it, we're doomed to repeat it."

I nodded, as I had come to the same conclusion. Except I wasn't thinking on the macro level. It wasn't the scholars who needed to process Margo and Caro's story—it was me. When I read their words, the narrative I found was my own and, in understanding their story, I began to see my family, my father, and myself. To learn from it, rather than repeat it, felt vital. Without redemption for Caro—without uncovering the truth about her life—was redemption possible for me? For any of us?

Mat caught the change in my expression and nudged my shoulder. "What are you thinking?"

There was so much I couldn't say. And one thing I could. I lifted the page I'd just read and tilted it in his direction. "We're nearing the end. Here is Rose's last mission, three days before that final letter to the Waites."

Mat tucked close.

MOST SECRET OPERATION
CLEMENTINE FIELD SUMMARY

17/18 October 1941

The purpose of this operation was to attack and do as much damage as possible to the engine facility in Paris twelfth arrondissement as it is extremely important in supplying engines for German troops. In particular, the construction of Arado Ar 240 aircraft.

It was thought that the maximum damage would be inflicted by blowing up the cement support structures in the main workroom area.

The party chosen consisted of 3 men equipped with automatic pistols, grenades, fighting knives, 4 specially devised explosive charges, incendiaries, rubber gloves, scaling ladder, wire cutters, and 2 days of emergency rations.

The above mentioned party and equipment were transported by one aeroplane in one container and dropped by parachute at a suitable point not far from the target. Cover was arranged by ROSE TREMAINE about 3 miles from the area where the party was due to be dropped and north of proposed target.

Reconnaissance led by ROSE revealed unexpected obstacles, and although these were successfully overcome, the operation was carried out later than expected on 17 October, with 2 additional German security officers on duty, as well as an alternate diversion employed 8 blocks from the factory entrance.

All 4 support structures were blown up. The party saw flames reaching 150 feet. Searchlights were seen probing the sky for hostile bombing aircraft. The results of that attack were as follows:

(a.) The 12 Germans who were in the station at the time were arrested and, it is believed, shot.

(b.) The railway and street traffic in the district was suspended for a considerable period of time.

(c.) The engine factory was completely destroyed—both production lines—and will be out of commission for a considerable time.

(d.) 3 agents reached the safe house organized by ROSE and left France via fishing boat off west coast. ROSE did not meet party at house nor at departure location. She has not been heard from. Presumed dead.

Mat rubbed his eyes as if trying to create something new on the page in front of us—answers to the myriad questions remaining. "That's no coincidence, Caroline. Arnim's transfer was cited in his record on October 17, and that's the last of him I could find. He vanished. There has to be a connection."

"How do we find it?" I turned the page.

MOST SECRET CIPHER TELEGRAM
To: War Office
From: Nelson, Frank

> 28/7 cipher 14/12
>
> Desp. 1425 12 December 1941
>
> Recd. 1632 13 December 1941

Two months post CLEMENTINE, reliable reports confirm the factory is still out of commission and will not be usable without significant German assistance.

In addition, despite a thorough search, ROSE TREMAINE has not been located since her deployment of diversionary tactics on the night of the operation.

"That's it. There's nothing more here about that night or about her . . . What do we do now?"

"I don't know." Mat blew out a long breath.

I tapped open my phone and read about the operation. "Wikipedia says, '*Operation Clementine was a military mission in October 1941 during the Second World War. The mission was organized by the British Special Operations Executive with assistance from the Royal Air Force. A German engine factory manufacturing light and heavy artillery aircraft was destroyed outside Paris.*'"

"That was a big win." Mat turned the page. Then another and another until the end of the file. "There's really no more. She's never mentioned again."

"Something happened to them both. You said Arnim was sent to Russia, and we know Dalton sent the note to Caro's parents on the twentieth. Did they close the books on her?"

"How could they? We read that Nelson valued, even feared, her strategic importance."

We stared at each other.

Mat finally spoke. "Maybe they didn't close the books on her. Maybe they lost her."

"You don't lose a spy . . . Keep reading." I returned to my file and sensed, in my periphery, it took Mat a few minutes to pull his gaze from me and do the same.

Hours later, I opened my final folder and discovered it wasn't an SOE binder at all, but the RAF personnel file for Randolph George Payne. "You requested my grandfather's records?"

"I hadn't before because I didn't know of any relationship with your aunt. It might be worth a look."

Inside I found flight notes, memos, and meeting summaries. My grandfather was respected, decorated, and consulted. I'd had no idea how much he had done. I'd had no idea of the sacrifice, the daring, and the losses his unit endured.

From the extra notes and memos, it was hard to reconcile his youth and action with the impassive, cold man I remembered. At first, the memos cited that his squadron handled air and sea rescue operations in France. Then I discovered, in 1944, they flew sweeps over Normandy landing zones.

"Hey . . . he was part of D-Day."

Suddenly my grandfather was a new man to me. After the disappointment of the last few hours, believing I'd lost my aunt, I was happy to find him. There were no questions here. His entire service was outlined from commission to discharge. There were notations that he signed up for extra missions when a friend was sick or needed out of the rotation. There were memos extolling his competency and ingenuity. There were even a few personal notes relating funny stories. I wondered if my dad knew and almost reached for my phone to call him.

In that second, I understood. It was eighty years ago, yet reading of my grandfather's demeanor and heroism elated me—today. The antithesis of that—the shame of a treacherous story—also had implications for today. Rather than elation, the loss would still feel unendurable.

Dad and Shakespeare were right. "The evil that men do lives after them; the good is oft interred with their bones." No one in my family was ever going to forgive or forget what Caro had done—what they thought she had done. So to mitigate the damage, they absorbed it. Great-Grandmother sold Parkley and moved into London's anonymity. Margo never fully lived, trusted, or loved again—nor did Randolph. And when Dad grew old enough to ask questions, rather than remember the good, they fashioned a lie to hide the bad. They erased Caro from the family tree and left my father with no understanding, only a dark shadow of shame.

I turned the page and, lips parted in shock, I poked Mat again.

MOST SECRET CIPHER TELEGRAM
MARRIAGE
To: War Office
From: 91 Military Section RAF

Recd. 12 May 1940

P 5006 cipher

Officer R. G. PAYNE serving with my squadron proposes shortly to commit matrimony with British citizen in Saint-Nazaire. Under Foreign Marriages Order in Council 1938 British Consul is expressly forbidden to solemnize marriage on grounds that sufficient facilities already exist under Foreign Marriage Act 1892.

(1.) Our reading of section 22 of act of 1892 is that I am empowered to appoint an officer to perform civil ceremony. Since I have a priest in Holy Orders serving as Officer, if our reading is correct, he could be appointed by me to perform ceremony and thus ensure legality for all purposes. Request confirmation.

(2.) If our reading is correct please advise what exactly is entailed by "observance of all forms required by law."

TCO Palmore

"He went to marry her." I sat back and smiled. "She misjudged him . . . She thought he didn't have the courage and was too damaged to step up and ask, but he went to France to marry her. How life would have been different if she'd gotten there on time."

Mat furrowed his brow, not following me.

"It was in the steamy May letter. Caro wrote Margaret that George had gone to Saint-Nazaire to meet her, but she didn't show and he had to return to duty. He never told her why—at least it wasn't in the letters. Look . . . he went to marry her." I spread my hand over my heart. "It makes me so sad for all the years of pain ahead and all that came between them. The whole expanding triangle—Margo, Caro, George . . . all of us."

"Come on." Mat reached for my hand. "Let's take a break."

We walked outside and circled a path along the Thames. Mat was right. We needed fresh air and sunshine. We needed a breather from 1941, WWII, and a stuffy research room with uncomfortable chairs and bad lighting.

We stopped at the river's edge and watched people navigate small paddleboats in circles across the Thames. A few rowers crewed shells down the center.

"If they'd married, she'd never have joined the SOE and that factory might have pumped out weapons for years," Mat offered.

"There'd have been no secret to hide. No shame," I countered. "We'd have never wondered about her defection."

He gave me the side-eye. "*You* wouldn't wonder. Because *you* wouldn't be here."

"Excellent point." I rolled my eyes but couldn't help returning his smile. "No pondering the what-might-have-beens."

Mat squeezed my hand and gently tugged me away from the railing back along the path to the Archives. "I, for one, am very glad you are here."

"Thank you." I glanced down at our hands, certain he'd forgotten he still held mine. I willed every finger to stay still so as not to bring it to mind.

But he caught me. He followed my line of sight and lifted our linked fingers before dropping them again, still entwined. "Your hand is actually warm today."

I smiled.

He hadn't forgotten.

TWENTY-FIVE

We worked until the Reading Room proctor kicked us out at closing. Despite an almost desperate need for answers still clawing at us, we were beat. My eyes could barely focus at short distances.

"What now?"

Mat led us back up Ruskin Avenue to the Underground. "We order files from Paris? That's where Operation Clementine happened, so we know that even if the Arnim part of the note was a lie, Paris wasn't. Something happened there. Then, if Arnim was involved, was he sent east as punishment? Did he disobey orders? Take her with him? Honestly, I thought once we found Rose this morning, we'd find the end. I didn't expect them to lose her as well."

I push out a tired, worn, and pathetically thin laugh. "You just answered my question with more questions."

Mat replied again . . . with more questions. "Maybe they didn't lose her, and I was right all along? If she was a traitor and if that was known, it could have hurt the program. What better way to cover it up than to conveniently misplace her and never record the truth?"

I didn't want that to be true, but it needed to be said. It needed to be faced.

Mat answered his own questions, talking more to himself this time. "There'd still be a record. Something. Somewhere . . ." He sounded unconvinced and discouraged. He bumped my elbow as a train approached. "Is your mom expecting us back for dinner?"

"She had plans with friends she couldn't cancel."

"Then let's catch this train."

I looked up to find a District line train approaching. Edgeware Road flashed on its side. I pulled Mat back. "We want the Upminster. This one won't go through Victoria."

"Trust me." Mat stepped on the train as the doors opened.

I hopped in after him right before the doors closed.

Neither of us said anything as we balanced in the center of the crowded car and were carried back toward London. While I had no clue where we were headed, I couldn't bring myself to care.

Mat led me off the train at Notting Hill Gate. A few blocks south and I stalled in front of what looked to be a corner pub—under an explosion of flowers. Hanging baskets of bright blooms covered almost every visible inch of the pub's exterior. Looking between and among them, I found a painted sign for The Churchill Arms.

Mat opened the door for me. "Seems appropriate after our day, and they have the best Thai food you'll ever taste."

"In an English pub?"

He led us through the crowd to the back corner and an open doorway. The quintessential English pub experience with pints, flags dangling from the ceiling, and gleaming wood morphed into a Thai paradise with green plants everywhere—mounted on every wall, hanging from the ceiling, and positioned on pedestals between tables.

A waitress came over and left us two menus after taking our order for a pint of Dark Star Hophead for Mat and a pint of London Pride for me.

"I needed this." I sank deeper into my padded plastic chair and relished a long sip as soon as she placed the beers before us. "We have no idea what happened to her any more than we did before."

"Yes and no." Mat leaned forward. "I thought about this the whole way here . . . SOE records state Giliana Gerson, active as of May '41, was the first female agent sent to France, closely followed by American Virginia Hall in August. We read, in official SOE files today, that your aunt became an agent in the fall of 1940. *She* was the first, Caroline. That changes history . . . Between your letters and the files, we can match her person with her code name and with operations. That's huge, any way you look at it."

He reached across the table and tapped the back of my hand for my attention. "I seriously doubt she was a traitor. What we read indicates she was a hero. That should make you smile. Your family should be proud of that. You need to tell them."

"I agree." I dropped my head, absorbing all he said. I discovered I felt more disappointed than elated. "My definition of success has changed."

"It always does. The never-ending chase." Mat lifted his pint. "Here's what we know. She was valuable to the SOE, and whatever happened occurred during Operation Clementine. Nothing we read today implied they purposely forgot her. Rather, I believe they lost her."

"Paul Arnim?"

Mat lifted his hands. "I don't have an answer for him yet. Why the romance angle? A ruse? A lie? A grain of truth? Was he an informant? A German traitor? We know he warned her at Schiaparelli's salon. We'll keep looking, or maybe we'll never know. But . . . don't forget. Everything you wanted to prove to your dad, you did."

"What are you going to write?"

A genuine smile emerged. His eyes crinkled shut. "This. It's big enough to warrant a series. I'd like to start with your family and the original story, hinting at the truth. That'll give me time, with your permission, to solidify all the research. I'd also ask you speak to your dad and request the British government open an official query. Your aunt should be honored. Not forgotten."

"I can't." I slumped in my seat and Mat's expression morphed from happy crinkles to wary surprise. "It feels risky. I don't know the ending."

"True. To a degree. But you are the ending, Caroline. You must see that. Being here. Doing this." Mat's gaze flickered. He reached across the table and didn't merely tap this time. He held my hand within his own and repositioned them halfway between us. "Even with what we know, good can come from this."

I felt my eyes water and my focus shift inward. His assurances pulled like a lifeline, dragging me from someplace gray. Yet the moment I envisioned holding tight and claiming that bright hope, I saw my dad, heard his calm dismissal, and felt his rejection all over again.

"What if Caro did live for years in Germany for some unknown reason? She could have run away with Arnim. We can't be sure."

"I highly doubt that."

"You said yourself we have no proof it's not true." I jerked his hand as if that would make him see and agree. "I need the end of the story. Dad warned me it would cost me everything, but maybe if I knew the end, that'd be okay."

"You're not going to lose everything, Caroline."

I picked up my phone from the table, tapped it open, and handed it to him with an email displayed. "Let's see . . . Dad said goodbye. That felt pretty final. Then this arrived a couple hours ago. Either I'm back at work by our staff meeting Friday afternoon or I'm fired."

"Then we go home. You can't lose your job over this."

"I'm answering questions I've had my whole life. Questions I didn't realize were always there. It's a good job and I'm good at it, and in this economy those aren't small things, but . . . what about Margo? What about Caro?"

What about me?

My voice cracked with need. I covered it with a sip of beer.

"Okay, then." Mat handed my phone back. "We've got two days.

We'll take a morning flight Friday and still get you to work midday. Will that do?" Without waiting for an answer, as I suspected he'd already supplied his own once more, he picked up his menu. "Let's order dinner, walk back to your mom's, and start on the letters again."

TWENTY-SIX

Revived by another pint, pad Thai, and The Churchill Arms' congenial atmosphere, we stepped out onto Kensington Church Street. During dinner the sun had dipped and its last rays of summer glow shot across the horizon under the growing clouds to the west.

I turned to Mat as we walked down the sloping hill to Kensington High Street. "Tell me about you . . . I remember siblings and Sunday dinners, but update me."

Mat's sudden grin surprised me. Then I recalled more than siblings and Sunday dinners. Stories of a close-knit family and antics beyond imagining flooded in.

"I'm third of four, you know, with two older brothers who still bully me, and a baby sister. You might have met Luke. He came to visit a couple times. And Aris visited. She's twenty-four now and runs circles around the rest of us."

He shifted his gaze as if lost in some memory from his childhood. "Well, my five nieces and nephews run the show really. Luke has three kids. Peter, a year older than me, had one, until a baby girl arrived a few months ago. Mom is driving Helen, my sister-in-law, crazy over her first and only granddaughter. But she has to bite her tongue because Mom is the queen of the kids' department at Nordstrom in Phipps Plaza—she's worked there for fifteen years—and gets an amazing discount. Helen loves herself some tiny smocked dresses."

I laughed. "Everyone still comes for Sunday dinner?"

"For now . . . They're all in Atlanta, but I suspect Helen will put a stop to that soon. The battlefield is extending beyond dresses." Mat looked into the street and stepped forward. "And to think, before reading Caro's . . ."

His words faded away as time slowed for me. In an instant, my mind consciously synthesized what I'd unconsciously noted. Mat had looked left before stepping into Sheffield Terrace. Midstride I glanced the opposite direction, the direction from which cars in London would hit you first—to the right.

I heard it as I saw it. A deafening horn, a black cab. Mat twisted slightly, perhaps to talk to me, his face lit with a smile. I watched as his mouth slackened and face paled in horror as the cab filled his vision.

The next thing I knew, Mat was tumbled across me on the edge of the sidewalk. The cab was screaming by us in a bluster of wind and noise. The horn still blowing loud. I couldn't move. I couldn't breathe.

"Caroline. I— Caroline." He scrabbled off me and pulled me away from the curb.

"Stop!" I called out. Yet with no air, it fell between us in a soft whimper. Every bone rattled. My head felt heavy. My vision blurry.

"I can't believe you did that." Mat was sitting next to me, his hand under my head. "Are you hurt? You landed hard. I—I can't believe you did that. Can you sit up?"

I lay there watching the crowd build above us. The curious and concerned pushed closer. Mat lifted me to sit upright and I drew in a few deep breaths. My ribs hurt, my shoulder burned, and my left elbow felt like it was on fire. I lifted up my arm, pleased that it moved properly. My white blouse was torn at the sleeve, my elbow scraped and bloody.

"Let's get you home. Let's—"

One look at Mat and I burst into tears.

"Hey . . . hey." Mat, with a hand beneath my good shoulder, helped me stand. He tucked me close as the crowd pressed in. It took several pleas of "I'm okay" and a few repetitions of "She's okay" from Mat to get everyone to disperse.

"Let's get a cab."

I tried to shake my head. It still ached, but my vision had cleared. "I want to walk. Please. I need to move a little."

"Okay." His voice was full of doubt. He probably thought I might break—I was certain I already had.

We walked slowly, with his arm tucked tight around me, for several minutes before Mat spoke again. "Thank you. I didn't see it coming. I— You saved my life."

"I had a sister," was all I could say.

In twenty years, I couldn't remember more than a few times I'd willingly spoken about Amelia. After her death, none of my friends wanted to talk about her; they wanted to help me heal, forget, laugh, move on. They meant well. After all, at eight, what else do you do? You watch movies, play games, eat junk food, and pretend.

Then it simply became awkward. Amelia faded from collective memory, and to bring her up stifled any gathering. In college, I seized a fresh start. No one knew. So when asked, I told the truth. "I have an older brother."

"I remember you telling me about a brother, but I didn't know you have a sister."

"Had. She died when I was seven, almost eight. She was only nine." I stepped away and looked behind us, turning my whole body as my neck was already sore and stiff. "Just like that."

Mat reached for my hand as I told him the story. He didn't interrupt. He didn't ask questions. He merely looked the proper direction at every street crossing and let me talk on. I told him things I'd never shared—like how cool that Rube Goldberg machine was and how far it stretched across our rooms, like how we used to make tents out of sheets and furniture and live in them during the summer, like how we would sneak through the door between our rooms after bedtime and talk late into the night. How she was my best friend and I didn't really think I'd ever found another. And how I dreamed about that moment—all the time—and woke up in a sweat, racked with guilt at my inability to move, to yank her forward, or to do anything but watch her die.

"You can't think that way. There is nothing you could've done."

"You don't know that."

"I do. Because when there was something to be done, you did it." Mat gestured to a high curb and watched me step up with solicitous care.

I thanked him and continued. It felt important to get it out, almost like Margaret turning to Beatrice after a painful event. She wrote to process. Talking felt equally cathartic. "I always thought it was only Amelia. That what I did, that what happened to her, broke us. But after all this, I wonder if we were already broken and I was too young to notice."

We crossed another street.

"Right after her funeral, my parents moved me to Jason's old rooms on the third floor. I think they were trying to do what everyone else was doing—distract me, surround me with new colors, shapes, textures, anything. But those rooms, Amelia's and mine on the second floor, and that life we had together, just sat abandoned behind our closed bedroom doors. We never talked about it. Ever. And that stupid Rube Goldberg machine sat in there for three years before I kicked it down one afternoon. Now we say nothing real to each other and soon . . ." I shivered, unable to draw closer to my lunch with Dad and what was to come. The motion sent a shuddering gasp through me.

"You okay?" Mat paused.

"I am. Everything moves, but everything hurts."

"Just wait until tomorrow. Or the day after."

We walked on at an interminably slow pace. The perfect pace. My mind returned to Caro and Margo, Amelia and me. It was as if those split seconds had opened a dam and memory was washing in, bringing with it insight and even acceptance.

"I understand my great-grandfather had to bury this shame and go command a ship. Take action. But my grandmother carried it her whole life and let it destroy everything she loved—including my dad. He said something like that when he told me to back off. I don't want to live like that, Mat. Not anymore."

As I wound myself down, we turned the final corner to Eaton Square. I stopped and stared up at the house. White-painted stone and brick. Glossy black door. Stark and imposing. Four stories high. It held every secret that weighed me down. It embodied them. Yes, buildings had personalities and, until entering it days before, I had always dreaded this one. Now I wanted to love it—wanted to. I was ready for something new and Mom's renovations had brought in light. It even felt like the house wanted something new. But there was still no clarity. Not yet. And without that, I feared the darkness would swallow whatever light we'd so recently found.

I pulled the key from my shoulder bag and let us in the side door. We descended the short flight of stairs to the kitchen. The room glowed with soft evening light, graying to night. I flipped the light switch.

"Tea?"

"Sure, but let me do it." Mat pulled a chair out for me from under the table. "Then let's get your elbow cleaned up."

He reached high for Mom's tea tin and filled the kettle. Without prompting, he then filled a small bowl with warm water and a drop of soap and tilted another chair to face me. "Shift my way."

He laid my arm on the table and dabbed at the elbow with the wet corner of a tea towel. His face was so close to mine that I noticed, like Caro had of George, that his skin was translucent. I really could see where the razor hadn't scraped close, or where a vein passed at the corner of his eye, or the small scar tracing up the left side of his chin.

"I'm sorry about what I said yesterday." At my questioning glance, he toggled his head to encompass the kitchen and the entire house beyond. "About envy?"

I followed his darting gaze and gave a rueful snort I had to cover with my free hand. "Don't worry about that. I envied you, so I guess it's all good." He continued to clean my scrape with tremendous care. It wasn't deep so much as a wide gravel burn. "I was overly sensitive. I look at this house and I wonder what my dad feels. He'd never tell me, of course, but it must hurt."

"Were they close? Your grandmother and your mom?"

"Maybe at the end. Mom came over to help, but no . . . No one was close. No one is close." I stared down but could now see only the top of Mat's head. His black hair held a hint of wave that only broke into a curl at one ear. "Jason tries. His wife had a baby girl a few months ago. They named her Carolina, after me . . . I . . . I'll be so sad when he stops."

"Stops trying?" Mat sat straight. "Why would he do that?"

Because everyone does.

I couldn't say the words. I couldn't lump Jason into that group, not yet. But I wasn't wrong either. "Dad did. Mom did. She filed for divorce and walked out the door the same weekend I left for college. Sure it was ten years after Amelia's death. But there are lots of ways to leave while living side by side."

"She's trying." My befuddled expression made Mat shake his head like I'd missed something terribly obvious. He continued, "Your mom. She's trying her best to connect with you. I hope you see that. She's like a pseudo-British Alice Waters down here."

The kettle whistled. He stepped away to pour our cups of tea.

"It's just food."

Mat chuckled. "You still really know nothing . . . What was that snack plate she brought up yesterday? Carrots, hummus, celery, a nut mix, turkey rolls with fig jam, brie, and a thin stalk of asparagus to 'give the whole thing a bit of crunch'? And macarons—don't forget those 'delightful' raspberry and lavender cookies."

The memory of my mom's tentative "*I don't want to disturb you, but I thought you might be hungry*" and his perfectly toned recitation made me smile.

"What do you think love is, Payne?"

His question caught me. The playful intimacy of using my last name caught me. He'd done it earlier, he'd done it in college. But I had no answer—I didn't know.

Mat set my tea on the table and gestured to my elbow. "It's all clean. If you can find a Band-Aid, I'll help you put it on."

I nodded, picked up my mug, and led him out of the kitchen and up to the attic—slowly. I'd noticed Mom had a first aid kit on one of the bookshelves, probably left over from when she lived up there during the renovations.

Mat taped a large piece of white gauze over my elbow then looked to the center table and the chaos of letters and diaries strewn across it. "We've got a lot to do, but it can wait for you to get some rest." He gently pulled me toward him by my hand. "Let me see your eyes."

He lifted his phone to my face. I touched the scar on his chin and wondered aloud if a brother gave it to him and when.

"Luke, playing King of the Bed. I fell and hit the bedside table on the way down."

"King of the Bed?"

"A no-rules wrestling match. Last one standing wins. The trick is to get really low." He shined the flashlight again into each eye. "Good," he whispered. "No concussion."

"Thank you," I whispered back and turned toward the stairs.

"Wait a minute." He closed the distance between us in one step, arms spread wide. "In my family, an event like this ends in a hug. We were once friends, Caroline, and I could use a hug after tonight. That was scary close."

Without hesitation, I stepped within the circle of his arms. My head nestled in the curve of his neck. A perfect fit. "Aren't we still friends?" I whispered.

He held me close and hesitated for what felt like a beat long. "I hope so. I'd like that." He laughed softly. "You have to squeeze. Standing there limp is hardly a real hug. I'll accept one arm, but give it that at least."

I gripped him tight as laughter rumbled in his chest. "Better. Thank you for tonight . . . And I'm sorry about your sister . . . I'm just sorry."

"Thank you." I spoke into his shirt, inhaling him. He carried notes like citrus, cedar, and old ink and paper from the Reading Room. "I'm sorry too."

"For what?" His voice arced in question.

"Something . . . I'll figure it out."

A sigh lifted then dropped his chest. I held tighter.

TWENTY-SEVEN

I slept hard but woke early, tossing with questions and concerns. That no one talked about Amelia suddenly bothered me. That no one, in eighty years, had searched for Caro bothered me.

Rather than ask questions, those who loved her accepted the story they were fed and gave up on her. Publicly and privately. SOE files held no records of a search or questions posed over the following months and years, and her family effectively erased all memory of her.

In the early hours of the morning, mid-dream, Caro's story became my own. If Dad was told something dreadful about me, like that memo relayed about my aunt, would he believe it? Would he never question, never search, never come for me? What about Mom? Sure, I'd told Mat they had shut down and shut me out, but wasn't that mostly a reaction to loss and pain back then? Or was it now our true reality? Would they believe something harsh or hard today, figuratively wipe their hands of me, and be done?

I made my way to the attic room before Mat awoke. I wanted to revisit Margaret's 1940 diary and Caro's letters alone. The cacophony in my head was too loud to invite another voice.

I had already marked everything within Caro's and Margo's writing I believed significant, but Mat was right. He had mentioned the night before that now knowing Caro was Rose changed everything. Reading again, we might catch more crumbs along her trail. He even wondered if Margo's diary entries might prove more revelatory than

Caro's letters, as Caro could say things to her sister she might never commit to paper—but unknowingly Margo might.

I skimmed to the dairy entry on May 1, 1940, then slowed to absorb select entries, as that's when things started to get interesting . . .

1 May 1940

Dear Beatrice,

Randolph came today, but not to see me. Usually we walk and talk alone when he comes for an evening, or when he stops by for a few hours on his way somewhere else. He doesn't say where he is going anymore. But we still have a ritual. I ask where he's been, he asks the same, then he teases me for my concerns here, and I tease him for having none out there. It's all fantasy, but the banter feels good, normal, light, and fun. And he always brings me a gift—a book, a pen, a flower . . .

Today he barely waved at me as Trent showed him straight into Father's study.

The door was cracked, yet there was little I could hear, despite arranging the flowers on the hall table for a full fifteen minutes!

I did hear he has a leave coming up and has convinced a buddy to drop him into France. My heart started racing and I stepped forward. My move brought me into Father's line of sight so I had to retreat and missed the next few sentences. Then I caught . . .

"Tell that to my daughter." By his tone, Father was speaking of Caro. I remembered that tone well. It was full of the notes once reserved only for me. It was derisive, almost to the point of mocking.

In that moment and in that tone, I finally recognized what Caro has been telling me for years. That tone is uniquely hers now—I'm not the one causing quarrels, chaos, and "challenges" anymore. I'm not the one he is set against.

"The window is closing, sir. She must listen now." The urgency in Randolph's voice pulled me from my thoughts.

Something more was said before a booming laugh sent me to the other side of the hall table. I thought their discussion had ended and they were coming toward me. "You do that, son, and you may just have the moxie to win the day."

Whatever Randolph said, my father liked a great deal. Father has to be in very good humor to pull out his "American slang," as he calls it.

I shoved the last flower back into the vase as Randolph pulled the door fully open. "Eavesdropping, Moo?"

Silly as it is, that old nickname, now shortened from Margo Moo to simply Moo, still makes my heart flutter.

"Practicing reconnaissance." I smiled. I heard the note of flirtation in my voice and ducked my head, hoping he hadn't caught it and terrified he did. What a fool I am.

When I looked up, his face was mobile again, relaxed. Whatever had upset him, the conversation with Father cured it. As playful as ever, he pulled me into a hug. "Carry on, Moo. No going rogue and turning spy. We need you to keep us on the straight and narrow." He kissed my forehead. "Drive safely."

I can still smell him. He is the most wonderful mixture of peppermint and spice soap. His is sharper than the shaving soap Father uses. I can't put my finger on what it is. I only know I will never forget it. I can't . . . I still have a bowl of it from when Caro and I stole it from his bathroom during a long-ago visit. We were fourteen that summer. He was eighteen. I'd die if anyone ever found that little bowl now. Such a silly treasure I've made of it. Does my absurdity know no bounds?

"Drive?" I called after him. "How did you know I transferred to the motor pool?"

He turned and winked. "I keep my eye on you."

I love that he does, Beatrice. He always has. I just wish he wouldn't keep such a close eye on Caro.

I've tried to let this go. Goodness knows, it's been six years . . . Six years? That's a very long time. I hadn't thought of that. Six years and they've gone no further. No engagement. No marriage. Could it be over?

Caro declared she'd marry him at eighteen. We're almost twenty-two and she hasn't come home for him and, as far as I know, he hasn't asked her to. He hasn't proposed. He visits her in Paris when there for work, but he would visit me if I lived abroad. Maybe—

"Randolph," I called after him.

He heard the panic in my voice and was back to me in four quick strides. "What's wrong?"

"I . . . I . . ." I had no idea what to say, what to ask. It was out of the question to simply ask, "Are you still in love with my sister?" So instead I settled for, "Please be careful out there."

His eyes curl into half-moons when he smiles. It's extraordinary. With a small genuine smile and a sigh that tipped toward a moan, he pulled me close again. He folded me completely within his arms, tucking me tight. "No worrying about me. If you do, I'll have to start worrying about you worrying about me and—"

"Vicious cycle. Yes, I know."

He kissed my forehead again and left. This time I watched him go, saying nothing more.

He's twenty-six, Beatrice. It's time for him to marry. Randolph is caring, relational, and he needs someone to love and someone to love him.

And yet . . . Perhaps it's not that he doesn't love Caro but that he fears marriage. Frederick is such a horrid matrimonial model.

In fact, Adele has been awarded a decree nisi. It doesn't mean they'll finalize their divorce, but it probably means Frederick should stop his affair with Maribelle Cummings. My bet is he won't—he's just like their father. And yet Randolph did always worship that reprobate—both of them.

Or maybe it's the war. How can one consider marriage in a world like this? We are in such an odd, terrifying place right now and I doubt life will ever return to the cadence we once knew—the safety and comfort I confess that I believed would last forever. And to make it worse, I feel as though we haven't really begun this war at all . . .

I wish Caro were here. We talk about everything—everything except this. Maybe it's time. Maybe she could help, understand, laugh me out of my fears, and banish these longings. If she does love Randolph, at least there could be clarity, and perhaps I could learn to let go.

I'm convinced that would be better than this—anything would be better than this.

26 May 1940

Dear Beatrice,

Mother asked one question at dinner last night. Only one. "Are we never to have peace in this house?"

Father glowered across the long table and held Caro in his sights. It was as if Mother and I vanished from the room. "Don't worry, dear. Peace reigns after tomorrow, at least here at Parkley."

Yes, Caro is home. Well, she was. She came to Parkley for two nights and stayed only one. Despite all the sentiment oozing from her last letter as she reached Hastings from France, she waited seven days to come here and has already returned to the London House this morning.

It's for the best. Last night, after thanking Father for working with Ambassador Campbell for her passage out of France, she launched into Schiap's politics, the horrors facing Jews in France, and the "Imperial bubble" she feels has skewed our perspective here in England.

She brought "spit and fire," as Creighton says, to the table and basically called everyone in England a coward.

Father turned beet red and ordered her out of the dining room—this was after Mother's question.

"The dining room?" Caro shouted back. "I'll leave the house."

And she did. She's not so independent as to have gone far or to have gotten a flat with friends. She simply returned to the London House—perhaps because Mother asked her to. I suspect Mother feels she will be safer there with its large reinforced basement than in a flat with friends, running the streets for a bomb shelter at night. Caro agreed quickly, seeing either the ease and comfort or the prudence of Mother's request.

Father is tired of Caro's "insolent rebellion," but it isn't that. She is wired for action. I can see it in her walk and wonder how everyone else has missed it. Her little bouncy step of old is long, firm, and directed now. She sees a way the world should work and is ready to make it so. She reminds me of that Archimedes quote, "Give me a place to stand, and a lever long enough, and I will move the world." I suspect she spouts these ideas, not even believing most of them, in an effort to get Father's attention and, perhaps, to find her way home. She's looking for that lever and a place to stand, and he's not making it easy.

"I'm sorry I have to go." She hugged me tight this morning as we waited for the train.

"As am I." I drove her alone to the station. I didn't want Creighton or anyone else to take her—I wanted it to be the two

of us. I wanted—I don't know what I wanted, Beatrice. I think I
wanted to test my strength. Test if, alone, I could look at her and
not scream and cry. If alone, I could love her again as part of my
own soul. If alone, I could reach out and help her.

Her latest letter arrived a few days ago—and I have cried
every day since. Betsy thought I was getting ill. Only Caro's visit
got me up and out—I couldn't let her see me down. I couldn't let
her sense my pain. And I was so afraid she'd bring it up and want
to relive it all, as she said in her letter, that I avoided being alone
with her. But when she didn't pursue me or say a word, it was
almost more painful.

How can she be so cavalier? How can she not blush constantly, recalling all she shared with him in Hastings? All she
shared with me in that letter? She never should have written such
things. That night changed my whole world—and I was not the
one making love to Randolph.

She called this afternoon, after reaching the London House,
and asked me to join her.

"We don't need to be apart. Come stay with me here. It'll be
just like you wanted when we were kids."

"I can't. I have work."

"Margo," Caro groaned. She heard it—my voice is flat and
dead now. "Don't let them bury you up there. Don't let them make
you afraid to live. Mother does that. She's the worst hypochon
driac there is."

I wanted to scream. Not only does she have no clue how I
feel, but she thinks me a coward? A sycophant to my parents'
every whim? I'm not sure my position can get more humiliating,
Beatrice.

"It's not that." I tried to lift my voice and muster some dignity, but it came out sharp rather than confident—and nowhere

close to kind. "Don't you think I have responsibilities? There's good and important work here, Caro."

"I wasn't saying that. I'm sorry . . . I just miss you."

We hung up soon after and I've felt sick all night. I keep snapping at people and I feel pulled apart. There are spaces within me, one near my heart and a couple openings around my lungs, that feel endlessly black and empty. I can't breathe. I can't relax. I hate feeling this way. I hate hurting her, and all I want to do is hurt her.

But as much as I yell and scream and dream of scratching her eyes out, part of me remembers she is innocent. Caro doesn't know—and would never suspect. We made a pact to never lie, never divide, and she never broke it. All those years ago, when I was so mad she left . . . That wasn't her fault either. I see that now. I was sick, and nothing, not even my twin, was coming between me and health. Mother and Father made it clear then and they've made it clear every day since. In many ways, Caro is right. I am trapped by their fear. Trapped by my own as well.

How did we get here? How did I diminish so completely? I barely recognize myself some days.

Worse yet . . . Does she get Randolph because my parents claimed me? I was once bold. I was once what he could have loved.

I should have told her. Right then, that summer we were sixteen and she came back and she glowed and it was all new—so new it could have ended. I could have spoken and she would have taken my side. She would have conceded and her weeks with Randolph would have been a summer crush that cooled with fall.

But I said nothing. I said nothing because she'd surpassed me in the short span of a summer. He had held her hand and spoken things I'd only dreamed of. He had never looked at me with anything close to what she described.

What would I have said anyway? That I had loved him since I was ten? That he was mine, like in a game of tag? It would have sounded ridiculous. It would have been ridiculous. But not one ounce of feeling has changed in twelve years.

That's a lie. Everything has changed. I love him more now than ever.

She can never know.

Even you and I, dear Beatrice, will never speak of this again.

22 November 1940

Dear Beatrice,

She didn't come home for our birthday. Twenty-two years old. For the first time in years, we are in the same country. We could have been together, but we weren't. We weren't because she didn't come home. She didn't ask me to come to her, and on the day, she didn't bother to telephone at all.

Even with bombs raining down upon London each night, I would have gone to her. If asked. And I telephoned the London House fourteen times.

Yet despite her cold silence and indifference, she asks me for a favor now. Eight days late, she finally telephoned tonight, but rather than open with an apology, she opened with a demand.

"I just talked to George and he's furious, Margo. He came by the London House when I was sick. I didn't know. I had told him I was coming home for our birthday, but then he spoke to you and learned I wasn't at Parkley, and now . . . he thinks I lied. Will you talk to him?"

"You did lie."

"I meant to come home, then I got sick. It was an accident, a misunderstanding, not a lie. He says after he talked to you, he came to the house and banged on the door."

"I telephoned you as well. Fourteen times, Caro. You didn't hear anything?"

"There's a war going on, Margo." She huffed. "Besides, the telephone at the house has been out for almost two weeks. I'm telephoning you from work. Talk to him, please. Do this for me. It's important. He'll listen to you. He'll believe you." She paused, yet I refused to acquiesce. "He wants to marry me, Margo."

My heart bounced up, then dropped straight through me. I glanced to the carpet fully expecting to see it splatted there. "What did you say?" I breathlessly asked her to repeat her statement, certain I couldn't have heard it right. But she misunderstood and continued on—sure I had.

"I didn't say anything, because he didn't ask. He said he had wanted to marry me, but now he's not sure . . . I thought we were getting through all that . . . You have to talk to him, Margo. He's not listening to me. He doesn't trust easily, but he trusts you. He always has."

That dagger struck deep.

"Trust . . . I can't lie for you."

"Margo," she barked. "I won't take that from you. Either you will help me or you won't, but you know I love him and I would never cheat on him."

That brought me up short, Beatrice. She said she would never cheat on him, not that she didn't lie to him—or to me. I've noticed Caro has become careful with language that way.

That said, I know she wouldn't cheat. We are cut from the same cloth. We are loyal. Why she lied, I have no idea, and such a silly lie. Because she does love Randolph. I see it every time she mentions his name. She glows. It's so cliché to say that, but clichés are born from truths.

"I love you, Moo, and I'm sorry. There's a lot I can't tell you, or him," she whispered over the line. I closed my eyes. As soon as Randolph had started calling me that, she joined in. Always with affection.

It never fails to wound.

"I love you too." I pushed out the words.

"You'll talk to him?"

"If I see him, yes."

"Thank you. I must go now. It's almost curfew and I need to race home." She hung up.

I'm afraid for her. Something isn't right. She never planned to come home. If she had, she would have telephoned me in advance to talk of plans and treats. She didn't.

And I don't believe she was sick.

She lied. But why?

TWENTY-EIGHT

I laid down the book and backtracked over lost time. Margaret had written nothing in her diary between the May of Caro's return in 1940 and the following November, six full months of lost time and two months after Caro joined the ISRB.

For a split second it surprised me. Margo had started her diaries in 1928 barely writing anything and always apologizing to her fictional "Beatrice" for her failure. But by 1940 she had hit her stride and recorded much of the world around her on a regular basis. What had happened?

I cast back to Caro's May letter, and to George.

Margaret answered my question—sometimes writing helps one heal, and other times it opens the wound. I suspected that she hurt so much after Caro's May letter and subsequent visit she couldn't bring herself to commit anything to paper.

That meant anything important from the summer of '40 and Caro's initial months at the ISRB came directly from her. If crumbs were to be found, it was because she had purposely dropped each and every one . . .

LONDON HOUSE
30 JULY 1940

Dear Margo,

London is too hot, too hard, and beyond quiet. All I want to do is cry. I want to hang my head in shame and cry. That's not doing my bit, I'm fully aware, but . . . I didn't realize how weak I truly am. I was so full of fire when I landed in Hastings. All that's gone now.

And I've been a fool. All those platitudes—"Fashion is politics." Bollocks!

I claimed it had meaning, substance, and power. I drank it in, believed it, even as rations were cut and Jews I knew and loved fled. I still believed I was doing the right thing and taking a stand. With silk and buttons? Buttons fashioned like birds, bugs, swimmers, butterflies, and zodiac signs? What the hell was I thinking?

I'm in a typing pool now. I can't tell you where, and I may be transferring soon. At least I want to. There's a new group forming that could use me—and maybe my fashion acumen. I'm kidding. No one has a use for that these days.

You should be proud to be in the ATS, by the way. I was recording the minutes in a meeting today—don't worry, it wasn't classified—and they talked about how brave the ATS women were. Did you know some of them—some of you—were the last to leave Dunkirk? ATS women worked the beaches with the troops, bombs and bullets cutting through them. I got a ride west, caught a train and safe passage home—all secured by Ambassador Campbell weeks earlier.

That's why I feel like a coward, Margo. Everything I hear makes me realize how privileged I am and how little I saw. My version of reality was not reality. It was nowhere close to reality—and probably still isn't.

This house is what I deserve—and even it is a beautifully gilded cage. Father refuses to unboard the windows, but I don't mind. My large, dark prison feels appropriate. Mr. and Mrs. Coffey moved out to Richmond to be with family, but one of them comes in most days on the train. I'm not sure exactly what they are protecting me from. Loneliness? Starvation from my own cooking?

Germs from my poor cleaning? Or perhaps I have that wrong and they are protecting the London House from me.

I remember how you wrote about the children leaving. I didn't understand how that would feel. My reply to you was so pragmatic and rational—patronizing really. You must have despised me.

It's the quiet that gets to me. With little petrol, the streets are cleared of cars. With no children, the parks are emptied of laughter. They carried away all our hope with them, I think, and left behind the robbers. Crime is trebled in London at last week's report. That makes me so sad. Shouldn't we all be on the same side? War should rally us and draw us tight, not make us turn on each other and regard another's loss as easy pickings.

Did you tell me Father has meetings at White Hall next week? If he does, please ask him to call on me. I would love to see him. I need to apologize for my last visit home. My behavior was inexcusable. It is past time for me to stop fighting. I need to forgive Mother and Father for not being who I needed them to be. That sounds self-absorbed and patronizing as well, but I don't mean it that way. I simply mean they strive to be the best parents they can—I see that now—and simply because it's not what I wanted does not mean their efforts aren't right and true.

Does that make sense, dear Margo? I guess a more appropriate way to state it is that I need to forgive the gap between what is and what I want or need. It is wrong to believe my perception is the only reality, and a true one at that. There are absolute truths in this world, Margo, and I am slowly learning I do not determine them.

I'm sorry I sound blue. I don't mean to burden you, and I'll be better soon. You pick yourself up and you move on, right? You always did when we were kids. You always bounced up, brushed off your knees, and tried again. A tree. A river. A fish. A nest of squirrels. Nothing got you down. Nothing stopped you.

You still have that fight in you. You are the bravest person I know. Could you share a little with me?

I love you, Margo, with all my heart.

Caro

I turned the page. The next letter had a pink Post-it on it, marking it as one of Margaret's "favorite four," as I'd dubbed them.

I read her August 26, 1940, letter again, with new eyes and insights gleaned from the SOE files. It was so clear now that Martine, from the House of Schiaparelli, hadn't written to Caro at all. Rather Caro had traveled to France to talk with her in person. Caro wrote to her twin of Schiaparelli's political leanings, German movements in the streets, German "gluttony" alongside the "cold efficiency" of their troops—things hard to convey in a letter from France to England, as they would have been censored by those same cold and efficient soldiers—but easy to see in a visit. Caro wrote with too much texture for it not to be, as Mat called it, a "lived experience."

She also wrote that "other work" was important and needed her now. This played in stark contrast to earlier letters in which she'd written of feeling weak, impotent, even cowardly, while at the same time yearning for action—needing to help more, do more, and be more.

As of August 26, her tone became calm, directed, and focused. She had found her place to stand and, perhaps, even that lever to wield. According to National Archive files, the August letter came right after Dalton had accepted her into the SOE.

I also noted that Caro's closing lines to her twin signaled the beginnings of her double life, the rivalry in her heart between action, affection, and loyalty—the start of secrets.

Remember that. Remember that no matter what happens tomorrow, next week, or next year, you and I are one—and you, of course, are our better half.

Mat emerged from his bedroom as I laid the letter aside. "Finally," I quipped, but it was only seven in the morning. His hair was tousled, his feet bare, but he was sporting a smile.

"I thought I heard you out here." He gave a sleepy squint toward the window.

"I couldn't leave them alone. I just revisited all the 1940 entries and letters and am moving on to '41. You were right—they read very differently now." I poured him a cup of coffee from the thermos I'd brought up. "If Margaret didn't have access to the files like we did yesterday, I don't see how she could guess beyond what she was told. To be fair, no one could read between these lines unaided."

"I wondered about that." Mat stepped up to the other side of the table. "But they were twins. There are nuances they'd understand that no one else ever could."

"Maybe. But if Margaret didn't glean them, it doesn't leave any hope for us."

"Wait—" He put his hand up as if tamping down my negativity. He then reached for his notebook, splayed upside down and open on the table. "I couldn't help myself last night and worked a little . . . I made a note . . . Here, listen to this:

"'I find solace tonight in remembering everything between us, every story we've shared and every tidbit of our letters. They tell our story and, feeling lost and alone, they lead me to you. Do the same when you need me. Please? Pull out our letters and find me in each shared story and in each detail. It's all there.'"

Mat laid the notebook down, both palms pressing into its green cover. "That's from Caro's last letter and I believe her. It's all here. We just need to stay the course."

One sister's last words led me to the other. Needing to read Margaret's final, heartbreaking entry again, I pulled the last diary toward me . . .

20 October 1941

Caro is gone. She is gone and she's taken a part of me with her, a part of all of us, and I don't think we'll survive.

An officer came tonight. I don't remember his name, only his message. At first, Father was delighted to see him. The officer's father was one of Father's closest friends, forged in the Great War, and Father said there wasn't a stronger bond than that. The young man's face lost colour as Father walked down memory lane. That cued me that something wasn't right. Father noticed and shifted into a discussion of the Army's requisitioning of Parkley and our plans to move to the South Cottage next week.

"Don't worry. We'll be ready for you," he boomed.

The officer cleared his throat twice before Father stopped talking. "Dr. Dalton asked me to come in person, sir. He didn't feel a letter alone was appropriate."

"Dalton? What letter?" Father stiffened. I could see the soldier in him.

With a grim expression, the young man handed the letter to Father.

He raised a brow as he grasped it, read it in silence, then handed it to Mother. I couldn't help myself. I hovered over her shoulder, and for the first time ever, she didn't stop me.

It was short—only a few lines—but certain words will

remain seared within my mind. "Transport . . . identified . . . Gruppenführer . . . loss."

"Thank you." Father nodded to the officer, who glanced to me and left.

His face was so full of sympathy in that quick look, I wondered what he wasn't telling us. The note didn't say Caro is dead. It implied she has been having an affair. It implied she ran away with her German lover. It implied she is a Nazi now. But that she is alive—isn't that good?

As soon as we heard Trent close the front door, Father walked to the sitting room door and shut it as well. We three stood alone.

Mother clutched the letter between us. "What do we do? What does this mean, John?" Her voice tipped up in a plea for reassurance.

Father had none to offer. He held out his hand for the letter and she passed it to him. He threw it into the fire.

"No!" I called out. It felt as if my last connection to Caro was burning.

"Never." Father spoke over me while watching the letter blacken, twist, and disintegrate into ash. "We will never speak of this again. Nor of her. Do I make myself clear? She has betrayed us and . . . we should have known better."

"What—" I balked.

Mother trembled but kept her lips pressed tight.

"Enough." Father turned on me. "She worked for that woman and believed every lie fed to her. At first she was headstrong and got caught up with things she didn't understand. But at some point, your sister made a choice, Margaret. Never forget that. She chose to run away with a Nazi and cast her future with that lot."

"We don't know it's true."

"Of course we know it's true. She's avoided commitment

here—to the war, to Randolph. She has had one foot here, one foot there, and now . . . it's over. She made her choice."

Mother reached for my hand and squeezed. She was begging me to submit and be silent.

Everything cried out that he was wrong, but I'm weak. I couldn't hurt him. I couldn't fight. That's what Caro never discerned—what a personal affront her words and actions were to him. She meant to spar and incite conflict to engage him and to make him notice her, but her statements were knives slicing at everything he held dear. I doubt she believed ninety percent of what she spouted. But he did. He believed that, with every declaration or insolent comment, she was choosing another way. This letter confirmed his every fear. In many ways, it felt as if he'd been expecting it all along.

I said none of that. I pressed my lips shut until I could command my voice. Then I simply said, "Yes, sir."

Father's gaze swept over me, not pausing, as if I was difficult to look at. And considering we are—were?—identical twins, I am sure I was. I expect I will be for a very long time.

Father disappeared into his study. Mother rang the bell and told Trent we would not dine tonight. She then left through another door. I suspect she went to Caro's room before seeking sanctuary in her own.

I retreated here.

I passed Caro's room on my way here. It looked the same. It felt the same. I expected somehow it would have changed, felt colder and reflected her loss. Yet, I felt her presence in all her warmth and could almost see her rounding the corner from her closet to laugh with me. I walked to her bookshelf. Her four journals from Father sat on the top shelf. If I wanted to know what happened, I thought to start there.

They were all empty.

I ran my finger across her other shelves. Her books from Mother filled two of them. *The Wind in the Willows. Briar Rose.* Hans Christian Andersen. *The Complete Grimm's Fairy Tales.* All of Austen. *Jane Eyre. Little Women* . . .

Stories we have loved. Stories that created and defined us. Had she changed so much? Could I be wrong about my sister? Could our father be right?

Caro's room is such a soft purple. It's beautiful and sophisticated, just like my sister. I remember feeling jealous when she picked her colours first. My room is green. And while I've grown to love it more over the years, I have never felt more grateful for its bright tones of light and life as I do tonight. Caro's purple feels like death, and I wonder if she actually is dead. Would I feel it? I think I would.

Closing my eyes, I trust she is still alive. But I sense nothing more than that. Even that might be wishful thinking.

Father came to my room moments ago with the announcement that he will report to the Navy tomorrow. He had planned to continue to work here and assist with Parkley's transformation into an Army hospital. He's past the age required to serve, though he does in every way possible.

"It's not enough anymore. They need ship commanders."

He will pay penance for Caro.

"You and your mother will leave for the London House tomorrow as well. You can be of more help in the city, and General Leighton has Parkley well in hand."

"I thought you said we were needed here."

"Things change. We can no longer let others sacrifice for our freedom."

"I didn't think we were," I retorted.

I expected Father to snap at me. He only sighed.

We will all pay penance for Caro.

He looked around my room, his arms hanging limp at his sides. He looked so old and broken, I backed down. In my words and in my heart. I can't protest. I can't refuse. I can't add anything to his pain.

"What will it be like?" I asked. I'm not sure what I was asking. What will London be like? What will life without Caro be like? What will this betrayal be like?

Father chose the one he could answer.

"You'll be fine. The bombings have stopped. You'll find good work with the ATS there. You'll also find that it's surprisingly easy for the mind to adapt to a new reality." He offered a ghost of a smile. "I have faith in your resilience. I also know you will take care of your mother."

He glanced to the connecting door to Caro's room. I'd left it wide open, needing to feel her presence. He stepped toward it and pulled it closed so slowly and carefully, I didn't hear it click shut.

"Pack what you need tonight. Tomorrow you both will take the afternoon train. I'll have the staff dispose of Caro's things while they're storing ours for the transition."

"Dispose of her things?" My voice cracked.

"She's gone, Margaret. I hope you understand what happened tonight. Your sister, if she survives this war, will never be allowed back into this house nor into our lives."

I remembered reading almost an identical line in literature, always finding the father's stalwart declaration funny—especially as he failed to uphold it three chapters later and invited his wayward daughter home. But I didn't say that—because it wasn't funny and my father would never show such inconstancy. He will never back down.

I dread tomorrow, Beatrice.

I dread all the tomorrows yet to come.

What has she done? And how will we survive it?

TWENTY-NINE

was shredded. It was seven in the morning, and while Mat had been at this for twenty-four hours, I'd been immersed in these letters, and these sisters, for well over seventy. It was heartbreaking and I was losing hope, not to mention running out of time.

"Hey . . . Don't look so gloomy." Mat circled the table with a letter in hand. He lifted the diary from me and turned to its beginning. "Read this entry. Then this letter. They'll cheer you up. The crumbs are there."

2 January 1941

Dear Beatrice,

I've just come home. After Christmas, I got a few days leave and went back to the London House with Caro. She wasn't going to stay at Parkley, and our time is so short. I feel it. It's not just the war either. Something is off . . .

She is keeping something from me and it's not good. She's pale, withdrawn, fidgety, and skittish. She doesn't light up when I mention Randolph. Yes, I'm that desperate to reach her—I mention Randolph frequently.

I thought that in coming to London we could break through whatever is wrong. We would have long evenings to talk and it would be like I'd imagined when we were young—the two of us striking out on life together.

What naïveté . . .

Just as Caro couldn't understand England while in France, I failed to understand London from Derbyshire. I was fully aware of the facts—the bombs, the crime, the rations, and the quiet. I knew no children played there or lived there. I knew sandbags covered the entrances to buildings and Underground stations were converted to bomb shelters last year. Yet nothing prepared me for the reality of it. It has probably been three years since I visited London last. I didn't recognize it or myself within it.

The London House looks sad and forlorn. It is no more so than any other house on the street, but that surprised me as well. All the windows are either blacked out or boarded shut. Only Caro's bedroom has the thick blackout drapes that she can open and close.

But the house still stands and that's something. A bomb hit one block over last month. Half of three homes slid like a rubble waterfall into the street. Caro said it quaked the neighborhood so badly her head hurt for a day after.

She led me down to the kitchen upon our arrival. We were both cold and wanted tea. The London House's kitchen isn't a single room. It's a mass of tiny ones I recalled as being warm, lit, and full of life when we were young. They are grim, dark, and silent now.

"Since it's just me"—Caro passed straight through the main kitchen to a smaller one at the back of the house—"I only use this servants' kitchen and my bedroom. I haven't opened any other room because I basically flop into bed as soon as I get home each night."

She pulled a teakettle off the most massive table I've ever seen. It could seat at least sixteen people. She laughed as I marveled at it.

"Have you never seen this? It's where the staff used to cook and eat. Mrs. Coffey thinks they built the house around it."

"She still comes?" I questioned, remembering the kind woman who used to hide treats for us in the library.

"Once a week to clean and make sure I'm still alive. She always brings me a pie that lasts a few nights. Mostly vegetable with a potato crust, but a little meat now and then."

"That's hardly enough. You can't live like this." We've never fended for ourselves.

Caro gave me a small, almost mysterious smile. "You'd be shocked at how little you need to survive."

I wanted to call her bluff. How could we know how little one truly needed? When have we ever been deprived? In our world, such talk is as tasteless as it is disingenuous. But I kept myself from commenting as I wasn't talking about surviving. In that instant, I realized I was thinking about comfort. Comfort, Parkley still afforded.

I almost said as much, but something in Caro's eyes stopped me—an awareness I had never seen before. I realized Caro knows of a world I do not. She actually may know something of deprivation and survival after all.

"What aren't you tell—" I only got that far before she cut me off with a sharp slice of her hand. The discussion was over before it began as Caro busied herself making a weak tea and chatting nonsense.

That night, curled together in her huge bed, I broached the subject again. "What are you hiding, Caro?"

She turned my question back on me. "I was going to ask you the same thing. In this last year, you've gone away."

There were many things to say and maybe, if I had the courage, pure truth could have been ours. But I shrank from it once more.

"I didn't go anywhere. That's just it. I stayed." I arched away from her to see her more clearly. "You keep saying I stepped away from my true self, but I didn't. Yes, I got scared. I almost died, Caro, and it scared me enough to finally recognize what I had and who I had, and it was enough. I grew up and stopped chasing every rainbow."

Caro swiped at her eyes like she used to do. "They thought you would—die, that is. Not quit chasing your rainbows. They sent me away. They didn't let me say goodbye."

"I'm sorry."

"You don't need to be, and I'm not angry anymore. But I can't deny it happened and that it changed everything. I felt guilty and sad, and then just angry. I've been angry for so long now . . . But perhaps that was the plan all along. You are where you need to be and I'm doing what I can."

I gripped her hand. "You told Father you were going to Scotland, to Arisaig to scout fabrics. There's more you can do. Rejoin the ATS here in London, come serve in Derbyshire. Parkley has just been commissioned for the Army. We will have lots to do. Come help us."

"I can't. Please understand." Caro's fingers traced the quilt's counterpane as if counting the stitches. "You'd be surprised at how important a working zipper and sturdy canvas are to an army." I sensed the smile in her voice, the secret, and the lie.

She scooted closer. "I need you to believe in me, Margo. Now. Can you do that?"

"I'll try." I wrapped my arms around her.

She spoke, her head resting against mine. "I'll be gone for a month and there may be more trips throughout this year as the Army implements uniform changes. Please don't let Father go sideways about all this. Trust that what I am doing is right and important, and defend me. Can you do that?"

She had asked the same question twice. What was she really asking?

Caro twisted to search my face. She needed an answer.

"Yes. Of course."

She nodded as if committing my answer to memory. And, rather than feel like everything was clear or assured between us, I felt the gulf open wider.

LONDON HOUSE
16 JUNE 1941

Dear Margo,

Martine wrote from Paris last week. I don't even know how she gets her letters out, but I suspect she employs Schiap's connections. Word had it that, at some point, Schiap was even using the diplomatic mail of the German ambassador to Vichy France, Otto Abetz, to get her missives out. Then again, Bettina's husband is in the Nazi ranks. Maybe he's helping Schiap.

Either way, Schiap or Bettina would have Martine's head if they knew what she wrote . . .

I shouldn't, but I have to tell you. I can't keep this horror inside. Writing it somehow lessens the pain.

Élisabeth de Rothschild came to a showing a couple weeks ago and some stupid girl now working at the salon signed her death warrant. The girl either didn't realize de Rothschild converted to Judaism when she married or she purposely sat her next to Abetz's wife out of spite. De Rothschild moved seats.

Martine said she didn't make a fuss about it; she simply got up and quietly moved. But the offense was noted, a warrant issued, and now she's been arrested.

She'll be shipped to Germany, if she hasn't been already. They have camps there. They call them work camps. Others call them prison camps. Either way, it is beyond belief and she will not survive. The stories of those camps would sicken you.

It's a mess at the salon, and Martine must clean up what she can. Bettina, Schiap's number two, is furious and ready to fire everyone. And Schiap is gone. She fled—there is no other word—to New York and is not returning. Yet somehow she has arranged for her precious House of Schiaparelli to stay open and poor Martine is trying to survive within it. I feel Schiap's duplicity in this—and cowardice.

I feel France's collusion as well. She has let Germany swallow her once again. You should have heard the bravado before the Germans invaded. Bravado I believed and joined in—that France would embody the call of *La Marseillaise* and run her streets with the blood of her enemies before she'd ever bow to invaders.

The streets are silent now. Silent because the Germans order them to be so.

Will they cross the Channel?

Will the Germans silence us as well?

I'm sorry, dear sister. I'm so tired tonight I can't see clearly. Work has drained me and depleted my hope.

Tonight I passed a police officer arresting a man on Chesham Place. He was robbing a bombed home and carrying two sets of identification papers. I surmise he was trying to pass off the second set so that false information would be recorded and he could return home with no record, safe in his anonymity.

Is that the best we can do? Turn on each other as long as no one sees our true selves?

It reminded me that I'm no better. Remember that brassier I wrote you about long ago? The one I adapted from the Lobster

Dress design and rolled papers into the supports? Something feels treacherous about that innocent project now. I actually designed that bra to hide something. Identification papers? Perhaps.

I'm beginning to doubt there's any innocence left in the world. There certainly isn't in me. I have another trip coming up—this time to Morar. You won't be able to reach me, but I'll telephone as soon as I return to London.

Be safe, dear sister.

Love,

Caro

While I read, Mat scrolled through his phone. He tilted it to me as I looked up. "Put that letter with this and we know she was heading to Morar for training."

MOST SECRET FIELD OPERATION SUMMARY
06/08 June 1941

I met with Martine at our usual spot. I provided her with 50,000 francs to secure a safe house for October and needed supplies. She has grown increasingly nervous of exposure as three arrests have been made within her group. She fears there is a mole.

There is and, I believe, he is still active. I suspect Christophe, but Martine refused to consider his duplicity. He began to work for Schiaparelli in April 1940 and quickly became a trusted bodyguard for her person and the salon. He kept watch over everyone rather than integrate into the workforce, remaining distant from the salon's daily rhythm. Many grew to suspect German affinities within him during the early weeks of his employment, even while I still worked there. While Martine has noted he is now more aggressive and more secretive, she believes that he can be trusted—he guards the House of Schiaparelli. I reminded her that is not the same as guarding her.

As I left out the back courtyard door, I met him outside her studio—close enough I suspect he heard bits of our conversation. He grabbed my arm and insisted I tell him what I was doing there. I said Schiap called me back to help transport designs to America. He half believed my lie. His eyes then narrowed and he pulled a knife from a holster on his calf. He demanded I come to the French police and try my story again, as Schiap told him everything and she had not mentioned this request. I tried to assert my command, but it failed.

At his strike, I lifted my arms in defense. He cut a four-inch gash into my left forearm. I then raised my knee to his groin and dropped him to the ground. I yelled at him for attacking me and I rattled off several plans, all fake, of which he knew nothing, to prove he was not in Schiap's confidence. I hope my lies and bluster will keep him from calling the police and putting Martine in their crosshairs. He may now feel he was in the wrong and could get into trouble with Schiap.

I left quickly, doubling back and forth over a mile of streets and alleys to make sure I was not followed to the safe house. Dr. Montreau stitched my arm.

Martine is no longer safe. She knows nothing of his attack on me. He has grown bolder, and I believe Christophe will sell any information he gleans to the Germans and will turn Martine over to them without compunction. Another agent needs to reach out and make certain Martine is warned and her network is secure. Christophe is a threat, and my continued involvement will endanger Martine and her contacts.

MOST SECRET CIPHER TELEGRAM
To: War Office
From: Nelson, Frank

28/7 cipher 14/12

Desp. 2242 8 June 1941

Recd. 0015 9 June 1941

Your para 1, ROSE's June trip signaled her unpreparedness and the heightening dangers. Please arrange for her to report to Morar for training as soon as she lands from Douarnenez. I strongly suggest enough time be given for field drills in sabotage if you expect her to augment CLEMENTINE.

Your para 5, I agree she is compromised. Infiltration prior to CLEMENTINE should be kept to a minimum and on an emergency basis only. I strongly recommend, after that time, she be pulled from the field.

"That's the Christophe from Arnim's file I told you about, the one sent to Auschwitz in November '41. I expect that his deportation was related to all of this, but we may never know."

"I wish we could know about Martine." I rested my head on my arms. "Caro loved her. I'd like to believe she survived, at least, and was happy."

"She was," Mat whispered.

I lifted my head and was met by an adorably sheepish grin.

"You mentioned her yesterday at the Archives, and after last night, I wanted to do something nice for you . . . I followed Martine."

"How?" I sat up.

He circled the table carrying his computer with him. "It wasn't so hard really. I started with what Schiaparelli's had online and from there I went to all the databases I could think of—regional, national, and international for World War Two. A few didn't get fully online until 2018 so we're lucky that way, but look . . ."

His screen displayed a compilation of screen shots, marking his way across the Internet and Martine Hervé's travels across the globe and through time.

"Ordino . . . Barcelona . . . She went over the Pyrenees?"

"She and about thirty-three thousand others throughout the war. But she was early. See, she's registered in Barcelona in spring of '42. Then I found a marriage license in 1946, birth certificates in 1953 and '55 and . . ." He pointed to a last box.

"She has a grandson living in California."

"And several other kids and grandkids still in Spain, but this one has a wife, three children, and a dog . . . People should be terrified with how much information is out there."

"I know." I laughed through sputtery tears. "But I'm so glad, right now, that it is." I reached up and hugged him. His arms slowly wrapped around me and held.

This morning he smelled like lemon and mint. It was a good early morning scent, relaxing in a sunshiny way. I breathed him in and it brought hope to another of my senses. "Thank you. Thank you so much. I can't tell you how much I needed some good news."

I felt Mat stiffen within my embrace. He stepped back and closed his computer. The glow I felt tracing Martine's trail across Europe and her family's journey to the United States vanished with his laptop's click. Suddenly our reality, rather than Martine's successful escape, loomed before us—and, with Mat's sudden retreat, there was awkwardness, a distance, and something yet unnamed between us I still couldn't put my finger on.

"Mat?"

He backed away—all the way around to his side of our worktable. "I just wanted you to have that."

"It must have taken hours."

He fussed with the chaos of pages in front of him. "A few. But it's good to have that loop closed." He located what he was looking for and stretched a list across the table to me. "After those field notes, read the diary entries I listed here. It all comes together. The story is forming a cohesive whole. Caro gets cut in France, comes home, gets assigned more training, and in these entries we read what she told Margaret about it all."

9 July 1941

Dear Beatrice,

Another disastrous dinner. Why does she bother to come home? Does she simply come to fight? Again, I left the table early with Mother on my heels. I don't think Father and Caro even noticed we left.

As usual, Caro came to my room upon leaving the dining room. I sat on my bed and listened to her pound up the stairs and down the hall. She stomps like an elephant when mad.

She didn't bother to knock, just burst through my door. "I'm not coming back."

"Don't be so dramatic. The Blitz is over. Things will calm down. He'll calm down."

"It's not him. It's me. I keep picking needless fights. I just get so angry." She plopped onto my bed. "But it won't calm down, Margo. Don't believe that. This war will get far worse before it gets better."

"Listen to you." I laid down my book and sat upright. "This is a new tune." I didn't want to revisit all that claptrap she used to recite, but couldn't help teasing her a little.

She stared at me. "I know more now."

I lifted a brow. She says that expression makes me look like a hawk. She noted it and banked her fire. I sensed she caught that she had accidentally signaled something by her tone, something she didn't want me to know.

The air thickened between us, but rather than share with me, she flicked her fingers as if shooing a ladybug. "It's nothing. Just talk in the RAF. Randolph is worried."

She was lying. So I decided to dig—and I sometimes play dirty. "You're still stringing him along, are you?"

She's not, but the charge reddened her face. "I'm not stringing him along, Margo. Don't say that. I love him and I would never hurt him."

"I believe you did. Once. But you lied to him, Caro, and you used me as cover over our birthday last year. You had never planned to come home, yet you deliberately told him that. You lied to him then as you're lying to me now. Isn't that a form of betrayal? A form of cheating?"

She moved as if ready to leave. I reached for her arm. "Just talk to me. You can trust—" She jerked back, toppling off the bed to stand. Noting a flash of red, I pounced forward after her. "Show me."

"What?"

I grabbed at her other arm to keep her from leaving. "Show me." I repeated the command with such force she wilted and lifted her sleeve.

There is a huge red, raised, and jagged scar across her forearm! It had to have been a horribly deep cut that required stitches to close.

"That's fresh. Who hurt you?"

"No one. It happened about a month ago." She stood at the foot of my bed, feet braced to either flee or fight. I wasn't sure which.

She traced the scar with her finger. "It was a fallen wire . . . I didn't see it heading to work one morning and walked right into it. If I hadn't raised my arm at the last second, it would have sliced my face."

"I'm so sorry." I stepped toward her. "You poor thing. Did I just hurt you?"

"It's still tender, that's all." She slid her sleeve back down as if needing to hide it again.

All my anger evaporated, but my fear for her increased. She lied to me, Beatrice. Right then and there—again. No wire can create such serrations.

But what was I to say? Push her and lose her? Accuse her again? Then she really might not come back home—ever. I sit here safe in the north while she lives and works in London, braving bombs and who knows what else each night.

"Remember how well you know me, Margo. You know my heart and I love you." She fixed me with an intense stare. "George too."

"I know." A sigh signaled to us both that I was backing down. It's true; I've never doubted her love for me or for Randolph.

She didn't leave. She climbed back onto my bed. "Will you be sad to move to the South Cottage in the fall?"

"Not at all." I climbed up next to her. "It would be impossible to stay when the Army takes over. And it's what we must do. Sometimes we don't have a choice with the situations handed to us. We'll make the best of it."

She smiled up at me. "See? I always said you were our better half. I'd be put out."

"Somehow I don't believe that's true." I glanced to her arm and her now-hidden scar. "I've got an uneasy feeling you're giving life and limb and I'm simply moving to the end of the garden."

"Do you think if you do something well and good that how you get there doesn't matter? Can the end justify the means?"

I sat straighter. "What are you talking about?"

She hung her head "Nothing . . . I hurt Father tonight. More deeply than I intended to. I simply . . . I can't have him worry. That's why I said I wasn't coming back. It's better to have him angry at me than to make him worry about me. I can't have any of you worry."

"You're poking him on purpose?" I gestured toward her arm and watched her tuck it behind her back. "There's more to that cut, isn't there?"

She climbed off the bed and backed to the door. I knew I was right, but also knew I couldn't push.

"Don't discount your work or your value, Margo. And I'm sorry I've jabbed you about Mother and Father. They need you. Right where you are, doing what you are."

"And you?"

"I'm doing what I can." She shrugged, one hand on the knob of the connecting door between our rooms. "Maybe one day they'll even be proud of me again."

Her last sentence lingered long after she left. It brought to mind a long-ago letter. She once wrote that Father told her she was "amounting to nothing" and that those words now sat between them.

What is she willing to risk to prove him wrong?

I fear everything.

THIRTY

Mat and I sat for another hour, passing letters and diaries between us. He was right: putting them alongside the SOE documents started to paint a complete picture of Caro's activities, her lies, and her sacrifices.

It struck me again and again, how each sister claimed to tell the other everything yet held back so much. How much did they know of each other? How much do we know of the people we love? Is complete truth with another, complete knowing of another, even possible?

I began to think it wasn't and, while one part of me wanted to hang my head and give up—on everything—another part recognized this was what I needed to understand.

I didn't know everything, and I never could. My grandfather's pain. My grandmother's sorrow. My father's childhood. His complete retreat after Amelia's death. I saw it as abandonment, but how did he see it? What did he feel?

Endless questions filled my mind, but they all had one answer—honesty. Perhaps understanding could never be complete, but that didn't mean it wasn't worth the effort. If these sisters had been more honest, from Margaret's illness on, so much pain could have been spared. And if I chose that path now, perhaps our present—and our futures—could be something new.

Mat's gaze caught mine. There were questions there too. He was angry with me, hurt somehow—I sensed it. Yet he'd stayed up late to locate Martine because I'd been upset yesterday, certain that whatever happened to Caro had harmed her. I wasn't sure if Caro had created another victim or had just been unable to save her. Yesterday I had handed Mat a file with the glum proclamation, "If Caro was a traitor, her friend will have ended up dead. That's more devastating than anything that's happened in our family."

At the time, he'd dismissed my concerns and told me to read on. Then all through the night, he'd sought the answers to bring me a gift—the truth. There was so much I wanted to say. I dropped my attention to the page, ready to share, but still unsure how to begin.

LONDON HOUSE
6 AUGUST 1941

Dear Margo,

Did you hear the BBC Broadcast Talk tonight? It was that writer I told you about, C. S. Lewis. He's giving a series of talks on the BBC and tonight's was "Common Decency." I'm sure you heard it. It felt as if all Britain listened.

Everything stopped at work as we sat mesmerized by the radio, trying to find understanding, meaning, and perhaps motivation.

Lewis's words rolled off a few coworkers, but I found them reassuring and thought-provoking. He talked about right and wrong, and that it exists outside of us. It is an absolute, not a perspective.

I have felt that lately. The issues we deal with now carry greater consequences than the world of our childhood and, in pondering them, I have come to realize that my "right" is subjective and must be in line with something higher, absolute, and fully formed. Otherwise I can twist and turn, perhaps through no fault of my own, into a horror. I used to think it was all mine, that my view carried weight, importance, even a stamp of absolute truth, but events lately have proven me wrong.

Yet looking around, it seems that subjective knowing still prevails. Everyone seems to cling to their own idea of right and wrong, and perception forms reality. But if that was true—objectively true—this war would make no sense. We would only fight together because, by happenstance, we agree that the Nazis are committing evil. Yet that opens another question . . . Would we also happen to agree on what is or is not evil?

But if these truths exist outside us and we do not determine them—nothing is dependent on our whims or happenstance. The truths are fixed, immutable, and eternal. We are the ones who will come and go, not truth.

Isn't that reassuring? I find such comfort, as the world falls apart, that some things will last—even if they are only ideals.

Only? What a silly thing to write. Sometimes ideals are the most solid, truest, and best things we can strive for. And we should strive for them. It's when we stop trying to find and chase true right that we stumble and degrade ourselves.

I was at the grocer's yesterday and one woman's ration of meat was a better cut, I gather. It certainly couldn't have been larger, as everything is so scrupulously weighed. But another woman called out that it wasn't right, that she was as important as everyone else in the shop, and she deserved her "fair share." She yelled on, starting a row, until the police arrived. I left as three officers hauled the butcher and five women into the street.

You see, just as Lewis said, the woman knew there was a "right," a standard of behavior, even in that shop—a standard she expected everyone to understand and follow. Otherwise she might have just been yelling nonsense for all the good it would do her.

But the standard does exist—everyone in that shop was shocked, alerted, then nervous that something had been violated.

Her idea of "fair" clearly had a true objective reality, even if her chase for it ended in a row rather than a calm resolution.

I needed Lewis's words last night. I'm so tired of everything tipping on edge and pressing to the point of destruction. I needed that call to action, that assurance that some truths are so inviolable that they are worth striving for, fighting for, and even dying for.

There are so many things I want to say to you, Margo. No, that's not quite right. I think I'd rather just be in your company than burden you with all these questions and concerns. Besides, even if I have not been able to articulate everything well over the years, you know my heart.

I am missing you tonight. I am also missing Mother and Father. You are my bridge to them, Margo. It's a lot to ask, but could you fortify it? When they think the worst of me, could you remind them of the best? I have been working so hard these last months to bring that best out. I only hope I haven't overstepped.

Isn't it odd how things have turned out? Could you have ever guessed? When we were young, I hated our roles. I was put on a sugary pink pedestal, idealized as all that was delicate, feminine, and obedient. Your pedestal was much lower, if you had one at all. But you had all the fun. Somehow, being out of their spotlight left you free—free to climb, fish, run, dig, and create.

I'm outside that bright light now and my pedestal is ground to dust. Yet I don't embrace my freedom like you did. Perhaps I am not strong enough. I chafe and strike out, guilt becoming anger. As much as I try to convince myself I am protecting them, I am honest enough tonight to recognize I strive to punish them as they punished me.

It was never on purpose—on their side and even on mine. Please believe me. Unlike Lewis—or maybe like the rest of humanity—I believed my view was reality. I'm only now under-standing that it isn't and never was. It's quite remarkable what five nights alone will do.

I am alone because you are not here. I am alone because I have sent George away. I still love him, Margo, but there is a gulf between us right now. I can't carry his vulnerability and he can't trust my love. I am causing him pain. If I could control my reality, George and I will still marry and still live happily ever after some-day soon. But we know that's not in my power and, as I once told you, it's easier for him—for anyone—to be mad at me rather than worry about me. Please don't let him in on that little secret, dear sister. All will be clear in time.

I leave tomorrow. Perhaps that's what makes this night so poignant. The bombings are worse now. The papers said four hundred planes come each night. How much longer can this last? How much longer can we last? It feels like an apocalyptic fireworks display ramping up to the finale. But tomorrow, I leave the city behind and pray she stands until my return. I'll be gone a few days, then I'll try to telephone or at least write again. Don't worry—in fact, by the time you get this I may already be safely tucked back in bed here at the London House.

Anyway, back to the broadcast and to my point. Goodness, I'm meandering more than our fishing stream tonight! I hope you were listening because I'd like to believe we were linked in that moment. I laughed aloud when Lewis cited, as proof points of a higher law, sayings such as, "You promised," or "You can't do that." Those were hallmarks of our childhood. Sisters bound by love, promises, our own language, and what I thought was our unique sense of fairness.

Yet, that's just it. It wasn't just ours. And if not only ours—we are part of a larger story. And that's what presses upon me tonight,

Margo—my part in this larger story. Because, when in danger, my world shrinks to only us again. When the telephone lines fell, you were the first one I wanted, the first one who felt out of reach, and it was physically painful. I need to hear your voice sometimes to feel well.

I'm sorry to sound so grim. As I said, I am worn out and writing to you is the only true moment when I can drop the facade and stop pretending to be brave. Again, please don't share any of this with Mother and Father, and never with George.

This is for you alone.

Mother and Father would try to solve these fears. They'd try to solve me. And George, dear sweet George, wouldn't understand. He sees me as something shiny and bright and, when I am with him, he is not wrong. I feel that way. I can do anything—and that's why I sent him away for now. While I still love him, my vulnerability would terrify him more than my defection. He's up in the skies tonight—keep him in your prayers, dear sister.

I'm sorry to lay all this on you and you alone, Margo. I can only trust I am not too heavy a burden for you to carry.

Love,

Caro

P.S. The announcer mentioned in the introduction that C. S. Lewis's friends call him "Jack" and that he made up his own nickname when he was young. There is something to be said for that . . . I may have to devise my own nickname someday. That would be a project, wouldn't it? Something reflective of my past, but fitting for the circumstances? Something secret. Maybe one I only share with you. Maybe that, rather than all these dark musings, should occupy my time.

However . . . if you had done that, there would be no Margo Moo and, for Randolph, there would be no George. The world would be a darker place for me without those endearments. But I do love the name "Jack," don't you?

I love you, my Moo.

I gasped.

Mat's head shot up.

"Jack. She says she loves the nickname Jack, after C. S. Lewis. My father's nickname is Jack. He said my grandfather constantly questioned why Grandmother insisted on giving John an equally long nickname . . . This is why."

Mat cleaned his glasses with the hem of his shirt. Somewhere in the morning, he'd pulled out a set of round wire-rimmed glasses—a must for every true scholar. "I suspect, now that you've met her, you'll start to see Caro's stamp all over your lives. Your grandmother never forgot her sister."

"Did you catch that she broke up with George? Her defection comment?" I lifted a brow, remembering Margo's hawk comment.

"I did." Mat laughed.

"She meant withdrawing her affections." I gestured to the diaries. "But Margo never mentioned it in her diaries, because she knew it wasn't real. Caro didn't really break up with him. Her 'defection' was to protect him."

"Yes, and the word plays both ways, doesn't it? I sense she was laying the groundwork for that final letter her parents received. Maybe cueing her sister to its double meaning? And she's not subtle about her intentions either. Over and over Caro said it was better to be angry with her than to worry about her. Here, I just reread her last letter to Margaret. It's a whole new letter now."

15 OCTOBER 1941

Dearest Margo,

I can't sleep tonight. I'm not sure why, but I'm wide awake and all I see is you. Two halves of the same coin. How does one survive without the other? How is one whole if the other half is not near?

Do you remember when we were seven and I got lost in the village? You searched for me for hours. It was dark by the time you found me. I had followed the river the opposite direction from home. I still don't know how you did it, how you knew where to search, and why you kept looking so deep into the night. You got in so much trouble and you never told Father I was the one lost. You let him believe you were the one who led us astray. You shouldered the brunt of every misstep back then and I always wondered why. I understand now.

There could only be one of us.

Be careful, dear sister. Mother and Father need you, but don't let them make you their sun. They revolve around you now and I fear they will keep you from growing your own roots and soaring on your own wings. They were so frightened in '34. We all were. But you have recovered. You are strong. And you do not need the pedestal upon which they've lifted you. I'm not giving you this warning from a place of jealousy. Please know that. I'm thinking of you, only of you. I don't want you to be so lonely forever.

You were wild once and you taught me to be brave. When you climbed that tree higher than anyone ever had, I was so proud of you. I was even more proud when you didn't cry after falling. No girl could touch you. No one could touch you. You were the brightest and most alive of us all.

I need that strength from you now, Margo. Somehow I know

I need you. We've always had each other's backs and tonight I feel very alone. I am heading out to research new fabrics and may be on the road for a week or so. As before, you won't be able to reach me, but I'll telephone or write the moment I return to London. I will not lie to you—something about this trip has me anxious. Perhaps it's only in my mind.

I find solace tonight in remembering everything between us, every story we've shared and every tidbit of our letters. They tell our story and, when I'm feeling lost and alone, they lead me to you. Do the same when you need me. Please? Pull out our letters and find me in each shared story and in each detail. It's all there.

I'm sorry I called you Tresse last year. I have felt bad since the moment I posted the letter. You never betrayed me and, please remember, I will never betray you. Remind Father and Mother of that . . . They can be angry, they will be angry, but don't let them doubt my loyalty and love.

As for you, you know me. You know how I feel and who I am. We are sisters. More than that, we are twins. We are we.

I love you. Forever.

C

"Oh my . . ." I leaned over the table. "I thought it was just sentiment before the Archives. A tearful goodbye of sorts, and it was, but not like I thought. She was nervous, but it's not even that . . . She knew. They all knew about Christophe and the danger—why'd they let her go? Despite extra training, it was suicide. She'd been compromised. Why would she do it?"

"Her Lewis letter answered that one. It was the right thing to do. An absolute right ranks higher than perception or fear." Mat angled toward me. "That letter? Coupled with the Lewis one? I'm sorry. I truly thought I wasn't leaping to conclusions, but I was wrong."

"Seems we all were."

"It's a relief really." Mat chuffed. "The *Atlantic* aside, I did not want to tell the Arnim family about her."

"I still wish I knew what happened. She said Margo could find out, and if she could, so can we. She can't have just disappeared. You said she was too important for that—a woman with connections, a peer's daughter. She would have been a prize and used for leverage."

Mat circled the table. "Everything points to Paris. For her and maybe for Arnim." Mat paused until he had my full attention. "Follow one and we might find the other?"

"Where? In Paris?"

With a side smile, Mat lifted and dropped a shoulder. He looked like a kid offering a dare. "Why not? If England doesn't know what happened, we expand the search." He raised his hand before I could interrupt. "We've got about thirty hours. She's worth the effort." He stared straight at me. "You're worth the effort."

My pulse raced as he broke the connection to check his watch. He continued, "It's eight. We've got a few hours before the noon Chunnel that'll get us there by 3:30 p.m. Paris time. We can get to the Police Prefecture Archives by four o'clock and they stay open until seven o'clock. Three hours. If we find nothing, we go back first thing tomorrow."

"Whoa . . . How do you know all this?"

"Research," he quipped. At my glare, he curved his lips into a self-deprecating smile. "It's what I do. I didn't have the funds to get over here on my own, so when the Arnim family paid for a Paris trip at the beginning of their project, I planned every second to get some of my own research done. I can tell you how to get Research Cards at national libraries in a dozen different countries, the cheapest trains and routes, how to arrange your ticket so you can get a free table on which to work, the most economical places to stay, the opening and closing times of countless municipal and government facilities, who's got records online and who doesn't . . . We have a window, Caroline. A small, closing window. The Paris police files were made public in 2015, but they aren't online. What do you say?"

"We can still fly back to Boston Friday?"

"Out of Paris."

So much was at stake, but what I told my mom was true: I wouldn't pass this way again. "Let's go."

THIRTY-ONE

While Mat organized train tickets and file requests from the Police Prefecture Archives, I went in search of Mom.

I found her in my grandfather's former study. What was once wood paneled and dark had been transformed into something truly special—a jewel box. The walls were still wood paneled, dark and smooth, but the furniture was light and airy, cream with threads of gold and touches of pink and red. A huge modern painting of the silhouette of two girls, white against a lime background, hung above the tiny fireplace. Matching armchairs sat perfectly positioned across from each other in the bay window to catch the morning light.

She sat in one of the armchairs, staring out the window. She was threading a gold chain through her fingers with a pile of letters resting on her lap.

"Mom?"

I startled her. She looked to me, to the letters, and motioned for me to sit. "I remembered these this morning. I'm sorry I didn't before. They were never with the other letters."

She handed the small collection to me. "Those are Caro's letters to her George. Your grandmother mentioned them to me in the last weeks before she died, but she couldn't remember where he kept them. I suppose she wrestled with that, the diabolical pull between remembering where he hid them and trying to forget, her whole life."

I dropped into the chair across from her. "Maybe it wasn't about remembering or forgetting, but forgiving."

"I think you are right . . . Why is that so hard? Especially forgiving ourselves." Mom closed her eyes. I sensed her focus shifted from me to something deep within.

She opened them and motioned for me to hold out my hand. "She would want you to have this. You know her and her sister better than anyone now." She dropped the gold into my palm. A beautiful gold heart covered in filigree rested in the chain's nest. "They must have gotten mixed up somehow."

"I read about these." I looked closely within the tangled vines wrought into the gold and, after a heartbeat, found it. The *C* woven into the center. "The necklaces didn't get mixed up. They traded."

"Ah . . ." Mom nodded. "Margaret never removed it, but she also requested not to be buried with it."

"Thank you." I closed it within my palm. This entire journey I felt I'd been bucking my family, caught between railing at all that went wrong and longing for all to be made right. This necklace felt like acceptance, confirmation, even love. I swallowed to regain composure and to try not to read too much into the moment.

"We are headed to Paris." My words came out rushed.

"Today?"

"Mat thinks we can find answers there and we don't have much time. I'll fly home to Boston from Paris on Friday."

"So soon . . ." Mom pushed forward in her chair, perching on its edge. "I thought we'd have more time. There is so much we should talk about—things I need to say."

I stared at her. Part of me wanted to sink into this moment and hear her out. Another part grew angrier with every breath—angry because, like Caro wrote, it felt so much safer than feeling guilty, rejected, and scared.

"You've had twenty years, Mom."

Her eyes flickered, full of questions and shock.

"I don't want to go through this. I can't right now. Again, I'm sorry. But I was eight, Mom."

"Again? You're sorry? What are you talking about?"

"I'm talking about Amelia . . . I came to apologize twenty years ago and you yelled at me. You sent me away and never said anything about any of it ever again."

I was no longer sitting in the London House's lovely study. I was hiding behind a doorway. I was eight and trembling, and we had just buried my sister two weeks before.

School had gotten out early that day for a teacher planning conference and I'd let myself in the back door. A crash had brought me to the kitchen and a second shattering of glass kept me hiding behind the swinging door, peeking through the crack.

Plates flew and shattered against the refrigerator. Mom fired water glasses one by one onto the marble floor. Glass shot up and her hands were bleeding. More plates. Crystal. It was mesmerizing in its terror. Everything within her sight was grabbed and smashed in a nightmare of sound and shards. But it wasn't her actions that kept me hidden. It was the screaming.

I drew myself back to the present. "You were yelling, swearing. Words I'd never heard before. That she was to blame, that you hated her, me. Then you fell into all that glass . . . And I stepped out to come to you . . ."

My words ran out, unable to describe what came next. She hadn't crouched to the floor and cried, or sobbed, or moaned. She had dropped like a rag doll with a sound I've never found words for, a keening that ripped open my heart even in memory. But the second she saw me, she leapt to her feet in fury, arms stiff and stretched toward me, screaming. "Get out. Don't you dare take a single step into here. Go upstairs. Now. Go!"

Mom pressed her hand to her mouth. "You were there? I yelled? I . . . You saw me?"

"Don't you remember?"

In a flash, she was on the floor clutching my knees, reaching for my face. "No, I don't. But it wasn't you. It was never you." Her eyes moved quickly back and forth as if seeking the memory. "Socks. You were wearing socks, right? Blue ones . . . There was so much glass . . . I was talking about the driver . . . She'd been typing on her BlackBerry. She never saw the light. She never saw your sister. And I was so angry. I was so angry with her. With God. With me. But never with you. I promise, never with you."

"But you said just the other day that sometimes someone else is to blame." Eight-year-old Caroline was talking now. I could feel her within me. The child who hadn't understood. The woman who still didn't.

"Sometimes someone does do something like that and it causes pain . . . But after all these years, I don't even think about that woman anymore. I'm the one I've hated. I'm the one I was talking about." Mom swiped at her eyes. It wasn't delicate. It was as snuffly and aggressive as I had done the day before. I almost laughed at the feeling of connection such a small gesture wrought.

She reached for my hand again. "I caused pain. I was to blame because I wasn't there for Amelia. I missed being with her when she needed me most. Then I caused you more pain . . . You needed me and I . . . I'm so sorry, my darling. I am so very sorry."

"You told me to get out, then you left me."

"I know . . ."

"No." I cut her off as tears built and spilled. "You don't know. You weren't there, but I was. I was the one rushing home. I was the one who darted when the light turned, and I couldn't pull her away. I still feel it. I was that close to the car, Mom, and you . . . you never said it wasn't my fault. You never came after me and said it."

"Darling . . ." She lifted onto her knees and pulled me into a hug.

"It was never your fault. This is late in coming, but I'm saying it now. Do you hear me? It was never your fault. Never . . . I got lost. I'm so sorry I got lost and I couldn't find my way back to tell you that. I pretended you were fine because I couldn't bear to believe your world was as dark as mine. I'm so sorry. Please forgive me."

She repeated her words again and again, as if repetition would lay them into my heart. And it did. After several minutes, I felt my tears subside and every tense muscle soften within her arms.

At my first sniffle, Mom tilted back onto her heels and reached for a tissue from the small table beside my chair. She dabbed at my eyes.

I reached for it with a blubbery laugh. "I'm old enough to do that."

"Yes." She offered an equally wavering smile. "You are, aren't you?" She tipped into a sitting position on the floor in front of me. She watched me for a long moment before speaking, her hands still wrapped around mine. "I want to say it again, Caroline. Now that we aren't crying . . . I fell into someplace very dark when Amelia died. I was drowning and, if I'm being honest, I didn't come out until I came here to help your grandmother. I should've reached out then. I should have flown home when I recognized it and begged your forgiveness. I've been a coward." She pinched her nose. I handed her a tissue.

"What happened here?"

"Your grandmother saved me by showing me I wasn't alone in all my pain, regrets, and loneliness, but that I would be . . . I was headed to where she had been." Mom closed her eyes in memory for a beat before continuing. "She loved your dad, but never knew how to show him. She could never break through her own black hole, I guess. That's why she left me the house, so he wouldn't sell it and be done with it, be done with her."

Mom squeezed my hands tighter. They felt warm within her grasp. "And refinishing it brought me back to life . . . I nailed boards, cleaned out generations of junk, sanded floors, oiled that huge kitchen table. By the time I hired a crew, I knew almost as much about construction and restoration as they did, and even more about myself and letting go."

She gave me a small eager smile. "I tiled your bathroom floor. It's a little crooked around the toilet."

"I hadn't noticed." I sniffled.

"I'm sorry," she repeated. At my expression, she giggled. "Not about the toilet . . . I'm sorry because you are right. I chose my pain over you. I left you alone. I left your father alone when he needed me as well. I can't undo any of that. I can only ask you to forgive me."

"I thought you hated me." Kleenex soaked, I dragged the back of my hand across my cheeks. "Not hated, but blamed me, and that felt pretty close."

"Never." She was up on her knees again, pulling me into another hug. This time I cooperated and hugged her back tightly, breathing in that fresh scent of jasmine and lily I'd caught before.

We pushed out sputtery laughs a little longer, more as a way to stop the tears and catch our breaths than anything else. It filled the spaces within and between us. I had been alone, and so had she, right next to me. But we weren't anymore.

"So, Paris?" She rocked back to sitting on the floor again.

"Yes." I nodded, back to business. "We may not find anything, but we have a few hours to search today, not to mention all day tomorrow. Mat's ordering files from the Police Prefecture right now. We'll take the noon Chunnel, go straight there, and hope for the best."

She twisted a strand of hair that had fallen from my loose bun and tucked it behind my ear. "And . . . Can I come to Boston? Will you come back here?"

"I'd like that." I felt my heart swell. "Both options."

Mom glanced to her watch and pushed up off the floor. "You go throw your things together and I'll make a lunch you can take with you and, while you're on the train, I'll get you a dinner reservation and a place to stay."

"You don't need to do all that." I faced her. "Mat says he knows a cheap place by Notre Dame."

"My darling." She cupped my cheek within her hand before pulling me into another hug. "I want to do this for you. Please let me."

THIRTY-TWO

During our train ride, Mat and I dug into the letters and the diaries we'd brought with us. As he opened Margaret's final diary, I unfolded the first of the small letter pile my mom had given me. Here again was the swirling fast script and large loops of a hand seemingly incapable of keeping up with the pace and emotion of the heart that drove it.

LONDON HOUSE
20 AUGUST 1934

Dear George,

London is not the same without you. I will drive home to Parkley tomorrow. We will both be gone and summer will be a memory. A beautiful memory. It didn't start out that way, but you made it that way.

Yes, write to me. I didn't answer your request last week because I couldn't believe you were serious. I thought you were making fun of me. You did once tease that sixteen was awfully young.

But I will take you at your word and believe you are not laughing at my age or my gullibility. Write to me. Tell me all about life at Oxford, tell me about your studies, share with me your friends, regale me with all the stupid things you University boys do. I want to know it all. I want to know you.

If I have assumed too much interest on your part, forgive me, and tear up this letter.

And write to me—if you want.

Yours,

Caro

BRILLIANTMONT, LAUSANNE, SWITZERLAND
10 JUNE 1936

Dearest George,

Two dozen red roses? A girl could get ideas—all my friends certainly have. And I didn't dispel a single one. Let them imagine all sorts of things. I certainly am. Just looking at them, I feel your arms around me. Touching the soft blooms, I feel your touch and your kiss.

How I wish you were coming to graduation next week. You're the only one I want here—well, you and Margo. How I miss her! But having her here wouldn't change that. I'd still miss her.

Do you sense she is gone as I do? Do you miss your friend? You used to ask about her more. Do you not because you feel she has stepped away? Does she confide in you? I hope she does. You and she have always been close and she needs that. She shares, or always used to, more naturally than I ever did. I don't want her to be alone, George, but I won't be there with her at Parkley or in London. I can't.

Thank you for your encouragement. I don't think I could be so brave without you. It still feels like a dream, but the tickets are purchased and I head to Paris with Renée right after the ceremony. I promise I will spend my first weekend mapping out perfect evenings, restaurants, cafés, and walks, so that when you visit I'll be a capable guide.

Oh . . . Thank you for the roses! I don't think I actually thanked you. Goodness, my head is all over the place today. Blame it on these gorgeous roses and this heady scent. I am wrapped up in you when I must be about other things. I have final examinations, and packing, and we're having a special dinner for those who are leaving next week.

Write again soon and plan your first visit to Paris now.

All my love is yours,

Caro

PARIS
14 SEPTEMBER 1938

Dear George,

What do you want from me? I will not come home simply because you say I should. I will not leave my friends and my work here—work I love—simply because it's on the wrong side of the Channel for you and my family. I am not some girl you can order about on a whim or for your convenience. And never question where my loyalties lie.

I love you.

I love you so much more than you know. Some days I almost think you understand and believe me. Other days you choose not to—you let other voices drown out my love.

Frederick's marriage is a disaster, yes, but Frederick is a disaster—and Adele isn't much better. I may be quite a bit younger, but girls talk and Adele was always a very spoiled girl. I can't imagine that marrying your bother matured her.

But you are nothing like your brother and I am nothing like his wife. How can you not see that, my darling?

I'm sorry about your parents . . . I didn't know everything you shared during your last visit. Growing up in that tension must have been terribly difficult. But again, that is your past, not your future. You must not project their pain onto our love. Not every marriage is like theirs nor like Frederick's. You and I? We talk, we fight, we are honest with one another, we listen, we make up, we kiss with more passion than I thought could exist in the world, and we love each other. Why can't you accept all that to be true and rest in it?

Honestly, my darling, if you can't believe in us and you can't trust me, how do we go from here?

This isn't an ultimatum, it's an honest discussion. Please do not write or telephone with another frantic sideways marriage proposal. Like I told you—when it's real and not a reaction to some horror you've created in your head, I will say yes.

But I am not returning to England right now. I'm not staying in Paris to punish you or to punish my parents. I'm staying because my life here works and the dangers are far less than all your imaginings.

I can breathe, think, create, and debate here. I feel like "me" here—the best version of me. The only time I feel even better is when I am with you. And someday we will be together. You have to believe that. Otherwise we are not moving forward. We are stuck, and for the wrong reasons.

Believe that, darling. Believe in me. Believe in us.

And don't fret . . . I'm right here.

Always yours,

Caro

PARIS
16 APRIL 1940

Dearest,

I've been foolish, dangerously foolish. I'm sorry I haven't

listened. I'm sorry for all I've put you through . . . And I hope . . . I hope I can deliver this apology in person, darling.

Something is going terribly wrong here. I can feel it and, for the first time, I am frightened.

A couple weeks ago that German industrialist, Paul Arnim, came into the salon. Remember I've told you about him and his lovely wife? They remind me of us . . . Anyway, he pulled me aside and said I needed to get out of France, and to take Martine. He didn't say more, but he scared me. He has the palest blue eyes that looked like the sky when he was with his wife and like ice as he warned me.

I'm sorry I didn't telephone or write to you immediately—I thought I was overreacting, that my panic wasn't rational. I felt dizzy and shaky and didn't want you to see the worst of me . . . my cowardice. But it wasn't irrational. To not see it for what it was— that was the cowardice. I am so sorry.

I should have known when Schiap left Paris at the beginning of the month. We thought it was another of her "inspirational jaunts," but she's running the business from Lyon. She says she is on vacation, but instructions, telephone calls, and couriers arrive by the hour. She is not on vacation. Bettina is tense as well. She seems antagonistic now, like sides have been chosen and she stands with her husband, a man with definite German affinities, and no longer with us.

I suspect that is closer to the truth than anything we've been told. Sides have been chosen and no one will escape unscathed. This Phoney War has soured to something new. The fear and tension are palpable. They thicken the air. They cling to us. The propaganda says the Germans are trying to peacefully work toward solutions and the British, supposedly on our side, are harming us out of spite. But I know that to be false—I've sat through countless dinners with your father and mine.

Only now do I trust my instincts. They tell me to be afraid and they tell me I am too late.

I'll write to Father next to ask if I should go see Ambassador Campbell. I don't want to ask favors I have no business asking, but I'm not sure where else to turn.

If I've been a fool, I'm so sorry, George. I thought I was being modern and mature. I conclude I've only been young and spoiled.

I love you—remember that. I hope to be able to tell you this in person and hold you close soon, but—

No, I will not think like that. I will reach you.

All my love,

Caro

LONDON HOUSE
22 NOVEMBER 1940

George—

Please come see me tonight. I told you things were tense and busy and upsetting. But it's war. It's supposed to be all that and more, right? I shouldn't have been so rude last month when you visited.

I got scared, George. I hope you can understand that. I let my dark imaginings get the best of me and I regretted my behavior as soon as you left for base again. We don't get enough time together and I wasted an entire evening with you.

Thank you for coming on my birthday. I am also sorry I didn't hear you knock at the door. I wasn't avoiding you and I didn't lie. I had planned to go home, but I got terribly sick. Other than a stuffy nose and a headache, I am well now—and desperate to see you.

Come to me tonight, George. Forgive me.

Caro

LONDON HOUSE
15 OCTOBER 1941

Dearest George,

You're on duty tonight. You're somewhere above me and I can't reach you. I pray you are safe. I trust you are because I think I would feel if you were not—it would wrench something deep within me. I'm not sure I'd survive.

I always told you that you could trust me—and I betrayed that trust. When I told you in August we should stop seeing each other, I wasn't honest about my reasons. I got scared. I got scared about your work, my work, and all the secrets between us. You said you thought I was cheating on you and, perhaps I am, but not in the way you think. I want to explain. You deserve my honesty. I want to share with you what I can. Although I can't share everything, at least not yet, I hope it's enough for you to love me again.

I told you I was typing, driving, and working fabrics these past months. I never told you I knew or did anything that might put me in harm's way. That was my lie. My only lie. Given to serve my country—just as there are confidential things you've done and secrets you've kept in serving as well. War has required it.

I leave tomorrow on a research trip. My commanding officer says communications are spotty at best and not to assume I'll be able to maintain contact while I'm gone. I've had such trips before and they've been fine, but this one fills me with trepidation. I don't want to be outside your reach. I don't want you to be outside mine.

Marry me, George.

I know after all I have put you through, this feels out of the blue. But it's not—we've been heading this direction since I was sixteen and you invited me for our first stroll through Mayfair. Goodness knows, you've asked me before—now I'm asking you.

Put aside all your doubts, fears, hesitations, and jump with me. This war is stealing our time and our love. And, if we don't prevail, I want to leave this world as your wife with no regrets. Right now I carry so many—I regret every missed kiss and every night you aren't lying next to me.

If for some reason my return is delayed, try not to worry, my love. You do that so well, but I can't have any of your mind on me during your missions. Trust I will be well and I will race home to you as soon as I am able.

If you hear anything that— Never mind. You and Margaret know me. With the two of you in my corner, I will always succeed.

God bless you, my beloved.

Caro

THIRTY-THREE

I felt myself melt into the seat with my exhale, unaware I'd been holding my breath while reading. It was so tender.

She loved George—always had, always would. It broke my heart again that Caro never married her George as much as it broke my heart that he waited nine years for her and kept the letters his whole life. He must have felt so lost and confused. From what Caro wrote, she knew he'd doubt her—he'd been taught that, modeled that, his whole life—but her letter had to have inspired hope. It was that powerful.

So powerful it haunted my grandmother as well. How could such tender sentiments, written by a sister she loved to the man she married and once adored, not always bring fresh pain?

I looked out the window and found myself, in the blackness of the Chunnel, staring at my own reflection.

How alike we were through the generations, I mused. How resistant to trusting, feeling, relaxing, being . . . loving.

I shifted my focus to watch Mat through the window's reflection. He was bent over the table again, paging through his notebook, that same lock of hair having fallen over his eyes, shielding them from view. So intent. In many ways, so caring.

"Have you ever been in love?" I blurted out. "I mean, have you ever had a serious girlfriend?" My rudeness, and my assumptions, surprised me. "Or . . . I'm sorry, you don't have to answer . . . Do you have one right now?"

Mat's eyes flashed panic. His gaze flicked to the letters in front of me, then back to mine, full of questions. "I have. Not now. Maybe one."

"You think you've been in love once?"

"I . . ." He blinked.

"Can you tell me about her?" He clearly heard the need to connect in my voice, because his look softened. "Please."

Mat shifted in his seat. I did the same, getting more comfortable, as his gaze lifted up and over my head. I felt like he was about to take me back in time. Perhaps not eighty years, but back to a few that mattered to him.

"Her name was Bethany. She was blonde and blue eyed, and I only say that to give you a mental picture and a sense as to how surprising it was my mom liked her."

"No blue eyes for your mom?" I have blue eyes.

"Not that. It's just that my brothers both married women of Greek heritage. My family is loud and opinionated." Mat's brows met above his nose in a deep wrinkle. "How telling you that Bethany had blonde hair and blue eyes conveys that she was the complete opposite of that— and quiet—I have no idea, but that's where I was going . . . Anyway, we met during my first year in grad school while she was working in a biology lab a few buildings away. We were together a couple years and, for most of it, I thought we were good."

"You weren't?"

"I suspect I idealized what love should look like rather than seeing what Bethany and I actually had." He shook his head as if he'd phrased it wrong, again.

And he had—I needed less philosophy and more details.

"I eventually noticed, but we lived parallel lives, not interwoven ones. I'd have my day, she'd have hers, we'd recount them and spend time together, but—" Mat rubbed his chin. "Bottom line, I don't need someone to say, 'Oh Knight-in-Shining-Armor, come save me.'"

He pitched his voice high and I clenched my jaw to keep from giggling. He was not trying to be funny.

He continued, oblivious of my struggle. "But I do want someone who believes 'Guy-I'm-in-love-with, hold my hand because we're stronger together.' I want a woman to believe that about me, with me. It's what my parents have and, without it, marriage has too many obstacles to tackle. Bethany was never going to figuratively hold my hand. She didn't need that from me and I didn't need it from her."

My mind drifted back to Mat holding my hand the night before. Saying nothing, just walking beside me holding my hand. I hadn't wanted to let go and felt the coldness of separation the instant we did.

I coughed to cover the heat crawling up my neck. "So you broke up?"

"Not quite." Mat scrunched his face. "While still dating me, she found a guy, engaged to another woman, mind you, whose hand she did want to hold. Last I heard, they married and may even have a kid by now."

"Ah . . . the Arnim issue."

Mat's blush matched my own. "Yes, well, I did confess my reaction was experience-born."

I waved his concession away. "All along you've said everything is subjective, and that's all, to a degree, experience-born, right?"

"True. So I merely confirm my own assertions." Mat gave me a crooked smile. "And you? Turnabout is fair play." He glanced down to his notebook as if unable to maintain eye contact. "Any true loves?"

I hesitated, now understanding why he paused a few beats when I first asked him the question. We hadn't treaded into these waters. It felt like we were trespassing upon a friendship long dead, like guests at a class reunion hoping to ignite a lost connection. I wasn't sure if I had the courage for such a vulnerable life update.

Yet in studying Mat for those few heartbeats, I discovered that, even after all these years, I still knew him. I still trusted him, and he was still my friend. The connection wasn't long dead. Quite the opposite.

"I came here for my junior year abroad." I motioned out the window. "To Paris."

Mat's jaw flexed. "I remember."

Something about his expression hit me wrong, but I skipped over it as memories of Paris and that year flooded in. My mind wandered to Caro's final letters and her love story, then back to my own, which had felt as gilded and surreal as Caro's time in Paris.

"I met someone. His name was Caden and I . . . I really thought I loved him."

"Caden," Mat repeated. "What happened to Caden?"

I swallowed and found the best way to explain was to simply start from day one. "I met him right after Christmas. I didn't go back to Boston for the break; there was nothing there for me, and I loved Paris. I felt free there. New. It was like everything I hated about my life and myself got left on the other side of the Atlantic. And one day, wandering the street vendors in Montmartre, he was there. We spent the next six months falling in love—at least I did."

"Was he a student?"

I shifted deeper into the seat. "He worked at the Kenyan embassy. It was his first time out of Kenya, and his worldview, family, experiences . . . Nothing was like my own and he was like air. I even considered leaving school and staying to find a job."

"But you didn't." Mat prompted me with a statement, not a question.

"I didn't. The plan was for me to return for senior year and he would put in for a transfer. It was all very *An Affair to Remember*. We were going to meet post-graduation in New York."

I was lost in the past until Mat prompted me with a soft, drawn-out "But . . ."

"But he changed his mind. We called and texted for about a month, then he called at the end of September . . ." I closed my eyes, remembering that final night. "He said I'd changed. I wasn't the same woman, and he wouldn't come. He never called again."

"That was it? Nothing more?"

See? I lifted both shoulders and let them fall. *Everyone leaves.*

I dropped my eyes to the table, seeing nothing. At the time, I'd been hurt. Beyond hurt. But seven years had given me one perspective. The last few days had given me a different one. This morning's talk with my mom, yet another.

I could finally recognize and admit Caden hadn't needed to say anything more that night. I had felt the truth of his statement like a heavy blow back then, but comprehended the nuances of it now. Whatever I had become and whatever freedom I had found in Paris, it hadn't been real. I couldn't sustain it, because I hadn't owned it and made it mine. I'd played a role, that of a happy, carefree young woman, and I left her in the Charles de Gaulle Airport the afternoon I flew home.

How alike we were through the generations, I mused once again. How resistant to trusting, feeling, relaxing, being . . . loving.

A new thought pierced through my memories. "When we met last Friday, you said I *hadn't* changed. What did you mean?"

Mat's Adam's apple lifted and sank with tension. His eyes reflected a glint of challenge. "You haven't . . . You're exactly the same and you still drive me crazy."

I remembered that feeling—that dance between us our first two years in college. Mat and I had fought, laughed, argued, eaten more Red Vines than humans should, and always tiptoed around the fact that there was something between us—electric, exciting, terrifying. I cycled through freshman year, sophomore year . . . senior year.

I *had* ghosted him. He'd been right about that. After Caden called, I had retreated—from friends and from him, just like I'd been taught to do growing up. "Lived experience," as he called it.

I finally got it. "Mat?" I waited until his eyes met mine. "I'm sorry."

"It's okay. You were in love with him and he hurt you . . . And I was in love with you." His eyes widened at his sudden admission—as did mine. He quirked a shaky, almost sad, smile. "That can't surprise you. You had to have known."

At that moment the train emerged from the Chunnel into a blaze of yellow sun, blue sky, and green fields. We were instantly thrust from our world of two back into our larger story.

I opened my mouth to reply, but he cut me short with a raised hand. "Don't say anything. I shouldn't have mentioned it."

"We can't just leave it there."

"Why not? That's what you did. You talk about feeling free and leaving everything bad across the Atlantic, but I was across the Atlantic, Caroline. And unlike Caden, I knew the real you, not some pretend version you tried to create. And when you came back and I asked you out, tried to reach out, then accepted that we'd only be friends, you still ignored me. You wouldn't return texts, calls; you dropped a class we planned together. Then you blew up at me one night and told me to leave you alone . . . so, yes, I get to 'just leave it there' no matter what you might want to do with it." He flicked his fingers in air quotes, but he needn't have. The disdain in his voice made the quote marks audibly clear.

"I . . . I didn't know."

Mat closed his eyes. When he opened them, all the fire was gone. "What didn't you know?"

"That I was enough. For anyone."

Mat, watching me, blew out a long slow breath. "I'd say none of us are, in any relationship, until we accept the other person may simply believe we are." He then cleared his throat and changed the subject. "You'd better start packing up. We'll be there soon."

I started gathering our papers. Tucking the letters away into my bag, checking and rechecking references, and seeing nothing on the pages in front of me.

Our charade of nonchalance lasted until the train pulled into Paris's Gare du Nord. Mat jumped up to grab our bags from the rack above us when I reached out and grasped his hand. He dropped back into his seat.

"Before we go and start this hunt, I want to say I'm sorry, again, and thank you."

He tilted his head in question.

"I hurt a lot of people that year. I ghosted everyone. My room-mates yelled at me after a couple months and we worked it out, but . . . you are right. We had something special and I abused it. I didn't mean to, but . . ." I thought of my mom and her comment about getting lost. "I did. I got down on myself and I never looked up. I'm sorry and I thank you for telling me."

"I shouldn't have said anything . . . It's in the past." He jumped up, seeming eager to put space between us.

I let him go. After all, I knew he didn't believe his own line.

To Mat, the past meant everything.

THIRTY-FOUR

Paris took my breath away.

When people say such things, they usually refer to the city's beauty, soft light, and air saturated with flowers; heat off the cobblestones, and patisseries redolent with rich chocolate. Not me. I was reminded in an instant of the freedom I'd felt, the strength and joy I'd tried to grasp, and the disparity between trying to manufacture those feelings versus allowing myself to simply trust they could be mine. I saw Paris through new eyes, or more accurately, a new heart.

Mat stretched out his hand. "We doing this thing?"

I clasped it tight, accepting it for the olive branch it was. "We are."

We hopped in a cab right in front of the station's iconic red Angel Bear and Mat rattled off, "25-27 rue Baudin, 93310 Le Pré-Saint-Gervais."

While the car sped through traffic, down small streets and around monuments, I tried to absorb Paris at the car's breakneck speed.

Mat chuckled. The first notes felt forced, but not the last. "You look like a kid."

"I feel like one. I let that ending with Caden cloud my memories. I let a lot of things dictate how I felt and what I saw." I willed him to understand, and in one long look, a second of silent communication, I felt he did. It was enough.

The Arc de Triomphe flew by. I twisted to catch it through the rear window. We next crossed over the Canal Saint-Martin. We zipped past the orchestra hall and the philharmonic as well as the National

Music Conservatory. Mat toppled into me as the cab cornered a fast right turn and stopped at the archives for the Police Prefecture.

He jumped off as if I'd scorched him. "Your shoulder. Did I hurt you? Are you okay?"

I assured him I wasn't hurt, but that didn't stop him from opening my taxi door, carrying my bag, and basically clearing the way for me into the building.

After gaining our security passes, Mat and I found our assigned desks and the files Mat ordered for us stacked high upon them. I counted thirty.

I groaned. He sighed.

"I ordered everything from October 15 to 22." He pulled our two chairs close together and laid the first file before me. "You ready?"

"Ready as I'll ever be." I opened the first folder. It was structured very similarly to the British files with a trifold cover binding and a varied number of copy sheets bound by thin strings within.

We again found ourselves slogging through hundreds of papers, with only three hours in which to do it. Each file was a mishmash of arrest reports, officer notes, and official dictums. When we reached the seventeenth, the day of Operation Clementine, it alone filled six folders worth of papers.

"They were certainly busy arresting people." I turned another page.

"This is unbelievable." Matt moaned, grabbing a new file from his stack. "I've read about people rounded up, shot, thrown in jail, handed over to different German agencies, Germans taking prisoners, stand-offs between the French and the Germans. It's like the Wild West. At least I think that's what I'm reading. My French sucks."

Mat was starting his third file. I was well into my eighth. "Just skim for the names we need."

We refocused on our individual piles and, now only looking for names, Mat moved through them much faster.

"Wait . . ." I reached out to Mat. "Paul Arnim. I found him." Mat's chair screeched across the stone floor as he drew it even closer to mine. "It says here . . . wait . . ." I turned the page. "This isn't an official report. Look, there's no stamp at the top. It's an officer's private notes."

"How do you know?"

"I found a few of these in that file." I pointed to the one I had just scanned. "Reading between the lines, it looks like the French police filed these reports when the Germans demanded no official record from the French. Perhaps situations in which the French got nervous, and rather than comply without question, they made unofficial notes, kind of like backup plans if there were issues later. So that means . . ." I turned another page, then back again. "Whatever happened with Arnim made the French officers on the scene uncomfortable."

Mat crowded closer. "What does it say? Anything about Factory du Carte?"

"Stop reading ahead . . . It says here there was an explosion at twenty hundred hours in the twelfth arrondissement and that, when reporting to the scene, nearby officers found Gruppenführer Arnim and a young woman fleeing an alley."

I looked at Mat. He wiggled a *hurry up* nod back to the page.

"They detained her and had decided to let her go when a German patrol surrounded them. It says here Sturmbannführer Brunel arrived, quarreled with Arnim . . . then shot him in the head." I froze.

"What?" Mat leaned forward. "Read that again."

"It says right here, Brunel shot Arnim in the head. Then the woman broke free in the ensuing chaos, and was shot by Brunel in the shoulder as she rounded the corner."

Mat slumped back in a whoosh of breath. "He was executed? In an alley by a fellow German? His transfer order covered up a murder?"

I dropped against the hard back of my chair to absorb the news with him. I was speechless. Mat looked baffled.

"I don't understand," he whispered. "What happened next?"

I pushed myself forward and read on. "Another explosion then occurred at Factory du Carte, a munitions factory eight blocks north, and Brunel sent half the patrol to it."

I glanced to Mat. His eyes were closed as he listened. "A French officer unrolled the woman's papers and tried to take her into custody, as she was a French citizen with a Paris address—Nanette Bellefeuille, 21 rue Saint-Joseph—but Brunel refused. He stated Germans had authority as everyone present had just seen her shoot Arnim in her attempt to escape. He challenged the French to defy his explanation then ordered them to stand down. They left. End of story."

"This is unbelievable. He was murdered by his own side." Mat opened his eyes. "What about Rose Tremaine? That has to be the diversion Caro set. It's eight blocks from the Clementine factory, exactly like the report."

"She's not here." I turned the page and found nothing. "Maybe Nanette was part of Martine's group that Caro mentioned? Maybe Christophe got to Caro and she passed on the assignment? She may have been nowhere near there. Christophe could have killed her the day before and we'll never find her."

Mat shifted to face me. "You've been thinking about all this."

"It's like a nonstop reel in my head. One with no ending."

"Don't race ahead of what we know." He gestured to the page again. "Keep reading."

Together we turned the next fifty pages, scanning for Rose Tremaine.

"How is this possible?" Mat pushed his hands from his brow to the base of his neck, ruffling his hair straight up with the motion.

I shut the file and pulled the next toward me. "You know what happened to Arnim. Hard as it is, knowing will bring his family some comfort."

"You know . . ." Mat sighed. "I had a hard time taking this project at first, knowing he was a Nazi. But all those dresses for his wife and their stories gave him an intriguing personality so I took it. Then Caro's letters gave him humanity . . . Now I'm not sure what to think about him. Regardless, that was an awful way to die." Mat shifted toward me. "You're right. Now they'll know . . . And what about you?"

I pressed my lips together. I wanted that comfort as well, but I needed to acknowledge that it might not come. Telling myself that over the past several hours and accepting it were two very different things.

"We've got a couple hours left. Let's keep going."

I tipped into him, shoulder bumping shoulder, in thanks. It was so clear he was trying to generate optimism for me. I'd lost my own.

An hour later and halfway through arrest records for October 20, Mat's buoyancy waned. It fizzled out completely when the proctor kicked us out.

"I can't look at another word anyway." I closed my eyes as we hit the sidewalk.

The natural light, though softened at the end of day, stung. We'd spent the last three hours in a small one-window room, crouched in plastic chairs, under florescent lights, frantically scanning documents and finding nothing that solved our primary problem.

I felt Mat's hand on my back and, without intending to, I sank into him. He stepped down next to me. "Let's get a cab to the hotel, drop our bags, and walk around. We could use a stretch."

I tapped my phone. Mom had left a text with an address and a dinner reservation.

"Not a hotel. Friends of hers are lending us their apartment." I showed the text to Mat. "You good with this?"

"Like I said, your mom is trying." Mat lifted our bags and headed for the curb. "Come on, Payne. Show me your city."

THIRTY-FIVE

My city.

I let Mat's words become my own as a cab drove us to the sixth arrondissement. Even though I felt frustrated and exhausted, the Paris light cast an exquisite spell over me. The sky's bright cloudless blue was softening with evening's shards of pink shooting to gold across the horizon.

The sights added to the glory. In one short ride, we saw the best of Paris—at least the tourist's version. We passed parks and memorials, the Place de la Bastille, the Louvre, and Notre Dame, among much more. Notre Dame welcomed me like an old friend and surprised me as well. I'd seen pictures of the great fire and its destruction, but looking upon the two iconic towers, I commented that it appeared intact and standing strong.

"Deceiving, isn't it?" Mat tilted his chin toward it, but said nothing more as the cab turned and pulled up to a building on Boulevard Saint-Germain. We left our bags with the doorman and walked back into the evening as neither of us wanted to be inside yet.

I instinctively turned us back toward the Seine and our pace slowed to a stroll down a typical Parisian street, flanked by a series of beautiful six-story limestone buildings. Each, connected to its neighbor, featured long windows with wrought iron detailing and a tall, sloping slate roof. The mansard roofs had always reminded me of hats—and in this neighborhood, expensive hats. I said as much.

"Hats?" Mat studied them. "I like that." He dropped his wandering gaze from the rooftops back to the trees dotting the sidewalk. I savored the interest and delight in his eyes. Mat was seeing what I felt—the beauty of a completely and utterly French moment with a broad cobblestone sidewalk, tony shops, and expensive cafés. No one had their cell phone out. It felt almost outside time as everyone appeared present, savoring the city and the simple joy of ending a workday.

As we strolled, I shared with Mat how much I had loved Paris, and how I had forgotten that. New York crowded me, hemmed me, and kept me walking faster than I liked. Boston, while feeling like home, never let me feel settled. I was always striving. London, in the short time I'd been there, intimidated me with its history and secrets. But Paris? Despite the fast pace of traffic, Paris felt like a dance with all the pieces moving in a complex choreography. Paris felt like warm butter spreading in the sun. Smoother, silkier. I breathed slower and, tonight, I felt comfortable in my own skin.

He laughed at my descriptions, but as the evening light hit the buildings on the other side of the river, warming the cream stone to a rose pink, I sensed he felt it along with me. He grew quiet. His smile softened.

No longer chasing answers at the Police Prefecture, I let Mat's train admission wash over me. It filled me with a sense of effervescent wonder. It wasn't so much that he'd once loved me; it was that he once saw me, knew me—not some "pretend version" I'd tried to create—and had loved me still. In many ways, I figured it was best I hadn't known back then, as I might have ruined it. For I never could have believed back then that I was enough. As he said, I could not have accepted that another "may simply believe we are." But now I knew with a deep conviction, I wanted to try. I wanted to try to break that generational resistance to trusting, feeling, relaxing, being . . . loving.

I wanted to reach out and somehow share all this, but his confession had wrought an equally powerful yet opposite reaction in him. He kept his eyes averted, his head turned away. It felt as if he now chased the wonder of Paris and the evening to avoid the more complicated reality of me.

Mat pointed beyond the bridge to the Place du Carrousel and the Louvre. "Do we have time for a detour?"

"This is all a detour. The restaurant's behind us." I laughed and continued walking. "Yes, we have time."

We crossed the bridge and found ourselves at the edge of the famous Tuileries Gardens at the Arc de Triomphe du Carrousel, across the street from the Louvre's pyramid.

Mat gestured to the Arc. "Did you know this one was built before the one on the Champs-Élysées?"

I kept my face blank. Even if I'd known, I wouldn't have said. The gleam in his eye told me this was important to him.

He continued, "The Champs-Élysées Arc honors those who fought and died in the French Revolution and Napoleonic Wars and was completed in 1836. This one is about half its size and was finished earlier, in 1808. It celebrates Napoleon's victories from his 1807 campaigns."

"You're well informed."

"I've been writing about memorials for years. How we view them. What they mean across time. I'm still trying to break into that public forum." He looked down at me. "We need to talk about the article."

"Now?" I asked.

Mat opened his mouth. I could tell from his expression that work was his next safe landing spot. Mid-exhale, he changed his mind. "Later is fine. Let's enjoy Paris."

I led him around the Louvre to the right, following the Seine, and soon reached the Pont Neuf bridge. Paris's oldest bridge surprises people. It surprised Mat. It was simpler than he expected, and more beautiful. That made me smile.

He pulled at my hand to stop midway across the bridge. "I forget how north we are, even here. It's after eight and the sun has a long way to go before it's gone."

"I'm glad." I rested my hands on the stone wall. "If we'd come out of that building in the dark, it would have felt even more depressing."

I needed the sun. I needed a gentle ending to our journey to find Caro. Darkness would have been abrupt, and mirrored how I felt about our search. Because I couldn't help it—I was sad. My expectations had grown far beyond our abilities. It was too far to leap—and I'd missed the landing.

"*It's not your job,*" my mom had said when I outlined my plan to find answers last Sunday. "*It was never your fault,*" she had assured me this morning.

She was right on both counts, but when are emotions rational? If what had started a domino chain of pain, retreat, and dysfunction could somehow be reversed or reimagined, then couldn't a domino chain of hope replace and even heal it? That's how high I had aimed— because the corollary to Mat's statement that history is subjective meant that we could change it, by shifting our perspective.

It meant my dream wasn't impossible. If our perceptions changed our reality, our minds could also adapt to something new. As Mom had more than implied—I could stop being a prisoner of a past I hadn't understood, because I no longer imagined myself to be one.

Standing on the Pont Neuf, I began to wonder if it was possible. Not to change my father, but to fundamentally change me. Could I reach for something new, like I had here all those years ago? This time, could I hang on to it? Not play a role, but grow into something new. I glanced to Mat, wondering if it had already begun.

"*You aren't the woman I fell in love with.*" Caden had been right. I shed the courage, the optimism, the *joie de vivre*, I found in Paris like a borrowed coat and shrugged on the familiar, the heavy, and the ponderous, simply because I didn't understand I had a choice.

Now this new lightness teased me. I could almost feel it covering me like Schiaparelli's soft—and as Caro called them, "free and comfortable"—knits all those years ago.

"You're awfully quiet." Mat leaned against the wall next to me, but not with me. At the Archives in Kew and the Police Prefecture, our shoulders had touched. With our focus no longer outside us, I missed the closeness. Mat maintained distance now.

"I am, but I'm okay."

"What's that?"

I looked down. I'd been unaware I was playing with the gold heart around my neck. I held it out to him. "Do you remember the necklaces mentioned when they turned sixteen? This was Margaret's. Caro's actually. They traded."

"No way." He placed his fingers beneath it. "It's so delicate. Where'd you find it?"

"Mom gave it to me this morning. She said my grandmother would have wanted me to have it."

"I agree." Mat smiled and released the heart. It dropped back into place, warm against my skin. "You probably know her better than anyone now. Except me, of course." He winked.

"I'll let you wear it on odd days."

"Deal." A light lingered in Mat's eyes for a heartbeat more. It felt as if, in our awareness that the light existed, he extinguished it.

He cleared his throat and I pointed across the Seine. "Let's circle Notre Dame then take the Pont de l'Archevêché over the river again. The restaurant is just a few blocks back toward the apartment."

We walked down the street and when Mat turned to the left, I gently pulled his hand to the right. Once redirected, he didn't let go and I moved my fingers to find that perfect intertwining within his hand. The fact that he didn't shake free felt deeply compassionate with the tantalizing hope of something more.

"Painful to see, isn't it?" He gestured to Notre Dame as we passed from a towers-only view to her battered flank. He was right. I hadn't been to Paris since 2014, five years before the devastating fire. I hadn't seen her wounds. Almost three years post-fire, they were still overwhelming.

"They've put up scaffolding?" I pulled him to a stop and pointed with my free hand. "I thought they were still debating the approach."

"That scaffolding was there before the fire and much of it got infused into the church."

"I wonder what will happen. I can't imagine it being anything other than what it was." I stared at the cathedral and, after a few moments, felt Mat staring at me. I twisted toward him.

"And what was it?" His look held a teasing gleam. Again, I got the impression I was about to get a history lesson. I smiled. This was Mat.

"Notre Dame." I swallowed the bait and fully faced the church. "The beautiful and impressive church you see right there."

Mat did the same, and launched. "What you see started small in 1160 with a simple broad, low building." He swiped his hand wide as if painting a picture in the air before us. "Then they laid a cornerstone for something grander, adding the choir and the double ambulatories in the last years of the twelfth century. In the early thirteenth, they started building the spine to the west, the basic blueprint of what you see today. Then during the late thirteenth to mid-fourteenth century, the two towers got added, as well as a spire at the intersection of the nave and transept. In the eighteenth century, while reconstructing the roof, they removed the spire and the lines changed again. Then, after an extensive reconstruction project in the mid-nineteenth century, another spire was added. That's the one you see under the scaffolding now and believe has been there all along." He turned toward me again. "We face that point again—an ever-changing discussion between the past and the present with an eye to the future."

"Applicable to both life and a building." I smirked.

"I couldn't pass on such an easy setup." Mat chuckled and started walking again to the next bridge, the Pont de l'Archevêché.

I smiled and half-skipped to catch up. In talking of history, he'd forgotten himself and the awkwardness between us. We were going to be okay.

On the other side, we followed a charming street in the sixth arrondissement, allowing only one lane of traffic, with wide stone sidewalks and again flanked with expensive shops and cafés. Our final turn was onto a pedestrian thoroughfare. It reminded me of Boston's Acorn Street. It was equally narrow and cobblestoned, sloping to a rise in the center. But the similarities ended there. This street was bustling with restaurants, cafés, people, and languages.

Le Procope sat halfway down like the grand dame she was, with her sidewalk tables and bright red and royal-blue striped chairs. Inside we found more red. Red walls, red leather banquettes, and red and blue carpet running up her sweeping white marble staircase. I gestured to a plaque on the wall. *Le Procope. Cafe-Glacier depuis 1686.*

"It's the oldest restaurant in Paris."

"Your mom must be well connected."

I nodded. "I'm beginning to think she might be. She always was the extrovert parent before . . ."

The words drifted away. I had no need to go back there anymore.

Soon settled in the rich leather banquette of a cozy corner table, we ordered. I started with escargot and tried not to laugh as Mat gingerly pulled his first snail past its plug of parsley, butter, and garlic with a tiny fork. One bite and his skepticism vanished. He brightened and dug those buttery dollops out as fast as he could snag them. He commented he couldn't taste the snail, but loved escargot.

I grinned. "That's because it's only a conduit for butter, garlic, and parsley. Three of my favorite foods."

We then moved on to *cassolette de ris d'agneau* for Mat and *filet de boeuf, sauce Bérnaise, and frites maison* for me—basically a country stew and steak and fries. Every bite worked its magic and I soon found we leaned toward each other more, smiled with greater ease, and truly laughed without holding back.

The real surprise came at dessert. Before we even ordered, a chocolate soufflé and the house tiramisu arrived without prompting.

"Your mother ordered these for you and paid the bill, with her compliments." The host arrived aside our waiter.

Mat raised a brow in an annoying *I told you* so manner.

Rather than give his smug look any reply, I reached forward and snagged a bite of tiramisu. He countered with a spoon to my soufflé.

"I don't think I've ever eaten so well." He finally laughed, swiping my ramekin and scooping out the final bits of chocolate. "I live on a chicken I cook every Monday and a heap of salad fixings. I can stretch the whole thing out a week."

He surveyed the room, now filled with the harmonious sounds of tinkling glass, china, and soft conversation—like an orchestra playing the first notes of a perfect night. "I couldn't have imagined something like this." He looked at me and tilted his head. "But you . . . the London House . . . I didn't know that about you in college. You must go to places like this all the time." His gentle lilt lifted his sentence to a question.

My mind shifted back to my Sunday arrival, reading letters with my mom. Something she had quoted . . . "There are very few of us who have heart enough to be really in love without encouragement."

Mat's tentative question was all the encouragement I needed.

"Not really." I cracked the door open to my childhood a little wider, for him and for me. "When I was young, my brother was a teenager and into every sport imaginable, and he was a good student. Weeknights were spent following his games or his studies. After he left for college, the same fall Amelia died, there weren't many family dinners. And now, fancy dinners out aren't my style, nor any of my friends. We're more of a pub burger than Neptune group."

The high-end Boston oyster bar somehow reminded me of Le Procope. It wasn't the decor, other than the almost matching black-and-white tiled floor, but the exquisite attention to detail, bustling vibe, and robust prices. I'd been there once, on a date, a couple years back. Now I longed to return. Mat would enjoy it. It would remind him of tonight . . .

"And Caden?" Mat's question stopped my musings. "No special dinners here in Paris?"

My heart shifted. Mat was cracking the door open to his heart as well. We were stretching beyond the topic at hand.

I sipped my wine and, this time, I prepared to take him back in time. I shared with him the details of that spring, wandering around museums and eating picnics. I shared with him who Caden was and who I thought I'd been in his company. And as I talked on, I realized my experience was more aligned with my aunt's than I'd accepted. Just as she had written to her sister, ideas and thoughts shared late at night about life, politics, art—along with good food and wine—had made Paris, and me in it, feel alive. It wasn't Caden as much as it was that I had stepped outside myself and my narrow perceptions of my world and my place within it. Perhaps the coat hadn't been borrowed after all.

I felt my face warm. "I've been hanging around you too much. I'm beginning to believe how I think changes who I am, and I can hang on to that brighter, even happier woman I found here."

"You were that woman before Paris." Mat kept his eyes trained on me. "Maybe you forgot, but I was serious when I said you hadn't changed . . . You still drive me crazy and you're still the woman I fell in love with."

THIRTY-SIX

While we'd been inside Le Procope, Paris had transformed once more. This time from pale pinks in blue-graying skies with white stone and yellow streetlamps, to colorful restaurants, wine bars, and neon store signs brightening the black backdrop like pinpoints. Notre Dame, the Louvre, and the Place du Carrousel were all lit and the Eiffel Tower shot resplendent with gold on the hour. Without talking about it, we found ourselves meandering back toward the Seine, making a broad loop, before turning toward the apartment. Cars, zipping through the streets, added a sense of modernity to the night that disappeared completely across the quiet bridges. There they slowed and the streetlamps' golden glows invited us to stroll again and take in the moment. It was the evening's perfect denouement.

As we crossed back over the river, I reached for Mat's hand again, sliding mine down his wrist until our fingers interwove once more. "Mat?"

"Yes?" He stepped closer to me.

I stopped and, before I lost my nerve, I kissed him. I didn't ask. I didn't explain. I simply lifted up on my toes and captured his lips with my own. In the first second, I sensed his hesitation and feared I'd misjudged. I lowered myself down, my mind racing through how to explain, retrench, and recover. But as our lips parted, he stepped forward, gathered me in his arms, and drew me up closer.

"You're not getting away that quickly," he whispered against my lips.

Instead of replying, I looped my arms around his neck and deepened the kiss. Margaret had said it felt like tiny bubbles. She'd been right. A bubbly sensation had danced through my head and heart for days. Now the champagne had been opened and a fizzy sensation rose from the tips of my toes to the top of my head, unlike anything I'd experienced. While I'd had a series of casual boyfriends over the years, there had only been two men I deeply cared for. First Mat, then Caden. And no two men could have been more different. There had been an intensity about my relationship with Caden. It felt fraught, and only in this moment did I understand I had mistaken an edgy anxiety for passion. Mat, on the other hand, had always felt like a delicious promise forever out of reach. Except he wasn't.

After a moment more, Mat pulled back. His eyes held such warmth I felt saddened by the time lost and the distance I'd put between us. But, I reminded myself as I sank back to earth, I wasn't the same woman back then, despite what he claimed, and that kiss wouldn't have been, couldn't have been, so glorious years earlier.

Without words, he tucked me close and we walked on toward Boulevard Saint-Germain. As we rounded the abbey, Mat stopped so abruptly I stumbled in surprise.

"Caroline?" I tracked his line of sight. "Isn't that your dad?"

It was, dressed in dark pants and a sports coat, standing outside the apartment building. He was pacing small circles on the sidewalk.

"Dad?" I dropped Mat's hand in my rush forward. "What are you doing here?"

Without answering, my dad pulled me into his arms and engulfed me into what might have been my first hug from him in over a decade. I discovered my forehead fit perfectly in that soft spot right beneath his clavicle.

I breathed him in. Lime shaving soap. Acqua di Parma. And his favorite cinnamon mints.

He stepped back, still holding my shoulders. "I came to see you . . . Can we talk?"

"Of course," I replied as I felt Mat step behind me. Flustered, I turned between them. "Mat Hammond, you remember my father, Jack Payne. Dad, this is Mat. You met him, but—"

Dad cut across me with both words and a handshake. "I owe you an apology, Matthew."

"Just Mat, sir." Mat paused mid-handshake as if trying to rewind correcting my dad. "I mean—"

"Just Mat?" Dad teased with a side peek my direction. He and Mom chided us as children when we didn't introduce ourselves by our full names.

"Moraitis," Mat replied. "Moraitis Papadakis Hammond. Greek mother. English father." Mat waved his hands, clearly undone. "My brothers got Luke and Peter, and I got Moraitis, my grandfather's name. 'Mat' was my idea." Mat looked between us, eyes wide. "Sorry. That was more than you needed to know. More than anyone needed to know."

"Not at all, Mat." Dad laughed.

Dad teased? Dad laughed? My focus swung back to him.

"I spoke with your mom. She said this apartment has three bedrooms. Do you mind if I stay with you?"

"Not at all."

"Please do."

Mat and I raced over each other in nervous agreement. If Dad caught the currents, he didn't comment. He turned away and led us through the building's front door.

Six floors up, the elevator opened into a stunning apartment. The living room, with broad windows, black leather furniture, and massive modern art, boasted a view across the building tops and distance to the Eiffel Tower. To the left, I caught a glimpse of books in a small library. Mat gravitated that direction. To the right, I found the edge of an oven range through an open doorway. Dad headed there and soon returned with a bottle of wine in hand.

"Would either of you like a glass?"

Mat spoke first. "Not for me, sir, if you don't mind. I'll leave you two to talk." He looked toward me with an encouraging smile.

I nodded to Dad, unsure what to say. While he returned to the kitchen, I dropped onto one of the living room couches and tucked my feet under me. I recognized the gesture, tucking tight into a safe ball, but I couldn't force myself to unwind. Soon he joined me, carrying two glasses of red wine and sporting a tense expression. I tucked tighter.

"Thank you." I reached for the glass. It was an amazingly big, dark, earthy red, most likely a Bordeaux blend, and chewy enough to count as a meal. Although I wasn't hungry, it was exactly what I needed, rich and grounding. I shifted my attention from the wine to the window and straight upon the top of the illuminated Eiffel Tower. The whole effect—the day, the wine, the company, and the view—was surreal.

Dad still had not spoken.

I turned back to him. "What are you doing here, Dad?"

We both heard my tone. It lay between us sad, defeated, and worn on so many levels. I also had failed to banish a note of wariness. All those feelings of light and hope I tried to envision as my own in the preceding hours vanished when faced with the reality of my dad.

"You're exhausted," he replied.

I nodded. I was exhausted. I also felt young, hurt, and very small. In the instant he hugged me, I had realized how much I missed and still needed my dad. Breathing him in had felt like coming home. I wasn't sure I could withstand another lecture or another walking away. I scrubbed my hand across my eyes. "It's been an unbelievable week, but you were right, the price has been high. I fly home first thing Friday to get to work."

"I'm glad you won't lose your job."

"Yes, well . . . I've been thinking about that."

His lips parted. It was clear he wasn't sure what to do with that comment, but I wasn't ready to deal with it myself so I pressed on. "Why are you here?"

"I drove to Derbyshire."

It was not the answer I expected.

He continued, "I was headed to the airport Monday, but—I can't tell you why—I ended up getting a rental and heading to Crich. I think I needed to say goodbye."

He glanced at me. Speechless, I could only stare. Jason and I had endured a year of Dad "saying goodbye," so this detour didn't surprise me as much as it seemed to have surprised him.

"We didn't stay for my mother's burial, so you didn't go, but all the Waite side of my family are buried in Crich. Generations of them. Grandparents, great-grandparents, great-greats. There is so much history there I've never felt a part of or appreciated before." He paused. "She wasn't there."

"Grandmother?" I sat straight.

"My aunt. No one had ever put up a gravestone for Caroline Waite. Not a fake one with her death marked at age seven, nor another as if she died when that letter was delivered in 1941. She simply wasn't there. It was like she never existed."

Dad leaned forward, elbows resting on knees. He set his wineglass on the table in front of him and steepled his fingers together. I could see the tips of his nails whiten with the pressure.

"I have never been so angry in my life, Caroline, and I've carried a lot of anger through the years. Her life mattered. I don't care what she did. She lived. She was my aunt, my mother's twin sister, and she had parents who loved her, and they . . . they erased her. They erased her life like it never happened. And . . . I . . . I can't abide that. There isn't a minute of Amelia's life I would want to miss. I could never—never—" He stuttered to a stop and swallowed. "I could never do that . . . I wouldn't have missed a minute of Amelia's life."

Dad drew in a shuddering breath and blew it out through circled lips. It wavered between us and his eyes glistened. It was the closest I'd ever seen my dad to tears. His Adam's apple rose and sank, catching with the strain, as he thought what to say next.

"I was so angry standing there. I was furious with all of them. Then this wave of red anger like nothing I've ever felt turned back on me . . . It's what I'm doing, isn't it? Right now. I'm erasing a life."

I couldn't reply. Nothing had prepared me for this.

Dad nodded as if I'd asked him to go on, as if we'd had a conversation and sat in agreement. "You had the courage to ask questions and to try to understand. You came to me and I was no better than all of them. I denied her to Mat, then to you. I wanted to erase her like they did, because that's how I was raised. Without realizing it, I toed the party line."

He smiled, tiny and flat. "Have you ever read *The Picture of Dorian Gray* by Oscar Wilde?"

I nodded and felt the clenching in my chest ease. This was the dad I knew. I still couldn't speak, but felt a yielding in my eyes and posture. He saw it, or at least sensed it, for he blinked in acknowledgment.

"My family was like that. We looked so perfect. All hiding a secret no one could bear, corroding us from the inside . . . until you tried to understand. Your motives were good. You were trying to protect me. But what did I do? I turned on you. I . . . I haven't been a very good father, Caroline. In that instant on Monday, as I realized I wouldn't miss a minute of Amelia's life, I recognized I've missed a lot of yours, and I'm throwing my own away."

He paused again.

"That sounds like a powerful visit." It was not the most sensitive thing to say or even what I wanted to say, but it was the only thing that occurred to me.

Dad chuckled. It cracked through the tension surrounding us. "Not one I want to go through again. I once read a biography of Saint John of the Cross. I gather he went through a forty-five-year 'dark night of the soul.' One afternoon was enough for me."

He reached for his glass, drank deeply, then returned his attention to me. "I'm no better than my own grandfather, I guess. Caro wrote he could only see one of them. After Amelia's death, I could only see her, the one I'd lost. That's how I've measured most things in life, by what I've lost. Amelia felt like one thing too many and I decided no more—look at the loss that has led to."

"You've read the letters?"

"I went to see you this morning, to apologize, and to say a lot of this. Your mom said I had just missed you again. I didn't expect her to, but she invited me in and walked me through a selection of the letters and diary entries you'd found. She even invited me back to read them all." He smiled at something warm and private. "She also fed me a marvelous lunch . . . When did your mom learn to cook?"

I felt my first genuine smile since hugging my dad break free, thinking of Mat and his Alice Waters comment. "I think she went through your 'dark night of the soul' a few years ago and came out a chef."

Dad stilled, pondering this statement, but didn't ask anything further. Instead, he looped his hand in a small circle as if resetting our conversation back to the letters. "I never knew my mother had scarlet fever. I never knew what she was like as a kid. I only knew her after years of loss. She also had one too many, I expect." He nodded to me. "Your mom said you remind her of a young Margaret, and maybe an older Caro. You would have done what she did."

Dad smiled with affection—and my breath caught in my throat.

"Run off with a Nazi?" I prompted, half joking, half testing. I wasn't sure how much he'd read, how much he believed, and where we had landed on the lie his family carried for years.

"Pursued a good cause with courage," he countered.

I felt myself nodding. Not in agreement, but in silent recognition that we'd gotten somewhere new. I bit the corner of my lip to keep myself from getting teary. When that didn't do the trick, I widened my eyes to dry away the pricking sting. I was someplace I never thought I'd be and someplace I never wanted to leave—with my dad.

Reality overshadowed the warm glow within a few heartbeats.

"It's over." I shrugged. "We found what happened to Paul Arnim, the Gruppenführer mentioned in the note. He was shot by a fellow Nazi officer on October 17, 1941. But we didn't find Rose—that was Caro's alias. There was nothing about her at all, even though she was in Paris that night for an SOE operation. Did Mom tell you about that?"

"She did . . . So she really was a spy?"

"A British one, yes. Perhaps one of the very first. Mat and I believe she orchestrated the note to her family because she wanted the SOE clear of any backlash for letting her work with them."

I leaned forward. "You see, those were early days and losing someone like Lord Eriska's daughter could have ended the whole thing. So rather than put anyone at risk, we think she scripted that note. And whatever happened to her, she also scripted that, as well as she could."

I sank into the soft leather as the search and the day drained away. "Nothing in the SOE files indicates they ever got a clue to her whereabouts. Her letters to Margaret imply she buried secrets within them . . . I'm sorry, Dad. We don't know her as well as Margaret did. We can't follow the clues. We've probably missed most of them."

Dad pushed off his couch and joined me on mine. He sat close, angled toward me, his knee touching mine.

"Don't be. Please. This is enough."

"It's not. I can't give you the ending. I can't make this right . . . You asked me to quit . . ."

He held my gaze within his own. "None of this . . . How we got here was never your fault or your responsibility." He pulled me close. "You've carried so much."

I squeezed my eyes shut.

"Believe it or not, I know how you feel."

A small gargled laugh escaped. That I could believe.

"What hurts now is knowing I could have lifted that from you. If I'd been paying attention. That's on me. So much of where we are is on me, Little One."

Little One. My nickname from when I was very small—smaller and younger than when Amelia died, younger even than when I learned I'd been named after an aunt who died of polio at age seven. It was his name for me, back at our very beginning.

Our conversation soon wound down. Dad sensed my exhaustion and headed to the apartment's far bedroom. He had generously left the master for me.

As I passed the second bedroom, I tapped on the door to say good night to Mat. He didn't answer, but the door was cracked so I pushed it another few inches to peek inside.

Propped against pillows, laptop tipping onto the blanket, he was fast asleep. I crossed the room, lifted his laptop onto the dresser, and covered him with the throw blanket draped across the bed's corner.

All that done, I couldn't help doing one thing more. I leaned over and kissed his forehead. His hair came to a small widow's peak at the center. "Sleep well," I whispered.

I turned back at the door, partly to make sure I hadn't woken him and partly just to see him again. Somehow, in a short amount of time, he had become deeply important to me.

Or maybe I was remembering he always had been.

"Good morning, Sleeping Beauty."

Mat met me at the doorway to the kitchen with a cup of coffee. He was fully dressed and inordinately chipper for seven o'clock in the morning.

"How long have you been awake?" I reached for the cup he stretched my direction.

"A couple hours. How'd you sleep?"

"Surprisingly well." I blinked, aware of our close proximity. We hovered together in the narrow doorway. "I came in and covered you with a blanket last night. I hope you don't mind."

"Not at all." He mussed his hair with his free hand. The scar on his chin flashed in the morning light. "Thank you. I never woke till five."

I tapped his scar. The gesture felt warm and intimate. I pulled back, again unsure if I'd overstepped and assumed. "Did you ever win?"

"Of course." His hand grazed over mine as he reached to trace the scar himself. "After Luke gave me this, they were scared not to let me win sometimes." His hand moved from his chin to my shoulder. His eyes morphed from the delight of feisty memories to tender concern. "Speaking of falling, how's this shoulder today? The day after the day after is always the worst."

"Not bad. Slightly sore." The accident felt like a lifetime ago rather than two days. Those two days had changed everything.

I turned into the kitchen when something in our conversation nudged me. Spinning back, I bumped into him, a bit of coffee splashing on both of us. "What did you call me? Just now, when you handed me the coffee?"

"Sleeping Beauty?" Mat replied. He stared at me, first in question, then in wonder. "Sleeping Beauty." He repeated the name as if it danced between us, just out of reach, out of memory.

"Sleeping Beauty." I gave the name conviction, grounding it for us both. "Briar Rose . . . She picked her own nickname. When you said that last night about yours, it was like a trail I couldn't follow. You picked your own nickname, just like C. S. Lewis, and just like Caro—Rose Tremaine. Caro even said she might do that. She wrote it." I held my hand out to him in a *wait here* gesture, set my coffee on the counter, and ran for my phone and notebook.

Racing back to the kitchen, I leafed through the notebook. "She said she was glad about Margo Moo simply coming into being, but that . . . Here! Nanette Bellefeuille."

I found the November 14, 1932, notes. "Claire insisted on role play for French lessons. Caro picked Nanette Bellefeuille, after her doll, and Margaret picked Bebe Dupont."

I leaned against the counter. "It *was* all there. In the letters. The report noted it as well. Her papers were rolled." I leafed through the notebook's pages so fast, I tore the edge off one. "September 5, 1939, she wrote about rolling papers into the support panels of bras, like Martine used to hold up the Lobster Dress. Then again . . . papers . . . papers . . . There's something else."

I paged through my notes, knowing that Caro had left another clue. She had written something in a letter that had made little narrative sense, something about papers and identities.

"Here." I nudged close into Mat to share the page. "She wrote about that man in London who carried two sets of identity cards so that when arrested his real identity couldn't be found—he could remain anonymous. The story makes no sense until you see she was leaving her trail of bread crumbs . . . Every story had significance."

"So she—what?—destroyed the Rose papers as soon as she got in trouble in Paris? Then pulled the string and released the Nanette ones?"

"If she was in real danger, yes."

"But Arnim knew her real name, and it doesn't explain why he was shot."

"I don't know." I shrugged. Mat was right. "But she is Nanette."

I waited. My last sentence was not a question, but I needed Mat's agreement. It was beyond clear, yet . . . I still needed him on board.

He dropped his eyes back to my notebook, brows furrowed in concentration. "Brunel shoots Arnim, point-blank range, execution style, and then shoots Caro and takes her into custody. If she didn't die from that wound, whatever happened to her next was probably horrible."

He accepted Caro was Nanette. I looped an arm around him in a half hug and, without thinking, planted a quick kiss at the corner of his mouth.

"We can find her, right? You said the Germans kept meticulous records. What would Brunel do? Question her? Torture her? Send her to a concentration camp?"

"All of the above, if not immediately execute her." Mat pushed away from the doorjamb. "I need my computer."

I followed him as far as the living room. Dad sat on one of the couches reading.

"We found her." There was no stopping my tears this time. "She really did leave every clue necessary, if one knew her well enough." I stopped short. "And knew they needed to look."

Mat returned, dropped on the couch across from Dad, and started typing. "The Arolsen Archives are the most comprehensive. If she went to any German camp under the name Nanette Bellefeuille, we have a good chance of getting a hit. The report said she was from Paris, right? Not another village?"

I found my picture of the police report on my phone. "Yes. Paris."

"I bet she'd kept her lies to a minimum . . . fake name, fake city, but real birthdate." He was talking to himself rather than to us. "Done."

He shut his computer. His elation lasted an instant and ended in a groan. Flipping his laptop open again, he continued. "I'm not thinking. They have the most complete records, but not the fastest."

"Who is faster?" Dad asked.

"The US National Archives . . . Name . . . City . . . Birthdate . . . Enter." He stared at his screen a few seconds then looked up. "One record found."

"Only one?" I dropped next to him. "It's her. It has to be. Can you open it?"

"There's the rub." Mat grimaced. "Arolsen will give us the most complete information, but it can take four to ten months. We can instantly see a match in the US National Archives, but it still takes a couple months to get the file . . . Unless . . ."

"Unless?" I drew the word long to prompt him.

"I've made friends with a tech guy at the Archives over the years. He may just . . ."

Mat started typing again. This time I didn't interrupt.

After a few minutes he closed his laptop and looked between Dad and me. We simply stared back.

"Now we wait." He nodded to each of us. We still sat staring. "We found her. You both get that, right? We don't know the details yet, but by getting that hit, we know she was a victim of Nazi persecution, not a traitor and not a defector. If you had any doubts, sir, banish them."

"No." Dad burst out into a laugh. It rushed out of him like a valve released of pressure. "I don't have any doubts at all."

"You should open an official inquiry in Britain," Mat continued. "Your aunt was a hero, and when you look at the SOE memorials in London, the Violette Szabo memorial or the one in Westminster Abbey, you should know she was a vital part of that. Her name not only needs to be recorded but added to the SOE memorial here in Valençay. She lost her life here, regardless of where she was actually killed."

My dad pressed his fingers to his mouth and nodded. "Not in my wildest dreams."

THIRTY-SEVEN

Mat left us to shower and dress. I sensed he was trying to give us time, but I had no idea what to do with the gift. I looked around the living room feeling lost. I had nothing to research, no lead to chase, and still no understanding of how it could or would change life today. I couldn't tell my grandmother. I couldn't ease her pain. I couldn't brighten my father's childhood. I couldn't refashion my own. Yet, despite all the couldn'ts, an odd elation gripped me.

I studied my dad, standing feet from me staring out the windows toward the Eiffel Tower. I suspected he wasn't seeing anything beyond his past either.

"Why don't I go find a café and get some pastries?"

He turned with a befuddled expression, as if trying to wind his way through a maze. He considered me and I wondered if he'd heard my question.

"Ah . . . I should come with you."

I swung my head, already halfway to the front door. "I'll only be a few minutes."

I needed out. I needed to breathe. I needed . . . I wasn't sure what I needed. I simply felt like the most meaningful thing I'd done had taken a prolonged intermission—and left me in a hyped-up interlude. What was I to do? Where was I to go? What came next? I had all these questions, but we were stalled right on the brink of answering them.

I wandered out into a quiet morning street and inhaled the deepest, most freeing breath I'd taken in years. It filled me all the way to my stomach and with it came scents of flowers, chocolate, yeast, sugar, coffee, and petrol.

Paris, like me, wasn't fully awake yet. It felt as if she was in that intermission between the busy night and the frenetic day with endless possibilities ahead of her. Few pedestrians traveled the broad stone sidewalks. White pillowy clouds rested above like cotton balls thrown onto a blue canvas.

I wandered down rue Bonaparte toward the Seine again and stopped at a corner café. The display case housed a typically Parisian, decadent pastry selection. After choosing a couple croissants, three éclairs, two canelés, four financiers, and a dozen macarons I should have resisted— along with three café au laits—I headed back to the apartment.

Dad wasn't in the living room upon my return. I caught sight of his profile in the small library and thought he'd retreated there to read. I placed the pastry box in the kitchen, transferred the coffees to proper café bowls, and headed to deliver his.

Dad and Mat, sitting close and talking, was such an unexpected sight, I stopped short by the door.

Dad glanced my direction, nodded to Mat, then pushed himself out of the brown leather chair. "I called your mom. She'll be here around noon . . . I'll let you two talk."

As he passed me in the doorway, I handed him his coffee.

"Thank you."

"Mom? What's going on?" I joined Mat. "I was gone for twenty minutes."

"He read my article, called her, then basically gave me an interview. He added a lot of good stuff, Caroline. Would you like to read the first draft?"

"It's written?"

"I'm submitting it tomorrow. I told you that."

Mat's words were slow and measured. He wasn't asking permission or a question, but I sensed he wanted my support. He needed me on board and I accepted—even embraced—that he needed me just as much.

"Yes." I lowered myself into the chair my father had vacated. "I do."

I handed him his coffee and he handed me his laptop. I sat and read, not an article, but a story. The story of a lie, pain, and a family; a story of misperceptions, misunderstandings, and loss; a story of heroism, resilience, hope, and truth.

Throughout it all, Mat sat silent. I cried.

"He said those things?" There were quotes from my father about his solitary and shadowed childhood, the pain of losing Amelia, even his "dark night of the soul." There were also comments about me, how proud he was, how grateful, and how he felt—three generations later—that I'd brought light back into his world.

"It's different from what you expected?" At my nod, Mat sat back. "Caro taught me a few things these last few days. While so much is perspective, it's not ultimate truth. In many ways, I've been doing history a disservice by claiming it is. She was right about Lewis and his BBC talk. Some truths, some absolutes, are above perception. I hope that comes across."

"Powerfully. It's what makes what we went through, what we fashioned for ourselves, all the more real and painful. No one got out of their own way to see what *was* rather than what they perceived it to be."

"Will you comment?" My nod inspired a bright smile. "Then, if we get the file, I'll add it to the end . . . The National Archives guy texted me. He'll try to get it to us today."

"It's the middle of the night there."

"Yeah, I woke him up. Who doesn't put their phone on Do Not Disturb at night?"

THIRTY-EIGHT

Mom arrived with lunch.

"I stopped at one of my favorite places, Pontochoux on rue du Pont aux Choux." She set down the bags. "It's a wonderful Japanese spot. Do you like Japanese curry, Mat?"

While he answered, she kissed me on the cheek then darted over to Dad to do the same. Her nervous energy bounced her between us like a pinball.

"Then after lunch let's go to Maison Schiaparelli. Don't you think that's fitting?" she chirped.

"Didn't it close in 1954?"

Mat shook his head and I remembered that was where he made his initial connection between his research subject and my aunt.

Mom replied, "It reopened in 2012 at the same address Schiaparelli left it, 21 place Vendôme. We can wander the boutique and imagine what it was like in Caro's day. It'll be fun."

And it was.

When the doorman opened the door, I felt like Cinderella—in her scullery clothes—trespassing at a royal ball. The gap between Schiaparelli's haute couture and my world felt vast. But the feeling only lasted as long as my walk to the small anteroom at the back of the salon.

On my way there, I sensed that the grandeur of the place swept over us all. Schiap's black-and-white knit sweater with its iconic bow rested front and center. The design that started an empire. Fantastical handbags, hair combs, and accessories filled every shelf and display case. And the dresses . . . color upon color. Embroidery, glass beading, extraordinary stitching. Everything was more splendid than I could dream and pricier than I could imagine.

"Wow," I whispered to my mom. "Was it always like this?"

"Always. Schiaparelli was the avant-garde designer of the day, of the world. This *is* Paris."

My aunt was part of this.

My yearning to find her in all this directed my gaze past the decadence on display to the history on the walls. Pictures from today— Cate Blanchett, Ella Balinska, Joan Smalls, Emilia Clarke, Michelle Obama . . . all dressed in gorgeous couture gowns—were displayed near the front. But as I walked back in the salon, I also walked back through time.

Pictures transported me to the fifties, the forties, the thirties. Wallis Simpson, Mae West, Katharine Hepburn, and Marlene Dietrich—all as Caro described—adorned an entire wall of the small back anteroom.

There was Wallis Simpson in the Lobster Dress, not at a showing, but at a fitting with young women surrounding her, displaying other dresses while their coworkers measured and served her. There was another of a mannequin—I'd read that's what they called models in the '30s—wearing the Tears Dress, and another displaying what must have been the ephemeral Butterfly Dress Margaret couldn't bring herself to wear. Caro had been right. The Butterfly Dress became one of Schiaparelli's most famous creations.

There were also pictures of openings and parties. There was one with young women in ice cream cone hats—the opening of the Circus collection. Caro had written about that night as well. I looked closely and felt certain I spotted her in the foreground of one of the black-and-white photographs.

I was probably only seeing what I wanted to see, but then again . . .

"Dad . . . Mat . . . Mom . . . ," I whisper-called to each of them.

There were so few people in the boutique, each heard me, turned, and hurried my direction.

"Do you think that's her?" I pointed to a young woman with short dark hair, dressed in a black calf-length dress, like all the others, with a cone hat on her head. A radiant smile brightened her eyes.

"Could it be?"

"Oh my . . . Maybe."

"Do you think?"

We all looked at each other. I beamed. "So we're agreed. That's Caro."

We spent the rest of the day wandering Paris slowly. Mom was so anxious that Dad not overdo it that we sat in more cafés than we wandered the sites. One could say we saw Paris one café au lait at a time. And despite my spending a year here before, Paris felt more complete, more inviting, and more bubbly—my new favorite word— than I remembered.

The sky's blue had deepened to a resplendent cerulean. And while sitting at a table in the Tuileries Gardens, I could not imagine a more wonderful moment or day. All my angst and discontent over our lack of answers had oozed away, probably helped by coffee and sugar, but certainly by the company as well. My history with Paris had been fast, exciting, young, and passionate. This was an older feeling, more secure yet more enticing, like watching a flower open to the sun. I sensed I could capture this feeling and hold tight. I could hold tight because, as I looked around the table, I wasn't alone—and perhaps never had been.

We found Caro.

A contented sigh escaped—one that only Mat, sitting close on my right, heard. He winked. I blushed.

Dad shifted his attention from the Roue de Paris—Paris's tower-ing ferris wheel—to me. "I've asked your mom to accompany me to Berlin."

"Berlin?"

Rather than answer me, he looked to Mat. "You said it could take months until we know anything, and all roads lead to German records. I know a little German; I can hire a translator and I can continue to search. We can even drive to Arolsen for a couple days." He glanced to Mom, me, then back to Mat. "I don't have months."

"You—" I tried to interject, but Dad stayed me with a waved hand.

"We're going only for a few days. Jason needs me in New York by next Friday for an appointment at Sloane Kettering. I don't have months, because I have work to do, but let's be honest, I may have squandered my best result by now. My 'no decision' was a decision, though perhaps not the right one."

I nudged Mat. He looked to me and an unspoken conversation passed between us.

You should tell them.

I don't want to raise their hopes if it doesn't come through.

You should still tell them.

The conversation might have sounded completely different in Mat's head and involved dinner or questions as to why we kept reaching for each other and pulling away all day, but I suspected I was right because of what he said next.

"I asked a friend for a favor and he's trying to send us the US Archives' file today. We may have answers—soon. Without need for Berlin." Mat pulled his phone from his pocket and placed it on the table between us. "That's why I keep checking my phone. I'm not trying to be rude. Just eager."

Dad gestured to it. "Check again."

THIRTY-NINE

As we wandered back to the apartment, we stopped at a grocer and a poulterer to make dinner ourselves. Upon entering, Mom and Dad headed to the tiny kitchen and Mat retreated to the apartment's office to edit his article. Last in the door, I watched them go their separate ways, wondering how so much could change so fast. In the span of less than a week, no aspect of my life looked the same—family, love, past, present, future.

Love?

I watched Mat drop into the library's leather armchair.

Yes, love.

I turned toward the kitchen. One glance and I knew I'd been right about Acorn Street and small houses all along. I watched as my parents bumped around each other, laughing and chatting, while unpacking our groceries. I joined them and soon found, after a fitful and giggle-inducing start, that the three of us moved well in and between the kitchen's tight spaces.

I even discovered that my dad and I didn't have only one conversation topic—my failures—between us. We were conversant across several others.

"How long until dinner?" Mat filled the doorway.

Mom answered while I poured Mat a glass of wine. "It's in the oven, but it needs a full hour. I can get you something to nibble if you're hungry."

"No, thank you." Mat stepped from the doorway, inviting us into the living room. "If you're not busy, and we have time . . . I got an email."

Mom and Dad trailed him into the room. I followed. "*The* email?"

He nodded first to me, then looked to both my parents in turn. He spoke to my dad. "Shall I open it?"

"Yes. Please."

Mat, laptop tucked under his arm, positioned himself on the couch between me and my dad. Mom sat on my dad's far side. I glanced around wondering if anyone was breathing—I wasn't.

The first PDF page was a copy of an old form, a mixture of a printed form and handwritten information. Cream paper. Black ink. Shadowed and smudged.

Mat slid to the floor, allowing us to tuck closer behind him. "Nanette Bellefeuille. Paris, France. Registered. 25 October 1941. #398869."

"Would that have been tattooed on her arm?" Dad asked.

"No . . . This is a registration form for Ravensbrück. Tattoos were unique to Auschwitz." Mat scrolled his cursor down as he scanned the information. "She was brought in on a train from Drancy and was assigned to Block 1." He pointed to a red triangle on the page. "This means she was a political prisoner, which is how they classified the French Resistance." He twisted back to face me. "The rolled papers . . . She really did sell her story."

"What happened next?" Mom leaned forward.

"She was assigned construction work for the men's camp next door."

"I didn't know Ravensbrück housed men."

Mat shifted to answer my dad. "The men's facility opened in 1942. There was also a facility for children." He clicked on the next page. "Personal effects and description. Twenty-two years old. 5'8". As we thought, she gave them her real birthday. November 14, 1918. Dark hair upon arrival—that would have been shaved off immediately—blue eyes, and—"

He stopped.

"And?" I poked his shoulder.

"A four-inch scar on her left forearm."

"Oh—" I pressed my fingers to my lips. "I knew we were right, but . . . it's her." I looked over Mat's head to my dad. "Christophe, the guard at Schiaparelli's, cut her arm on a June 1941 mission. She wrote field notes for the SOE files about that night and how it happened. Margaret also wrote about it in her diary. Caro told her she'd cut it on a wire and Margaret knew she was lying."

Mat continued, "It also says she came with a necklace, which again would have been taken immediately. A gold heart."

"My mother wore one," my dad whispered. "I never saw her without it."

I pulled the necklace from beneath my blouse.

Dad's eyes caught it and held. "That's it. How?"

"Margaret gave it to me before she died and I passed it on to Caroline, if that's okay?" Mom's solicitous respect didn't escape any of us.

"I'm so glad you did that." He clasped her hand and squeezed it before letting go and tapping Mat's shoulder. "What happened to her? Did she make it out?"

Mat clicked through PDF pages on his computer. "My German isn't great and this is really long. They kept scrupulous records."

"Skip to the end, if you can. Right now, I want the punch line."

Mat slowly scrolled past several pages of handwritten notes. "It's here." He tapped a line with his finger. "She was shot December 25, 1942."

"Christmas Day?"

"I'm so sorry." Mat lifted and dropped his shoulders. "I can't make it all out. I'll need to use a translator. But there is something about *singen*, singing . . . maybe Christmas carols? Officers came to enforce order. *Ungehorsam* . . . I've seen that . . . Disobedience? Insubordination? Maybe she challenged an officer?"

"She survived over a year there." I sighed.

"She survived only a year there." My dad rubbed a hand across his eyes. "What would this have changed for my mother had she known? Could she have . . ." He glanced between Mat sitting on the floor and me sitting at eye level. "Could she have found her? Without the files? With only the letters, and her diaries, and her memories? Could she have done it?"

Mat looked to me.

I needed to be the one to answer. While I wasn't sure, I felt I knew these women well and what was possible—even what was not. "No . . . Technically the information was all there. With tenacity and imagination, she might have guessed at the truth—a slim might—but Caro was asking a lot of her sister. There were natural misunderstandings between them . . . But she couldn't have found her and saved her, if that's what you're asking. That was not possible."

"'O, what a tangled web we weave when first we practice to deceive,'" Dad said, quoting Walter Scott.

I held out a hand. "It wasn't her fault. Caro's or Margaret's. That was Caro's job and it was important, and in leaving her clues, she was trying to respect a vow of secrecy while sharing her life with her sister, the only way she could. Caro never could have anticipated the length and the pressures of the war or Margaret's grief and the trauma of then losing their father only months later. Life simply carries misunderstandings along with consequences."

Of anyone, I figured the three of us could understand that. Mom's soft expression told me she did.

"And even if she had deduced any part of this, who was Margaret going to contact to confirm it?" Mat picked up my baton. "She knew nothing about the SOE. No one did, not then. Caro did the best she could to reveal herself, but she had no idea what Margaret was up against." Mat turned to face my dad more fully. "Not only that, the final SOE files, including much of their work in France, weren't declassified until 1998."

"What about my dad? He was in the RAF. He had to know something about the intelligence world, the Old Boys Network, something. Couldn't he have found the truth if he'd wanted?"

I thought back to the letters. While Caro loved her George, she protected him. She kept him at arm's length, even broke up with him, to keep him from worry. Anger is better than worry, she'd told her sister on numerous occasions. It was Margaret she trusted. Margaret alone. I shook my head.

Dad sank back, his thoughts miles away.

No one spoke. We were waiting on him.

"Maybe it's chauvinistic thinking, but we need to believe we can protect our families. It strikes very hard when we realize we cannot."

Mom reached over and took my dad's hand this time and squeezed. She didn't let go.

I watched their hands for a moment, and a peace I had never known filled me. It was time to lay some things down—hurt, pain, blame, and grudges—and studying Mom, Dad, and even Mat, I knew it was time to pick other things up and hold them tight.

Mom rose to check on dinner.

Mat moved over to the dining table and started cutting and pasting large blocks of the pdf pages into a translation program.

Dad crossed the room to the window and waved his hand toward me, inviting me to join him.

Tears flooded his eyes. "Thank you, Caroline. I see things so differently now. And they are good, aren't they? They can be good. They will be." He chuckled softly.

"But . . ." I gestured to his face.

"Don't mind me. They're happy tears." He swiped at his eyes. "They're also tears for what might have been. But for you, all this could have gone another way. You could have quit when I asked, and I . . . I wasn't headed anywhere good, was I?" He drew an arm around me, securing me close. "Yes, these are joyful tears . . . You have a beautiful name, by the way."

I laughed at that, and was surprised I could do so without a tinge of sarcasm or cynicism warping the notes. "We haven't been so sure about that these last twenty years, have we?"

His second arm reached out and I found myself tucked into a hug. Dad rested his chin on top of my head. "We are now."

FORTY

The next morning I found Mom already in the kitchen and Mat and Dad sitting together at the dining room table translating Caro's records from German.

After dinner, Mat and I had walked them through our notebooks and pictures from both the British National Archives and the Paris Police Prefecture. It was a night of laughter, tears, and more closeness than I'd felt between the three of us in—well, in my entire life.

"We're leaving soon after you today, darling." Mom handed me a cup of coffee.

"Why? There's no need for Berlin now."

"We're heading to Ravensbrück regardless. He needs to see it. Goodness, I need to see it. I love Caro almost as I loved Margaret. We need to do this for her, and for us."

I leaned against the counter, watching Dad through the open doorway. "Is he going to be okay?"

Mom followed my gaze, a thoughtful and loving expression lighting her face. "He's better than I've ever seen him. Can you feel it?" She peeked at me before returning her focus to Dad. "There's been a weight on your dad as long as I've known him. This morning it's gone. It is simply gone."

"From last night?"

She lifted a shoulder. "I think it started at the graveyard in Crich. I've never seen him so angry as when he came to the house Wednesday. It was good."

"Angry was good?"

The comment confused me as I'd felt myself shed the imponderable weight of far too much anger over the last couple days.

"Oh honey, after years of defeat masked as indifference, yes, the energy needed for a good shot of anger was very good to see. I think he might be ready to turn that energy to cancer now."

Her words brought Jason's text to mind . . .

If I have to pit him against you—so be it. You first. Cancer next.

As I sipped my coffee and parsed through the weight of anger, I recognized the energy it required, the energy it had taken from me. Mom was right. Jason was right. Dad had not been mild-mannered, deflated, indifferent, or absent so much as hurt. And I had not been seeking to please or to bring closeness over the years so much as reacting from anger.

Mat was right—we can change our perspective.

I pushed off the counter, pulled a second cup from the cupboard, and filled it with coffee. I headed to the dining room. Mat was no longer there. I found him in his bedroom packing his few things.

"Are you sure you shouldn't go with them? This is huge for your family."

"No." I sank onto his bed. I smiled, still feeling that peace, along with the bright flash of something more I was hesitant to label—or, more accurately, hesitant to label alone. "My role is over. This is for my dad, and after all my mom went through with my grandmother, this is for her. I answered my questions and I need to show up for work today. Besides, they don't need a chaperone."

Mat raised a questioning brow.

"Call me a romantic, but they held hands more yesterday than throughout their whole marriage."

FORTY-ONE

I spent the eight-hour flight parsing legalese and researching how to open an official inquiry in England for Caroline Waite. Mat spent the eight-hour flight editing. And as our connecting flight from New York touched down in Boston, he submitted his article.

My phone beeped with a text.

> Good afternoon from Ravensbrück. Soul-wrenching and healing. We needed to come. Going back tomorrow to search files in the information center. More soon. Love, Dad.

I held my phone to Mat sitting beside me. "I don't think I have ever received a text from my dad and never a 'love.'"

I pulled the phone back and stared at it. Only when the plane parked and everyone started moving about did I tap it off, still dazed by the wonder of it. I glanced to Mat, who again was gathering our bags from the overhead bins.

The wonder of it all.

There was one more thing to do. I tapped on my phone and texted my brother.

> I'm back. Dinner tonight? I have so much to tell you.

His reply was instantaneous.

What??? Dinner? YES! Come to the house. I can't wait to hear.
Talked to Dad. He sounds great.

Mat dropped back into his seat. "What now?"

"If I'm lucky I'll make that two o'clock staff meeting. Then . . . I'm going to return to Georgetown in the fall and finish my JD."

"You are?"

"Yes. It was something you said about truth. Perspective and truth. That's where I'll find the tools to think through those questions and help in the ways I want to help." I stared at him, inches away, willing him to understand. "But Boston is my home."

"Good to know, but I don't mind weekend visits to DC."

I laid a soft kiss on his lips. "I'm glad."

He closed the space between us for another, and a third, before the line to deplane shifted forward.

After we cleared customs, we each ordered Ubers—work for me, home for Mat.

Mine arrived first.

Mat held open the door for me and toggled his head to the Prius's interior. I hesitated, on the edge of another precipice.

"You'd better get going . . . I'll see you tonight. Dinner? My place?"

Relief flooded me. I hadn't ventured ahead alone. "I can't. I'm having family dinner at my brother's." Mat's eyes clouded and I quickly covered his hand on the car's door rim with my own. "Will you come with me?"

The clouds cleared. "Absolutely."

With that, he kissed me hard. Not long and lingering, but that prolonged claiming kiss of someone in love and confident in that love. It was exciting, assuring, and held a delicious guarantee of more to come.

I dropped into the car and watched him through the window as it pulled into traffic. He never looked away. With a hand raised, he watched me go.

A tiny butterfly feeling of delightful anticipation fluttered through me. It expanded with each breath. To know someone's heart, to want him like that, and to have him see you and reciprocate that desire—again I smiled.

The wonder of it all.

EPILOGUE

E ven if you have no proof of something happening, it doesn't mean it didn't happen. Just this way . . .

17 OCTOBER 1941

Staring at Christophe, it was Caro's last conversation with Frank Nelson that filled her mind. She had made provisions, left instructions. And even if Nelson had accepted them with reluctance, he had accepted them.

"You aren't serious. You can't be," Nelson had scoffed. "You'll tie my hands. If Dalton sends this to your parents, if we let everyone believe this lie, you stop me from searching through open channels. You're signing your death warrant." He rattled the paper in front of her. "And this? Telling them you're dead would be easier than this."

She remembered how she had stepped her feet shoulder width apart as if bracing herself against that moment and all the tough ones to come—if the letter was sent, if something went wrong. "Dead means there's no hope. My sister has clues and she'll need the hope within them, even if there is nothing she can do."

Caro pushed the paper back into his hands. "You said it yourself—if anyone knows who I am, who I really am . . . I'm too important." She lifted a brow with her half smile.

They both knew it was true. Some realities are objective.

Nelson sighed, small, sad, and full of resignation. "I'm sorry I ever said that . . . We can do this without you."

"Not the way the plan is structured, and our window is now. We can't leave that factory operational one day longer." Caro reached out and touched his shirtsleeve, right where his blue coat met the pristine white cuff. "You won't find me anyway. I won't be Rose. There are people who are made vulnerable if I'm linked to Rose Tremaine."

"What alias did you choose?"

"One you'll never guess, but someone will. If this goes poorly, the truth will emerge someday and no matter what happens, that'll be enough."

Now, gripped in Christophe's beefy fist, she regretted all her mistakes. Christophe knew Caroline Waite. He knew Rose Tremaine. Her only hope was that, as of yet, he didn't understand the implications, and the power, his knowledge held. If only she could get away . . .

Christophe dragged her across the courtyard. In the moonlight she could see the stubble on the back of his neck, his eyebrows growing together across his nose as he spun back to face her. The night was so clear she could see his nose hairs moving in and out with his breath.

"What? No lies to tell?" he growled at her.

She stepped back with her right foot and, twisting her body as Major-General Gubbins had taught her, she used her hips and Christophe's vise-like hold on her arm as leverage to thrust the heel of her palm straight up and out. It connected with his face just beneath his nose. She heard the crunch of bone.

He moaned and released her, dropping to the pavement. As he folded, she grabbed his head in her hands and bent her leg. She cut her knee up into his head, just as she had done last June. The whimpering stopped as he flopped unconscious on the slick paving stones.

Caro grabbed her identification papers from her pocket and shredded them between her cold fingers as fast as she could, shoving the important bits into her mouth and scattering the useless edges along the street as she ran. She then reached into her other pocket and shredded the drawing of the Butterfly Dress. She grimaced. Tearing the embodiment of such delightful hope felt like a crime. But no one could see that. No one must ever connect her to Schiaparelli again.

One block. Two. She was four blocks from where she was to set the explosion, but it would have to do. Only eight blocks from the factory — yet to backtrack meant failure. She was already twenty minutes late.

Improvising, she lunged behind a car and set the charge beneath it. She struck a match. It failed and she willed her hands to stop shaking. Catching it the third time, she lit the fuse and ran.

One block and . . .

"Arrêtez."

The voice was in front of her or she wouldn't have stopped. Looking for an alternate path and finding none along the narrow street, she slipped and skidded to a stop in front of the officer.

"Mademoiselle Waite?"

"No!" she cried, scrambling to stand. "You sailed for America. You said—Gestapo? You're Gestapo now?"

Paul Arnim reached for her, taking in her khaki trousers and wool sweater with the same startled expression she wore while absorbing his black uniform.

"All Germans were called home. I had to protect my family. My companies were seized and I was conscripted. I suspect it was their plan from the start."

Caro caught notes of disillusionment in his voice. They gave her hope.

"But—" The car's explosion in the next block drowned out her words. The sound was deafening. The glow in the sky almost beautiful with its yellow-orange tones.

She stepped closer to Arnim as smoke, dust, shouting, and footsteps filled the air around them. She chose to risk, and to trust him. "The Carlingue . . . Don't let them take me. I'd rather take my chances with the Germans."

"You can't want that . . . What have you done?" When she didn't reply, he pulled her into an alley steps behind him. "Through there. There is a small exit at the back. Run."

"Thank you." Caro squeezed his arm then dashed down the narrow corridor.

Noise was everywhere. Sirens. Shouting. Footsteps. Whistles.

Through the small archway at the end, she turned right and plowed straight into a French policeman. She spun back, but an officer approached from the other side as well.

One short young man, dressed in brown, grabbed her by the arm. *"Pourquoi cours-tu? Que se passengers-t-il ici?"*

Why are you running? What is happening here?

While trying to keep on her feet, Caro reached her free hand up under her sweater and pulled at the tiny thread. The papers dropped into her hand and she slid them, spreading them as flat as she could on the way down, into her trousers pocket.

"Rien. Je suis perdu," she pleaded. *"Un tel bruit. Je suis effrayée."*

He most likely wasn't going to believe she was lost or that the loud noise frightened her, but she couldn't think of anything else. Perhaps he would simply let her go. After all, they had bigger problems tonight—or soon would—than a lost woman.

The officer shrugged and loosened his grip, only to tighten it the next instant as Arnim raced through the alley's opening behind her.

In fluent French, he shouted to the soldiers, "She is a German person of interest, leave her be."

The officer let go. Caro sagged with relief. The street was clear to the river behind her. She still had plenty of time to make it across and to the rendezvous point.

Arnim nodded to her and she ran.

Within half a block, a piercing whistle blew and the scene changed again. German soldiers surrounded her from every direction. They pushed at her, shouting words she couldn't understand. After a few moments of being jostled between the men, she saw a senior officer, tall and officious, push through the circle they'd created. He briefly looked her over, head to toe. Steel eyes. No emotion. He motioned for a young guard to hold her.

Caro pushed down her defiance and let only a very true fear show in her eyes.

"What is going on?" He spoke English to her. She kept her face blank.

He switched to German and said something more as he reached outside the circle and yanked Arnim within.

Arnim straightened as he addressed the man as Sturmbannführer Brunel. Caro sensed he was explaining his actions and pleading for the right to bring her into custody.

Two sharp words from Brunel silenced Arnim and Caro felt his will crumble as his body slumped. She had no idea what had been said, but its effect on Arnim was devastating.

One flash of silent communication and Caro knew they were both in trouble. Brunel caught the look and, without another word, unholstered his weapon and shot Paul Arnim between the eyes.

Caro gasped and the soldier released his grip for an instant. It was all she needed. She kicked at his shin and ran.

A loud "Halt!" and a shot split the night.

She didn't stop. She ran faster and, as she rounded the corner, another shot rang out. She was thrown to the ground, her shoulder on fire.

Caro rolled onto her back the moment the factory blew. The ground trembled beneath every inch of her as she watched the sky light with a bright yellow followed by a deep, cloudy smoke that blocked the stars. Dust and rubble fell like rain. She curled onto her good shoulder to keep the debris from hitting her eyes. Through the pain, she felt her lungs empty with relief. They had succeeded.

With that, her mind turned to more personal matters and she frowned in the quiet space created by the chaos. It was as Reverend Foley said, she thought. Your life flashes before your eyes. But not quite like he said, either. For it wasn't what she had done that flooded her mind as she watched her blood trickle into cracks between the cobblestones. It was what she had left undone. Never marrying George; never letting him in on what she could share of her secrets; and therefore never letting him all the way into her heart; never apologizing to her father for their distance, and for fighting him long after she should have stopped; never forgiving him for his humanity; never hugging Margaret so tight she'd never doubt her love.

Margaret.

She could see her sister so clearly. Her twin. Her better half.

Sturmbannführer Brunel loomed above her. With slow precision he brought his jackboot down on her injured shoulder, turning and pressing her whole body into the street as he crushed it to the ground. "What do we have here?" he said in English.

She didn't react to his words. She kept her eyes shut tight.

"Qu'avons-nous ici?" He repeated his question in French.

Caro opened her eyes. She let her tears and every ounce of fear and pain pour out.

A spark of triumph passed through the man's gaze. "French traitor."

He gestured to a younger soldier who dug into Caro's pockets and pulled out her papers. Without questioning her or noting it, he unrolled them by smoothing them flat against his knee.

"Nanette Bellefeuille. Paris. Rue Saint-Joseph."

Caro pressed her lips shut, banishing English from her mind. *When the torture comes,* she told herself, *cry out in French and no one will know. No one must ever know.*

Brunel pointed to the soldier, stiff words matching stiff gestures. The young man, years younger than herself she guessed, grabbed her by her hurt arm and hauled her up. The pain sent bright shards of light through her vision. She couldn't catch air.

He held her papers to his torch. She stopped herself. *Lampe de poche.* Not torch. Not flashlight. *Lampe de poche.* She recited the words again and again as the soldier dragged her to a car.

French words. French thoughts.

Shoved inside, she toppled across the leather back seat. The officer leaned in, his face lit by the high flames from the factory eight blocks away. "You knew Gruppenführer Arnim, I suspect." He spoke a formal book-learned French. "He was soft. Questionable loyalties. Weak. Not so with me. You and I are going to get to know each other very well, Mademoiselle Bellefeuille."

Nanette squeezed her eyes tight against more tears.

"This is too risky, even for you. I'm not certain it's worth your sacrifice," Nelson had remarked in his office.

She'd been so quick, so sure in her reply. "Of course it is. It's the right thing to do, an absolute, and it's worth any sacrifice. I knew the dangers the day I walked in your door."

But had she? She wondered now what was true and what was bravado. She pushed herself upright in the car's back seat.

Yes.

Confirmation and a deep conviction settled within her. Peace flooded in behind it. A peace so enveloping Caro felt her emotions shift. The small smile she felt curve her lips surprised her, as did the change in her tears. No longer crying from pain or fear, she felt them trail down her cheeks in what felt close to joy.

It was enough. She had done well. And someday, she thought, the truth would come out, and that would be enough too.

More than enough.

AUTHOR'S NOTE

I hope you enjoyed *The London House*. I thoroughly loved the research and the writing and want to pull back the curtain on a little of that for you here. First of all, a lot of fiction is wrapped within fact throughout this story and I encourage you to dig in to anything that interests you—SOE memos, the Munich Agreement, the Phoney War (spelled in the UK with an "e" and in the US either with or without one), and especially the fantastic couture creations of Elsa Schiaparelli. Also, please check out my social media or my website to see pictures of several of the SOE documents I reviewed—because, yes, I was tempted to run my "greasy fingers" over Churchill's penciled signature. It's also true that only about ten percent of those documents remain due to a fire, but it is fiction that they are a mess. One will not find Egypt SOE files interspersed among France's, yet one will find that "slothful" memo that made me laugh and had to be quoted in the book, along with the "marriage" memo that added a nice twist to Caro and George's romance.

Additionally, other small stories are true. According to one recorded account, Elisabeth de Rothschild did offend Nazi Ambassador H. Otto Abetz's wife at a Schiaparelli showing and was subsequently arrested and sent to Ravensbrück, where she died in 1945. The stories of Dali and the Lobster Dress are also true. There really was a large jar of mayonnaise and a great yelling match. The Lewis radio talks were also real, wildly popular, and occurred between 1941 and 1944. Many of them were renamed and placed as chapters within his classic *Mere Christianity*.

Lewis's speech "Common Decency"—found in Caro's letter—became "Right and Wrong: A Clue to the Meaning of the Universe."

All that said, this is a work of fiction and sometimes I changed details to fit the story . . . Paul Arnim is fiction. German citizens living abroad were called home in 1935 then again in 1938, but I wondered what might happen if a few private citizens were strategically left in positions of potential usefulness—so Arnim and his factories were kept operational in Paris for a time. Additionally, the "private officer notes" that Caroline and Mat found in Paris are also fiction. But I'd like to think such notes might exist—that some French officers pushed back by recording the truth behind the atrocities so that someday it could come to light. Caro's prisoner number from Ravensbrück is also fiction. I wanted to make sure she had no real person's number, so I went outside the entire series; 202,499 was the highest number employed before the Nazis began using letter prefixes to keep the numbers from going higher.

And when I needed results fast, I took a cue from television—where lab results always come back immediately. So, while the Arolsen Archives and the US National Archives are very complete, I didn't want you all to wait months for the results. Hence, a "friend in the tech department" got them to us in a day.

There is so much more to share of the rich history and brave men and women of this time, and I hope you'll enjoy learning more. Please visit my website www.katherinereay.com where I have listed many of the books I read for research. I recommend each and every one of them.

ACKNOWLEDGMENTS

What a story this has been for me! I loved every bit of creating it and hope you enjoyed the journey as well. I didn't take it alone . . .

Thank you to Claudia, my agent and friend; to my new publishing family at Harper Muse—Amanda, Becky, Jocelyn, Jodi, Karli, Kerri, Margaret, Nekasha, Halie, Mallory, and the entire sales team! You all picked up this story and ran with it, making it so much more than I imagined. Thank you!

I also need to thank family and friends. Elizabeth—my first and best reader—your navigation is vital! Kristy and Sarah—you two are a lifeline! Team Reay—always my anchor! And thank you to all of my writer friends—an extraordinary bunch who support each other and lift each other up every day. I can't imagine this writing life without you.

Thank you, dear readers! Thank you for trusting me with your time and your hearts. I hope we meet within the pages of a book again soon.

Katherine

DISCUSSION QUESTIONS

1. What do you think of Mat's premise that history is subjective rather than objective, as it is changed by the lens we bring to our study of it?
2. During Caro's first days in Paris, she asserts that fashion is more than simply clothes. It is "political, theological." Do you agree that clothing is more than simply what covers the body? (Also, be sure to look up the Lobster Dress and Tears Dress—the Butterfly Dress too!)
3. Do you agree, as Caroline comes to believe, that Mrs. Dulles was right and "the eyes are the windows to the soul"?
4. What do you think of Jack's statement that a ghost was worse than an affair because ghosts never age or die?
5. Do you agree with Jack that "one generation never truly understands the perspective and needs of another"?
6. How might things have changed if George had met Caro in Saint-Nazaire and married her?
7. When talking about Caroline's mom, Matt asks, "What do you think love is, Payne?" What did he mean?
8. What do you think of Jack's "dark night of the soul"? Have you ever experienced a life-changing revelation?
9. Caroline muses that how she thinks about herself and her story can change her story. Do you think that the way we see ourselves (positively or negatively; as strong or weak, for instance) can change how we see our lives and the world around us?

10. Caroline wonders at one point how much we can really know about the people we love. What are your thoughts on this?

11. Was Caro's sacrifice worth it? Do you think she felt peace in those final moments?

12. What do you think was the source of Caroline's ending wonder?

Also by Katherine Reay

Books. Love. Friendship. Second chances. All can be found at the Printed Letter Bookshop in the small, charming town of Winsome.

Return to the cozy and delightful town of Winsome, where two people discover the grace of letting go and the joy found in unexpected change.

AVAILABLE IN PRINT, E-BOOK, AND AUDIO!

Don't miss these other stories from Katherine Reay!

"Katherine Reay is a remarkable author who has created her own sub-genre, wrapping classic fiction around contemporary stories. Her writing is flawless and smooth, her storytelling meaningful and poignant."

—DEBBIE MACOMBER, #1 *New York Times* bestselling author

Available in print, e-book, and audio!

ABOUT THE AUTHOR

Corrine Stagen Photography

Katherine Reay is a national bestselling and award-winning author who has enjoyed a lifelong affair with books. She publishes both fiction and nonfiction, holds a BA and MS from Northwestern University, and currently lives outside Chicago, Illinois, with her husband and three children.

KatherineReay.com
Instagram: @katherinereay
Facebook: @katherinereaybooks
Twitter: @Katherine_Reay